⫽ **W9-BAW-423**

ONLY THIS BEAUTIFUL MOMENT

ONLY THIS BEAUTIFUL MOMENT

ABDI NAZEMIAN

BALZER + BRAY
An Imprint of HarperCollins Publishers

Balzer + Bray is an imprint of HarperCollins Publishers.

Only This Beautiful Moment
Copyright © 2023 by Abdi Nazemian
All rights reserved. Printed in the United States of America.
No part of this book may be used or reproduced in any manner
whatsoever without written permission except in the case of
brief quotations embodied in critical articles and reviews. For
information address HarperCollins Children's Books, a division of
HarperCollins Publishers, 195 Broadway, New York, NY 10007.
www.epicreads.com

Library of Congress Control Number: 2022951835
ISBN 978-0-06-303937-7

Typography by Julia Feingold
23 24 25 26 27 LBC 5 4 3 2 1

First Edition

For Evie and Rumi
I will always love you most
in this beautiful moment

MOUD

2019

Los Angeles to Tehran

Being gay on the internet is exhausting. That's what goes through my head as I de-gay my social media. Gone are all my opinions about *Drag Race* and whether straight actors should be allowed to play gay roles. Gone is every picture I've ever posted of me and Shane kissing or holding hands or ironically painting rainbow flags on our chests (ironic because we're not the kind of gays who post thirst traps, not because we don't respect our flag). When I'm done deleting everything, all that's left is a void. It's like I have no past. Just possibility.

There's a knock on the door. "Mahmoud," my dad says from the other side. He'll never call me Moud, no matter how many times I ask. He just doesn't want to acknowledge the real me.

"You can come in." Ever since my dad walked in on me and Shane studying on my bed together, he won't enter without being explicitly told to. We were fully clothed, by the way. We had open copies of trigonometry textbooks in front of us. And my dad was *still* shocked. Maybe because our feet were bare and our toes were touching. Maybe because Shane was wearing a T-shirt that read *Make America Gay Again*. Maybe because despite having come out to him two years before, he had neatly compartmentalized that conversation away into the part of his brain where he stores the things he never talks about. Like me being gay. Like my mom being gone. Like my grandfather being sick. Deny, repress, avoid.

Well, he eventually told me about that last one. He had to before it was too late. I guess, given my dad's history of emotional evasion, I shouldn't have been surprised that he hid my grandfather's cancer from me until the very last minute. Hiding pain is a deeply Iranian thing, and my dad is deeply Iranian.

"Dad, I'm alone. You can come in."

He opens the door and peeks in. He hasn't shaved, which for him is a sign that he's not doing well. He thinks we look like terrorists when we don't shave. "We have to go back to the Pakistani embassy," he says. "Your passport is ready."

"Oh, wow." Something about the knowledge that there's an Iranian passport with my name and picture on it stops me cold, like a piece of paper has already changed me. I'm still staring at my computer, at the blankness of my social media profiles. I guess I expected the process of wiping away all those memories to be traumatic. Technically, I'm giving up my freedom out of fear that some

Iranian authority might punish me for it. But it's the opposite. Because the memories that matter feel stronger inside me the moment they belong only to me and not to some data center in the cloud. In a strange way, by giving up what should be a piece of my freedom, I feel more free. I wish I could talk to my dad about this, but I don't talk to my dad about anything. I wish I could talk to Shane about it too, but I already know he's going to be pissed.

I close my computer and stand up. "Put a coat on," my dad says.

"It's Los Angeles. It's never cold." Not entirely true. It's a crisp November day.

He stares me down, and I find a coat. It belonged to my grandfather. He gave it to me the last time we saw each other in Geneva. He said he was shrinking and I was growing, so it was time to pass his clothes on to me.

Iranians don't have an embassy in the United States, so we have to use a wing of the Pakistani embassy. There are a few families entering at the same time as us, and as they do, the women throw on their head coverings, preparing to enter a world with different rules.

Iranian passport in hand, I ask my dad to drop me off at Shane's house. He just nods and heads up the hill. He still refers to Shane as my *friend*, even though he knows we're more than that.

Mrs. Waters opens the door when I buzz. "Moud!" she says, that permanent ring of optimism in her voice.

She gives me a hug, then waves at my dad, still parked in the car. "Hello, Mr. Jafarzadeh."

My dad rolls his window down a couple of inches. "Hello, how are you?" he asks politely. My dad is always well-mannered in public, more concerned with what strangers think of him than his own son.

"No complaints. You want to come in?" she asks.

"No, no," he stammers. "I have a lot to do before our trip." He adds a "thank you" before driving off.

Mrs. Waters leads me inside, an arm around me. "Trip?" she asks. "Where are you going?"

"Oh," I say. "It's complicated." It's really not complicated. I'm going to Iran to see my grandfather before he dies. The complicated part is that I haven't told Shane about it because I'm scared of how he'll react.

"Is everything okay?" she asks, and the warmth in her voice immediately makes me long for a new parent. Would my mom have checked in on my feelings the way Mrs. Waters does? Would she have responded differently to my coming out?

"Yes," I say. "Well, no, actually. My grandfather is sick."

"Oh, I'm so sorry. The music teacher in Iran?" I'm shocked that she knows this. Shane really tells her everything.

I nod. "I haven't told Shane yet, so . . ."

"Well, I'm sure he'll be a great support to you. He's upstairs recording."

Mrs. Waters squeezes my hands and stares at me misty-eyed. She's already shown more emotion over

4

Baba's illness than his own son has.

I open the door to Shane's bedroom as quietly as I can. I know how seriously he and Sonia take their podcast, *Down with America?* It does have a surprisingly high number of subscribers for a show recorded by two teenagers in a bedroom.

"I'm sorry, but I'm not down with it," Shane says. "We don't buy music anymore, so we've forced our favorite musicians into creating makeup lines and perfumes, which then distracts them from doing the exact thing we want them to do, which is make more music!"

"I mean!" Sonia says, incredulous. "No one is *holding them hostage* and telling them to become a brand." A small piece of me bristles at the word *hostage*, which always reminds me of the Iran hostage crisis. "And how much time do you think a pop star really spends on their makeup brand? They're just licensing their name. Let's get real."

"I am real," Shane says, smiling at me. "And our listeners know how I feel about the word *real*, and the implication that anything in this world is fake. Everything is authentic, especially artifice."

"Anyway, maybe it's a good thing your favorite singers aren't making as much music as they used to. Less opportunities for them to enjoy a little cultural appropriation."

"We've already covered that in another episode," Shane says. "For now, we want to hear from you, our listeners."

"Celebrity brands. Are you down with them, America?"

"And now, I'm going to give my boyfriend, Moud, who just walked in, a *real* big kiss as we play some listener responses to our last show about queer pain."

Shane gets up and welcomes me in. As his lips meet mine, Sonia hits play on some tape from listeners. A strident voice fills the room. "I am not *down* with queer pain. I'm so sick of queer characters suffering in our stories. And let's talk about how our stories are always centered on coming out to *straight people*. Especially parents. Aren't we over that?"

"Yeah, Moud, aren't you over that?" Shane asks, his lips gently kissing my neck.

"Stop," I whisper. I know what he wants. He wants me to say I'm over my dad. He wants me to leave my dad all alone and move in with him and his parents, into an *accepting* home. He actually suggested that once when I was crying over my dad not acknowledging my sexuality. Like leaving my home would be that easy.

As he continues kissing my neck, I think of how much I love him. His power and authority. His fearlessness. He's the reason I came out in the first place. And also, I think of the language barrier between us. Sure, we know the same words. But we obviously approach things differently, and I often find myself defending my homophobic dad when Shane attacks him. I'm sure I would defend Shane if my dad ever attacked him, but he doesn't. He just never brings him up. Maybe the struggle isn't between me and Shane at all. It's between the side of me that feels a duty to defend my family, and the side of me that wants to unapologetically celebrate my sexuality.

What Shane keeps forgetting is that my dad is my only living parent. I said that to Shane once, and he said I could find a *chosen* family. That's what it really boils down to. Shane wants me to choose him. He and my dad aren't so different in some ways.

"So," Shane says. "What did you think?"

"What I heard was great," I say. "It always is. You guys are naturals."

"When are you going to be our guest?" Sonia asks.

"Oh," I say. "I'm not like you two. I wouldn't know how to express my thoughts on the spot like that. I'm just a listener."

"The world needs listeners." Shane smiles as he says, "Wait, I have a theory. Maybe in every successful relationship, there needs to be a listener and a talker. Like in ours, right?"

"You sound like my dads," Sonia says. "They have this whole thing about how one of them is a bartender and the other serves hors d'oeuvres."

"Sorry, what?" Shane asks. "I like my relationship theory better."

"It's kind of the same theory," she counters. "The bartender stands in one place and waits for people to come to him, and the other person is working the room, passing out finger foods. And speaking of fingering, I told Becca I'd go see her."

Shane and I both burst out laughing. To punctuate her point, Sonia flashes us two middle fingers as she leaves the room. Then she immediately adopts her sweetest tone when she says, "Bye, Mrs. Waters" while descending the stairs.

The air in the room is thick when it's just the two of us. The passport in my pocket suddenly feels like it weighs ten pounds.

Shane pulls me in for a kiss, but he must sense my hesitation because he says, "What's wrong?"

"It's . . . Well, can we sit down?"

"Moud, is everything okay?"

"Just let me figure out where to start." I sit on his bed. There's a copy of *The Velvet Rage* next to his pillow. His scent seems to waft up from the sheets when I sit on them, giving me a moment of strength. "So my grandfather is sick."

"Wait, what?" He sits next to me, curling his legs around me. "How sick?"

"Really sick." I hear the numb distance in my voice. "Stage four lung cancer sick." I shake my head. "I always thought he'd make it to a hundred years old, but I guess that was wishful thinking."

"But . . . I don't understand. How did he just find out?"

"He didn't just find out. I just found out." I hear the lie and immediately correct it. "Well, I found out a couple of weeks ago."

"And you didn't tell me?" I feel his legs stiffen around me. "That's a very *your dad* thing to do."

"Yeah, well, my dad hid my grandfather's cancer from

me for two years. I didn't tell you for three weeks."

"You said a couple of weeks. A couple is two weeks. How long has it really been?"

I push myself away from him and stand up. "Shane, my grandfather is going to die. Can we talk about that instead of how long it took me to tell you? I'm not good at talking about pain, okay? That's like, a hereditary cultural thing for me."

"That's so unfair," he says. "When you say it's a cultural thing, you totally shut down my point of view."

"Okay, whatever. I thought every successful relationship has a talker and a listener. Well, I'm obviously *not* the talker, so don't punish me for being bad at talking."

He bites his lip. He does that when he's nervous. "I'm sorry. You know I'm sensitive about being lied to. Of course I want to support you. What can I do?"

For starters, he can stop saying I lied to him when I didn't. There's a difference between lying and processing the truth, but that's a conversation for another day. "You can support my decision to go to Iran," I whisper, avoiding his gaze.

He says nothing. Just sits there biting his lip. I pull out the passport and show it to him. "Weird, right? I'm a dual citizen now."

"But you weren't born there."

"Yeah, but my dad was. All you have to do is have an Iranian father with a Shenasnameh, and you can get a passport."

"A what?"

"It's an identity card. My dad has one, since he was born there."

"What if you just have an Iranian mother?" he asks, cross-examining me.

I shake my head. "Then you can't get a passport, and you can't inherit property, or . . ." Sensing what he's going to say, I add, "Look, I know there's a lot that's messed up about Iran, but—"

"But they kill gay people!" he blurts out, finally saying it.

"They don't . . . I mean, yes, they have, but they don't always . . . What I'm saying is that it's rare and . . ."

"Are you listening to yourself? You're defending a regime that wants you dead." He's using his podcast voice now, like he wants to teach me something. Maybe he thinks me defending my dad and defending the regime are the same thing. That it means I don't love myself enough or something.

"I'm not defending anyone. I just want to see my grandfather before—"

"I get that. Of course I do. But your whole relationship has been on WhatsApp, except for a few trips. And those were to Europe or Turkey, not Iran."

"Well, he's too sick to travel, so this is the only option. And Turkey is part of Europe."

"A *part* of Turkey is a *part* of Europe," he says. Then, softening, he pulls me back to the bed and envelops me in his arms. "Okay, wait. I'm sorry. I'm sorry. I'm sorry about your grandfather, and I'm sorry about my reaction.

I just don't want you to . . . you know . . ."

"I'm not . . ." I can't say the words. Of course I'm a little scared. Like everyone else, I've seen the photos of two gay teenagers being publicly hanged in Iran. Isn't that why I removed any sign of my sexuality from the internet?

"Shh," he says. "Let me just be here for you right now."

"Okay," I say, closing my eyes.

"When do you leave?"

"The day after tomorrow," I whisper, awaiting another round of shock.

"Oh, wow." I feel Shane stop himself from asking why I waited until the last minute to tell him. He's not very good at repressing his urges, and I feel a wave of gratitude to him for doing it just this once. And a wave of gratitude to him for being him. Isn't he the reason I'm not still hiding who I am from my dad? The reason I've been able to accept and love myself? "What about school?"

"I can do an independent study so I don't mess up my senior year transcript," I explain. "I'll be back after the winter holidays, unless . . ." I don't finish the sentence. There are so many things that could go wrong. Baba could die before the end of the year. I could be arrested and thrown in jail.

"I'm really going to miss you." I gaze into his eyes, and when he closes them, I kiss his eyelids.

"Me too," he says. "I guess we won't be together for New Year's Eve. It'll be weird, bringing in a new year without you."

"I'll be back way before the Persian new year. All is not lost."

"All is never lost." He smiles and lies down.

I lie next to him, my head on his chest. As I gaze up at the blankness of his ceiling, I'm reminded of the blankness of my social media. All the Shane and Moud history I erased. Like that video of the first time he played his ukulele for me, composing a melody just for us. He called it "Shane and Moud's Theme." He explained that in all great romantic films, the lovers have a melody that repeats in the score when they're together. This was our melody. He told me to imagine it playing every time he kissed me, then he kissed me for the first time. We photographed it. Posted it. And now I've deleted it.

I should tell him about wiping my feed. I should say something. Because if there's one thing about me that annoys him, it's that I sometimes expect him to read my mind because I'm no good at putting my feelings into words. But I can't. Not when I'm staring at the Harvey Milk poster on his wall, the one with the words *Every gay person must come out* on it.

How do I tell my boyfriend, who believes that every queer person must be loud and proud, that I just went a little bit back in? And how do I tell my boyfriend, who expresses his every opinion online, that I already feel liberated by my online absence? That it feels good not to feel the pressure to engage in every debate and every meme. That I don't want to post another photo of a pop star and label it "gay rights." That I never really cared about stan wars, or

12

mac 'n' cheese recipes, or who was Mom, or who snatched our wigs, or who centered what, or who platformed what, or what went viral, or who *always* understood the assignment, or who *never* understood the assignment, especially 'cause when it comes to social media, the person who never understood the assignment was me. I never understood why I needed to document my dull life. People love to begin by saying, "I don't know who needs to hear this, but . . ." And the thing is, usually no one needs to hear it.

As my dad and I have a WhatsApp video call with Baba during dinner, the world of social media already feels so far away. Shane feels distant too, like he belongs to a completely different world from the one my dad and Baba inhabit. "Nivea," Baba says. "I need lots of Nivea. My skin is so dry, and they don't have good cream here."

"Write it down," my dad says.

I swallow a bite of pizza before saying, "I'll remember that he needs Nivea."

"Trust me, there's going to be more."

Baba continues. "Toothpaste. Sensodyne. My teeth feel terrible."

My dad gives me an I-told-you-so look as I start a new note in my phone and begin to list everything Baba wants us to bring to Iran with us.

"Advil," Baba says. "Or Aleve, if there's no Advil anymore."

"There's still Advil, Baba," my dad says. "It's America. They have an endless supply of painkillers to treat their endless supply of pain."

"Good, then Advil. The strongest they make. And Pepto-Bismol. Not the chewable kind. I hate the taste. The kind you swallow."

"Shall we just bring one of every item in the pharmacy?" my dad jokes.

Baba doesn't laugh. He just keeps listing what he needs. Foot cream, and hydrocortisone, and Valium.

"Valium is a prescription medicine, Baba," my dad explains. "We can't get that for you."

"Fine. Then get me an iPad. The latest model, please."

I throw my dad an incredulous look. For a moment, we're united by how funny we find this moment.

"It's not for me. It's for Hassan Agha's son. Hassan Agha has been a huge help to me since I've been sick, and I'd like to do something nice for his son."

"Are we allowed to bring all this into the country?" I ask.

"They won't confiscate anything," Baba says. "The worst they'll do if they open your suitcase is tax you. They don't care about sanctions and morals, just money."

"And how are you feeling, Baba?" I ask.

My dad's gaze tells me he doesn't like this question. We don't talk about feelings in our home, especially not when we already know someone feels bad.

"I'm in pain," Baba says. "My wife is gone. My son and grandson live so far away. I spend most of my time with Hassan Agha, and I pay him to be here."

My dad gives me another I-told-you-so look, like he

wants me to be sorry for asking the question, when I'm actually pleased to have received an honest answer. At least Baba speaks from the heart.

"We'll be there soon, Baba," Dad says curtly, before ending the conversation. "Now we need to finish our dinner."

"Pizza from a box is not dinner," Baba says. "I'll show you a meal when you get here. We've already done all the shopping and marinated the meat."

My dad uses a Persian expression of thanks that translates to "May your hand not hurt," then hangs up. We don't speak for the rest of dinner.

The night before our flight, I text Shane to come over. My dad's at his office wrapping things up before our trip, so there's no risk they'll cross each other. I show Shane the contents of my suitcase when he comes into my room.

"That's . . . a lot of Nivea and Advil," he says.

"Baba had a lot of requests, and I have one too."

"Anything."

"I just want to be careful going to Iran, and, well, did you notice I deleted almost everything from my social media?"

Shane shakes his head. "Why? Because you think they'll see it and put you in jail or something?"

"I don't know, Shane. I'm just being careful. But I realized, well, you've tagged me in a lot of pictures of us kissing and other super-gay stuff, and . . ."

"Super-gay stuff?" Shane asks, pulling out his phone

and scrolling through the photos he's posted of us. "Like, the Pride Parade, the Chick fil-A protest, the Gaga concert, the Lana pop-up."

"Well, yeah," I say. "I'm just being careful."

"You keep saying that," he says.

"Because it's true."

"Isn't it weird that you protested a chicken sandwich, but you're gonna be visiting a country that—"

"Stop, please," I plead. "This isn't about politics. It's about my grandfather. And even if it was about politics, then things are more complicated than boycotting everything we don't like. I mean, our whole economy revolves around oil from countries with horrible human rights records. We arm countries who are dropping bombs all over the Middle East. What does protesting a chicken sandwich accomplish in the grand scheme of things?"

"There it is," he says.

"There what is?" I ask.

"You never shared my values." He deletes a post of us as he says this, then moves on to deleting another. "You've always agreed with me just to pacify me." He keeps deleting the posts.

"You don't have to delete everything. You can just untag me." I speak as softly as I can, doing exactly what he just accused me of. Trying to pacify him.

"It's okay. I don't need to publicly celebrate something you're ashamed of."

"I never said I was ashamed." I pull him in for a kiss. "I'm not ashamed."

Just then, my dad pulls up to the curb. We both hear it, and we both stop. "You want to hide me so your dad doesn't catch us together again?" he asks.

"Shane, no," I say. "You know I'm out to him. Just like you wanted."

"You didn't do it for me," he says. "You did it for *you*. And you've kept me and your dad apart ever since."

"Because he won't even acknowledge that I came out to him."

"Then come out again. Maybe once wasn't enough. Don't you want him to know you?"

I feel the tears welling up inside me. "Of course I do. You know that. But it's not that easy for me. Your parents figured out you were gay, and they love you. You didn't even have to come out."

He looks away from me. There's guilt in his voice. "You're right. I'm sorry. I should go."

"Are we okay?" I ask.

"Yeah, sure," he says. "Why wouldn't we be?"

I kiss him again, but there's no passion in it. We run into my dad as I walk him out.

"Oh, hello," my dad says.

"Hi, Mr. Jafarzadeh." Shane extends his hand, and my dad shakes it. "I'm very sorry to hear about your father."

I can sense my dad's discomfort, discussing something so personal. "Yes, thank you," is all he manages to say.

"Well, I was just here to say goodbye." Shane looks at me, the love back in his eyes.

"Then goodbye," my dad says. I wish he would offer

Shane just a little warmth.

I walk Shane out to his car. We don't say much to each other. There's nothing left to say, especially not with my dad watching us. I promise Shane I'll WhatsApp him from Iran, and he tells me again how sorry he is about Baba. The last thing he says is, "Take care of your emotional immune system, okay?"

We fly through Dubai. The flights are long, and I'm too full of nervous anticipation to sleep. But my dad's eyes are closed for both flights. Maybe he's sleeping. Or maybe he's just avoiding talking to me. The only thing he says to me the whole way there is, "Most people used to fly through Frankfurt, but that ended because of the idiotic sanctions."

When we land in Tehran, the women who weren't already wearing a head covering throw one on. And then we line up to exit the plane, into a place that has defined my whole life. I'm hit with a wave of emotions as we enter the airport. The thing that hits me hardest is that everyone looks like me, and I realize I've never had that experience. I've always stood out because of my brownness, but here I blend in. It feels strange, and safe.

Then I'm hit by a wave of fear, because I might look like everyone else, but I *know* I'm different. And what if the wrong person finds that out? Like the guy holding a gun as we make our way to the immigration line. He looks like he's my age, but he holds the weapon like an expert. He wouldn't hurt me, would he?

Dad hands our passports to the immigration officer, and I can feel my heart beat out of my chest as the officer looks us over. "What's the reason for your visit?" the officer asks.

My dad solemnly says, "My father is ill."

"May God protect him," the officer says. Then, handing our passports back to my dad, he smiles and says, "Welcome home."

Those words linger in the air as we make our way to baggage claim, where Baba and Hassan Agha wait for us. Baba is in a wheelchair, Hassan Agha behind him. Hassan Agha might be smiling, but it's hard to tell with his giant horseshoe mustache. Baba waves to us, a welcoming smile on his face. His body's been shrinking fast the last few years, but his head has stayed the same size. His hair is a shock of white. His big dark eyes glimmer with life and mystery. And his smile still brightens the room.

I think of those words again. *Welcome home.* I realize that I may be coming to a foreign country, but my dad isn't. He's coming back to the place he was born in, the country that raised him.

"Does it feel like coming home?" I ask him.

He shakes his head, like he disapproves of my asking about his feelings. "It all looks different," he says.

I didn't ask how it looks. I asked how it feels. I want to shake him and demand answers. *How does it feel to be back? How did it feel to leave then? Why won't you talk to me? Why won't you tell me who you are?*

SAEED

1978

Tehran

"Come on, double six," Baba whispers as he shakes his dice cup like it's an instrument. My father turns everything into music. "Parvaneh, come here. I need you." On cue, Maman enters, holding a blueprint in her hands. Without being asked, she blows into Baba's dice cup.

"I'm done for," I say with a rueful smile.

Maman moves behind me. She puts a hand on each of my shoulders and kisses the top of my head. "Don't worry, I'll blow on your dice too. I have enough luck for both of my favorite men."

Baba rolls his dice. As expected, he rolls a double six. He removes four chips off his side of the board with an impish grin. "Your move, son."

I hold up my dice cup for Maman to blow into. When I shake the dice, it sounds nothing like music. Baba may have taught me how to hit the right keys on a piano or pluck strings on the tar, but he'll never teach me how to be an artist. That's not who I am. Peyman says all children must become the opposite of their parents in at least one important way, and I think he's right. Except sometimes I feel like the opposite of my parents in *every* way. I roll a two and a one. "Oh, come on," I yell in mock exasperation. "I'm never going to catch up now."

"Come to my side again, Parvaneh." Baba smiles slyly. "Your luck only seems to work for me."

"Don't you dare, Maman," I plead.

Just in time to save her, the doorbell rings. I move to stand up, the old wooden chair creaking under me. "Keep playing, I'll get it," Maman says.

"If it's my student, will you ask him to wait in the study?" Baba asks as he rolls a three and a two, then grimaces.

"Well, well, well," I say. "Looks like your luck's running out."

I hear Maman open the door and greet Peyman warmly. Their footsteps head toward us, the rhythm changing when they move from the creaky wood floors to the colorful rug that depicts a story from *The Shahnameh*. "Who's winning?" Peyman asks when he enters. He's wearing a black peacoat and holding a large covered tray.

"We're tied one game each," I tell him. "But Baba is about to go down. What's in the tray?"

"Homemade *yakh dar behesht* for you." Peyman hands the tray to my mother.

Maman peeks inside before placing the tray down on the long wooden dining room table. "Please tell your mother she doesn't need to cook something for us every time you come over."

"I can tell her, but she won't listen." Then, with a meaningful gaze toward me, Peyman says, "We should go, Saeed. We don't want to be late."

"Where are you going?" Maman asks.

"Please tell me you're going to have some fun," Baba says. "You're young. Youth is meant to be enjoyed."

"Should we keep the board here and finish tomorrow?" I ask.

Baba nods as he stands up. He turns a light on, and the bulb illuminates the calligraphy on the lamp. "You changed the subject," Baba says. "Where are you two off to?"

"We're going to the library," I say. "To study with some friends." I don't look at either of my parents. I hate lying to them, but what choice do I have? If they knew where I was going, they would stop me. My parents are open-minded about almost everything. They encourage me to go out and enjoy the city's bustling cafés and discos. The one thing they forbid me from doing is taking part in the protests spreading across the city.

"You're eighteen years old and all you do is study," Baba says to me. Then, turning to Peyman, "You seem like a fun kid. Can't you convince our son to let loose and enjoy his youth once in a while?"

Peyman laughs. "I wish my parents were more like you. They're always telling me to study more, work harder, think of my future." Peyman does let loose, often. But unlike me, he has an uncanny ability to balance school, protests, and nightclubbing without ever losing his focus.

"Study *more*?" Maman asks with a smile. "You two are already going to the best engineering university in the country. You've even been taking summer classes."

The doorbell rings again. "That must be my new student," Baba says. He starts to make his way to the front door, then stops and turns back to us. "Your mother and I don't want you to party all the time. Or to study all the time. Or to do anything all the time. What we want is for you to find balance. When you don't have balance . . . when you're laser-focused on one goal . . ." The doorbell rings again. Baba seems lost in thought.

"Babak," Maman says gently.

He snaps out of his reverie and continues to the front door to greet his student.

As they make their way to Baba's study, Maman grabs my coat from the dining room chair and throws it around me. She straightens the collar. "Should I get you a scarf?" she asks.

"I'll be okay," I say.

"It's already getting cold at night." Maman looks me in the eye with discomfiting tenderness.

The sound of Baba's tar floats toward us, casting its magic spell over our home. Then there's a brief pause, followed by the sound of the tar being played by the new student, who turns those strings into a screeching instrument of torture.

"Oh, wow." Peyman grimaces in playful shock, which

makes Maman and me both laugh. "I think we've found the key to convincing the Shah to change his policies," Peyman says. "We just force him to listen to the worst tar player in the world until he gives in."

Maman shakes her head as she laughs. "You'd be surprised at how quickly Babak turns a terrible musician into a decent one."

I want to say that she might be surprised at how quickly a mass of young students can do that with our government. But I can't say that. Because she can't know that we're headed to a protest. I wish I could explain to my parents that when I'm at a protest and my voice is raised in chorus with my fellow students, I feel alive in a way I rarely do.

Peyman's car is parked next to mine in our driveway. "Get in," he commands.

"My turn to drive," I say. We both love the Paykans our parents got us when we were accepted into university, and we always want to be the one who gets to maneuver our magic vehicle through Tehran's bustling roads.

I park five minutes away from Shahyad Square, and we walk toward the protest together, alongside other students headed to the same square. Peyman greets our classmates warmly. He's a social creature. He makes friends wherever he goes, which I suppose is why I've always felt lucky that he chose me as his best friend.

As Peyman chats with two guys he plays soccer with, I see the most beautiful girl I've ever seen in my life. Her long black hair glows. Her brown skin shines. It's as if she's radiating light.

"Saeed!" Peyman calls out to me.

I'm entranced by her, until she drops her hair tie as she fixes her ponytail. I swoop in to pick the hair tie up for her, and hand it back to her as if it's something rare and precious.

"Thank you," she says. She ties her hair back into a ponytail.

"Saeed!" Peyman yells at me. "Come here, I want you to meet my soccer buddies."

I look at the girl sheepishly. "I, um, have to go. That's my friend. . . ."

"Nice to meet you, *Saeed*," she says with a gleam in her hazel eyes. Then she walks away, just one more body in the crowd of people headed to Shahyad Square for the protest.

"Wait, what's your name?" I ask, but she's already too far away to hear me.

Peyman introduces me to his soccer friends, and then I chastise him as we walk toward the square. "You just pulled me away from the most beautiful girl I've ever met," I say.

Peyman shrugs. "I didn't get a good look at her, but if she's as stunning as you say, then she's definitely out of your league."

I slap his shoulder a little too hard. "Walk faster. I need to find her."

Peyman smiles, impressed. "Well, wow. Is my best friend finally coming out of his shell?"

The energy of our fellow protesters compels us forward. I push my way through the crowd, dragging Peyman along with me. Until I see her again, a few steps ahead of me.

I want to know everything about her. I know she has fire in her eyes and wears her hair in a simple ponytail, avoiding the elaborate European hairstyles so many young Iranian girls seem to emulate these days. I know she shares my values. Why else would she be out in the streets like I am, screaming for freedom, demanding a better country?

"Go talk to her now, before we reach the square and there's still time," Peyman says.

I feel suddenly nervous. "I don't . . . I don't know what to say."

He rolls his eyes. "Fine. If you're not brave enough, I'll ask her to have dinner with me. Imagine me and her, sitting real close at one of those cozy little spots at the foot of the Alborz Mountains, eating *kookoo sabzi*, drinking *doogh*—"

"I may be a bad Iranian for saying this, but *doogh* is disgusting. Yogurt should be eaten with a spoon. And you wouldn't dare." I give Peyman a sharp look.

"Of course I wouldn't. But someone else might. So go talk to her now." Peyman gently pushes me toward her, just like he gently pushed me into the streets back when I was too scared to raise my voice. I always believed in what the students were demanding—freedom of the press, freedom of speech, more opportunities for young people—but if it weren't for Peyman, I would never have been brave enough to defy my parents and join the movement.

Peyman's gentle push makes me stumble next to her. She looks over at me and smiles. "Oh, hello again, Saeed," she says. I smile too, but I don't say anything. My mouth feels chalky. "Are you going to say something?" she asks.

"I, um . . . I'm not sure what to say."

"You could perhaps start with hello."

"Yes, hello," I say with a smile. I swallow hard. I need water. And someone to teach me how to talk to girls. "Nice day, isn't it? I mean . . . it hasn't rained and it's not too windy, and . . . Well, hello."

Peyman, who is standing close enough to supervise my pathetic attempt at romance, puts an arm around me. "I apologize on behalf of my friend. He's just a little shy. But he's also ridiculously brilliant, unbearably handsome, and extremely well-mannered."

Looking at Peyman, she says, "Something tells me you're not to be trusted." Turning to me, she adds, "There's nothing extremely well-mannered about meeting a girl and not even asking her name." She starts to walk again, challenging us to join her.

"I'm sorry," I say. "What's your—"

"Shirin." She cuts me off with a smile. "I'm Shirin. If you're so well-mannered, perhaps you can introduce yourself."

"I'm Saeed Jafarzadeh. This is my friend Peyman, who is quite trustworthy, I assure you." I throw a hard stare at Peyman as I say, "In fact, he's so studious that

27

he's off to study for a test now."

"You're not attending the protest?" she asks him with a smile, like she can see right through me.

"Not today. But it was a pleasure to meet you, Shirin." Peyman pulls me into a hug and whispers, "Don't mess this up. And thanks for not letting me drive. Now I have to take the bus home."

Peyman leaves. My legs feel wobbly as I walk alone with Shirin. "Are you going with friends?" I ask, looking around at the people walking alongside us. Most of them seem to be students.

"I'm alone," she says. "Most of my friends are too scared. They say the real crackdown hasn't really begun yet."

"And what do you think?" I ask.

"Look at that, a man who cares what a woman *thinks*."

"I care what *you* think." Realizing that came out the wrong way, I quickly add, "Not that I don't care about other women's thoughts, of course."

"Of course." She suppresses a smile.

"Do you think the revolution will be good for women?" I ask.

"Would I be here if I didn't?"

"No, I suppose not," I say.

"We're marching for freedom. That helps *everyone*."

"Exactly."

Ahead of us, the sound of the protest gets closer. We hear the horns of cars in support of the chants of "Independence" and "Freedom." And also shouts of, "The Shah is a traitor! Death to the Shah!" A group of students walking near us repeat the words, but I notice she doesn't. She keeps her lips sealed instead of wishing death on the man we're all out here protesting.

She notices me watching her and says, "I just don't believe in wishing death on any human being, even one I want out of power."

"I'm starting to think you should run this country," I say. "Bravery and compassion, that's a rare combination."

A guy driving a shiny black Mercedes-Benz tries to speed through the light, almost running her over in the process. She jumps out of danger, grabbing ahold of my arm to steady herself. The feel of her hand on my arm makes my pulse race. "Watch where you're going," she screams to the bearded driver after he screeches to a halt at the light.

"Shut up, Miss Iran," the driver screams back.

As we walk away from him, she turns to me. "Miss Iran? Do I look like the kind of girl who would enter a beauty pageant?"

"You look like the kind of girl who *could* enter a beauty pageant, but perhaps not like the kind of girl who *would*."

She smiles. "You should talk more," she says. "I like what you have to say. And I don't always look like this."

"Like what?" I ask. "You look . . . perfect."

She rolls her eyes. "Well then, you should see me on a Friday night at Key Club."

As the chant continues—"Down with America, Down with America"—I look into her eyes, and we both stop for a moment, like we're lost. Or perhaps like we're finally found. Because we've reached the center of the protest now. We're in Shahyad Square, surrounded by greenery, dwarfed by the Azadi Tower the Shah built with money he could have used to feed his people. We're marching for our own future, but we're also marching for all the Iranians who can't afford to feed their families right now. Crowds of people march past us, bumping us closer to each other as they do. The men are a mix of older workers and younger students. The young men stomp across the square in their boots, their bell-bottom pants swaying as they move.

As we get swept up into the crowd, I realize I have no idea how to find her again. "What's your last name?" I yell over the sound of the crowd.

Before she can answer, there's a sudden commotion. "It's the army!" someone shouts from up ahead.

Panic invades my body. I've been to three protests now, but so far they've ended peacefully. If the army is here, then violence will follow. I hear Baba's and Maman's voices, telling me this is exactly why we stay away from politics—because protest leads to violence. And they don't want to lose their only son.

"Shirin, take my hand!" I scream. I try to reach for her, but the crowds are charging ahead too fast, running from the army. It's no use. We're separated.

I keep my eyes glued to her, but everything is a haze. Guns are shot, bullets flying into the sky as a warning. A stampede of people push past me, escaping the threat. Screams pierce the air. The screams don't have the strength of purpose anymore, just the cold metallic sound of fear.

"Shirin!" I cry out desperately. I can't see her anymore. Where is she?

"Saeed!" her distant voice responds.

I search for her in the smoke and the blur of fear. But she's gone.

I close my eyes and say a silent prayer that she won't be afraid to show up to the next protest. Because how else will I ever find her?

And then I run to my car and drive to Lalehzar Street. Thinking of her the whole way there, picturing her in my arms. Every thought that was consumed by revolution is now consumed by her, like she has become the revolution of my life, the change I need.

I'm still out of breath when I reach the house, the sound of gunshots ringing in my ears. I try to calm myself before I enter, but I'm doing a terrible job of hiding my emotions. Baba and Maman rush to the front door when they hear me. "Where were you?" Baba demands.

"I told you, studying with Peyman." My breath is too heavy. They can tell I'm lying. This could be my moment to tell my parents what I believe in, who I am. But I know what they'll say, so what's the point?

"Saeed." Baba speaks my name softly. "You know you can talk to us about anything, don't you?"

"Of course I do." I avoid his gaze.

"You don't need to keep any secrets from us," Baba continues.

"I know that," I say.

Baba waits for a few uncomfortable moments before sighing in resignation. "All right, then, my student is waiting for me."

Maman lingers next to me for a moment. She doesn't say anything. She just kisses my forehead, then lets me head to my room. I open an engineering textbook and daydream about Shirin. My concentration isn't helped by the sound of the tar that comes from the study. Baba is the one playing now, and his music captures all my emotions. There's hesitation, longing, passion, and a hint of fear in the sounds drifting toward my room.

I skip dinner. I'm not hungry. I'm filled up by the energy of the day, and by the memory of her. I read a poem aloud before bed. Khayyam.

"'Ah, my beloved, fill the cup that clears today of past regrets and future fears.'"

I hear rustling outside. A light knock on my door. "Good night, Saeed." Baba knows the last thing I do before bed is read a poem. It's his tradition, after all.

"Good night, Baba," I say.

I feel him outside, probably considering whether he should ask more questions about where I was and why I skipped dinner. Finally, he pushes the door open. He's holding the backgammon board. "We have unfinished business," he says. He puts the board down on my bed and hands me the dice cup. "I think it was my turn."

The next day, in between classes, I tell Peyman everything about my fleeting moments with Shirin. He kicks me in the shin as he says, "I told you not to mess this up, and now you're telling me you didn't even get her last name."

"There were gunshots," I say incredulously.

"You're going to let a little thing like gunshots keep you away from the first woman you've shown any interest in?" We exit into the fresh air of our university. All around us, students head to their classes, textbooks and bags in hand.

"I'm sorry that unlike some guys, I don't lust after every woman I see."

Putting on a high-pitched voice, he says, "I don't know who you're talking about." Then, back to his regular voice, he adds, "Now how are we going to find her?"

"When's the next protest?" I ask.

Peyman shakes his head in disappointment. "My best friend. So smart when it comes to engineering and calculus. So utterly stupid when it comes to women."

"What did I do this time?" I ask.

Outside the university, a man grills corn. Peyman buys two cobs and hands one to me. "Given what happened, have you considered that perhaps a political protest is not the ideal location for the start of a romance? Next time, I recommend talking to her in a place where you won't be interrupted by the army."

I take a sizzling bite of corn. "But where else can I find her? I don't know her last name, or where she lives." Suddenly, my eyes open wide. "Key Club. Friday night."

Peyman speaks through a mouthful of corn. "Yes, I've

been. It's fantastic. The girls all wear miniskirts, and the ones who don't wear tight pants. Very hot."

"No, listen. She told me I should see her at Key Club on Friday nights."

Peyman smiles. "And see her you shall." I laugh, because I'm giddy with excitement, and because Peyman looks so silly with corn stuck between his teeth.

Friday after class, Peyman comes over to help me get ready for our night out. Baba and Maman peek in and find all my clothes strewn around my bedroom. I'm in nothing but my underwear, waiting for Peyman to tell me what to try on next.

"Studying hard?" Baba asks.

Peyman leaps up when he sees them. "Mr. and Mrs. Jafarzadeh, please come help me." I gaze hard at Peyman, silently warning him not to tell my parents too much. "You see, I've convinced your son to go dancing for the first time ever."

Baba and Maman enter. They give Peyman a kiss on each cheek.

"You wanted me to have more fun. Well, I'm trying. But Peyman says my clothes are depressing."

"Follow me," Baba says commandingly, and we all do. Baba leads us to his closet. He pushes back the items on the front of the rack until he reveals some clothes I've never seen, hiding in the back. He pulls out a button-down shirt with a beautiful, almost architectural, design on it. Colors swirl around each other, deep purple, navy blue, chocolate brown. "This was my father's shirt. It once fit me. Perhaps it will fit you now."

Baba throws me the shirt, and I put it on. Peyman gives me an approving nod. "Now we're talking." Peyman pulls a navy-blue blazer from the closet. There are camel-colored suede patches on the elbows. "May I?" he asks.

"You may," Baba says. "My father bought me that jacket before a recital. I think I was just a little older than you, Saeed *joon*."

I throw the blazer on and look at myself in the full-length mirror. I look a little silly with no pants on. And as cool as Baba's old clothes are, they're not me. But maybe that's the point. Maybe I'm changing.

"Now we're going to have to do something about the hair," Peyman says. "Do you have scissors?" He sees the look of horror on my face and laughs. "I'm joking. We'll just use some gel."

Maman tousles my mop of hair. "And what inspired you to finally go have some fun?"

"Just taking my beloved parents' advice," I say, with a forced smile.

Baba squints, clearly not buying my answer. "Take a taxi, please. I don't want you drinking and getting behind the wheel."

"Baba, I don't drink," I protest.

"And before tonight, you didn't go dancing either." Baba gives us a sharp look. "Take risks, but not stupid risks. I'm not losing my only child to a drunken car accident or to a pointless political protest. Do you two hear me?" Baba's eyes land on mine. He seems to know everything.

The taxi drops us off outside Key Club in Shemran, where a group of guys in bell bottoms smoke cigarettes. As we approach the club, I turn to Peyman. "Wait, before we go in, tell me if the rumors are true."

"What rumors?" he asks. Peyman also wears bell bottoms, with a polyester shirt and an off-white blazer. I've never gone out dancing with him, so I've never seen him dressed like this.

"You know, that it's called Key Club because everyone who gets in is given a key to a private room where they . . . you know . . . where they . . ."

Peyman puts a hand on my shoulder. "Unfortunately, those rumors are not true. Now get that look of fear off your face. We still need to get in."

Peyman is a member, so we're let in with no problems. No one asks how old we are. No one asks to see documentation. When the doors open, my senses come alive. The scents of perfume, cologne, cigarettes, and sweat hit me hard. The sensual sound of Donna Summer singing about having a spring affair transports me. And my eyes, they can't quite believe what I'm seeing. Peyman was right about the girls. I've never seen skirts this short, pants this tight. They dance with abandon, drinks in their hands. "I know you don't drink, but what do you want to drink?" Peyman asks me.

I laugh off the question. "Do you see her?" I search the room, but I can't find her in the sea of feathered hair and polyester and flashing lights.

"I'm getting you a vodka with tonic," he announces.

"I don't—" But he's already gone to the bar, leaving me standing awkwardly alone.

I'm searching for her when another girl approaches me with a smile. "You look like a lost lamb," she says.

"Oh, I'm just looking for someone. A friend."

She takes a sip of her brightly colored drink. "I've always found lambs very cute." She bats her eyes at me, and I realize she's flirting.

"Her name is Shirin. My friend. Do you know her?"

Disappointed, the girl says, "I know at least ten Shirins. Have fun."

As the girl walks away, Peyman returns with our drinks. "Who was that?" he asks.

"I don't know," I say. "Just some girl who isn't Shirin."

Peyman shakes his head. "You idiot, the best thing you could be doing when Shirin gets here is flirting with someone else. Don't you know jealousy is the way to a woman's heart?"

I take a sip of the drink. It burns the back of my throat. "I don't want to make her jealous. I want to make her happy."

"You're hopeless," he says, as he takes a much bigger slug of his drink than I did.

The song changes from Donna Summer to Aretha Franklin. I'm taking another sip when I turn and see her.

She's standing on top of a table, wearing a fitted black suit with a sparkly silver shirt under the blazer. She's holding a bottle of champagne, her ponytail swinging from side to side as she screams the lyrics at the top of her lungs. "*What you want, baby, I got it,*" she yells when she catches my gaze. With her free hand, she waves to me. I wave back.

Peyman slaps my back so hard that some of my drink spills. "Go dance with her."

"What, I can't, I don't know how—"

"Finish your drink," he orders, and I do as I'm told, polishing off what's left in one painful chug. "Now go."

I stumble my way toward her. I can't tell if the alcohol is going to my head, or if it's just nerves. When I reach her, I just stand there, staring up at her on the table. "*R-E-S-P-E-C-T,*" she screams as she offers me her hand. I take it and she pulls me up on the table. She hands me the bottle of champagne, and I can't say no to her. I take a sip, the sweet bubbliness much more pleasant than the sharp taste of vodka. I try hard not to look foolish dancing. As the song hits its crescendo, Shirin and I are facing each other, mouthing the words, each of us telling the other to "sock it to me," whatever that means.

When the song ends, she collapses down into the booth.

I blush and sit next to her. "Hello," I say.

"So you found me? I'm impressed."

"How do you know I came here looking for you?" I ask.

She rolls her eyes. "You don't strike me as the kind of guy who spends his nights dancing. If you were, I would've seen you here before. Or at Cheminée. Or at La Bohème. Or at Cave d'Argent."

"Do you speak French?" I ask, stunned by the ease with which she speaks the names of the discos. In Tehran, the discos and restaurants love to use French or English names.

"I'm a woman with many hidden talents." She picks up the bottle of champagne again. Takes a quick sip. "And you? What are your talents?"

"I don't know," I say nervously. "Obviously not dancing, as you could see a moment ago."

"You weren't so bad." She looks at me for a long beat, and I suddenly feel self-conscious about my exposed chest. Peyman insisted I leave the top two buttons of my shirt unbuttoned. "I like the outfit."

"They're my baba's clothes." Why did I have to bring my parents into this? Quickly changing the subject, I declare, "My talents are engineering. Mathematics."

"I take it you're a college student too," she says.

"Aryamehr," I declare proudly, because saying I go to Aryamehr means something. It means I was chosen from the countless candidates trying to secure a place at the school.

"Thank God, you're not dumb." I know my parents hate that I'm always thinking of the future. But right now, I'm happy that all the studying got me into a school that impresses Shirin.

"What would happen if I was dumb?" I ask with a laugh.

"I'd get bored with you after one meal, and then I would have to find a way to tell you I don't want you pursuing me without hurting your feelings. It would be awkward for both of us."

I smile. My head feels light. "And you're a student too?"

"Tehran University," she says. I nod. Like Aryamehr, only the brightest get into Tehran University. And unlike in Western countries, university is free in Iran, so no one can buy their way in. It's one place where the corruption infecting the rest of the country doesn't exist. The royal family controls billions while their people starve and their opponents disappear. But at the universities, there's real equality. Maybe that's why all the students are in the streets. Because we know how equality feels. "I'm studying biology. I want to be a doctor. Perhaps medical research. But this isn't the place to be discussing school, is it? Shall we dance again?"

A new song begins. Don McLean's "American Pie." "I'm not sure I know how to dance to this song."

"I can lead you." Shirin stands up, and I follow.

"Do they play any Persian music here?" I ask as we head to the dance floor.

"No, you have to go to the cabarets for that."

On the dance floor, Peyman is snapping his fingers. "It's just a bit hard to make sense of it all."

"What?" she asks.

"Well, on the one hand, we're protesting because we want America to leave our country alone, right? But on the other hand, we all love their music and their movies.

How can a place that makes such incredible art do such horrible things?"

We're standing at the edge of the dance floor now. She thinks a moment before saying, "I suppose that a country's government doesn't always represent its people. The government is responsible for the atrocities. The people make the art. And it's not just the Americans who have meddled in Iran." With a smile and a perfect upper-crust British accent, she adds, "The British have been doing it longer."

"Where did you learn to speak like that?" I ask.

She switches back to Persian as she says, "I've traveled. London. Paris. Rome."

That's when I know that even if we share values, she's not like me. Sure, I'm educated. I speak English. I go to a top university because I worked hard. But only the wealthiest families travel through Europe. "And . . . what's your favorite city?" I ask.

She smiles wistfully. "Tehran." Then she pulls me onto the dance floor and we all raise our arms toward the sky as we sing that this'll be the day that we die. When the song ends, a group of her friends crowd around her and say they're heading to the next destination.

"I'll see you again soon?" she says as they pull her away.

"Of course," I yell over the music. I want to stop them so I can get her phone number, or ask what her last name is, but it's too late. Will I spend the rest of my life scouring protests and discotheques for her?

41

By the time I get home, it's two in the morning. I sneak into my bedroom quietly. I throw my clothes onto the floor and pick up a poetry book. Saadi. I get into bed and am quietly whispering the poems to myself when I hear the creak of my door. It's Baba. He stands at the threshold of my room. "How was it?" he whispers.

"It was nice," I say. "I didn't wake you up, did I?"

He comes in and sits on the edge of my bed. "No, I was up reading."

Memories of Shirin dance around my brain. "Baba?" I ask tentatively. "Did you know you loved Maman as soon as you met, or did it take time?"

He turns away from me as he says, "That's too long a story for this hour."

"Was she the first person you fell in love with?"

Baba stands up. He runs a hand gently through my hair. "It's late," he whispers. "Go to sleep." There's a distant look in his eyes as he leaves my room.

BOBBY

1939

Los Angeles

"Bobby, hurry up," Coach Lane says impatiently as I tie my shoes. "I want to see some great tennis." But the thing is, I don't want to play tennis. I play for one reason, to be near Vicente.

We're playing doubles, and thankfully Vicente is not on my team, which means he'll be in front of me, right where I can see him. He serves, and I'm distracted by the way his shirt rises when he tosses the ball up. The momentary view of his bare, hairy abdomen sidetracks me, and the ball whizzes past my racquet. An ace.

"Fifteen-love," Vicente says as he moves to the other side of the court.

"Fifteen-*love*," I repeat. This is a game I play with myself, finding covert ways to speak my feelings for Vicente out loud.

He serves the ball to my partner, and though we all know every serve in his arsenal—flat, slice, high, low—most of us can't return his balls. Vicente is the best player on our team—our star. He's the reason our little school has a chance of going to the state finals. Coach Lane says he has the potential to go all the way, as long as he works on his sportsmanship. Coach Lane is *very* big on sportsmanship. He's not training tennis players. He's training gentlemen athletes, Southern California boys who will someday need to compete in the elite world of East Coast tennis, in the all-white world of Wimbledon. He expects us to be perfect on *and* off the court.

"Thirty-love," Vicente says. He serves to me again, and this time I manage to return it. My racquet swings on instinct, a forehand that somehow lands deep in the court. He shuffles backward, effortlessly hitting a crushing ball to my backhand side. He knows my backhand is weak. He's not afraid to take advantage of me, and I hope someday he'll be taking advantage of me in other ways. But first, I have to tell him how I feel.

My backhand lands in the half-court, a setup for him to hit a winner. He runs forward, gets into position, and whacks the ball down the line. I clap my hand against my racquet strings, congratulating him.

"Forty-*love*," I say.

My partner and I haven't won a single game, but I don't care. Before we know it, Coach Lane announces that it's match point. Vicente bounces the ball three times. When he throws it up into the air, Coach Lane yells, "Foot fault."

Vicente turns to Coach Lane. "Seriously, Coach? I didn't cross the line."

"You did. It's forty-fifteen now."

Vicente beelines to the coach. "You never call a foot fault for anyone but me."

"No one ever footfaults but you," Coach Lane says calmly.

"Oh, please." Vicente rolls his eyes and turns to the rest of the team. "Patrick footfaults every time and you don't say a word."

Patrick doesn't dare speak. None of them say much when the coach is with us. They act like the perfect gentlemen Coach Lane wants them to be. Calm. Polite. Their skin as white as their tennis clothes. Vicente and I are the only dark-skinned kids at our school. The Mexican and the Mother's Boy. That's what they call us when we walk down the halls.

"We're at forty-thirty now," Coach says in his usual icy tone. "Keep arguing with me, Vinnie, and you'll lose another point and get to deuce."

"This is so unfair," Vicente says. "I didn't footfault. You just don't like me."

I want to cross the court and put my arm around him. Tell him that no good will come of fighting back against the Coach Lanes of the world. Of course Coach Lane hates Vicente. Partly because he's Mexican. He probably blames men like Vicente's dad for taking jobs away from "real" Americans like the fathers of all these pasty-skinned boys we go to school with. But Coach Lane also hates Vicente because he's got the talent to be a *real* professional, not just a coach.

"Get back on the court and finish the match," Coach Lane says. "Tennis is a gentleman's sport and you're acting like a savage."

"A savage? Really?" Vicente spits the words out, his rage growing. He raises his racquet up in the air, ready to smash it into pieces.

"Don't you dare throw that racquet," Coach warns. "You will behave like a gentleman if you want to represent this sport, this school, and this country."

Vicente squints in disgust. He knows exactly what the coach is saying. He looks at me, and I try to convey all the support I can from across the court. I try to tell him not to bother arguing with someone who isn't worth the time. His shoulders drop.

"Okay," he says. "Okay."

"You're at forty-thirty," Coach says.

Vicente takes the court. Throws the ball into the air. I squat down, readying myself for his power. And . . . smash. The ball whizzes past me. He always manages to play his best when he's angry.

"Game. Set. Match," Coach Lane says. "Get to the showers, boys. And Vinnie, you're lucky this was a practice match. If I ever see you acting up during a real competition, you're off the team."

Vicente and I walk to the center of the court. We shake hands, gripping each other tight. I love the feel of his warm, sweaty palm against mine. He pulls me ever so slightly closer to him.

"Good match," he says.

"Good match," I say back. And then, whispering, I add, "Ignore him. He's an ass."

The public courts we practice on are a five-minute walk from school. We walk toward school slower than the rest of the team. We always do this. In part because we don't want to shower with those gross guys, who like to tease each other mercilessly about their penis size, who deal with the discomfort they feel around other naked boys by saying lewd things about girls. These boys might act like perfect gentlemen in front of Coach, but in the privacy of the showers, they turn into something else entirely.

"Is your aunt still sick?" I ask.

"She is," he says. "She has a really bad cold. She'll probably join us for dinner, but she definitely won't be cooking it."

"That's great," I say.

He laughs. "You *want* my family to be ill?"

"I'm sorry, that came out wrong." I laugh too. "I just thought, well . . . It could be nice to have your place to ourselves for once."

He glances at me curiously. "Yeah?"

"Yeah." I smile. "Well, at least for an hour. I have my piano lesson this evening, which I wish I could cancel. But you know Mother."

"I sure do," he says, laughing.

We reach the entrance of school. All the other boys have already gone inside. They're probably under the cold showers by now, spanking each other's bare bottoms as they talk about which girls they want to screw. Perfect gentlemen indeed.

"Move it, you two," Coach Lane screams from behind us.

Vicente turns around. Coach is pushing his cart of tennis balls toward us. I can tell Vicente wants to share a few more choice words with Coach Lane, and I look to him sharply. "Let it go," I say. "He's not worth it."

Vicente takes a calming breath as he heads into school. We walk toward the locker rooms side by side. Thankfully, the other boys are drying off when we get there.

"Oh, look, it's the Mexican and the Mother's Boy," one of them says. "Take it off, boys. Let's see if either of you grew overnight, or if you're still the smallest among us."

I cringe at how stupid they all are.

"Did you cut off that extra skin yet, Vinnie?" another boy asks snidely.

"Nope," Vicente says. "But I'll cut your head off if you don't shut up. And I don't mean the head above your neck. I mean the one that looks like an infected mushroom."

A few oohs and aahs as the boys laugh.

"Don't have too much fun in here when we're gone, you two," one of them says. "You know what they say about Mexicans, don't you, boys?"

"What's that?" another one asks.

"They love being on their knees. My dad says it's 'cause they're biologically made to be farm workers."

Vicente gets close to the guy. "Yeah, well, my dad works in an auto factory," he says. "And he's as American as you and your idiot of a father. He even has the passport to prove it."

The guy backs away from Vicente. "Don't get too close to me. I heard it smells when it's not cut."

I want to beat the guy to a pulp. But instead, I blurt out, "Who told you that? Your mother?"

The room stops cold. No one says a word. Here in the locker room, we mock and tease. But mothers are perhaps the only sacred thing left in their world.

The boys throw their clothes on. Before they leave, they leer at me with violence in their eyes. One of them runs two fingers along his neck, a silent warning that he'll kill me next time I dare cross him.

"Sorry," I tell Vicente when they're gone. "Did I go too far?"

"No, it was funny," he says, as he strips his sweaty clothes off.

"Okay, but . . ." What I want to say is that I'm sorry for saying something nasty about anyone's mother. Because if mothers are sacred to anyone, it's Vicente. He lost his mom when he was seven.

"Bobby," he says. "I know what you're thinking, and it's okay. You didn't say anything about *my* mother." Of course he knew I was thinking of Mrs. Madera. It's like he can see inside me with X-ray vision.

He's standing naked before me now, his skin gleaming under the overhead locker-room lighting. "Come on," he says. "Let's clean up so we can go to my place and be away from all these assholes."

He leads the way to the showers. I join him. We stand under side-by-side shower jets, the cold water hitting us hard.

I want so badly to reach over and soap up his body, to confess my true feelings for him. But Coach Lane could come in at any second. So could one of the boys. And what if Vicente doesn't feel the same way? What if by telling him how I feel, I lose my best friend? My heart is beating fast as I stare at his body. I tell myself that today is the day. We'll be alone at his place. This is my chance to tell him the truth.

Mother never picks me up from school. And yet, there she is, leaning against the front of our new jet-black Buick. She's wearing her best skirt too, which she most definitely never wears unless there's a reason.

"Isn't that your mom?" Vicente asks me. "I thought she was meeting you at your piano lesson."

We're holding our books as we head out of Hollywood High. On a normal Monday, I would say goodbye to Vicente, study in the library for an hour and a half, and then make my way to piano class before going home for some cold dinner with Mother, my stepfather, Willie, and my tiny little poodle, Frisco, who I love with all my heart. But this isn't a normal Monday. This is the day I'm finally going to say the word *love* to Vicente *off* a tennis court.

But here's Mother, unannounced, with her chocolate-colored hair in a tight updo. She waves to me with one hand and reapplies lipstick to her rigid lips with the other. Jungle red ever since we saw *The Women*.

"It is indeed my mother." I take a deep breath. I always make a point of taking the deepest breaths before spending time with Mother, because it's hard to breathe when I'm with her. I know she pushes me because she wants me to succeed, but sometimes the pressure feels like a noose. "Let's say hello and then go to your place, okay? I really want to . . . There are things I want to tell you."

"Sure," he says nonchalantly. "That's some car," he tells Mother as he runs his hand across the shiny hood.

"A big honey for little money!" Mother quotes the ad for the car.

"*Big honey*," I whisper, eyeing Vicente covertly.

"With dynaflash ignition," Mother says with a smile, still quoting the ad. She showed us the ad the day before she sent Willie to buy the car. No more trolleys for us. Although Willie bought the car, it was all Mother's decision. It's always Mother who decides how we spend the money we make as the Reeves Trio. Willie on guitar. Mother on vocals. Me on piano.

"What are you doing here, Mother?" I ask. "I thought we were meeting at the piano—"

Mother clutches my arm tightly. "Change of plans. Big change of plans."

I look at her curiously. My plans rarely change. Piano lessons. Violin lessons. Voice lessons. My life is over-scheduled.

She puts her hands on my cheeks. She smiles. There's a smudge of red lipstick on her front teeth. "You have a screen test, baby."

Vicente looks at me proudly. "Wow, is this what you wanted to tell me?"

"No, I—I didn't . . ."

"Well, don't act surprised." Mother starts fixing my collar. She spits into her hand and slicks my hair back. "We always knew this day would come. It was just a matter of time before the right executive came to our show and saw what I see every time I look at you. A beautiful, talented star."

I can't help but feel proud at hearing her describe me as beautiful and talented, but I wish I was more to her than a ticket to stardom. The unspoken truth of our unhappy family is that Mother and Willie both failed at becoming the stars they want to be, and they use me to hear the applause they've craved all their lives.

"Mother, I . . ." I try to tell her how nervous I am, but how can I when she's running her nails through my thick eyebrows? She used to hate my eyebrows, before she decided that what separates me from the current crop of stars is my black hair, my olive skin, my mysterious dark eyes.

"You ready for this?" Vicente asks softly.

"Of course he's ready," Mother says. "He's been

preparing for this moment his whole life." Correction: *she's* been preparing for this moment my whole life.

"I can come with you," Vicente offers. "If you're nervous."

"That won't be necessary," Mother says. "Besides, nerves are good. If you're not nervous, you don't care. We should always do the things that scare us most."

The thing that scares me most is telling Vicente how I feel about him. I can only imagine how Mother would react, knowing I want to rip my best friend's clothes off. She's never liked Vicente. She blames him for the fact that I use precious rehearsal time on tennis when music is my calling.

"Okay, let's move," Mother says. "You're about to become a star."

"First of all, it's just a screen test," I counter. "And also—"

Mother cuts me off. "You need to stop saying 'first of all' so much. Don't use superfluous language. If it's the first thing you're saying, then 'first of all' is implied. You'll be interviewed soon. Magazines will want to speak with you. You need to be eloquent."

A few of the other kids from school overhear her and laugh.

I want to hide. Maybe it's hard to believe for people who've seen me perform, but I'm painfully shy. I always have been.

"*Just* a screen test?" Mother says in a snide imitation of me that makes me sound like a spoiled toddler. "Do you know what I've done to get you this screen test?"

I don't want to think about what she did. I know all too well that Mother will do anything to see our last name in lights. When I was a little boy and we were low on money, she would beg music teachers and vocal coaches to train me for free. She'd pay them back when we made it big, she'd say. They would always say no. But then Mother would ask me to wait outside so she could have a private chat with the instructors. And by the time Mother emerged, they had changed their minds. I didn't think anything of it when I was six or seven. But as I got older, I noticed that the only teachers who agreed to give us free lessons were men. And I started to wonder what exactly Mother was doing to change their minds.

"More than a decade of work, my love." Mother practically pushes me into the car. "All those lessons. All those evenings I took you to the movies, skipping meals sometimes. So you could study the greats. And you think this is the first offer I've had to test you? No. But I wasn't about to let you sign a contract with some B studio. I want the best for you."

That's when I know we're not just headed to any studio. We're headed to the biggest one. Metro-Gold-wyn-Mayer. They say that Metro has more stars than there are in heaven, and it's true. How am I ever going to fit in there?

"Good luck, Bobby!" Vicente calls as Mother enters the driver's side.

I look out the window at him. The longing inside me

feels like a physical object. It gnaws at me. I wave to him wistfully.

Mother drives toward Culver City, past rows and rows of single-story homes and restaurants. I've seen pictures of New York City, and I've always wanted to see it in person. How would it feel to stand in a city where the buildings reach for the stars?

"Sit up straight, like you do at the piano," she orders. "You're a powerful man."

I do as I'm told. It's easier than fighting with her.

"Honestly, Bobby. How you're so poised at the piano, and so . . . unpoised the rest of the time . . . Well, it's a mystery to me."

I don't dare say what I'm thinking. Which is that maybe I get my shyness and slouchiness from my dad. That I'm a mystery to myself because I have no idea who he is. I first asked Mother about him when I was five. She seemed panicked and told me he was a soldier who died in the World War. I guess she thought a five-year-old could tap-dance but *not* do basic math. That night, I told her it was impossible that my dad had died in the war. It ended before I was born. She told me to stop asking so many questions. And I did. Because once I started piecing together what Mother did with her time, I realized my dad was probably some music teacher she made a deal with before I was even born.

"If you do good today, I'll treat you to an ice cream," she says with a forced smile.

"I'm seventeen. I'm graduating in four months." I

scoff. "And you still think bribing me with ice cream will work."

She laughs as she turns the radio on. She sings along with Mary Martin to "My Heart Belongs to Daddy."

When the song ends, she silences the music and says, "We're almost there." I notice the slightest tremble in her usually controlled voice.

"Mother, is everything okay?"

"Of course it is." She avoids my gaze as she drives into the gate of the studio. The glamour and grandeur of it all suddenly hits me. It's almost like you can smell the stars in the breezes of this place.

"Mother, are you sure? You sound, I don't know, emotional. Look at me."

"I'm fine," she insists. She pulls the necklace she never takes off into her palm and clutches the decorative items dangling from it tightly. A silver bunny. A blue eye. A gold key.

"Where did you get those lucky charms anyway?" I ask.

"A jewelry store, where else?" She quickly hides the necklace back under her blouse.

"Here in Los Angeles?" I ask. "They look so—"

"Stop asking so many questions," she snaps. "And remember, our Reeves Trio rules apply at MGM. I'm not Mother. I'm Margaret. Please."

"Okay . . . Margaret." Calling her by her name always sounds so strange on my tongue. At least she doesn't ask me to call her Mags like Willie does.

She puts on white gloves and grips my arm tight as she leads me toward the soundstage where I'll be taking my test. My eyes dart around, distracted by all the movie people whizzing past us. Five showgirls in silver dresses smoke cigarettes outside a replica of a New York City street. Giant men carry lighting equipment from one stage to another. Bicycles zip past us. There's a clown on one of them. And there's . . . Joan Crawford on another.

"Mother," I whisper. "Mother."

"Margaret," she snaps.

"Sorry. Margaret, look. Look, quick."

She follows my gaze to Crawford, who bikes past us, hair billowing in the wind, the sun hitting freckles that I never knew she had. Of all the movie stars we worship together, Crawford is our favorite. On Joan, we can agree.

"What a face," Mother says.

I remember her saying those exact words when she took me to see Crawford in *Possessed*. I was nine years old. *What a face.* She said the same about Garbo. And Gable. And Dietrich. And I agreed. This is our bond. When we go to the movies, we escape together.

That's when I realize that of course I want this. Maybe I'm scared, but there's nothing I want more than escape. As a picturegoer, I get two hours of it. As a movie star, my whole life would be fantasy. Maybe then I could buy a house with enough room for Vicente in it. Maybe then my father would see me up there on the silver screen, know immediately I'm his son, and come find me.

And then Crawford is gone. we're back to reality. From her purse, Mother pulls out some pages. "Here's the scene you'll be doing."

"Scene?" I ask.

"They already know you can play and sing. They saw you last night at the club. Now they need to see if you can act."

"But . . . I can't act," I say. "I don't know how to. I never took lessons."

"You never took acting lessons because acting isn't like singing or dancing. Acting is just being natural." I nod. "So just act natural, okay?"

I look over the dialogue. It's a mother-and-son scene. In it, the mother tells her distraught son that his beloved grandfather has died. I have no idea how to act this character naturally, especially since I've never known either of my grandfathers.

We enter the soundstage. The vastness of the space dwarfs us. The lights above us brighten and warm the space like the summer sun. Mother sees the executive in the distance. "That's her," she says. Before she leads me to her, she takes a very deep breath. Wipes a single tear from her eye.

"Mother . . . Margaret," I say. "I can tell you're hiding something from me."

"Stop asking," she says quietly. "I didn't want to tell you until we got home."

"Tell me what?" I feel my heart beat fast. Mother

never cries. It must mean something awful happened. "Is it Willie? Is he okay?"

"It's Frisco," she whispers.

The executive walks toward us. She holds a clipboard. Her skirt-suit is perfectly tailored. The heels of her shoes click on the hard floors. "Mother, what about Frisco?"

"I can't . . ." Her voice trembles. "Please . . . I'll tell you later . . . at home." And then, with a loud sob and her face in her hands, she says, "It's just too awful."

"What happened? I can't go through with this if you don't tell me."

The executive is stopped by a shapely woman in a tight-fitting sweater. They debate something passionately, and Mother takes the opportunity to quickly say, "Fine, I'll tell you. But I need you to stay calm, do you hear me?"

"I hear you," I say.

"Do you promise?" she asks.

"I promise."

Mother takes my trembling hands in her gloved ones. "I went out to get the mail this morning, and Frisco ran right out the door. You know how he barks at the mailman."

My body suddenly feels weak. I don't want to know more.

"Well, he chased after the mailman as he drove away, and . . ."

"Mother, is he . . ." I can't say the word *dead*. My heart

59

feels like it's in my stomach.

"A car turned the corner." She looks me in the eyes. I can feel her holding her tears in. "I'm so sorry, Bobby. Tell you what. If you get this contract, I'll get you another dog. Just like Frisco. Even cuter."

"There's only one Frisco," I whisper.

I can feel the tears coming, but not yet. Right now, there's just shock. My dog is gone. The only member of our home who loves me unconditionally. Who doesn't judge me for who I am.

"Margaret and Bobby Reeves," the executive says brightly. "Are you ready?"

"Born ready," Mother says, digging her sharp nails into the skin of my arm.

"Bobby dear, I'm Ida Koverman, Mr. Mayer's executive secretary," the woman says. "And I'm very happy I got to see you perform. I heard about your show from the woman who does my dry cleaning, and she wasn't wrong. How many instruments do you play, anyway?"

I hear myself say, "Four, but piano is my favorite," but all I can think of is Frisco.

As the executive leads the way, Mother whispers to me. "I bribed that dry cleaner into convincing Ida Koverman to see our show."

I turn to Mother. I could care less about her machinations. "But . . . Frisco," I begin.

Urgently, she whispers, "We'll talk about this later, okay?"

I feel like the ground is falling out from under me

as Ida says, "What a little musician you are. And it's so sweet that you play with your father."

I glare at Mother. She knows how uncomfortable it makes me when people think Willie is my real father. Mother met him three years ago. Married him two years ago at city hall, and made me take his name because she thought it would look better on a title card. She liked the sound of Bobby Reeves. Loved the ring of the Reeves Trio.

When we reach a camera operator, Ida stops. "Here we are. Now we find out if you can act. You go stand there." She points to a chair, illuminated by a bright light. "I'll read the lines that aren't yours."

"I was thinking," Mother says. "Perhaps Bobby would be more comfortable if I read the part of the mother."

Leave it to Mother to turn my screen test into *her* screen test.

"Why not?" Ida says.

Mother leads me to the chair. Sits me down. She leans in, her face so close to mine I can smell the egg salad she ate for lunch. "Remember," she says. "Don't think about Frisco."

"And action," Ida says.

Mother crouches next to me, playing the part of the consoling mom with unnerving tenderness. When it's my turn to speak, I can't think about anything but Frisco. The shock has worn off and all that's left is sadness. I say the lines on the paper in front of me, but what I'm thinking of is my poor dog. The tears come and they don't stop. I manage to speak through them somehow. I make it through every line on the page until Ida yells, "Cut!"

I catch my breath as Mother leaps up and approaches her. "What did I tell you?" Mother asks. "My boy is a musician *and* an actor. How about those *tears*?"

"We'll be in touch," I hear Ida say. "Mr. Mayer needs to see this."

Mother unlocks the door to our house. We take our shoes off. Mother has strict rules about shoes. We are a no-shoes-inside and no-dust-under-the-beds home. As I place my shoes neatly next to hers, I hear those *pat-pat-pat* footsteps and the *yap-yap-yap* that underscores all my entrances.

It's Frisco. Alive and well and happier than ever. My shock quickly turns into relief. He leaps into my arms when I crouch down. I hold him tight, like he could disappear any moment. I don't want to look at her. I hate her. And yet, I can't help it. I have to glare at her.

"Don't look at me like that," she says when she catches my judgment. "I lied for you."

"How could you do that! I thought Frisco was . . ." I still can't say the word.

She speaks to me with the same unnerving tenderness she brought to the scene we performed. "I know you did, and I'm sorry. But they needed you to cry, and you did. In time, you'll thank me, I hope."

I'm too shocked to speak. All I want is to be alone with Frisco. And the only way to get away from Mother is to submit to her. And so, I say, "You're right. Thank you, Mother." I thank her for lying and telling me my dog died. Just like I've thanked her for all the years of lessons when other kids were out playing.

"You're welcome," she says without a trace of regret as I put a leash on Frisco. Then, "Where are you going?"

"I'm taking Frisco for a walk." I put my shoes back on.

Sensing the snideness in my tone, she follows me to the front door. "Bobby boy, look at me." I don't want to, but I obey. Her eyes are misty. "I know I can be tough on you, but I'm doing it *for* you. So you can have the life you deserve."

Frisco bounces at my feet, excited to go outside.

"Just wait until you have kids. Then you'll understand that a parent will tell any lie for the good of their child." There's a weight to what she says, like the anger inside her has been replaced by sadness. Maybe even regret.

"Well, I'm not planning on having children," I say, thinking that Vicente and I could never have kids together. "So maybe that's a lesson I'll never learn."

"When I was your age, I didn't want kids either," she blurts out. "But you'll be a parent someday. You'll see. You'll be a star *and* a parent. You'll have it all. I'll see to that."

As I walk Frisco out of our claustrophobic home and into the fresh evening air, I do the math and realize Mother was pregnant with me when she was my age. If she didn't want kids, then she didn't want me. Which would explain a lot. But then again, Mother is Mother, and she probably lies about her age to make herself more youthful.

"Come on, Frisco," I say. "Let's go to Vicente's. Maybe his dad is working late."

On the twenty-minute walk to Vicente's house, I talk quietly to Frisco. I tell him how desperate I am to tell Vicente how I feel. Frisco looks back at me often, his sweet eyes giving me support. His pitter-patter leads us to Vicente's home. Through an open window, I can see and hear Vicente, his dad, and his sniffling aunt eating Chinese food out of the restaurant containers. They're chatting about their days and laughing at each other's jokes. I don't knock, not yet. First, I close my eyes and say a silent prayer, that someday I'll have a family that feels like this. I lied when I told Mother I didn't want to have children someday. Of course I do. I want a family just like this one. Happy. Connected. Whole.

MOUD

2019

Tehran

Dad and I are in the back of Baba's car, which Hassan Agha drives through the streets of Tehran, narrating as he goes, like he's a tour guide. "We're going to be driving through Eslamshahr on our way north. You've never visited, have you, Mahmoud?"

"No, I haven't. First time." I look out the window at the life outside. This whole country has just been history to me. My own hidden history. When I FaceTimed with Baba, I never saw more than the wall of one of his rooms. But now it's a living, breathing country. It's late afternoon and families walk into stores, groups of boys play soccer in parks, drivers honk at each other with road rage on their way back home from work.

"Mahmoud *jan*, how can this be?" Hassan Agha says in shock. "This is your homeland."

"I guess so," I say hesitantly. "I mean, I was born in America, though."

"Does America feel like your homeland?" he asks.

I pause before answering the question, because the truth is, I'm not sure. It's the country I was born in. The only country I've ever lived in. But I've never felt I truly belonged. Maybe because I look different. Maybe because the rules of my home aren't the same. Maybe because my dad speaks to me in Persian. Finally, I just whisper, "I don't know."

"If after seventeen years, you don't know if your country is your home, then there's a problem, Mahmoud," Hassan Agha says.

Baba turns to Hassan Agha. "He likes to be called Moud."

"Moud?" Switching to English, he asks, "Like a bad mood?"

"Or like a good mood," I counter.

"But that's a ridiculous name. There's no history to it. We are no one if we don't carry our history in us. Who are the Mouds that precede you?"

My dad laughs. It's the first sound he's made since we got in the car. Until now, he's just been silently staring out the window, living in his head like he always does. "I agree, Hassan Agha. But I've never been able to articulate it as well as you."

"There was a king named Mahmoud," Hassan Agha says. "Eldest son of Mirwais."

"Mirwais," I ask excitedly. "Like the guy who produces Madonna's stuff?" I think of Shane, who argued passionately in one of his podcast episodes that every musical artist's least successful album is in fact their best, using Madonna's *American Life* and Lana Del Rey's *Honeymoon* as his primary examples.

"Who?" Hassan Agha asks.

My dad gives me the side-eye, like he's afraid I've just outed myself to Hassan Agha with this too-gay piece of trivia. Of course my dad cares about what this guy who works for Baba thinks of me. God forbid I shame my family in front of Hassan Agha.

"Mahmoud was the Afghan who overthrew the Safavids, if memory serves," my dad says, trying to get the conversation back on track.

"You're right," Baba says. "Very good, Saeed *jan*. But of course back then, we were one people. Afghans. Iranians. So many people now living in Turkmenistan, Uzbekistan, even India. We were one people connected by the Persian culture and language before new borders were created."

"Before the British forbade people in the Indian subcontinent from speaking Persian," my dad adds sadly.

I feel embarrassed by how much I don't know about my own culture, so I keep quiet.

"Borders are fluid," Baba says. Then, glancing my way, he adds, "And so are names, Moud."

"And why do you call yourself Moud?" Hassan Agha asks.

I don't dare tell Hassan Agha the primary reasons I changed my name to Moud. First, to make it easier for Americans, which seems so silly now that I'm in a place where everyone could pronounce it. Would an American ever change their name to make it easier for *us*?

The second reason is the more serious one, though. It's that the only Mahmoud I knew of when I was a kid was the former president of Iran, Ahmadinejad, the asshole who said, "In Iran, we don't have homosexuals like in your country," and who called being gay "an ugly deed," among other atrocities he was a part of. I was eleven when I heard what he said and did on CNN, the exact age I was when I realized I was thinking of boys all the time, the exact age I was when Shane and I became inseparable. We weren't boyfriends yet, just best friends. But we recognized a kinship in each other, a sense of otherness that bonded us. Why would I choose to share a name with a man who wanted me not to exist, who thought the very core of me was ugly? So I changed it. I told everyone my new name was Moud. And it stuck. Everyone but my dad has called me Moud ever since.

"Now we're in the heart of Eslamshahr," Hassan Agha says. "Did you spend time here when you were a boy, Saeed *jan*?"

My dad looks out the window, his eyes foggy. "Not a lot. It was called Shadshahr back then."

"Iran is just like my grandson," Baba jokes. "It likes to change names around. The country changed its name after the revolution, and then it changed the names of the streets, and of the neighborhoods."

"But you can't change our spirit," Hassan Agha proclaims proudly. "Our passion. You tell me one other country that has as many great poets as we have. Rumi. Hafez. Saadi. Khayyam."

"That's true," Baba says, looking at my dad as he speaks. "Poetry is in our bones."

Hassan Agha begins to recite his favorite Saadi poem. *"Of what utility are the rich, if they are . . ."*

To my surprise, my dad finishes the poem. *". . . clouds of August, and do not rain upon anyone."*

I stare at my dad, who has never expressed interest in poetry to me, and who can suddenly recite this one by heart. What else is he hiding? I feel desperate to know what this is like for him. What is he thinking?

"And now we are in Lalehzar," Baba says. "Home."

"It's beautiful," I say, as the car winds past leafy streets, past hip galleries and restaurants, and eventually toward gorgeous old homes.

"This used to be the place to be," Baba explains. "It was the north of Tehran. The Shah wanted it to be like the Champs-Élysées, and it was. Then after the revolution, the city kept growing north, and the wealthy moved up, leaving our little neighborhood behind. But now it's hip again."

I look over and see two young girls in bright patterned head coverings. They pout as they take a selfie together.

Baba shakes his head. "Maybe too hip. It's become overrun with young people who come here just to take photos for Instagram."

I'm immediately reminded of my own social media, of all the photos I deleted, and of Shane. I haven't even told him I landed. I immediately pull out my phone to send him a WhatsApp message, but I have no Wi-Fi.

"Our family has lived in Lalehzar for many generations," Baba says. "Our house was my grandfather's house. It's a miracle we held on to it this long, but some things are meant to stay in the family, I suppose."

Hassan Agha pulls the car into the driveway of a stunning old home. I'm immediately taken aback by the architecture. In Los Angeles, a home built in the 1920s or 1930s is considered historic. The whole city is a modern fever dream. This home looks like it was built centuries ago, like it should be a museum instead of a family home. Everything inside is colorful and mysterious. The pictorial rugs tell ancient stories. The floors creak with secrets. Some rooms aren't separated by doors, but by pointed horseshoe arches that feel like entrances to a magical land.

"Well, come on in," Baba says, as Hassan Agha helps him into his wheelchair.

When Dad tries to help Hassan Agha lift the chair up the front steps, he's shooed away. "Leave me be, this is my job," Hassan Agha says. "You go eat the food your father made for your arrival."

"Baba, you didn't need to cook for us," Dad says.

"Who cares about needs?" Baba says, laughing. "I *wanted* to cook for you. Cooking and music are my passions. They've sustained me for almost a hundred years, and no illness can take them from me."

Once Hassan Agha gets Baba up the steps, he shifts

his attention to getting our suitcases. "Follow me," Baba says, wheeling himself into an ornate dining room that stuns me with its majesty. Everything in this room is a kaleidoscope of details. The wooden chairs have decorative motifs carved into them. The humongous rug on the floor is bursting with colors. There are lamps in every corner that shimmer like gold, calligraphy etched into the middle of the lamps. And on the long wooden dining table is a feast of food. Rice and *tahdig* and stews and *kotlet* and *kookoo sabzi* and yogurt and pickles and lavash and *barbari*.

"Wow," I say, taking it all in.

"I didn't know what you would be in the *mood* for, so I made a little of everything," Baba says. "Luckily, Iranian food is always better the next day, so we can keep what you don't eat."

I approach one of the glowing lamps. "Can I touch it?" I ask.

Baba laughs. "Of course you can touch it. These lamps have survived for a long time."

"What does it say?" I ask, running my hand along the calligraphy.

Baba wheels himself close to me. "It's a verse from the Quran. It says, 'Do good. Allah loves the doers of good.'"

I nod. "I didn't know your family was religious."

"Not terribly religious," he says. Then, taking my hand in his, he adds, "My grandfather, and then my father, owned a furniture factory. Most everything in this home came from their factory."

"Really?" I ask. "It's amazing."

"Yes, it is," Baba says. "Now, let's sit and eat. You've had a long flight. You must be starving."

We all sit around the table as, in the background, Hassan Agha takes our suitcases up to the rooms we'll be staying in. As Baba puts a little bit of everything on plates for us, he says, "Saeed, I put you in your old room. And Moud, you'll be staying in Maman's old room."

"She had her own room?" I ask.

My dad makes himself a tiny *kotlet* sandwich with lavash and yogurt as he says, "Baba and Maman always slept in separate bedrooms. She was a bad sleeper."

"She couldn't stand my snoring," Baba says, laughing.

When I take my first bite of food, my taste buds feel overwhelmed. "Baba, how does this taste so good?" I ask. "I've had this stuff at Persian restaurants back home, but it doesn't taste like this."

"It's the produce," Baba explains. "Wait until you taste our fruit."

We eat in silence for a few moments, Baba smiling as he watches us appreciate his dishes. And then, the silence is interrupted by a flurry of activity. First, the slamming of the front door. And then, the click of high heels on the wood floors of the foyer. Followed by the unmistakable sound of Britney Spears saying, "You better work, bitch." The second time Britney says it, I realize it's the ring of a cell phone.

"Allo?" a loud female voice says. "Why are you calling me now? I told you I was busy today . . . I told you to handle it . . . Don't call me again."

"That would be Ava," Baba says. "She insisted on coming to greet you."

Before I can ask who Ava is, she makes her presence known by entering, holding two presents wrapped in gold paper with silver stripes. She puts the gifts down on an old wooden box at the entrance of the dining hall, strips off her sequined head covering and black trench coat to reveal that she's wearing a tight sweater and tighter black jeans that hug her curves. She wraps the head covering around her waist like it was always meant to be a stylish belt. "*Vay, vay, vay*, and *vay*," she says, using the Persian expression for "wow" in a voice that drips with drama. "I can't believe my American relatives are finally here. I've only waited twenty-one years for you to come. Which is how old I am, by the way."

I look over to Dad, and then to Baba, in utter confusion. Who is this relative I've never heard of?

"Ava *joon*," Baba says, trying to stand himself up to greet her.

"Baba *joon*," she says, rushing to his side and kissing his forehead. "Please don't get up on my account. Look at this. Are you happy now that your son and grandson have landed safely?"

"Hello, Ava *jan*," Dad says, standing up. "It's nice to finally meet you." He formally kisses each of her cheeks. "Mahmoud, this is Ava. She's your . . ."

"Cousin," Ava exclaims brightly. "I'm your cousin."

"But how?" I ask. "Both my parents were only

73

children." And then, realizing the secrets Iranians like to keep, I turn to Baba and ask, "Wait, Dad *was* an only child, right? Or do I have an uncle or aunt I don't know about too?"

Ava laughs. "Technically, I'm more like your second or third cousin. I'm Maman's sister's granddaughter."

My head spins as I put it all together. I never even met Maman's sister, let alone her granddaughter, but now here she is, in front of me.

"I brought gifts, of course," she says. "First, for Uncle Saeed." Ava hands my dad a gift, which he seems embarrassed to accept. "And next, for my cousin Moud. I love the name, by the way. So fun."

"Oh, thanks," I say awkwardly.

She whispers in my ear after she kisses my cheeks, "We're going to have so much fucking fun together, just wait."

I can't help but smile.

"Ava *joon*, what are you whispering about?" Baba asks.

"Just telling him how happy I am to finally meet him," Ava says politely. I'm impressed by how expertly she filters her tone and language in front of her elders.

"Shall we open our gifts now or later?" my dad asks.

"Whatever you wish," Ava says. "But if you open them now, I can tell you a bit about them." She pulls a chair out and finally sits.

Dad and I unwrap our presents at the same time. Dad pulls out a scarf, with different patterns sewn together.

And I reveal a big brown coat with a bright orange collar.

"So they're from a new company my friend works at," Ava explains. "They find the most amazing vintage clothes and refurbish them. Sometimes they sew pieces of one vintage fabric together with other ones, like that scarf. Everything old is new again. You should see their Instagram, Moud. It's so cool."

"Oh," I say, my eyes on my plate. "I'm not really on Instagram much. But thank you for this. I love it."

"Yes, thank you," Dad says, folding the scarf back up and placing it on the empty chair next to him. "This is very thoughtful."

Ava seems to do most of the talking for the rest of the meal. She tells us all about how she was an economics major in college and now works at a music-streaming app—"It's basically the Spotify of Iran. We even play Rihanna, we just can't show her picture, which is so dumb 'cause we all know what she looks like"—and how all her friends are doing the most amazing things—"Iran is the new Silicon Valley. We have everything here. America can't make us use their apps, so everyone's starting their own. We have a ride-sharing app and a food delivery app and everything"—and then, eventually, she mentions that her father wants to build a high-rise on the land Baba's house is on—"I only bring it up because my parents will certainly bring it up when you meet them."

"They'll say it's life-changing money," Baba says. "And

I'll remind them that I don't want my life to change."

"I'm with you, really I am." Ava waves her hands across all the antique furniture. "I'm all about preserving our history. But my parents never give up, and I've begged them to let it go."

"Which is why you're the only member of the family I welcome in my home," Baba says with his slyest smile.

"And what an honor that is." Ava smiles. Her teeth are blindingly white.

When we've all polished off dessert—saffron ice cream and *faloodeh*—Ava begins to clean up all the plates.

"I can help," I offer.

"Absolutely not," she insists. "You're a guest. And you haven't even unpacked." I try to lift my plate up, and she slaps my hand. "Leave it. Go."

"Come on," Dad says. "I'll show you to Maman's old room."

As Dad leads me back into the foyer and up the steps, I try to imagine him growing up in this house. These were the first steps he must've climbed. These are the walls that first heard him speak.

"This is it," he says, pointing at a bedroom door on the second floor.

"Where's your room?" I ask.

"Just down the hall. That one." He points to the last room down the hallway.

"Baba seems good," I say. "I mean, he seems the same."

"Yes, he seems good," is all Dad says before walking down the hall toward his own room.

I enter Maman's old room and immediately send Shane a message. *Hey, I'm here in Iran. It's weird. I miss you.* I put the phone down and then take the room in. My suitcase rests on an old wooden bed with a huge bedspread on it. The walls are covered in gold-leafed wallpaper that's peeling at the edges. In the corner is another one of those shimmering gold lamps with calligraphy on it. I open my suitcase and pull out all the items inside we brought for Baba, the Nivea and Pepto and foot cream, the iPad for Hassan Agha's son. We purchased all these items less than forty-eight hours ago, but it feels like a lifetime since we were in America.

I unpack my own stuff and start to put it away in a creaky armoire. But when I open the two bottom drawers of the armoire, they're filled with Maman's work. I stare in awe at blueprints and images of buildings my grandmother devoted her life to.

I close the drawers when my phone dings. It's a text from Shane. Los Angeles is eleven and a half hours behind Tehran, so he's probably just waking up. He sent a photo of himself frowning with the words *I miss you* written on his forehead. The photo is followed by a text that reads: *I hope your baba is okay. And I'm sorry if things were weird when we left. This whole fucking country feels empty without you in it.*

I smile and open up my podcast app to listen to the latest episode of *Down with America?* I want to hear his voice. But the app doesn't work. I've saved a few old episodes in my computer files, so I open up my laptop and press play on one of them.

"This is Shane Waters." The sound of his voice fills the room, and it feels so anachronistic in this space, like he could never belong here.

"And this is Sonia Souza."

"Are you ready for another episode of *Down with America? America?* Because this is gonna be a good one."

"Today we're talking cultural appropriation. What is it? Who's guilty of it? Is it ever okay? Be sure to call in and let us know what you think, 'cause we want to know if you're down with it. So Shane, I want to ask you, when I say the words 'cultural appropriation,' what's the first image that comes to mind?"

"I mean . . ." Shane laughs, then says, "Katy Perry as a geisha. Gwen Stefani with a bindi. Elvis's whole career."

I'm putting my clothes away when I hear a voice that isn't Shane or Sonia. "You know what I think?" Ava asks as she sweeps into the room and throws herself on the bed.

I instinctively close my computer, trying to remember if Shane mentions his boyfriend in this episode. Unlike the men in my family, Shane likes to talk about *everything*.

"I think Americans are so bored that they talk about things that don't really matter," Ava says, kicking her heels off when she realizes they're on my comforter.

"That's my friend's podcast," I say, a little offended that she just said it doesn't matter, and more than a little disgusted with myself for calling Shane my "friend" like my dad does.

"Then tell your friends I want to be their next guest. Cultural appropriation. I would love people to embrace Iranian culture. Better than thinking of us as terrorists or victims. Look at Beyoncé. She appropriated our culture when she named her kid Rumi, and I loved it. Good for her for even knowing who Rumi is."

"Sure," I say, closing my sock drawer. "But by the time *her* Rumi grows up, they'll patent the name, turn it into a brand, and the whole world will think *the* Rumi is Beyoncé's kid, not our poet."

"You're cynical," she says, squinting in disapproval. "Don't be cynical."

I feel a deep desire for her to leave the room. So I quietly say, "And you're loud and presumptuous, and not even my cousin."

At this, she laughs and claps her hands together. "*Vay*, I'm obsessed with you." Then she immediately makes a phone call. "Siamak, you have to meet my cousin. He's feisty just like me. He just called me loud and—" She looks up at me. "What was the second adjective again?"

"Presumptuous."

"Presumptuous!" she repeats. "Such a good word for me, right? Wait, I'm putting you on speaker."

"No really, it's okay, I'm tired," I say, but it's no use.

"Siamak, meet my cousin Moud."

"Hello," the voice on the other end of the line says. "Welcome to Tehran."

"Oh, thanks," I say.

"Are you coming to the party tonight?" he asks.

Before I can say no to going to a party I haven't even been invited to, Ava says, "Of course he is. He's gonna wear the new coat I gave him. It's so chic."

"I'm really jet-lagged," I say quietly.

"Don't be rude." Ava shakes a finger at me. "This is Iran. You don't turn down an invitation from an elder."

"You're an elder?"

"I'm older than you," she says with a smile. "Besides, jet lag, time zones, all of that, it's just a state of mind." She leaps off the bed and kisses me on each cheek. "I'll pick you up at eleven. Meet me outside. Don't tell your dad or your baba. They'll think I'm corrupting you!"

"The party *starts* at eleven?"

"What time do parties start in America?" she asks. But she doesn't wait for my answer. She's out the door, talking to her friend as she leaves. "Siamak, will there be anything to drink?" Is she talking about what I think she's talking about? I thought alcohol was illegal here. "Do you need me to sneak some whiskey from my dad's cabinet?" I guess she doesn't care much about legality. Laws, like time zones, are probably just a state of mind to her. As fluid as borders and names. But the thought of drinking in Iran fills me with fear.

When I'm confident she's gone, I look at my phone and FaceTime Shane. He answers immediately. He's at the breakfast table with his parents. "Hey!" he says. "You know my parents have a no-cell-phones-during-meals policy, but they made an exception this time."

He moves the phone over to reveal his smiling parents.

"Hi, Moud." They both wave.

"So?" Shane asks as he walks away to talk to me privately. "What's it like?"

I tell him that Baba seems to be in good spirits, and that the house is incredible, and that I met my second or third cousin, but somehow my words don't capture any of the emotion of it all.

"Well, I gotta get to school," Shane says. Jokingly, he adds, "You know, that thing you bailed out on."

"I didn't bail," I say. "I'm only missing a few weeks of school. The rest of the time is vacation anyway. And I'll keep up with my work."

"Three and a half weeks," he says. "That's how much school you're missing. And three and a half million tons is the weight of how much I miss you."

I smile. "I miss you too."

"Call me tomorrow?"

I nod and say goodbye. I feel a strange emptiness when I hang up. I don't want to be alone. I miss Shane. I miss the ease we once had, the feeling that we were one being.

I walk down the hall to my dad's room, wondering if I should ask him about the party. The door to his room is cracked open, and I can see him inside. He hasn't unpacked. He hasn't even taken his shoes off.

He holds his phone tight in his hands and speaks in a low voice. "Yes, is this the alumni office? I was wondering if you could help me find someone I once knew. . . ."

Just as I'm leaning in, Hassan Agha slaps me on the shoulder. "Mahmoud *jan*, are you hungry?" I turn to see him holding a space heater.

"Hungry?" I ask in shock. "After what we ate, I don't think I'll be hungry for another few months."

Hassan Agha laughs. "You're a growing boy." He holds up the space heater. "It gets cold at night. If you want one for your room, I'll bring you one too."

Hassan Agha enters my dad's room and sets up the space heater, just as my dad hangs up the phone, leaving me desperate to know who he wants to find.

At eleven, I can't sleep. My mind is reeling, and one of the things keeping me up is curiosity about this party Ava wants to take me to. Against my better judgment, I throw on a pair of jeans and the coat she gave me, then tiptoe down the stairs. I can hear Baba snoring in the living room. He's moved in there, since he can't get his wheelchair upstairs. And it's right next to the room where Hassan Agha sleeps, so he can help if Baba has an emergency.

I find my shoes at the entrance of the house and put them on. It's cold outside, and the freeze in the air makes me second-guess my decision. Maybe I should go back in. But before I can get out of going, Ava's car pulls up. She rolls the window down. "Get in," she says.

I do as I'm told. To my surprise, I'm happy to see her. Yes, she's abrasive, but she's also fascinating. When she hits the gas, she turns the music up. It's a remix of an old Dalida song. "I love her. Do you love her?"

"My dad listens to her," I say. "She's heavily featured

on his card night playlist. All those Iranian men sing along to her when they play poker."

"All your dad's friends are Iranian men?" she asks.

I nod. "I guess sometimes he plays golf or tennis with someone who isn't Iranian, but yeah, for the most part, it's all Iranian men. I mean, their wives too. But the wives never come over, because, well, my mom's not around."

She offers me a warm smile as she says, "That must've been hard, losing her so young."

I nod but say nothing, because we don't talk about how hard it was to lose her.

"Don't say a word about this to any of the parents by the way, especially not mine."

"Aren't you twenty-one?" I ask. "Why do you still have to sneak out?"

She laughs. "Welcome to Iran, where parents treat their daughters like children until they get married. Thankfully, mine are deep sleepers."

"So you still live with them?" I ask, thinking I would never live with my dad at that age.

"I always have." She shrugs. "I thought about living in the dorms during college, but the dorms are even more strict."

"Where are we going?" I ask as she makes a sharp turn.

"My friend Siamak works part-time at an art gallery. He's a freshman at the college of fine arts, the baby of our group, and probably the most talented. Anyway, the gallery owner is letting us have a party at his house in

Niavaran. It's going to be fabulous, you'll see. You'll love my friends. They're the best, obviously. I only surround myself with the best."

She pulls up to a quiet street and screeches her car to a halt in front of a gated home. She presses a button outside the gate, and we're buzzed inside. She takes my hands and leads me in. Music is blaring, something ambient and dreamy. There's smoke from cigarettes in the air, obscuring my view of the guests. She wasn't kidding: they are fabulous, one more stylish than the other. "There's Siamak," she says, pointing to a tall, lanky, and scruffy guy. His curly mop of black hair is pulled back by a hairband, letting his open face catch the light. He quickly glances our way, then turns his attention back to the guy he's huddled with in a doorway. "I'll wait to introduce you later. He looks busy."

"Do you mean . . ." I want to ask if she means that he's flirting with the other guy. It certainly sounds that way.

She clearly gets what I'm thinking. With a smile, she says, "A lot of my friends are queer."

As the smoke clears, I start to piece together what I'm seeing. Scattered among the crowd are men holding hands. Women flirting with each other. I don't know what I was expecting to find at an Iranian party, but it wasn't this.

"Not everyone here is queer, obviously," she says. "But everyone is open-minded. It's a lot of art students." I look around. So many of these young people have turned their bodies into art, experimenting with hair color, piercings, tattoos. One guy has half his head shaved, the other half buzzed and dyed turquoise. Almost all the guys have at least one piercing in their ears; most of them have more. There are girls with smoky eyes, people who wear all black, and people who stun in bright colors.

I should tell Ava I'm gay. I should tell her I've had a boyfriend for four years. But somehow it all feels like too much for this moment. So all I say is, "This is so cool."

She smiles as she ties her head covering around her waist. "You see, Tehran isn't just nuclear power plants and prisons like the Western media wants you to believe."

The underground party plays tricks on my brain. It's not just what I'm seeing. Queer life in Iran. Persian fashion. Contemporary art on the walls. People leaning on sculptures as they blow smoke rings from their lips. No, what's messing with me is the way my fingers reflexively reach for my phone, wanting more than anything to post pictures of all this magic. I find my brain turning every detail of the room into captions.

#ThereAreNoGaysInIran, a little nod to my namesake Ahmadinejad and his idiotic catchphrase.

#UndergroundMood, a little nod to my nickname.

#WhyAmIThinkingInHashtags when I felt so happy to be liberated from social media?

Ava holds up a decanter of red wine. "Have you ever had a drink, my young cousin?"

I smile. "Yeah, but I'm a lightweight, so just a small glass."

She pours a small glass for me, a big one for her. I'm

deep in thought as I take a sip, still thinking about how much I'd love to post about all this, share it with the world.

"A rial for your thoughts?" Ava asks, her teeth already stained red from the wine.

"Just taking it all in," I say.

"You were obviously thinking some kind of really deep thoughts." She takes another sip of the wine. "That was a Tori Amos reference," she says. "You like her?"

"Um, my—" I'm about to say *my boyfriend likes her.* He discovered her when he did a podcast on female artists who produce their own records. "My musical knowledge isn't as vast as yours."

"I know you don't want to tell me what you're *really* thinking," she says. "But all in time. I'm nosy. And pushy. And . . . what did you call me again?"

"Presumptuous," I say, a nervous smile on my face. But she still seems to love the word. I take a sip of the wine, and the sourness of it shocks me. Then relaxes me. "It's stupid. I was just thinking that this is the first place I've been to in ages that actually deserves to be shared on social media. Because it really is so cool. And people should know that *this* is Iran."

"Well, not really," she says. "This is a very small, very secret piece of Tehran."

"Yeah, but maybe if more people knew it was here, then it wouldn't be so small, or so secret."

She raises her glass up. "Hashtag truth bomb," she says with a laugh.

"Hashtag truth be told," I joke.

"Hashtag the truth shall set you free," she says with a wink.

"Hashtag truthful Tuesdays." I take a sip of my drink. I'm already feeling warm and floaty.

"Well, it's not Tuesday, so I'm not sure that works," she says.

"And we're not actually posting anything, so what's your point?" Another sip.

She cackles. "Touché Tuesdays," she blurts out, and we both crack up.

"Anyway, real truth bomb here. I just deleted all my social media, so I have nowhere to post this party. No Insta, no TikTok."

"How do you even exist?" She pokes me. Pinches me playfully but firmly. "Just checking to see if you're real."

"That actually kind of hurts," I say.

She stops the pinching with an apologetic look. Then she squints at me hard. "I think I'm stating the obvious here, but just in case . . . You do know that if you posted any of this, you could put everyone at this party in danger. Especially if your profile were public. Or if you were an influencer."

I laugh. "I'm definitely not an influencer. And I wasn't saying I would post it. Just that in a sea of stupid photos of people's dinners and their pedicures and sunsets and shit, this is actually something that *should* be shared."

"And the reason it should be shared is that no one knows about it," she says. "Therein lies the conundrum."

I smile. She's loud but wise. She's a little like Shane that way. Maybe that's why she puts me at ease. "There should be a word for when you're like, writing social media captions in your head while you're living your daily life."

"There is," she says firmly.

"What, dissociation?"

"No. Withdrawal. What you're going through is withdrawal. You're an addict. We all are."

"Yeah," I say solemnly. "That feels . . . true."

"Maybe it's a good thing we're not allowed to be as open here as you are in America." Her eyes take in the party crowd. The canoodling couples. The gossipy friends. The loud drunks and the sad drunks. "I mean, it's not a good thing that queer people here aren't free to be themselves. That's not what I'm suggesting."

"No, I know you weren't. You're not—"

"But maybe not documenting every moment allows us to, I don't know, be in the moment."

"Yeah," I say.

"The bright side of living under a repressive regime," a voice from behind me says. I turn and see Siamak, no longer flirting with the object of his affection.

"Siamak is always looking on the bright side," Ava says as she pulls him into a hug. "That's what I love about this baby." She squeezes his cheeks so hard that his lips turn into a fish mouth.

"I'm not a baby. I'll be eighteen in a month."

"A baby!" Ava screams. "Look around, you and Moud

are the youngest people here."

"That's because I didn't invite anyone my own age. Most people my age are so boring. I feel so much older than my classmates."

"And Siamak is a year ahead, so he's the youngest in his class," Ava says proudly. "Our little genius."

"I'm not a genius. I just work hard. And I'm definitely not always looking on the bright side." Siamak glares at Ava until she finally lets go of his cheeks. He eyes the guy he was flirting with. "He's not interested in me. He said he only dates older men. I told him I'm almost eighteen, and he told me to call him when that number is doubled."

"It's an epidemic in Iran," Ava says. "Our fathers are stoic and don't give us enough love, so we search for the love of older men."

I think of my own stoic Iranian father and all the love I've craved from him and never gotten.

"So, my fellow teenager," Siamak says to me. "You're Ava's cousin, but you look nothing alike."

I correct him. "We're second cousins. And in America, *everyone* would think we look alike."

Siamak laughs. "Americans think we're all the same person. I attended my second cousin's wedding in Houston, and thirty-two Americans congratulated me on being married. Yes, I counted. They thought I was the groom, who happens to be a foot taller and ten years older than me. But we're both Iranian, so . . ."

"I'm sorry," I say. "America can be the worst."

"No, no," Ava says. "Never say America. Always say Americans. Using the noun takes the agency away from the people who did the dirty work."

"Do the dirty work, present tense," Siamak says.

I look into my cup, feeling guilty. America is the country I was born in. It's my home.

"Siamak lived in America for years, so he's allowed to be as harsh as he wants to be," Ava explains.

"Why did you come back?" I immediately hate how that sounds, as if America is the superior place.

Siamak raises an eyebrow. "Well, it's my family who moved back. They could barely make ends meet in lovely New Hampshire, especially not after the recession. And they wanted to reclaim the property that was taken during the revolution."

"Did they?" I ask.

"Still working on it," he says with a shrug. "Bureaucracy. So much bureaucracy. In any case, I want to be here. I had the option of moving to Houston. My aunt and uncle were willing to take me in. But I chose to come here. And you know what? I prefer it here. These are my people. I want to be a *Persianate* artist, representing my culture."

I nod, wondering if I could ever live here permanently. "What's Persianate?" I ask.

"Not now, please," Ava begs. "I've heard Siamak's sermon about Persianate society too many times now. Look it up later. It's a party."

"Academic theory isn't fun for you?" Siamak asks with a wink.

Ava laughs. "What I want to know is . . . If your Houston cousin is your second cousin, then your Houston aunt and uncle are technically not your actual—"

"Stop," Siamak demands. "None of it matters. Because you know as well as I do that all Iranians are second cousins. We're inbred."

Ava hoots. "It's true, it's true."

"One more reason to be gay." Siamak side-eyes me as he says this. "We need to stop all those heterosexual Iranians from procreating with their second cousins."

"My great-grandmother was married to her first cousin," Ava announces proudly.

"Really?" I ask, a little shocked.

"That wasn't a big deal here back then," Siamak says. "Lots of people married their cousins. Mostly rich people who wanted to keep the wealth in the family."

"Oh," I say.

"Maybe you'll marry Ava," Siamak says with a sly smile that tells me there's more to the joke than just us being related. Does he know I'm gay? Can he smell it on me? I've always had terrible gaydar, but maybe Iranians living in Iran have to develop great gaydar as an act of self-protection.

"I would make a terrible wife," Ava says. "I hate cooking. I hate cleaning. I'm loud. And all I want to do is party and gamble."

"Sounds perfect to me," Siamak says, licking her cheek playfully.

"You know what I want?" Ava asks. Answering her own question, she says, "I want to marry some filthy-rich Arab with multiple wives. I want to be his *least* favorite wife, so he leaves me the fuck alone but gives me enough money to live my fucking life my way."

My phone vibrates in my pocket. I pull it out and see Shane's face pop up. He's holding a cone in front of the Big Gay Ice Cream truck in the photo. I quickly silence the call.

"You can answer it," Ava says.

"No, it's okay," I say. "It's just my . . ." I pause a beat before saying, "Friend."

Ava and Siamak share a glance.

"What?" I ask.

Siamak looks away from me. "Nothing," he says.

But Ava can't contain herself. "This is so silly, Moud," she says gently. "Look at where you are. Why are you hiding from us? We're not undercover police."

I swallow hard. I feel so strange. Why have I been hiding from them?

Siamak puts a hand on my shoulder. "You can be yourself around us. You don't have to be ashamed or anything."

I feel my face get hot. I'm not ashamed of who I am. At least I don't think so.

"I'm sorry," Ava says. "It's all my fault. I lurked on your

social media before you got here to see who you were. We know that was your boyfriend, Shane, calling. I should have told you right away, but I figured you would tell us first, and when you didn't . . . Well, I'm sorry."

"Oh," I say, feeling stupid for hiding who I am from people who would obviously accept me. "Well, you don't need to apologize. My social media was public. You didn't do anything wrong. And yeah, I'm gay and I have a boyfriend. I'm not ashamed of it or anything. . . . I just, I don't know, didn't think I could be open here. I definitely wasn't expecting . . . this."

"You did the right thing wiping your history," Siamak says.

The words he chose—*wiping your history*—hit me hard. I don't want to wipe my history. I want to honor it, carry it inside me.

Ava speaks as quietly as she can. "You could've just set your socials to private. That's what we do here."

"Yeah," I say. "I didn't know how *private* a private profile is, I guess."

"Anyway, we're your friends now," Ava says. "All of us. If you're queer or an ally in Iran, you have to stick together."

"Because no one else will," Siamak adds sadly.

The word *shame* keeps swirling around my brain. Siamak was right. I do feel ashamed. I feel the shame of lying. The shame of allowing myself back into a closet. The shame of judging my own people.

"I assume, since your social media was public, that your dad knows," Ava says. "But does Baba know that you're gay?"

"He does know," I say. "And you might be surprised that he's been more accepting than my dad."

"I'm not at all surprised," Ava says, with a quick, covert glance to Siamak.

Siamak glares at her hard. I can tell they're hiding something from me, but I'm not as nosy and brash as Ava, so I don't push them to tell me what they don't want to.

"Baba is very kind," Ava says. "I'm sure your dad is too. He is Baba's son, after all."

"I mean, my dad is reliable. He's there. I don't know about kind. He doesn't talk about me being gay, ever. He never invites Shane over for dinner or anything." It feels so good to be talking to someone I'm related to about my dad. With Shane, I always feel like I have to defend my dad. With Ava, I can be honest. She's family, after all.

Ava nods. "I know it's no consolation, but your dad raising you on his own like he did, and staying quiet about your sexuality . . . well, it's pretty progressive for an Iranian man. If my dad had a gay son . . ." Ava shakes off the thought and offers me a supportive smile. "Well, your life, your boyfriend . . . none of it is my business if you don't want it to be. But if you want it to be, I'll be your biggest supporter."

"Thanks," I say. "I actually could use support, so yeah, I'll take it."

"Good, then call him back," she demands. "I want to meet him."

"Let's go outside," Siamak suggests. "It's too loud in here, and there's more light on the porch."

Siamak leads the way outside. We stand under an outdoor sconce. I hesitate before dialing Shane back, but it does feel right. He feels a world away from me, and I don't want to feel distant from him. Maybe if he meets Ava and Siamak, sees me in this new context, he won't feel so far away from me.

Shane answers from the school courtyard. Sonia is in frame too. The Los Angeles sun shines directly onto their faces, making them almost invisible. In the small box at the bottom of the screen, I'm barely visible too.

"Hi!" he says. "I figured you'd be jet-lagged. Tossing and turning."

"Well, not really," I say sheepishly.

Ava grabs the phone. She holds it too close, so her red lips take over the screen. "Shane *joon*, I'm the cousin. Ava. *Salam, azizam.* It's so nice to meet you."

"Oh, hi, you too. Um, where are you guys?"

"We're at my friend Siamak's party, which is at his boss's house. Say hi, Siamak."

Ava moves the phone to an embarrassed Siamak. "Hi." Siamak waves. "We're taking good care of your boyfriend, don't worry."

"Oh, wow, so he told you about me?" Shane asks.

"We're all open here," Siamak explains. "Lots of

queer people, and we even tolerate those of us who aren't queer, like Ava."

"I WISH I WAS A LESBIAN," Ava screams joyfully into the air.

Siamak gives her a stern look. "Ava *joon,* stop."

"Wow," Shane says. "I thought . . . I mean, isn't it illegal to be gay in Iran?"

"Yes," Siamak says. "And sodomy was illegal in the United States until 2003, was it not?"

Ava whispers to me. "I told you Siamak is a genius. He researches everything."

"Only the things that interest me," Siamak says. "And queer life interests me."

"Well, I mean . . . That sodomy law was rarely enforced," Shane says.

"And clearly ours is the same," Siamak snaps. "Because here we are."

This is rare. Shane at a loss for words. Shane conceding that he may not be right about something.

Sonia interjects, "I'm sure Iran is full of surprises. I read this article about trans people in Iran. Doesn't the government pay for trans people's surgery in Iran? Like, that's wild. It's not only legal, it's actually paid for. Like, who would've thought Iran would be ahead of Western countries on trans issues?"

"I'm not so sure about that," Siamak says. "Trans people might be able to get surgery here, but they're not treated well at all. Most are shunned by their families and by society. Many become sex workers, drug addicts, live in shelters. Not everything is what you read in an article. Sometimes you have to see something with your own eyes to understand it. If you ever visit Iran, you'll understand."

"Wow," Sonia says. "That would actually be really cool. I'd love to see Iran someday."

Ava beams. "You're both welcome here anytime. One of us always has a boss who's traveling, so we can put you up in style."

"I mean, yeah, maybe . . . ," Shane stammers. He's not about to tell them that he had a moral issue with *me* coming to Iran, let alone him visiting.

I can only imagine Ava's and Siamak's response if he tells them that he views visiting Iran as the same thing as eating a chicken sandwich from Chick-fil-A. Both are putting precious pink dollars in the pockets of homophobes.

A handsome thirtysomething man comes out of the darkness and toward the front door. His thick black hair is slicked back, like he's in an Iranian production of *Grease*. He wears a tight black T-shirt and even tighter black jeans. "Siamak, Ava, *salam*," he says.

"Please leave, Hormoz," Ava says coldly.

"We didn't even invite you," Siamak adds, even icier than Ava was.

"Is that so?" Hormoz asks. "Well, many of your guests requested my presence here, so I'll be heading inside to put a smile on their faces."

"We don't want trouble," Siamak begs. "And you only bring trouble."

Hormoz throws his arms up into the air, pretending he's been shot as he stumbles backward. When he's entered the party, Ava turns to me and whispers, "Stay away from him. He's a drug dealer. He preys on vulnerable people who need to escape their pain."

"Which sadly describes so many queer people," Siamak says. "I'm going to make sure he leaves." Siamak walks into the party without saying goodbye to Shane or Sonia.

"It's really too bad," Ava says. "Hormoz used to be sweet. And he's so hot, isn't he?"

I glance at Shane, still on the phone. I'm not about to call another guy hot in front of him. We're allowed to fantasize about celebrities and Instagays, but real-life guys, not so much.

Ava continues. She has a gift for filling life's awkward silences, and I appreciate that about her. "He used to get his hands on things that didn't hurt people. CDs from all over the world. Books. You know, healthy escapes. But the internet destroyed his black market media business, so he switched to selling drugs instead. Opioids. Methamphetamines. The internet hasn't figured out how to distribute those yet."

"Jesus," Shane says. "I think of the opioid epidemic as such an American thing."

"Where do you think opium comes from?" Ava asks. "Anyway, I once had empathy for Hormoz, but I don't anymore. And blaming the internet for dealing drugs is a little silly, no? Can't we all blame the internet for *everything*? I blame the internet for my body image problems!"

"You have body image problems?" I ask.

"Well, I used to," Ava says. "You think being a fat girl in Iran is easy? Please."

"I think you're beautiful," I say.

"You're gay." She rolls her eyes.

"I think you're beautiful too," Sonia says. "And I'm a major bisexual."

"You can barely see me in this light, but thank you both."

"We gotta get to class," Sonia says, off-screen. "Bye, Moud. I miss you."

"Bye, Sonia. Bye, babe. I . . ." I want to tell Shane I love him, but it feels weird in front of Ava, and again, I'm reminded that maybe I'm holding a little shame I didn't even know about.

"We'll talk soon," Shane says. "Send me photos of everything."

"Not everything," I say. "A lot of what happens here can't be photographed."

"Please tell that to the Rich Kids of Tehran and their horrific Instagram account," Ava jokes. "They should keep some things private."

Shane and Sonia say goodbye. After I hang up and put my phone away, Ava cocks her head toward the front door, where Siamak practically pushes Hormoz out, threatening to call the authorities if he comes back.

Hormoz has an unbothered smile on his face. "I'd be

more than happy to call the authorities myself."

"Hormoz, please," Siamak begs. "This house belongs to my boss. If there's trouble, I'll lose my job."

Hormoz shrugs. "I wonder who the authorities would want to punish more. One heterosexual drug dealer, or a room full of perverts."

Siamak breathes heavily. Ava moves to him. Puts an arm around him. She reaches her other hand out to Hormoz. "We've known each other since I was a kid," she tells Hormoz. "Let's just get along."

"Okay, fine." Hormoz changes his tone. "I have more parties to go to anyway."

We watch as Hormoz disappears into the darkness, off to the next party, to the next customers.

The French hip-hop song that was playing ends, and a Persian song I've never heard comes on the loudspeaker. "*Vaaaaaaay,* this is my song," Ava yells out as she rushes inside, and single-handedly turns the open space near the coffee table into an impromptu dance floor. A group of twentysomething men surround her. She's in the middle of the circle, twirling and shaking and hollering, living her very best life. The guys who surround her cheer her on by putting their hands together and snapping their fingers the Iranian way.

Siamak and I stand side by side, watching the fun. "I could never do that," I say.

"What?" he asks. "Be as uninhibited as your second cousin?"

I laugh. "No, snapping my fingers like that. The *beshkan.*

My dad does it, but I guess, well, he never taught me."

"Come on, put your hands up," Siamak says. "I'll teach you."

I raise my hands up in front of me.

"Fingers together," he says. "Take the tip of your ring finger on your right hand—"

"Which one's the ring finger again?" I ask.

He looks at me, shocked. "You gay Americans, obsessed with gay marriage, and you don't even know your ring finger from your other fingers?" He takes my hand in his. His hand is warmer than mine. "It's this one," he says quietly. "Now we press that finger against this one." He leads my right hand to my left, pressing the ring finger to my middle finger. I don't say a word. I feel nervous, because my mind is thinking things I wish it wouldn't. Like how Siamak is hot in a Brooklyn indie rocker by way of Tehran kind of way. He could be the new Iranian member of the Strokes. And also . . . what would it feel like to make out with another Iranian? Would it be the same as being with Shane, or would I feel more seen, more deeply understood?

Siamak continues the instruction, but when it comes time to snap, I fail miserably. "I suck," I say. "I'm sorry. I'm a bad, bad Iranian."

"It takes time to master it." He takes my hands in his again and leads them to the right position. "But I won't let you leave Iran until you have. What kind of Iranian man doesn't know how to properly snap his fingers? It's part of who we are."

"You're setting yourself up for failure," I say.

"Perhaps," he says. "But I love a challenge."

My hands are still in his. I don't move. Neither does he.

Ava is out of sight, surrounded by her adoring friends. I may not be able to see her, but I can hear her screaming, *"Vaaaaaay"* and *"Baaaaabaaaa"* from within the circle. *Baba.* It means "father." And yet Iranians use it as an interjection that can literally mean anything. It can mean "wow." It can mean "shut up." It can signify support, shock, surprise, happiness. Kind of like a father, it can shape-shift so often that you never know what it really is.

Siamak pulls his fingers away. "Would you like a tour?" he asks. "The art in the house is truly incredible. It's like a museum. My boss is the coolest."

I nod. "Sure, I love art." I sound so stupid. Who doesn't love art? "Which one's your boss?"

"Oh, he's not here," he says. "He's in Qeshm with some friends."

"Wow, he really is the coolest, letting you guys party here while he's gone. How long have you been working for him?"

He starts to lead me through the stunning home. "I started last summer. It's just part-time while I'm in school. He liked my art and agreed to hire me, which is great, 'cause I would've needed another job to get by and I don't want to work anywhere but in the arts. A lot of the people at this party are rich kids, but not me. Maybe that's why I work so hard, I don't know."

"It's cool you know who you are. What you want to be. Shane is like that." I wish I was like that. "What do you do at the gallery?"

"I update our social media pages and the website. Photograph all the art. Someday it'll be *my* art on the site." As we walk, he tells me where everything came from. The bathroom tiles were created by a Moroccan artist. That chandelier used to hang in the home of the Shah's sister. The photographs in the hallway are of Elizabeth Taylor when she visited Iran with her photographer friend Firooz Zahedi in 1976. The sculpture in the study is by an artist who won first prize from the Tehran Contemporary Sculpture Biennial four years ago. Siamak's boss now represents the artist.

"And finally, my boss's bedroom." He leads me to a gorgeous room. A sleek, modern bed sits on a colorful ancient rug. He points to a painting above the bed. "That's my favorite piece in the house. We don't represent the artist because she had to leave the country, unfortunately."

"Why?" I ask.

He shrugs. "Asking why people have to leave Iran is like asking why your ancestors died."

"Wait, why did my ancestors die?"

He laughs. "Because people died back then. When I first moved back to Iran with my family, I realized I had all these relatives I never knew about."

"Sounds about right," I say.

"And so I decided I was going to make a family tree."

I should do that, I think to myself. There's so much I don't know about Baba and Maman, let alone those who came before them. "I asked everyone about my ancestors. My parents. Aunts. Uncles. There were so many people I knew nothing about. My great-great-grandfather was a dervish, which I really love. But anyway, mostly there were just people who died young. I asked my only living grandparent how this person died, or that person died, and every time she laughed at me and said that people just died back then."

"That's so bleak," I say.

"I guess so." He smiles. "I asked my aunts and uncles and parents the same question. Every time, the same answer. People just died back then." He takes a breath. "Anyway, that's how I feel about people who have to leave Iran. The reason is that they had to leave. That's all there is to say. The reason is obvious, *especially* if they're an artist. This country is good at looking the other way, but not when it comes to politics. And art is political."

"But you work at a gallery," I say.

"A gallery that is very careful about our selections." He sighs. "There's so much art I wish we could display."

"So the woman who painted that," I say, turning my attention back to the painting. "She said too much, or she was too political, or . . ."

"What do you think the painting is saying?" he asks.

I stare at the painting. It's of a veiled woman standing atop the ocean, like she's walking on water. Or maybe like she's about to sink. There's a wave behind her that looks like it could swallow her whole. But also, there's a smile on her face, like she knows exactly what a precarious position she's in, and she doesn't mind at all. In fact, she welcomes the danger. "I think it's saying that you can't live in fear," I say.

He nods. "Me too. Can you see what it's painted on?"

I shake my head.

"Get closer to it." Sensing my hesitation, he adds, "It's okay, you can get on the bed. My boss is very relaxed."

I kick my shoes off and crawl onto the bed to get closer to the painting. Only when my eyes are inches away from it can I see that it's painted on Persian writing, hidden behind all the paint. "I can't read Persian," I say.

"It's a poem by Forough Farrokhzad," he explains.

"I don't . . . I've never heard of her."

"Of course you haven't. She should be revered, but most people don't even know who she is."

"Is she still writing?" I ask, wishing I had his breadth of knowledge.

"She died when she was thirty-two," he says, "in a car accident."

"That's horrible."

He pulls his shoes off and joins me on the bed. We're both on our knees, staring at the painting close-up. "*How comfortable I am*," he says, and I think he's talking about how inviting this bed is until I realize he's reciting the poem behind the paint. "*In the loving arms of the motherland. The pacifier of the glorious historical past. The lullaby of civilization and culture. And the rattling noise of the ratchet of law. How comfortable I am.*'" Those words underline exactly what the painting is about, the illusion and trap of comfort in a world that needs to be shaken up.

"I don't know how you read all that," I say. "You can barely see half the words behind the paint."

"I wasn't reading," he says, looking over at me. "I know it by heart. Every Iranian should know at least five of our great poems by heart."

I laugh. "Five? Who makes these rules up?"

"I do," he says, as he flips his body around and lies down on the bed, his head on the crisp white pillow.

I follow his lead and lie down on the bed. I feel so nervous, lying in bed with a boy who isn't Shane. And yet, at the same time, I feel like I'm exactly where I belong. "Well, I know a total of zero poems. My father wasn't exactly a poetry guy. He's an engineer."

"And your mother?" he asks.

"Oh," I say. "She died when I was four. I thought maybe Ava had told you, but why would she, right?"

"I'm sorry I asked." He puts his hand on mine and squeezes it. "You don't have to talk about it unless you want to."

"I mean, she had cancer. Pancreatic. She . . . I don't know what to say. I know her from photographs, but . . . We don't talk about her much. Baba only met her once. Maman never did. My dad didn't stay close to her side of the family, and . . . I guess I don't know a lot about her."

"Have you asked?" His voice is gentle.

"Not really." I avoid his gaze. "I don't know . . . I've

always felt like asking my dad about her would be like rubbing salt in his worst wound. I mean, *he's* the one who lost her. I don't even remember her. But she was his wife, and he hasn't even gone on a date since she died. He must've really loved her."

"I'm sure he did." He moves his hand up to my cheek. "But Moud, you lost her too. And you deserve to know who she was."

I nod. I want to escape the painful intimacy of this moment. I wish Ava was here to fill the silence with her effervescence. "Are you going to teach me five poems when you're done teaching me how to snap my fingers?" I ask, attempting a jokey tone to change the atmosphere in the room. "Because I'm feeling like a very bad Iranian right now."

"Don't listen to my stupid rules," he says. "There's no one way to be a good Iranian. And you're pretty great just as you are."

I smile. "Thanks."

He leans in closer to me. I know what's happening. He's going to kiss me. I want him to, and I also need to stop it from happening. "What kind of art do you make?" I ask.

He pulls away. "You want me to show you?"

I nod.

He pulls out his phone and lets it hover above our faces. He pulls up his photos. Scrolls past photos of him and his friends, him and his family, sunsets and sketches and meals and paintings and sculptures. Finally, he stops on what looks like an ancient Persian miniature. "This is my favorite," he says.

"You made that?" I ask. "It looks like it was made centuries ago."

"Zoom in," he says, laughing.

I use my fingers to zoom in on the details, and that's when I realize he's filled his miniature with scenes right out of a gay bacchanal. Men cupping each other's asses. Men kissing. Men dancing for each other. It's stunning. And embarrassingly, it turns me on. "Wow, this is incredible," I say. "I really mean it."

"Thank you." He scrolls to more pieces he's made. Each piece takes ancient Persian art and fills it with gay imagery. Then there are photos of young men. Their poses match the poses from the paintings. They kiss. They hold each other. They dance ecstatically. I recognize a few of them from the party. "Oh, sorry. I shouldn't show you those."

"They're your models?" I ask.

"Yeah, and my friends." He shuts the phone down and puts it away.

"You're really talented," I say.

"I try." He shrugs. "I just hope someday I can show my art in my own country. For now, I can only dream of a show in the West. And when that happens, I'll probably have to leave. Which I don't want to do. But what choice do I have?"

"Your teachers, your boss, they've all seen these?"

"Sure," he says. "They're all supportive."

"Well, I really love your stuff."

He laughs as he glances at my crotch. "I could tell."

I feel my face get hot. I'm so embarrassed. But he's smiling as his head moves closer to me. "Seeing you excited made me excited," he whispers. His lips part. I don't move. I could gently push him away. I could tell him to stop. But I don't. I let him kiss me. I want to know what it feels like to have another Iranian's lips on mine. And it feels great. Connected. Beautiful. Until I remember Shane, and how much we've been through, and how we've always been honest with each other.

That's when I push Siamak away. "I'm sorry, it's just . . . I have—"

"A boyfriend." He shakes his head. "I knew that, and I shouldn't have—"

"It's okay." I stand up and nervously put my shoes on. "It was like, two seconds long. It doesn't mean anything. Not really." What am I even saying, when I know that two seconds can change everything? How many seconds did it take for Forough Farrokhzad's car to crash? How many seconds does it take to destroy the trust in a relationship, in *my* relationship? I can't do that.

"I really am sorry." He moves to the edge of the bed. Puts his shoes back on. "I was just in the moment, which is—"

"Fine. It's good to be in the moment." I move to the door.

"It's not good when you're not thinking through things." He joins me at the door, but neither of us opens it yet. "We don't have to tell Ava about this if you don't want to."

"Maybe that's a good idea," I say. "Not because I think what we did is so wrong, but just because—"

"Ava thrives on drama. I love her so much. She's like a big sister to me. But she'll want to make more of this than it is."

"Exactly," I say. Putting on a forced smile, I add, "Thanks for the tour."

He laughs. "You're very welcome."

I open the door, and we head back to the party. Ava is by the bar now, pouring drinks for a group of people. "*Vay*, there you two are," she yells out at us. "Did Siamak give you the grand tour?"

I nod and smile.

"*Babaaaaa*, come have another drink. The night is young and so are we!" She looks at me sternly and adds, "But I'm older than you, so don't take it too far, 'cause I'm watching you."

I don't take her up on the drink, but she's right about the night being young. The party lasts until the sun rises. These soulful people keep singing, dancing, laughing. By the end of the night, Ava has introduced me to everyone. There's Roshanak, a lesbian who goes out in the streets dressed as a boy because she doesn't want to wear women's clothes or a chador. There's Farbod and Aryabod, a gay couple who have been together since their first year of high school. There's Goli, an underground theater director who is working with a group of trans women to create a theater piece that shines a light on their experience. I'm fascinated by everyone I meet, by their life force and joy. There's nothing jaded in them, and it's shocking in a world that feels steeped in irony. These incredible people live in hope, soaking up every second of freedom and connection they can get in the dark of night before trying to make their world a better place in the light of day.

I fall asleep with the sun streaming through the cracks in my curtains. I don't think anyone heard me tiptoe in. I'm woken up way too early by the ring of the doorbell. I will myself back to sleep, but it's impossible with all the screaming downstairs. I'm too tired to listen to who is screaming or what they're screaming about. I throw a pillow over my head, desperate to drown it out and get some more sleep. But here's my dad, hovering over me, already dressed. "Wake up, Mahmoud," he commands. "Ava's parents have invited themselves over for breakfast."

"I'm so tired," I croak.

"Didn't you sleep?" he asks.

I quickly say, "Jet lag." My dad obviously can't know where I was last night.

As he walks out of my room, my dad says, "Jet lag is made up. I can sleep anywhere, at any time." That's classic my dad, thinking everyone else is just like him, or maybe that everyone else should be just like him.

I pull the covers off me and realize I fell asleep in my clothes. Good thing my dad didn't see that. I also didn't brush, and I can taste my own rank breath. I take a fast shower, brush my teeth, and throw some casual clothes on.

As I make my way downstairs, I can hear the argument gaining steam.

"Please, Baba *joon*," a woman's voice pleads loudly. "This money could change everything for our family."

"I don't care about money," Baba says, his frail voice straining to be as loud as hers. "And if our family needs money, then it can make some money of its own."

"In fairness, it's not like you made the money to buy the house," a man with a shrill voice says. "The house has been in our family for generations. You just happened to inherit it, and now you're stubbornly refusing to consider what this house could do for you. For us. Let me build on this land. People with half this land have become millionaires. You're sitting on dynamite when we could all live comfortably for the rest of our lives."

I enter the dining room, expecting to find it set up for breakfast. But it's empty. The voices are coming from the kitchen.

The shrill voice keeps pleading. "I'm not asking for anything from the sale of the land. Just for you to let me build. You'll be the one who stands to gain the most, Baba *jan*."

I make my way to the kitchen. Baba sits in his wheelchair, directing Hassan Agha, who stands above the stove, cooking. Sitting at the kitchen table are my dad, Ava, and her parents. I'm shocked at how fresh Ava looks. Why does she seem like she got a full night of sleep when

I can barely get my eyes open?

"*Salam*," I say.

Everyone looks my way. Baba smiles. "There's my grandson. Moud *joon*, Ava's parents have decided to pay us an unexpected visit because—"

Ava's parents rise up to greet me. They both give me a kiss on each cheek. Her mother squeezes my cheeks and tells me how handsome I am.

"Moud, this is my mom, Shamsi, and my dad, Farhad."

"You can call us Ameh Shamsi and Amu Farhad," her mom says. "We're so happy you're here."

"Thank you," I say. "It's really nice to meet you."

"Our apologies for discussing money in front of the children," Farhad says. "Though perhaps it's good they learn about such things."

I smile dutifully but say nothing. I'm not getting involved in this debate, though I am surprised by the value of Baba's land.

"You must be on our side, Saeed *jan*," Farhad says. "You're an American now. You understand the importance of seizing an opportunity. If more of us thought like Americans, maybe Iran wouldn't be the devastated country it is now."

"And what do Americans like me think like?" My dad's tone is cold.

Farhad raises his hands apologetically. "I'm not implying anything bad about you. You did what none of us in the family dared to do. You went to America and made a success of yourself."

"Success," my dad says, his eyes traveling to Baba. "It's one of those words that can mean anything."

"Okay, okay," Farhad says. "I understand, and I ask you to please understand what it's like trying to make a living here. Your disgusting orange president bans us from your precious country—"

"He's not my president," I say quietly.

"Or mine," my dad says, and I'm so thankful for that.

"Well, he represents your country." Farhad won't give up. "And his sanctions have made it impossible to live here. To raise a family. Who do you think these sanctions hurt? The mullahs? They're fine. They're sitting on their billions, moving their money to foreign countries. The billionaires of the world are the same no matter where they're from. They find ways to hide their money. But us, the regular people. We're the ones who are afraid that soon, our children won't be able to eat. Do you know what Ava makes at that app she works at? Practically nothing."

Ava, who clearly inherited her passion from her parents, takes her father on. "Daddy, you know I agree with you about the sanctions and the mullahs and all that, but don't use me to make your point. I don't want this home to be torn down so you can build a high-rise."

Ava's dad seems genuinely hurt by this.

"I'm sorry, Daddy," she says gently. "You know I love you and I'm grateful for all the work you've done and the life it's given me. But the history of our family is in this home."

"History is a concept," her dad argues. "It's just an idea. It's not food on the table. It's not a roof over your head."

"Actually, it is," my dad says. "In this case, it's quite literally a roof over our heads."

I smile at my dad, impressed.

Baba cocks his head at Hassan Agha and tells him it's time for the vegetables. Hassan Agha picks up some chopped vegetables and throws them into a pan. They sizzle in olive oil. "Let the vegetables cook for a few minutes before you throw the eggs in," Baba says. Turning to me, he adds, "This is what cooking is now. I used to do it all myself. Now I can't even reach the stove or the cupboards. Aging is horrible."

"Better than dying," Hassan Agha says.

Ava howls. "So bleak. So true."

"You have a way with words, Hassan Agha," Baba says.

"I see what you're doing, Baba *joon*," Shamsi says. "Changing the subject."

"The subject is closed," Baba says firmly. "It's my house. I inherited it from my father, who inherited it from his father, who inherited it from his father. When I die—"

"Baba *joon*, don't talk like that," Ava begs.

"I'm dying," Baba says. "It's no secret. Look at me. And when I die, and I would have preferred not to say this now because believe it or not, I don't enjoy talking about the end of my life—"

Ava scooches to Baba's side and leans close to him. "Baba, you don't have to say any more."

Baba takes a breath. "When I die, the house will belong to my son. That is the tradition."

The silence in the room sizzles like those vegetables. Hassan Agha cracks eggs atop them. Sizzle, crack, sizzle, crack. I turn to my dad, who says nothing. I don't know what he's thinking right now. Maybe he assumed he'd inherit this home. Or maybe he didn't.

"So," Baba says, "if it's all right with all of you, I would love to never discuss the sale of this house in my lifetime again. If my son wants to let you turn it into a condominium, that's his decision. Are we done now?"

Farhad is not done. "Saeed may be your son, but he hasn't stepped foot in Tehran since he was what, seventeen—"

"Eighteen," my dad says.

"Over four decades ago," Farhad says. "Wouldn't it make more sense for him to inherit money rather than property in a country he visits once every four decades? My proposition isn't purely selfish. It's good for you, Baba jan. It's good for you, Saeed jan. And yes, it's good for us and Ava. And the market is still hot right now. If we wait too long, things could change. You know how this country is. Waiting makes no sense."

"Very few things make sense," Baba says with a shrug. "Now, you're in my home until I die, and you will abide by my rules of the house. Rule number one is hospitality. Saeed and Moud just arrived from America. How are we going to show them the beauty of this country?"

"I'd be happy to take you to see some sights," Shamsi says unconvincingly.

"That's all right," my dad says flatly. "I can show myself around."

Shamsi and Farhad both smile. "The offer always stands," Shamsi says.

"I have an idea," Ava says, a warm gleam in her eyes. Her eyes travel to Hassan Agha, who throws some *barbari* bread into the toaster and pulls some cheese and greens out of the fridge. "*Vay, barbari,*" she says. "My favorite."

"Do we really need to serve bread?" Shamsi says. "Some of us are watching our calories."

Ava rolls her eyes. "Some of us? Or me?"

"I wasn't talking about you," Shamsi says.

"Sure." Ava shoots an angry gaze at her mother as she stands up and pulls the *barbari* bread out of the toaster. She layers it with cheese and herbs. Takes a defiant bite of it as she sits back down.

"You had an idea, my beautiful Ava?" Baba reminds her.

She finishes chewing. "Oh, yes. If it's okay with you, Uncle Saeed, I wanted to invite Moud to Shemshak next weekend."

"Skiing?" my dad asks.

Ava nods. "See, I exercise," she says with a sharp gaze her mother's way.

Hassan Agha serves up the huge omelet he made with the bread, cheese, and herbs. The plates are stacked and

Baba passes them out as we all sit and serve ourselves.

"I mean, I don't really ski," I say.

"It's not really about the skiing," she says. "It's fun."

"It's fine by me," my dad says. "Whatever Mahmoud prefers."

"What do you say, second cousin?" Ava asks. "It'll be super chill. My friend Goli's aunt has an amazing place there. It's huge, but it'll just be four of us. And Goli doesn't ski, so she can keep you company if you don't want to learn."

"Who's Goli?" Shamsi asks as she cuts her omelet into tiny little bites. "Have we met her?"

"Not yet." Turning back to me, Ava says, "Anyway, it'll be me, Goli, and my friend Siamak." Ava expertly pretends I haven't already met her friends. A true master of family deception. "I think you'll like them."

I distract myself with the food. It really is the best bread, the best cheese, the best herbs, the best eggs. Everything here tastes better. What I'm trying to wipe out of my head is the taste of Siamak's lips on my mouth. I can't be in an apartment with him for a weekend. Not after what I let happen. And I can't tell Ava about the kiss.

"It does sound fun," I say once I've swallowed my food. "But honestly, I'm here to spend time with Baba. So I think I'll pass."

Ava brushes off the rejection. "Suit yourself," she says. "But don't go back to America without leaving the city a few times. Iran has everything. Mountains and lakes. Palaces and mosques."

For the rest of breakfast, we talk about Iran. Ava and Baba talk it up, telling us all the exciting things we can do and see. And Shamsi and Farhad remind them that for all the beauty and history around them, there's also corruption, poverty, injustice. And I realize that despite the specificity of what they're talking about, they could be talking about any country. We have beauty and history in America. We have corruption, poverty, and injustice too.

Ava gives me a big hug before she leaves with her parents. "Last night was so much fun," she whispers in my ear. "We'll do it again soon."

"Of course," I tell her, but I'm not so sure. It's not that I don't want to keep hanging out with her and her incredible friends. It's just that I'm scared. If one night made me kiss another guy, what would another night lead to?

Shane is on my mind as I go back to my room for a nap. I toss and turn, questions swirling around my restless brain. Did my two-second kiss constitute cheating, or did I stop the cheating from happening when I ended the kiss? Should I tell Shane the truth? Would the honesty prove my loyalty to him? Or would telling him the truth just hurt him for no reason? Because it will never happen again, right?

I must fall asleep, because I'm woken up in the early afternoon by a WhatsApp video call from Shane. His picture on my phone feels like it's judging me. I roll over and answer the call. "Hey," I say groggily.

"Were you asleep?" he asks from his own bed. "Did I get the time difference wrong? I thought it was—"

"It's one in the afternoon," I say, turning my bedside lamp on. "But yeah, I was napping."

"Long night, huh?" He smiles.

"Yeah," I say. "Iranians know how to party."

"I'm glad you had fun." He leans his head back on his pillow. Next to it is another pillow, the one I use when we lie on his bed together. I want to be there again.

"I miss you," I say.

"Me too." He kisses the air.

We stare into each other's eyes for a few beats, but really, we're staring at our fucking phones.

"So what was it like?" he asks.

"What?" I know what he's asking about, but I'm afraid to tell him about the party. I'm scared that I'll slip and tell him about the kiss.

"Well, I'll be honest. I was shocked that you were at a party in Iran with queer people and drug dealers—"

"Lots of queer people. One drug dealer."

"I stand corrected." He smiles. "Anyway, it's super-cool, isn't it? I mean, I'm sure it was powerful for you."

"Yeah," is all I say.

"Hey, Moud, it's me." Even through a screen, I can feel his breath, his heat, his body against mine. "Why are you hiding?"

"I'm not, I'm just . . . waking up." I put a pillow behind my back and prop myself up. "It was powerful. Very powerful."

"Tell me," he says. "I want to know."

"It's hard to describe." I close my eyes and remember the party. "I don't know how to put it into words, but it just felt, I don't know, like a real community."

He pauses. "What do you mean, 'real'?"

"I don't know if I'm choosing the right words, but . . . well . . . I mean . . ."

"I'm sorry," he says. "You know the words 'real' and 'authentic' have always kind of bugged me in certain contexts." Did I know that? I guess I did. He talked about it in one of his podcast episodes. He was talking about how people love to call queer culture fake or artificial.

"Yeah, I know," I say. "And I know everything that exists, even the most constructed things, are real and authentic."

"You *do* listen to my podcasts," he says with a smile.

"Of course I do."

Everything has substance, he said on that podcast. He said he misses irreverence. He said everyone takes everything so seriously, and that he takes irreverence seriously.

"Irreverence is the thing you're most reverent about," I say, quoting him back to him.

"Well, that and my love for you."

I relax again. We're back on track. "Anyway, I think you know what I meant. Not that the community here is more *real* than the community in America, but—"

"We're talking about the queer community, right?"

I nod. "Obviously, it's all real. It's all valid. But the feeling of it here, of being at this party . . . I mean, the people at the party don't have the same freedoms when they leave the safety of the party. And it just made everything feel so much more, I don't know, present. Important. And also, they were barely ever on their phones. Like people were actually focused on each other, not on performing their lives."

"Is that how you feel when you're here? Like you're performing your life?"

I know he's not accusing me of something, but it feels like he is. "No," I say. "Well, sometimes."

"Sometimes when? When you're with me?"

I'm digging a hole for myself. "Not with you," I say. "Of course not. What happens between us in private is . . . it's everything to me. But at school, or at parties . . . I don't know, yeah, sometimes I feel like I'm performing for people. Saying the things I'm supposed to say. Thinking the things I'm supposed to think. Writing the caption for a moment before I've even lived the moment."

He's quiet.

"Do you not feel that way?" I ask.

He shakes his head. "I try so hard not to be like that," he says. "But I get it."

"You do?" I ask.

"I mean, we're so different, right? That's why we're so good together."

"Yeah," I say, wanting to be comforted by his words but still feeling unsteady.

"I've always thought about how my parents just accept

me and love me unconditionally. And your dad . . ."

"He does love me." Once again, I'm defending my dad from Shane. Yes, he's tough. And no, he doesn't like to discuss my sexuality. But he's been there for me, and he's my father, and *I'm* allowed to complain about his flaws, but no one else is. Not even Shane.

"I'm not saying he doesn't love you. It's just . . . You had to hide more than I did. And maybe that's why you perform for people. Because it's what you had to do at home for so long. Because you're used to staying hidden. But silence equals death, right? We can't stay hidden."

I shake my head, but I don't refute him. Even though I hate what he's saying.

"And maybe that's why you felt the community there is more real than the community here. Because they match your experience more. They're hidden. It's sad."

I feel my heart race and my lip twitch. I wish he could hear himself. The condescension. I know him so well. I know he thinks he's being empathetic, but he's not. This constant judgment is his worst quality, and I never take it on because I'm not as good at debating as he is. And also, because everything else about him is wonderful. Or was wonderful. It's all a mess in my mind.

"It's not sad at all," I say.

"It's not sad that queer people there can't even post a public photo with their friends because it could get them thrown in jail or killed?"

"That's not what I meant. Of course that's sad. But

what I saw . . . what I felt last night . . . it wasn't sad. It was joyful. It was alive. It was necessary. I've *never* felt that in America. The things we talk about in America seem so, I don't know, small compared to—"

"Trans people being murdered isn't—"

"Oh, come on, that's not what we talk about. Most of the time, we're arguing about whether Harry Styles is queerbaiting or whether Doja Cat is allowed to use the word—"

"She's not," he declares emphatically. "And things like that, they have an impact on the world. If a kid out there thinks it's okay to use queer slurs, maybe that kid is more likely to commit suicide, or turn to drugs, or—"

"I'm not saying . . ." I don't know what I'm saying. This is why I don't take him on. "You're twisting it around to make it sound like I don't care about people dying or becoming addicted to drugs, and obviously I do! But maybe I don't think that arguing over pop stars is the right way to create change."

"Then what is?" he asks.

"I don't know, I'm not you. I don't think about how to create change all day. Maybe people like you shouldn't condescend to people like me when your culture—"

"Sorry, what's this *my* culture and *your* culture stuff? You were born here. We're from *the same* culture."

"But I've never felt American," I say. "And maybe I'm just realizing that now. I know I was born there. I know that. But I don't feel like it's who I am."

"But it *is* who you are."

"I'm telling you that maybe it's not. At least not completely. Who are you to say who I am? Why do Americans get to treat me and my people like one of them when it's convenient for them, and like a foreigner when they feel like it?"

"That's not . . . That's not what I'm doing," he says. "I always treat you like—"

"Stop defending yourself. Just listen to what I'm saying. You don't know what it feels like to be totally invisible in your own culture."

"What culture?" he asks.

"American culture. I mean, Iranians aren't even part of the cultural conversation in America. Nobody from the Middle East is."

"That's unfair. I've always asked questions about your culture, but . . ." I know what he's going to say. That it's hard to learn about my culture when he and my dad are always kept apart.

I take a breath. I got too heated, and the last thing I want is my dad or Baba overhearing this. "I know you do," I whisper. "I'm sorry. It's just . . . being here has helped me understand how different I've always felt in America. Which is maybe why I felt more connected to the queer life I observed here."

"Okay," he says. "And I think there's something deeper at play here. Like, what are you saying? That you need to be in a place where you're oppressed and hidden in order to feel a sense of community?"

"But that's not what I said." I feel lost, and so far away from him.

"It's really late here," he suddenly says. "It's almost midnight."

"Okay," I say.

"Are we good?" he asks.

"Yeah, sure," I lie. Because the last thing I want to tell him is that we're not good. That we weren't good long before this. Because there was always a disconnect between us that we never really talked about because I didn't have the words for it yet. I remember the first time he suggested I cut my dad off for not embracing my sexuality the way his parents did, and it dawns on me just what he was suggesting—to sacrifice not just my dad, but my connection to my whole culture.

"Okay, because I love you," he says. He might love me, but if I had taken his advice, I wouldn't be here right now. I wouldn't have seen Baba before he died. I wouldn't have met Ava, or experienced that incredible party. I wouldn't have known what it feels like to belong somewhere.

"I love you too," I say. I find myself thinking about me and Siamak in that bedroom. Not about the kiss—about the conversation. I told Siamak that I don't ask about my mom because my dad doesn't talk about her. And I resent my dad for not asking me more questions about my own personal life. Maybe all this time, I should've modeled the love I want from him. Maybe it's time for me to ask my dad about his own life instead of always wanting him to inquire about mine. I can't let my own silence be the death of my relationship with my dad.

He sighs. "I'm sorry. You know I get heated."

"Yeah, well . . . next time, let's not treat a phone call like a podcast."

"Deal," he says. "And babe, I'm proud of you for speaking your mind."

I feel so alone when he hangs up. I crave company. Connection. I call Ava, who answers immediately.

"Is there still room at the ski place?" I ask.

"The ski place?" she parrots back, laughing. "It's called Shemshak, and it's so amazing, and yes, there's room."

"Okay, I'm in." I don't know if it's the right decision, but after that conversation, I know that I can't stop myself from getting everything I can from my time here because of Shane. I do love him, but if he's taught me one thing, it's to prioritize loving myself. And the best way to love myself right now is to walk on water, unafraid to sink, unafraid of the waves I might create by asking questions.

I get out of bed and head to my dad's room. I don't know how I'll start asking him questions, or what I'll ask first, but I know that I need to start somewhere. I'm about to knock on the door when he opens it himself. He's wearing his coat and shoes. "Oh, hi, Mahmoud *joon*," he says. "Did you sleep the jet lag off?"

"The imaginary jet lag," I say, going for a joke but sounding petty.

He almost smiles, but not quite. "I'm going out for a

bit," he says brusquely, walking past me into the hallway.

"Where?" I ask.

He turns around, surprised. Back home, we rarely ask where the other is going. If I'm going out, then he knows I'm probably going to be with Shane, and he'd rather not know about it. And if he's going out, it's usually to his aerospace job, tennis, golf, or poker, and none of those things have ever been very interesting to me. "I'm going to see an old friend," he says.

"The one you called the alumni office about?" I ask, before I think through what I'm saying.

He squints angrily. "You were eavesdropping?"

"I overheard. I'm sorry. But . . ." I wish I could say that all I want is to be closer to him.

He looks stricken as he says, "The alumni office couldn't find her."

"Her?" I ask.

He looks confused. "I thought you overheard the call."

"Just part of it," I say. "I didn't hear who you were looking for. . . ."

He nods. "Then it's not important." Before I can tell him that it is important to me, he adds, "I'm going to see my friend Peyman. He was my best friend when I was your age."

"I've never heard you mention him." I shouldn't have said that. I'm trying to get him to be more open with me, but instead, I sound like I'm chastising him for the mistakes of the past.

"We grew apart." He shrugs. "I wish we hadn't. It's

my fault. But he's still here, and he has a family he'd like to introduce me to, so . . ." He trails off. The reason is obvious. Peyman wants to introduce my dad to his family. But my dad isn't jumping at the chance to introduce his gay son to his old friend.

I won't let myself get lost in hurt feelings. So I ask, "Can I come?"

He looks surprised. Maybe even moved. "Of course you can. I didn't think you would want to." Maybe I was wrong. Maybe the reason my dad didn't invite me has nothing to do with my sexuality, and everything to do with the lack of interest I show in him. "Brush your hair, though. It looks like you just rolled out of bed."

"I mean, I did just roll out of bed."

He almost smiles, and then he does smile. I remember what he said about how success can mean so many different things to people. And I'm feeling pretty triumphant right now. I made a small connection to my dad. That's something. That's success.

SAEED

1978

Tehran to Los Angeles

Maman and I are in the dining room playing backgammon, as Baba makes us *kotlet* sandwiches for dinner in the kitchen. I can hear the meat sizzling as Baba listens to the radio.

As I shake the dice in their cup, Maman claps her hands together and yells, "Come on, double three."

"Maman." I can't help smiling. You're supposed to be rooting against me—not for me!"

"I'm your mother, which means I'm always rooting for you."

I put the dice cup down and take a breath.

I want to tell her and Baba everything. I want to confess to attending protests despite their warnings. I want to tell them I met a girl at one of those protests. They deserve the truth, my parents who have always supported me. "Maman . . . ," I whisper.

But just as I'm about to confess, Baba turns the radio

up. An announcer shares the news that the Shah is seriously considering a declaration of martial law. Baba turns the radio off and walks in, looking stunned. "Did you hear that?"

I nod, and feel my throat tighten. How can I tell them about the protests now?

"This is why you can't go to those protests like those other students, Saeed *joon*." Baba sits down next to Maman. "People will get killed."

"They're killing political dissidents, not students," I say quietly, like I'm trying to convince myself this will always be true.

Baba nods. "For now," he says.

Maman looks at me. "Promise you won't go into those streets."

I close my eyes as I nod. I have to hide any evidence of guilt as I say, "I promise, Maman."

The following Friday after class, I ask Peyman if we can go to Key Club again. I don't know how else to find Shirin, and I can't stop thinking about her. But she isn't at Key Club that night, and without her presence, the whole place feels silly to me. Just a bunch of people in fancy clothes, drinking and dancing as their country crumbles around them. And still, I ask Peyman to take me again the next Friday. And once again, she's not there.

It's yet another Friday when Peyman and I walk out of class and hear students whispering covertly about a protest at Jaleh Square. They're arguing about whether to go. Peyman must know what I'm thinking, because he slaps me on the shoulder as he says, "Don't even think about going."

"What if she's there?" I ask.

"If she's there, then she's a fool and not worth your time. We're officially under martial law as of yesterday. We can't risk our lives for—"

A classmate interrupts Peyman. "If you're not willing to risk your life, then what's the point of protesting at all? Risking our lives is the whole point. We need to show the authorities that they can't scare us into silence."

"I'm sorry, were you a part of this conversation?" Peyman asks.

The annoying classmate rolls his eyes. "The whole country is a part of this conversation, coward." Then he walks away.

I pull Peyman to a quiet corner and plead with him. "Please come with me. She's not going to Key Club anymore, and I have to find her."

"Saeed, listen to me. Martial law is no joke. And you know I have a joke for every occasion."

"We won't stay long. But if she is there, then maybe . . . Maybe I want to be there to show her I'm brave."

"Risking death isn't brave, it's stupid. You know I believe we need more freedoms, but the best thing we can do for our country right now is stay alive. And you promised your parents—"

"They'll never know. It's just once. To find her."

Peyman puts a hand on my shoulder, gently this time.

He holds it there. "I don't want you to get hurt."

"I won't," I say. "I feel invincible."

"Well, you're not. You just feel that way because you're blinded by your first crush. But you don't even know her, Saeed. She's just a girl. There will be other girls. But you won't find them if you don't survive. Please don't go."

"You won't tell my parents if I do, will you?"

He shakes his head. "Of course I won't." As I rush away from him, he screams out, "Be careful, Saeed."

I park my Paykan blocks from Jaleh Square, then follow the sound of the chants. The closer I get, the harder my heart beats. I think of turning away. I hate breaking a promise I made my parents. I hate defying Peyman, who has always been a good friend, and who has never led me astray. And as much as I believe in the ideals of the student protesters, I also think Peyman might be right about staying alive being the smartest course of action. We can't be the future of the country if we're not alive. I take a deep breath. I decide to turn back, but then . . .

I see her. Her unmistakable ponytail. Her beautiful eyes. I scream for her. "Shirin!" But she doesn't hear me. My voice is swallowed up by the chaos.

I turn a corner into the square, searching for her. Screaming her name. But I can't find her. There are so many people here. Far too many to count. Thousands. Maybe tens of thousands. Maybe even more. Every single one of them brave, and stupid, and defiant. I feel unbearably moved by these people, each of them risking their life for their dreams.

I keep screaming her name in the commotion, but it starts to feel futile. And so I stop my search and join the crowds. I chant alongside them, for a free Iran. I raise a fist in the air. I feel something stir inside me with each pair of eyes I find, a sense of connection, of unity, of hope.

And then the hope is shattered by gunshots. They're not fired into the air this time. They're fired directly at us. At me. I duck down reflexively, covering my face with my arms. I squeeze myself into a ball, my body shaking in terror. I see flashes of my parents, disappointed in me for not listening to them. I hear Peyman telling me I'm not invincible. He was right. I've never felt more vulnerable, more scared. I'm just a frightened student, crouched down on the ground, praying to a God I'm not sure I even believe in.

The gunshots won't stop. One after the other. I'm overwhelmed by the terrifying sound of shots fired, agonized screams, and the panicked footsteps of people running for their lives.

I peek through my arms at the horrifying scene. And then I realize . . . she's here. I have to find her. I can't let her get hurt. "Shirin!" I yell out as I get back up and search for her. Another gunshot. The sound is so close to me that a part of me thinks I've been shot. My heart beats out of my chest. My life flashes before me. But there's no blood on me. I'm still alive. It's just fear. "Shirin!" I scream again.

I make my way through the frightened crowd. All around me is violence and tragedy. Screams of desperation. Bodies on the ground. Blood on the streets. So much blood. My eyes dart from one horror to another, and I pray that I find her.

Security forces seem to come from all sides, weapons in hand, shooting indiscriminately. I beg for them to stop, naively thinking that my voice might make a difference. But I can't even hear myself, just gunshots, just pain. And yet, I continue to beg. "Please," I cry out. "Please stop. Please. You've made your point."

I make eye contact with an officer. I see him point his gun at me. Quickly, I throw my hands up in the air in surrender. Still, the officer shoots. I close my eyes. I pray this isn't the end. But the bullet hits a man who runs in front of me in an attempt to escape. The bullet hits his leg, and the man falls backward. I try to catch him, but he's heavier than I am, and he takes me down with him.

His blood pours over me. It has a scent to it, like rust. I hold on to the man, pleading with him to stay alive, to keep breathing.

"What's your name?" I ask, pushing myself out from under him.

No response.

"Please. Tell me your name. Please."

He can barely manage a whisper. "Bijan," he says. "My name is Bijan."

"What's your last name?" I ask urgently. "Please tell me who you are."

"Am I dying?" he asks.

"You're bleeding," I say desperately. I want to ask for help, but from who? Chaos is all around us, the world sped up. "We have to stop the bleeding." I pull off my belt. I don't know what I'm doing, but I do my best to turn my belt into a tourniquet around his leg. He screams in agony as I tighten the belt. "I'm so sorry. I think this will help. Tell me your full name."

"Bijan Golbahar," he says. "Please tell my family . . ." But he doesn't have the strength to say more.

"I'm here, Bijan Golbahar. My name is Saeed Jafarzadeh. I'm a student. Just a student. I wish I was a doctor." I think of Shirin, and her future as a doctor. My heart sinks down my body, thinking she might be shot. I scream her name desperately, as if I can keep her alive by yelling her name to the heavens. "Shirin! Shirin!"

And then I hear her call back to me. "Saeed!"

There she is. Just a few feet away. Running toward me. I reach an arm out to her. But she's yanked away. I scream her name again, as if a word could save her. But it's too late. She's pulled back into the crowd. I can't see her anymore. I feel powerless. I am powerless, and I feel stupid for thinking I could make any difference at all by being here.

I look down at Bijan's face again and realize that he's around my age. Probably a student like me. A student who just wanted a country that allows him to have real opportunities. My God. I say a silent prayer that his life doesn't end today, and another prayer for Shirin.

"Shirin," I croak. I look up to the sky and close my eyes. I see blackness. I feel a fist. Or is it the side of a gun? It knocks me down. The pain radiates through my body, like a warning. Run, it tells me. Run. But I can't move. I just keep saying her name like an incantation. "Shirin. Shirin. Shirin."

The last thing I remember is her voice. Screaming my name. "Saeed." Again, closer. "Saeed." And again, so close I can feel her breath. "Saeed, I'm here. It's Shirin. It's me. I'm here."

I don't know where I am, or how I got here. My memory seems to have stopped in that moment when I was hit in the back of the head. I look down at my feet. Water from the shower jets above me wash the blood away. His blood. Bijan Golbahar. Maybe some of my blood too. Mixing together, becoming one, and then circling into the drain, disappearing forever. I look up for a moment. Three jets above me, one more powerful than the next. I've never seen anything like it, like something out of a guide for the best European hotels. Then I look down again. I have to watch the blood disappear. There can't be any evidence of me at the protest. If Baba and Maman find out I was there, they would kill me before the security forces get me.

"Are you okay in there?" It's her. Shirin. "Do you need help?"

I panic, thinking she's going to come in and see me naked. Instinctively, I pull the shower curtain around my body. "I'm fine," I say too aggressively.

She laughs. "Don't worry, I won't come in. Bahman Agha can help you if you need him."

"Who is Bahman Agha?" I ask, letting the shower curtain go.

"He's our chauffeur," she says. "He helped carry you into the shower. I tried, but you were a little too heavy for me. Your mother feeds you well."

"My father," I say.

"What's that?"

I look down at the drain. It's just water now. Clean, clear water. All the blood is gone. "It's my father who does all the cooking."

"How forward-thinking," she says.

I peek out into the bathroom and I realize . . . . I'm not in a European hotel. I'm in her home. White marble everywhere. A bidet next to the toilet. Embroidered towels. A mirror gilded with gold. Everything obviously imported from France, Switzerland, Italy.

"So are you ever going to dry yourself off?" she asks.

I take a breath. Finally, the blood is gone. I'm clean, but I know that no matter how many showers I take, I will never wash away the memory of Bijan's face. He will always be seared inside of me.

I dry myself with the softest towel I've ever felt. Next to the sink, I see a stack of clean clothes. "Whose clothes are these?"

"My father's," she says. She must sense my hesitation, because she quickly adds, "Don't worry, we're washing your clothes. You can change back into them when you leave."

Her father's clothes are like nothing I've ever worn. The pants are tailored and crisp. The eggplant-colored cashmere sweater feels like a second skin.

"Can I open the door now? Are you dressed?" she asks.

I open the door. She stands behind it. I want to hold her, to thank her, but I'm frozen. "What happened?" I ask.

"You don't remember?" She puts a tender hand on my cheek.

"The boy who was shot. His name was Bijan. Is he okay?" I hear the panic in my voice, like I'm right back there again.

"I don't know," she says sadly. "I wish I did."

"I used my belt. I tried to help him. . . ."

"I know you did." Her hand doesn't move from my cheek. "You were calling my name. I found you lying on the street, and I dragged you to the nearest restaurant. They let me call home. Bahman Agha picked us up. Helped me get you home. Got you in the shower."

"You were there the whole time?" I ask, my face hot with shame.

"Don't worry, I didn't see anything." She manages a smile. "Come on, you're not going to spend the whole day standing in the doorway of my bathroom, are you?"

I follow her into her bedroom. Her bed is big enough for four. She lies on one end. I sit at the edge of the other, uncomfortable. "I should go . . . ," I say. "Your parents . . . They won't like a strange man in your bed."

"You're not *in* my bed, you're *on* my bed. And you're certainly not strange. Besides, my father isn't even in the country at the moment. He's in France, doing business and furniture shopping."

I look around the room. The end tables are perfectly lacquered. The carpet looks freshly woven. There's a divan against the wall, upholstered in a fragile silk. "New furniture?" I ask. "Everything in here looks brand-new."

"Yes," she says. "Well, what's new to you may not be new to my father." She gazes across her bedroom. "It wasn't always this way. We're what the French call *nouveau riche.*"

She says it in a perfect French accent. She sounds like Catherine Deneuve, like a foreign film star.

"I know some French music," I say. "My father, he's a musician. Tar and piano mostly. But he plays other instruments. He says music is the only universal language."

Her eyes light up. "A musician. The highest calling there is. I couldn't live without music."

I take her hand in mine. "Is this all right?" I ask.

"Yes," she whispers. "But your hand is shaking."

"I'm nervous." It's not just my hand. My voice trembles too.

"About what?" she asks tenderly.

"About being alone with you."

"Let's not get too dramatic." The gleam in her eyes is blindingly beautiful. "You don't even know my last name."

I remember the monogrammed towels in the bathroom. *SM.* "I know it starts with an *M*."

"Good job, detective."

"Majidi. Mahdavi. Marilyn. Monroe."

She laughs and stands up. "I'll never tell. It's too much fun keeping you guessing." She squeezes my quivering fingers. "Are you okay?" she asks, her voice turning serious.

"Of course," I say, pulling my hand away and steadying it. "I'm fine."

"Were you raised to say that no matter how you're feeling? Men in this country think that stoicism is bravery. But it's not. Honesty is bravery." Her gaze pierces into mine.

"The truth is . . ." I can't get the words out. I curl my fingers into a fist. The truth is I'm scared. Scared that I'll always be haunted by that protest, and by Bijan's blood. Scared of what my parents will do if they ever find out. Scared of touching her, and of what she does to my heart, the way she makes it soar. But I can't say any of that. I don't have the words for all the conflicting emotions. I'm no poet.

"Are you thinking of that boy?" she asks.

I nod sadly.

"I wish I had brought him here." She sighs. "There was so little time, and so much bloodshed. If I could have, I would've brought everyone suffering back here, but I couldn't. . . ."

"You can't blame yourself," I say.

She looks at me with discomfiting sympathy. "Neither can you." She doesn't look away as she adds, "You strike me as someone who has a hard time forgiving himself, who feels the weight of the world on your shoulders."

I nod. "I thought . . . that we could create a better world without dying for it. I was so stupid."

"That's not stupid, especially if you've never seen death happen. It changes you." After a breath, she says, "I was holding my mother's hand when she died."

I look into her eyes. They're welling up with tears. "I'm so sorry," I say. I don't know what else to add. I want to ask her how it happened, but that seems invasive. I want to ask what her mother was like, but I don't want to cause her pain.

"My mother . . . She was the fairest girl in her village." She starts to tell the story of her mother haltingly, like it's the first time she's telling it. "Her parents . . . They told her that her light skin would be her ticket to a new life. Ridiculous, isn't it? That something as superficial as the color of our skin should have any impact on our lives."

I nod.

"They didn't let her go into the sun," she continues. "They didn't care to educate her or give her any tools she might use later in life. They simply made sure her skin stayed fair. If she ever went outside, she carried a parasol. That's how my father met her."

"He sold her a parasol?" I ask, confused.

"He was a young civil engineer touring villages," she explains. "He still hadn't made his fortune. But he had started his work. Planning how those villages could and would be transformed. Roads. Buildings. Schools. Shops. All the conveniences of modern life. That's what my father wants to bring to Iran. He asked for my mother's hand in marriage without ever speaking to her. He saw her walking home under her parasol. He followed her in his European car. Her parents had never seen a vehicle like that. They had never seen a man dressed in a tailored suit. They immediately agreed to let their daughter marry him. She was fifteen. She was sixteen when my brother was born. Seventeen when I was born. A child."

"Where's your brother?" I ask.

"Oxford," she says. "He doesn't like it here."

"You didn't follow in his footsteps?" I ask.

"My brother left Iran long ago. He went to boarding school in England when he was eleven years old. He's never been back, not once. But I'm different. My place is here. In my country. I believe . . . I believe that women in this country are just starting to live. There are doors waiting to be opened for us, and not by men. By other women. That's why I march in the streets. To make sure we have a voice in the change that will soon come."

I nod.

"If you read my mother's obituary, it will say she died of heart failure," she says faintly. "But she didn't. She swallowed too many sleeping pills."

I feel my heart beating too fast. "I'm sorry," is all I can think of to say.

"She didn't belong here. Going from a small village

to a big city overnight might seem like a fairy tale, but it wasn't for her. She had no role to play here. No friends who understood her. No purpose. And the more money my father made, the more lost she became. She was asked to entertain princes and Europeans and millionaires, all because she was beautiful. Sometimes I think what is happening in Iran right now is just a giant version of my mother's story. The country is modernizing too fast for the people. They're not ready for the changes. People can only handle so much change at once."

"I'm so sorry," I say again. I sound like an idiot. What is a person supposed to say when they've found out something so devastating?

"Thank you, but you don't need to apologize. You did nothing wrong. And neither did she. That's something that's taken me some time to realize. There's a poem by Shahriar I hold very close to my heart." She takes a breath before reciting, "*No, she has not died, because I am still alive. She is alive in my sorrow, my poem and my fantasy.*"

When she pauses, I complete the poem for her. "*Never will die the ones whose heart is alive with love.*"

She smiles wistfully. "You know it?"

"My father used to read me a poem every night before bed. Our literary classics. And even our contemporary greats, like Forough Farrokhzad. It's silly, but I still need to read a poem out loud to myself every night before bed. It's, I don't know . . . comforting."

She leans in a little closer to me. "It's bold of your father to introduce you to Farrokhzad. Most men aren't interested in the words and thoughts of women."

"My father isn't most men," I say, with appreciation for all the ways my father is different from the others. He turned me into the kind of man who might just win the heart of Shirin.

"And my mother wasn't most women," she says. "Her moods shifted like the breeze. It kept me on my toes. Taught me to be ready for anything."

"Shirin . . ." I'm about to say I'm sorry again, but I stop myself. Instead, I ask, "How old were you? When she . . ."

"I was ten," she says matter-of-factly. "It was the year my brother had left. My father was in Germany on business."

"My God," I blurt out. "You were alone?"

"Of course not," she says, with a sad smile. "I've never been alone. I've always had a staff full of wonderful people to care for me. And they did. They do. Perhaps that's why their loyalty is to me and not to my father. Why do you think I felt safe bringing you here?"

"What would your father do?" I ask. "If he knew I was here?"

It's not a question she wants to answer. "I'll go see if your clothes are dry," she says before leaving.

I sit alone for what feels like an eternity. It's all too much to think about. The protest. The blood. Shirin. I've never felt more lost, and at the same time, more found.

When she returns, I want to ask her to marry me. I feel so foolish. I just met her. I don't know her last name.

And wouldn't that just make me another version of her father, asking for her mother's hand in marriage without even knowing her? I won't make the same mistake. I'll get to know her first. Then, when the time is right, I won't ask her father. He doesn't own her. I'll never own her either. That's what I love most about her. She belongs to herself and to her country, just like I do.

"What are you thinking?" she asks when she sits down and places my dry clothes next to me.

I smile big, dreaming up ways to propose to her someday. Imagining my beaming parents at the wedding. "I'm thinking my parents would really like you."

"What a sweet thought," she says. "I'm certain I'll like them too. What's your mother like?" she asks.

"She's . . ." I hesitate because I realize my mother is like her. Opinionated. Ambitious. "She's an architect."

"Wow, there aren't many female architects in Iran."

"She's incredibly smart. Very ambitious, like you."

Her eyes open wide. She laughs. "You're a Freudian cliché, chasing a woman who's just like your mother."

I can't help but laugh too. "I will remind you that I'm wearing your father's clothes, so who's the Freudian cliché?"

I'm lost in the magic of her laughter. Everything else fades away. "I'm sorry, but I have to go now," she says.

"Will you be at Key Club tonight?" I ask, desperate to know when I'll see her again.

"I don't think so. After what we just witnessed, dancing the night away seems . . . I don't know, wrong somehow." She looks at her watch. "Oh wow, I've lost track of time. I'm already late." Then she calls out loudly, "Bahman Agha, I'm so sorry, but would you mind taking my friend Saeed back to Jaleh Square to pick up his car?"

"You won't be riding with us?" I ask.

"I drive myself," she says proudly. And I'm sure that unlike me, she doesn't drive a Paykan. Probably a Mercedes or a Cadillac. "And I'm late to meet my aunt at Cloop Shahanshahi, so this is goodbye for now."

As she throws on a jacket, I declare, "I need to find him. To know if he's alive."

"Bijan?" she asks.

I nod sadly.

"We'll find him together," she says with a decisive nod. Before she walks out, she leans toward me and whispers, "My father is gone for three more weeks. You can knock on my door any evening after seven or any morning before nine. You know where I live."

I want to say that I still don't know her last name, but there's time. Nothing but beautiful time.

When I pick up my car and get myself back home, I can hear the tar coming from the study. Baba is teaching. I check my watch—almost dinner. Maman is still working. I sneak into the house as quietly as possible. I make my way to my room and strip the clothes off my body, just in case there's still blood on them.

I put clean clothes on. I run down to the kitchen in search of a garbage bag. And I get rid of the clothes. As far as anyone is concerned, I was never there.

Anyone *but* Shirin, who knows everything.

Who will always know me in a way nobody does. She saw me at my most vulnerable, watched me become forever changed.

When I've thrown the clothes out, I join my parents for dinner. *Khoreshteh kadu, polo, tahdig, mast.* I stuff my face to avoid talking about my day. As I listen to them debate the Reza Baraheni book they're reading, I can imagine me and Shirin, decades from now, debating a new book as our own child listens on, maybe even keeping their own secrets from us.

How long should I wait before knocking on her door? This is the question Peyman and I are grappling with on Saturday as we eat some street kabob and walk.

"Three days minimum," Peyman says.

"Three days?" I parrot incredulously. "I want to spend every moment of my life with her, and you're asking me to wait three days?"

"Here's another option," he says. "You can go knock on her door tonight and scare her off. This is a long-term plan, isn't it?"

"Of course it is," I say. "She's the only woman for me."

"Then play your cards correctly or you risk losing her." Peyman slaps my shoulder a little too hard. "Chin up, young man. You have me. You'll survive three lonely days without seeing her."

* * *

On the third day, I drive to Shirin's house in the late evening. I hesitate before knocking on the door, and then, like magic, it opens. She stands on the other side of it, wearing a bulky sweater, jeans, and a smile. "What took you so long?" she asks.

"Well," I say, "my friend told me that if I came to see you too soon, it would scare you off."

She laughs. "It takes a lot more than that to scare me."

We stand still for a moment. I wonder if she's going to invite me in.

"I found an address for the Golbahar family," she says.

"How?" I ask. My own search for them was futile.

"I made a few phone calls," she says. "I'm very resourceful. Should we go see them now?"

"Now?"

"There's no time like the present," she says. "It's one of the best lessons my father taught me. I may disagree with him often, but he's right about that. If you want to do something, do it now. Tomorrow isn't guaranteed."

Bahman Agha drives us from north to south, from the affluence of Shirin's home to a neighborhood with no sewage, crowded with too many people sharing too little space.

"This is it," she says, pointing to a dilapidated apartment building. Outside, children play soccer, happily kicking, oblivious to the inequality that surrounds them.

Shirin throws a black chador over her hair. I've never seen her wear one before, but she does it here out of respect for the community we're in. I love her for that.

She exits the car first. I follow her out. "Wait here for us, Bahman Agha," she says. "Thank you."

A few kids circle the car, touching the cool, clean steel doors.

I follow Shirin up to the third floor of the apartment building, climbing narrow stairs. She knocks on a door when we reach the third floor. There's no answer. She tries again.

"Can I help you?" a woman asks. She looks about twice my parents' age. She clutches her cane tightly as she descends the steps.

"We were hoping to speak to the Golbahar family," Shirin says.

"What have they done?" the woman asks. "They're good people."

"They've done nothing," I say, realizing she thinks we're here to punish them somehow. Arrest them. Why else would we be looking for them?

"We don't need any trouble here," she says emphatically. "That family, they moved here searching for work, for a better life in the big city. And now, their son has been shot."

"Is he alive?" I ask.

The woman narrows her eyes as she considers my question. "Why do you want to know?"

"Do you know when they might be home?" Shirin asks. "I promise this is a friendly visit."

The woman sighs. "They've left the city, and I don't blame them. That's all I know. I don't know if that poor boy made it or not. Now please leave us in peace."

The woman continues her very slow descent down the narrow stairs. We follow behind her, stuck at her speed.

The fascinated children are still hovering around the car when we get back. Bahman Agha is explaining the intricacies of the vehicle's design to them. We let him finish, and then we get in.

"I'm sorry they weren't there," she says when we reach her home again. "For what it's worth, he was lucky the bullet only hit his leg. There's a good chance he made it."

"Thanks for saying that. I have to believe he made it." I sigh. "Can I call on you again soon?"

"Soon sounds good." She exits the car but turns back once more. "Don't wait three days this time, okay? Your friend's advice might apply to some girls, but I'm not some girls."

"No," I say. "You're most certainly not."

I arrive home as my parents are finishing dinner. "Where have you been?" Baba asks when I sit down and serve myself some *kotlet*.

"With Peyman," I say.

"Don't lie to me," Baba says.

I look down at my food, wondering how he knows.

"You've been seen out in the streets," Baba suddenly blurts out. "We've known for days. We've waited for you to tell us, but——"

"Millions of people have been in the streets," I say meekly. I swallow hard. Baba makes the softest *kotlet*, but it feels like a rock moving down my throat.

"Well, you're not millions of people," Maman says. "You're our only son, and you broke a promise." Her voice cracks as she adds, "And now your life is in danger."

"You were at the Jaleh Square protest, weren't you?" Baba asks.

One look at my parents tells me that they already know. But how? "Did Peyman tell you?" I ask.

They both shake their heads.

"I promise I'll stop. And I'll keep my promise this time. They'll leave me alone. I'm just a student."

"No, you're not," Baba says. "Not anymore."

I look up at them, confused. "What? Why?"

Maman gives Baba a heavy nod, and then he says, "Please hear us out, and trust us. We've arranged for you to leave Iran. You'll be going to UCLA. In Los Angeles."

"America?" I feel dizzy. I've never left Iran. I've never wanted to. This is my home.

"We've arranged everything. They have a fantastic school of engineering, don't worry."

"That's not what I'm worried about." I stand up. "I can't leave you. Or Peyman." And Shirin, I want to say. I can't leave her, ever.

"Don't worry about us," Baba says. "We're not involved in politics. They'll leave us alone."

"And I don't want to abandon my country," I say, feeling the strength in those words, the truth of them.

Baba stands up, facing me. "Saeed *joon*, your country has already abandoned you."

I shake my head, refusing to believe him. "No, it hasn't. Not yet. There's still hope. That's why we're out there. And you want to send me to the place that caused all this? You want me to be American? When America gives the Shah the weapons he uses to attack us? When America removed Mossadegh from power?"

"You don't need to lecture me about Mossadegh," Baba says. "I lived through Mossadegh. I remember the sense of hope he gave us. But that's the past."

"And it can be the future. If the Shah leaves, we can have that again."

"With who?" Baba's voice rises. "Khomeini? You think that corrupt prick is your savior?"

I'm briefly taken aback by the harshness of his tone. "Anyone is better than who we have now."

"You don't understand how power corrupts. You will someday. You'll see."

"No, it's you who doesn't understand anything," I spit out. "Because you don't care enough to get involved. You just sit in that living room teaching ancient music, stuck in the past. You're a coward." I regret the words the minute they leave my mouth.

"Perhaps I am," Baba says sadly. I can tell he's angry, but he takes a few calming breaths. "But I know the world. And I warned you not to get involved in politics. Your mother and I warned you. Do you think we want you to leave?" He waits a beat before whispering, "Our hearts are broken."

I look over at Maman. The heartbreak is evident in

her eyes, and I hate myself for causing her pain.

"Saeed *joon*, there are things we've wanted to tell you for a long time," Maman says. "And now is the time."

Baba sighs, a deep sigh, a sigh that holds secrets in it. "My mother is American," Baba says carefully. "I never told you because . . . well, because my history with her is complicated."

I feel like I'm floating outside my own body. This can't be real.

"Her name is Margaret. She lives in Los Angeles. I haven't spoken to her in decades."

"But . . ." I can't finish the thought. The shock is too great. How could my own father have kept this from me?

"Were you raised there?" I ask incredulously. "Is that why your English is so good?"

"Yes," he says.

"And your Persian. You always told me you had a slight accent because you went to an American school, but that was a lie, wasn't it?"

"None of it matters now. Maybe Margaret will tell you everything out of spite. Maybe she won't."

"Tell me what?" I ask.

"None of that matters," he says.

"How can it not matter?" I say too loud. "You tell me that my grandmother is American? That I'm moving to Los Angeles? That you've lied to me my whole life? But it doesn't matter."

"My past doesn't matter. The choices I made . . . I don't regret them. They were my choices. I never looked back. But I must look back now. You're our son, our life. And Margaret is willing to keep you safe."

"You did all this behind my back. Spoke to her. Purchased my plane ticket. Got me into a new school."

"We knew that you would only be upset if you knew," Maman says. "And we couldn't tell you until we were sure she would agree, and until we were sure the university would take you. She made it all happen, and she did it quickly."

"My mother is very effective when she wants to be," Baba says coldly.

Maman looks at him when she says, "And it was a big thing to ask of her, a mother who was deserted by her only son."

"And if I say no?" I ask. "If I refuse to leave?"

Maman looks at Baba, and I can tell there's more he's not telling me.

"One of the boys I tutor has a father who delivers packages for the SAVAK," Baba begins. "Your name is on their list. They've been tracking you. They have photographs of you at multiple protests. They don't know we have this information—this head start. Do you understand now? The SAVAK shows no mercy. We have to get you out of the country before they take you to prison, or—"

"I understand," I say, stopping him from saying more. I already know they could kill me if they wanted to. The shock of that reality turns into resignation. The conversation is over. I have no choice. I'm saying goodbye to my parents, and to my country, and to my best friend, and to a girl I love who I may never see again, a girl I can't bring myself to tell my parents about. Just saying her name aloud would bring tears to my eyes.

I don't read a poem to myself that night because I don't bother going to sleep. I just sit up in bed, staring at the wall for one last night, desperately figuring out how to propose to Shirin early tomorrow morning. It's not the way I dreamed of doing it, but if I don't propose, how can I expect her to come with me to Los Angeles? And she must come with me, because if they know about me, then they know about her too. We're both in danger now.

I sneak quietly into Baba's bedroom the next morning. He's a light sleeper, so I tiptoe into the closet as quietly as I can. Even though Maman sleeps and works in the guest room, she keeps her clothes and jewelry here. I find the jewelry box and rifle through it, wondering what I can borrow without upsetting Maman.

"What are you doing?" It's Baba. He stands at the door of the closet, wearing nothing but his underwear. That's always how he's slept.

"I—"

"Those are your mother's things," he says.

"I know that. I . . ." Why can't I tell him? Won't a man who teaches the art of music understand romance? "I thought I should bring Margaret a gift."

"She's not a sentimental woman."

"Still. You raised me to be a gentleman."

"Pick something else to give her," Baba suggests. "Not something that belongs to your mother. I have an idea. I'll wrap a gift just for her. Something that will hopefully soften her. Remind her of a better past." I nod, wishing he'd leave. But he just stands there, staring at me. "Now are you going to tell me what you're really doing in here?"

I look into Baba's eyes. I want so desperately to resent him for sending me away, for lying to me, but I know he's trying to save my life. I can see the fear in his eyes, the love, and I break. "There's a girl," I say.

"Ah." He moves closer to me.

"I just met her. It's too soon, but I can't think of another way."

Baba turns his gaze toward the jewelry box. It suddenly dawns on him. "My son," he whispers. "You want to ask her to marry you."

"It's the only way to convince her to come with me. I need her to come with me. I can't go to America alone. And . . . I don't know how to explain it, but I've never met anyone like her—"

"Shh," he says. "You don't need to explain yourself. The beauty of love is its mystery. When you try to explain it, you rob it of its power." He pulls a ring out of the jewelry box. A blue stone. "This is turquoise. I bought it for your mother the first time we went to Isfahan. Turquoise wards off the evil eye."

"Do you really believe that?" I ask.

Baba shrugs. "I can't afford not to be superstitious.

Especially now." His voice suddenly chokes up. "I'm scared. Imagining you in prison. Or worse."

"Don't imagine it."

"Still. Imagining you away from me. With her."

"Then come with me. Please. With me and Shirin. That's her name. We can all start a new life together." I suddenly feel the absence of my parents. I've never been away from them. I wasn't sent to boarding school like some of the wealthiest Iranians. How will I exist without them?

"*Aziz.*" He whispers the term of endearment with an ache in his voice. "I left America a long time ago and I've never been back. I don't know if I can."

"Why did you leave? Why don't you talk to your mother? What happened?" The questions pour out of me.

He clicks his jaw nervously, like he needs to stop himself from saying too much. Then he looks into my eyes and says, "There isn't much time left. Go to her now. Tell her you'll respect her and love her, through good times and bad times. Because there will be both in the road ahead." His eyes look wet. "Go. Be back in time for your flight."

He places the turquoise ring in my palm and wraps my fingers around it. Then he pulls me into a hug.

I let myself melt into his arms. My father. My baba. How can I say goodbye to him when there's so much more I need to understand about him?

* * *

I drive to Shirin's house, the turquoise ring in my pocket. I take a deep breath, imagining every version of what could happen next. The happy ending. The tragic ending. But no, I tell myself. This isn't an ending. Whatever happens, it's a beginning. It's just the start of the rest of our lives.

I approach the front door apprehensively and ring the doorbell. I can hear the bell from outside the house. I wait for her, or Bahman Agha. Anyone. But no one comes. I ring again. Still nothing. I knock on the door. "Shirin? Shirin, are you there?" I plead from behind the door. "Shirin!"

I hear the aggressive sound of a lawn mower and turn around. A bulky gardener stares at me from behind the loud contraption. "Who are you?" he asks in thickly accented Persian.

"I'm a friend of Shirin *joon*," I say meekly.

"You go to school with her?" he asks.

"No, I—Well . . ." I can't say how we met. I could get her in trouble. "We're friends, that's all. Is she home?"

"If you were a friend of hers, you would know she had to leave the country."

My heart sinks in shock. She's gone. Probably fled to a safer place forever, like I'm about to do. I've lost her. "Is she in Europe with her father?" I ask.

He walks toward me, but he doesn't answer the question.

"Could you tell me how to reach her?" I beg. "Where is she staying? Is there a phone number?"

"I'm a gardener. I can't give out personal information

159

about my employers to a stranger."

"But I'm not a stranger. I promise." I hear my voice speed up, panic setting in. "I'm a friend. My name is Saeed Jafarzadeh. Ask Bahman Agha. He'll know me."

"The staff is away visiting their families," he says with a shrug. "It's just me here. And I don't know you."

"Just give me her phone number. Or an address. Or even . . . Oh God, I don't even know her last name. Give me that. I'm begging you."

"You don't know her last name?" He shakes his head in disbelief, then laughs.

"Please." I'm deflating. The fire is leaving my body. I feel checkmated. Every fantasy I dreamed for us is gone. Maybe that's what they always were meant to stay. Fantasies.

"I'm going back to the lawn now," he says. "You should leave before I call the authorities."

My heart skips a beat when he makes this threat. The last thing I need is to be delivered to the same authorities who already want to put me away, or worse. "I'll go," I say. "I just— If she comes back— When she comes back . . . tell her that Saeed came to see her. And that . . ." I love her. That I was prepared to ask for her hand in marriage. Ready to get down on one knee and slip the good-luck turquoise stone onto her finger.

"That what?" he asks.

"Nothing," I say. "It's nothing." I turn away from him, and from the house, and from this city that holds my most beautiful memories.

* * *

Baba and Maman drive me to Peyman's house so I can say goodbye. He makes no jokes. Just hugs me tight and tells me he'll hunt me down if I ever lose touch with him. Then my parents take me to Mehrabad Airport. They hug me goodbye outside, tears in both their eyes. I hold my tears back.

"I'm sorry Shirin wasn't there," Baba says. "I promise there will be more love in your future."

"I haven't given up yet," I say. "Maybe you could find her for me." Hope fills me for a moment.

Maman eyes Baba before she says, "Every one of us experiences heartbreak at some point in our lives. But the heart grows back stronger when it breaks. And you'll need a strong heart for what's ahead."

"So you won't look for her?" I ask. "I can always ask Peyman."

"We will," Maman says. "Of course we will."

"But if it doesn't work out, you'll be okay," Baba adds. "That's what we're saying. Human beings are resilient. And the Jafarzadehs are very good at starting over. Runs in the family."

I give them one more hug. I don't want to say any more. I'm afraid that if I say another word, I'll break down in tears.

"I put the gift for your grandmother in your suitcase," Baba says.

"Thank you. I'll give it to her."

"Stay strong," Baba says.

"Don't forget to focus on your studies," Maman says. "And don't forget to let yourself have fun."

"There will be light in your future," Baba adds. "You'll see."

An annoyed official tells them to move their car immediately and stares at them until they're back in their car, driving away from me.

I wander through the airport in a daze. It all feels surreal. I've never even been on a plane before. Now I'm boarding my very first aircraft to take me twelve thousand miles away. Twelve thousand miles. The number alone feels daunting. What am I doing traveling across that much land and sea? Where do I think I'm going?

It's not until I buckle my seat belt in the airplane that I feel the ring in my pocket. It hits the edge of my pinky finger. I pull it out and stare at it. I clutch it tight in my palm as the plane takes off.

The man traveling next to me turns my way. "Turquoise wards off evil and brings good luck."

I give him a wistful smile, hoping he's right. I'll be needing all the luck I can get.

Margaret doesn't come to the airport to greet me when I land in Los Angeles. The very idea that a relative wouldn't come to the airport to welcome you to a new country would seem absurd in Iran. But I'm not in Iran anymore, which is evident from the views I take in from the window of my taxi. There are no Paykan cars here. No kabob and *balal* and *gerdu* being sold on the streets. I see mountains in the distance, but they look nothing like the Alborz Mountains.

The cab drops me off outside a small single-story home with a sad-looking rose garden and dry grass in the front garden. I ring the bell and wait for her to arrive, but she doesn't. Maybe she went out. Maybe she forgot about me. So I sit on the front stoop, facing her vintage jet-black Buick, and wait for her. I open my suitcase and pull one of my engineering textbooks out. I may as well use the time to study. An hour later, the front door opens and I hear a gravelly voice behind me. "Well, what are you doing out there?"

"I rang the bell," I explain. "You were inside the whole time?"

"The doorbell doesn't work," she says coldly. "Why didn't you knock?"

I stand up and turn to face her. "Hello," I say, unsure what I should call her. I'm not ready to call her Grand-mother.

I lean in to give her a kiss on each cheek, but she backs away from me and waves me inside, pulling her baby-blue house robe tight around her as she does. Her face is lined with wrinkles, and her hair is thinning but dyed a strange and unnatural shade of red that makes her look like a dry raspberry. "Well, come in already. Your room is in the back. Shoes off."

"Thank you," I say, as I take in the old house, which smells like cleaning solutions and potpourri.

When the door closes behind us, she pulls a pair of

glasses from the pocket of her robe and puts them on. "Well, let me take a good look at you." She squints and grunts. "You certainly look nothing like my side of the family. You're very dark, aren't you? Dark genes are dominant, so they say."

I stand still, letting her inspect me and my dominant genes. I want to run away from her, to be back home where I belong.

"Strange," she says. "A few days ago, I didn't know you existed. And now here you are, living with me. Did you know I existed?"

I shake my head.

"Well," she says, "I suppose your father has his grudges, but if I'm the evil incarnate he believes I am, then why would I have saved your life?" She puts the glasses away and smiles proudly. She believes she's my savior. "Well, don't just stand there. Go find your room. It's in the back, like I said. Dinner is at six thirty. I'll see you then."

"I brought you a gift," I say. "It's in my suitcase."

"You can give it to me at dinner. I'm tired. Why are your shoes still on?"

She leaves me to find my own room. Offers me no warmth or hospitality. But perhaps she's already offered me enough. I take my shoes off and go unpack my things. Before I know it, dinnertime has arrived. I make my way to the kitchen, where she's set up the meal at a small table. She's already plated chicken and vegetables for me. I sit and eat. It's bland. Nothing like the Persian food Baba makes.

"You like it?" she asks, as I fork some flavorless peas

and chicken into my mouth.

"It's great." The lie flows easily out of my mouth.

"It's healthy," she says. "I can learn how to make some Persian food, if you like."

I'm not sure how this American lady would learn to make a cuisine that is so much older and more refined than she could ever be. Just looking around her home feels like an assault on the senses. She has ceramic rabbits everywhere. The whole place smells like the overly fragrant potpourri she places in every room. Her fabrics are all floral, but she clearly has no respect for flowers, because all the vases are full of fake ones.

"It's very hard to make. You'd have to be home all day to stir the pot."

"I don't go out much anymore."

I shrug. "Whatever makes you happy."

She squints. "My happiness has passed me by, boy. As have your manners. Besides, it will bring back memories for me too. You know, I lived there when I was a girl."

I shake my head. I don't know that. I realize Baba told me his mother was American, but he told me nothing about how or why.

"In Abadan. In the southwest of the country."

"I know where Abadan is," I say.

"Yes, I'm sure you do."

I also know that Abadan is rich with oil, and that it's where the Anglo-Persian Oil Company built its very first pipeline. And now I know why Baba never told me about his mother. Because her father must've been one of the oilmen who robbed our country. Why else would she have been in Abadan?

I work hard to swallow the chicken. It's chewy. Nothing like the soft chicken in the *khorakeh morgh* that Baba makes. Clearly, he didn't develop his love of cooking from his mother.

"You're going to be an engineer?" she asks.

"Perhaps," I say.

"Just like my father. He was an engineer. You must get it from him. Too bad you didn't get his fair skin too."

I remember Shirin telling me about her mother and the fair skin that decided her fate in life. I wonder why and how this obsession with light skin travels from Iran to America. We have so little in common. Why this?

"Well, at least you have his brain," she says. "He was brilliant."

I want to tell her that I come from the civilization that invented mathematics, and don't need her father's brain. But instead I ask, "He was an oil engineer?" I hear the accusation in my tone.

"Well, yes," she says. "Why else would he have been in Iran?"

I bite my tongue. There's no point in discussing this with her. And besides, I'm jet-lagged and tired. I stand up when I'm done. I reach out to take her empty plate.

"I can do the cleaning," she offers. "You should get some sleep. You have school tomorrow. It's a big day."

"Thank you," I say. "But I don't mind helping." I'm an Iranian. I've been taught to show good manners to my elders, and I've already been accused of forgetting my manners once by her.

I wash the dishes at the sink and place them on the drying rack. Outside, I can see a dad playing basketball with his kids in a driveway, illuminated by lights above their garage. They're laughing, oblivious to the price of their ease. Don't they know who keeps their lights on?

"I thought you brought me a gift," she says.

"Oh, I did. It's in my room. I'll go get it." I rush back to my room and pull out the old parchment Baba rolled up and put in my suitcase. It's from my grandfather's collection. She's eating a chocolate bar when I find her in the kitchen again.

"I hate healthy food," she says. "Don't tell my doctor."

"I'm very good with secrets," I say.

She smiles as she swipes the gift from my hand and unrolls it. She looks like she's seen a ghost when she stares at the calligraphy.

I read the poem out loud, Shirin's scent coming back to me. I want these words to float to her somehow, float across time and space to my beloved. "*How can I know anything about the past or the future, when the light of the beloved shines—*"

She snaps at me. "I know how to read the language. I grew up there."

"You like it?" I ask. "You don't have to hang it on your wall if you don't want to."

"Your grandfather made this," she says. It's not a question.

And that's when I realize how little thought I've given to any of this. If this is my grandmother, then once upon a time, she loved my grandfather, and perhaps he loved her, as unlikely as that seems now. I didn't ask Baba why he packed this particular gift for her, but now I know. He wanted to remind her that I come from her past.

"Yes, he did," I say.

She rolls the parchment back up. She offers no thanks, and I fear I've made as bad a first impression on her as she's made on me. Perhaps for her, the past is something to be escaped, not to be remembered.

"You should call your father and tell him you're safe," she says. "Don't stay on the phone too long. The long-distance fees are exorbitant."

"I'm sure," I say, thinking it makes sense that the corporations of the world would find every way to discourage communication between America and Iran.

She walks away when I pick up the phone and dial home. She obviously has no interest in talking to her son. And Baba doesn't ask about her when he picks up. "Saeed joon," he says breathlessly. "How are you?"

"I'm okay," I say.

"We miss you so much. The home feels empty without you."

My voice trembles when I say, "I miss you too. Both of you."

There's a long pause. I wonder if he's going to ask about her, his mother. I can tell he wants to. But instead he says, "Your mother wants to hear your voice."

"Wait. Baba." Before he can hand the phone to Maman, I quickly ask, "You won't forget, will you? You'll go to Shirin. You'll tell her where I am, how to find me. Baba, please."

He sighs a deep sigh before he says, "I promise."

Then Maman gets on the phone and asks what I ate for dinner. She tells me there's a store in Los Angeles where I can find Persian spices, but I wonder if those flavors will just remind me of the past. Perhaps, like my grandmother, I need to put the past behind me for now. It's too painful. That's what I think about as I unpack and realize that everything reminds me of Shirin, of my parents, of the faraway country that I love.

I sit up in bed at night, unable to sleep. I don't want to sleep, anyway. My dreams are of Shirin, my nightmares of Bijan. Either way, it hurts. The pain I feel isn't just emotional. It's physical. In the Persian language, we don't say we miss someone. We say our heart is tight, and that's how I feel. My heart feels like a raisin, shriveled and dry. I pull out a poetry book. There are tears in my eyes as I read Saadi out loud, wishing my father was here to read it to me.

I'm nervous and apprehensive as I get ready for my first day at my new American college. Margaret hands me a banana for breakfast and tells me where the bus stop is. "I was hoping we could ride in your Buick," I say.

Margaret laughs. "That old thing just looks pretty. It's a big honey that needs a lot of money to start running again."

"Maybe I can walk," I suggest. "To get to know the neighborhood."

"Nobody walks in Los Angeles," she says. "People will think you're a foreigner."

"But I am——"

"Take the bus. The stop is just up the block."

I do what she says. The bus drops me off at the main entrance of the school, which is frightening in its size. Aryamehr felt like an extension of my home. I knew everyone there. And whenever I needed him, Peyman was there to make me laugh. But at UCLA, I feel like I stand out. Everyone seems *too* interested in me, starting with the dean, who welcomes me to the school's engineering department.

"So, how does it feel to be in America?" the dean asks.

Recognizing that this man holds the power to cancel my enrollment, I smile too broadly and lie. "I already love it here. It feels just like home."

"Hopefully, a little more free than your home. No one gets kicked out of our country for exercising his right to peaceful protest." The dean speaks to me of the values of their campus and their country: *decency, honesty, equality.*

I keep forcing the smile as the dean hands me off to a senior student, who is tasked with giving me a tour of the campus. The student asks me the exact same question. "How'd you like America so far?"

Once again, I smile and lie. "I love it here."

"Of course you do. What's not to love? And your English is already so good."

What I'm starting to piece together is that these people don't care about me. They only care what I think of them. And they don't want an honest response. They simply ask because they couldn't possibly imagine an answer that wouldn't make them feel pride in their country.

The student who gives me the tour tells me how quickly things on campus are changing. "It's amazing," he says. "We have people from so many different countries attending these days. Like, look at you. Just the fact that you're here is a testament to American values."

I nod and smile, which I do a lot of my first day at school, as I'm barraged with exhausting questions from students and teachers alike.

I'm so bleary-eyed as I make my way to the gates of campus at the end of the day that I run right into someone and make her drop all her books. "Oh, I'm so sorry," I mumble.

"It's okay," she says. "Where are you in such a rush to get to? Classes are done for the day."

When she looks up, I realize it immediately. She's Iranian. I can hear it in her subtle accent, and see it in her dark brown eyes.

"You're Iranian?" I ask, smiling my first real smile since arriving.

She laughs. "How could you tell? It's my nose, isn't it? My mother always says I have the most Iranian nose."

"I'm Saeed." I help to pick up the last of her books.

"Bahar." She smiles shyly. Bahar. Spring. The name reminds me of Bijan Golbahar, his blood on me. My breath speeds up when I think back to that horrible day. "Are you okay?" she asks.

"Oh, yes. Sorry. I'm, um, jet lag, you know."

She nods. "Well, nice to meet you, Saeed."

As she's walking away, I call out to her. "Bahar, wait." She turns around. "I don't know any other Iranians here, and I hate Americans. Will you . . ."

"Will I . . . what?"

"I don't know. Be my friend?"

She thinks it over. "I don't know if I can be friends with someone who hates two hundred million people."

"I don't—"

"How many Americans do you think there are?"

I see what she's getting at. "I'm sure there's one or two good Americans out there. I'm very fond of Aretha Franklin and Donna Summer."

That gets a hearty laugh from her.

"I wasn't in a rush, you know. I actually have nowhere to go. If you have nowhere to go, we could have coffee."

"I have somewhere to go," she says. "But you can walk me there and tell me what you're doing in a country you hate."

She leads me back across the campus, through parts of it I haven't seen yet, and asks me question after question. But these questions aren't about America, they're about me. She wants to know why I'm here, and finally I say,

"It's a long story, but here's the short version of it. My grandmother is American, a fact I only just discovered, and I'm here attending school and living with her."

She narrows her eyes and smiles. "So you hate yourself?"

"Perhaps I do."

"And how did you come to have an American grandmother?"

"I don't know, honestly," I say.

She laughs. "I take it back. How could you hate yourself when you don't even know yourself?"

"A fair point."

"This is my destination." She points to a brick building. "I'm part of the student feminist group. We have a meeting now. Men are welcome."

"I don't know if I'm ready for that, but . . ."

"But . . . what?"

"What's your last name? And can I have your phone number?"

I don't feel for Bahar what I still feel for Shirin. This isn't about heart-fluttering obsession. It's about not letting a potential friend slip away.

"My last name is Hosseini, and I'm listed. You can find me in the phone book." As she disappears into the building, she says, "You should really find out who you are."

I think about her as I head back to Margaret's house. When I get there, she's outside, tending to her limp rose garden. "So?" she asks.

"So?"

"How was school?"

"Fine," I say.

"Just fine? It's one of the best schools in the country. I used an old connection to get you in there. It was just *fine?*"

"It was good," I say, thinking of Bahar, the one truly good thing about my first day.

She shrugs as she prunes the garden.

"When did you leave Iran?" I ask. "Did you leave when Mossadegh was elected?"

"Who?" She doesn't look up.

I knew that most Americans wouldn't know who he is, but not an American whose family worked in Iranian oil. "Mossadegh. The democratically elected leader that America removed from power. The prime minister who nationalized the oil and kicked out all the oilmen like your dad in the early 1950s."

"Honey, we left in the 1920s, and I stopped paying attention to *that* part of the world when we left. Too depressing."

"Then why did you leave?" I ask.

"Why do you think we left?"

"I don't know. That's why I'm asking."

She finally looks at me. "Use your brain, child. My parents and I left because I was pregnant with your father. Ow." She puts her finger in her mouth, sucking on it as I process this latest revelation. "Well, now I've pricked myself on a damn thorn." And with that, she heads inside, leaving me with nothing but questions and longing. I look up at the sky, and I'm briefly filled by a thought that both comforts and frightens me. I'm gazing at the same sky Baba, Maman, Peyman, and Shirin are under. I hold on to this feeling of connection. It's all I have.

That night, I stare at a Khayyam poetry book as I think about what she said. If she left Iran because she was pregnant with Baba, then Baba was born in America.

The poetry has no answers, but I read it aloud anyway, lulling myself closer to sleep, letting the words bring me closer to my father. "*Come, fill the cup, and in the fire of spring / Your winter garment of repentance fling.*" My eyes flutter. It's not my voice I hear when I speak. It's Baba's. How did he find himself back in Iran when he was born here? When did he leave? And most importantly, why?

I make no friends at school. I simply keep my head down, do my work, and wait for news from Iran. Every week, I call Baba and Maman to hear their voices. I always ask Baba if he was able to find Shirin.

Tonight, he says, "I'm sorry, Saeed *jan*. I've been to her house many times. No one's ever home."

"They must have moved to Europe," I say. "But please, keep trying. Get her Margaret's phone number somehow."

"Tell me about America. How are you?" he asks.

"I'm good." I don't give him details, and I don't tell him about Bahar, because she's never home when I call her, and she has no roommate to take a message.

"Is your grandmother being kind to you?" I can tell he doesn't want to ask about her.

"She's fine," I say. "We don't talk much." That part isn't a lie. Margaret avoids me because she doesn't want to answer my questions. I've asked her how old my father was when he moved back to Iran, and why she didn't move back with him. She always shrugs the questions away with a cliché. *The past is the past.* Or, *Don't look back.* Or, *Never dwell on what you can't change.*

"Good," Baba says. "If she ever brings up, well . . . if there's ever anything she tells you that you want to ask me about, I'm a phone call away."

Baba hangs up, and I already miss the sound of his voice. I know there's so much he won't tell me, and I don't know why. I wish I could explain to him that it's impossible to build a future when you don't know the truth of your past. The Los Angeles sun might shine every day, but I feel like I'm in a fog.

A few nights later, Margaret knocks on my door. I'm drying myself from the shower. "Hold on," I say.

"There's a phone call for you," she announces.

"I'm still wet." I shake the towel over my growing hair, which I haven't had the energy to cut since landing in America. "Can you tell my parents I'll call them back?"

"It's not your parents," she says. "I don't know who it is." I assume it's Bahar. She's the only other person I gave this number to. Then Margaret says, "But he doesn't sound friendly, I'll tell you that much."

"I'll be right there." I quickly throw a T-shirt and sweatpants on. I open the door and cross into the living room, my hair and feet still wet.

Margaret eyes the water I drip onto the floor with disdain.

I find the phone receiver off the hook, sitting next to a ceramic rabbit on one of the living room end tables. I pick it up nervously. Perhaps it's one of my new professors. Or Peyman. We've exchanged letters, but no phone calls. He can't afford to call long-distance, and I don't dare run up Margaret's phone bill any more than I already have. "Hello?"

The voice that comes through the receiver is deep and serious. He speaks a formal Persian. "Is this Saeed Jafarzadeh?"

"It is," I say, my voice small. It suddenly dawns on me that this could be a government official calling with bad news. "Is it— Are my parents okay? Did something happen?"

"Something did happen," the stern man says. "You interfered where you should not have."

"I'm sorry, I don't know what you're talking about." I hear footsteps and notice Margaret hovering behind the couch. She holds a damp towel, having wiped the drops I left on her wood floors.

"My name is Ali Mahmoudieh," he says. "Does that ring a bell?"

"No, I'm sorry, sir," I say. "Could you please tell me who you are?" And that's when the realization punches me in the gut. Her monogrammed towels. Shirin's last name starts with the letter *M*. Now I know her name. Shirin Mahmoudieh. The most beautiful name on earth. Melodic. A symphony in two words. Now I'll always be able to find her. My heart soars.

"Your father paid our home a visit. He asked me to give my daughter this number so she might contact you."

"Yes, how is she? I—"

"Don't speak, just listen," he commands.

I nod, even though he can't see me.

"You won't contact Shirin again. You won't write to her, or call her, and you certainly won't send your *artistic* father to my door anymore."

He says the word *artistic* with a strange lilt, an emphasis that reeks of hatred. Iranians are meant to revere the arts. We are the culture of poetry, music, beauty.

I close my eyes. I don't want to see Margaret's beady eyes staring at me. I find the courage in me to ask, "Is this what Shirin wants?"

"It doesn't matter what she *wants*. She's a child. My child."

I feel my fingers twitch with hate. I've never wanted so badly to hurt someone.

"If I find that you've tried to contact my daughter again, your beloved mother and father will be turned in to the authorities," he says without a trace of emotion.

I open my eyes again. I look at Margaret. She's sitting

on the couch now, one leg crossed over the other, her lips pursed.

"My parents aren't political!" I argue. "They've done nothing wrong."

"So you don't know that your parents are deviants," he says, a diabolical iciness in his voice. He's enjoying this.

"I don't . . . I don't understand."

"Good thing that what your parents were able to hide from you is easily discovered when you have friends at the right agencies. They're lucky the Shah and his European sensibilities look the other way at such transgressions against nature. But I don't. I'll destroy their careers. Your father teaching young boys. It's disgusting. And if your precious ayatollah takes power, you can bet your life your parents will be first in line to be executed."

I feel the ground shake under me, like my own personal earthquake.

"I think you understand what I'm saying now," he says. "So you have a choice. You stay away from my family, or you sacrifice your own father and mother."

I close my eyes in silent shock. My heart feels broken. Torn into pieces. In a few horrible minutes, I've lost Shirin, and I've found out that my whole family is one big lie. I feel sick with despair as I plead, "Just let me say goodbye to her. Hear her voice one more time. Please, that's all I—"

He hangs up. I'm left with nothing but a dial tone. I know her name now. I know how to look for her, and I also know I'll never see her again.

I put the receiver back and turn to Margaret, my eyes frantic and desperate. She avoids my gaze as she says, "I once knew who I was and what I wanted. But no one cared what I wanted."

"What?" I ask.

"Like this girl you're fighting for," she says.

"You understood us?"

"I still know a Persian word or two," she says. "Some things never leave you, especially if you learned them when you were young. The things we experience when we're young . . . they mark us forever."

"I need to know who my father is," I say. "This man. Her father. He claims . . . He says that my dad . . . that he's . . ." I can't bring myself to say the word, but I know exactly what he was implying.

"Ah," she says. "So your father's sins destroyed my life, and now they've destroyed yours. Welcome to the club." She pulls the ears off a pink ceramic rabbit and fishes a pack of thin cigarettes from inside. She holds the pack out to me.

"No, thank you," I say.

"I try not to smoke." She pulls one out. "Not because of my lungs or anything. Screw my lungs. But they say it ages the skin." She flings a lighter at me. "It's bad luck to light your own cigarette. Be a gentleman, won't you?" I catch the lighter and flick it, holding it near her. She leans in, cupping her hand around the flame as she takes a deep drag of the cigarette. "Mmm." She exhales the smoke through the side of her mouth. "Why does everything that's bad for you feel so damn good?"

"Margaret," I say. "Please. Tell me about my father. I want to know everything."

"Let's walk," she says curtly.

So we do. She smokes. I listen. The ground under us shifts, the earth reorients itself. A new past emerges. A strange and frightening history. This isn't a conversation. It's a seismic event. My life will never be the same.

I bang on her door desperately. "Bahar!" I scream. "Please open the door. Bahar!"

She opens the door in a nightgown, a book in her hand. "Saeed?"

"I'm sorry. I didn't have anywhere else to go," I say. Are my eyes red from crying? From rage? I don't even know. All I know is that when Margaret finished telling me about why my father left Los Angeles, I needed a friend. Someone who might understand.

"Come in." I follow her inside. She lives in one-half of a duplex. It's small but quaint. She's managed to turn this half a house into a full home. There are framed photos of her big extended family on the mantel. Persian rugs. Calligraphy on the walls. Blue eyes hanging near every door. "Sit down. I have tea."

"I don't need tea. I need a friend." I sit on the couch, my head in my hands.

"I can be a friend." She sits on a chair, facing me. She leans in. "What happened?"

How do I even begin to explain it all? I start with Shirin. With the proposal that didn't happen. With why I left Iran. And then I slow down as I get to Baba and Maman, and to what I just found out about them. "Shirin's father, he told me that my parents are both . . . They're both . . ." I switch to English because there's no good word in Persian for what they are. "They're both homosexuals."

"Okay."

"You're not shocked?" I ask. "Their whole marriage is a sham."

"You don't know that," Bahar counters. "People are complicated."

"What's complicated about this?" I ask. "They can't possibly love each other. My own grandmother confirmed it all. The reason my father left America is disgusting. It's—"

"Don't say that," she says. "He's your family. Your father."

"I know that all too well." I look into her eyes. "I'm the one who has to give up the woman I love to save my parents from being exposed. It makes me sick."

She waits a beat before asking, "Have you ever met a gay person?"

"I just told you that *both* my parents are—"

"Not your parents. But, you know, a person who says they're gay. Who isn't afraid to live openly."

I shake my head. "Of course not."

"Here in America, things are changing," she says

gently. "People live openly. Men can have relationships with each other. Women too."

"I don't want to know," I say.

"Why?" she asks.

"Because it's not natural." I stand up. I pace the room. "Think about it. If my father was allowed to live that way, then I would never even exist. Nobody would. There would be no children left!"

"You're being dramatic," she says.

"I'm Iranian, we're all dramatic. It's in our blood."

Bahar laughs at this. And I laugh too. I suppose I need to laugh. Even if I'm sad. Even if I'm enraged. Laughter might be the only way to release sadness and anger.

"No one is saying the whole world has to be gay," she says.

"But they convert people," I say. "If they're allowed to live openly, they'll multiply until they're all that's left."

She really laughs at this. "You do have a lot to learn," she says. "Do you know the only way to overcome your fears?"

I shrug.

"You face them." She stands up and faces me. "Let me take you out tonight."

"Now? It's already past dinner."

"We're not going to eat," she says. "We're going to observe."

"Observe what?" I ask.

"You're afraid of what your father is, what your mother is. But you don't even understand it. I can call my friend's brother. Luis. He's gay and wonderful."

Those aren't two words I ever imagined going together.

"He's funny. Very easy to talk to. His sister is in my class at school. We're in a book club together, actually."

"A book club?" I ask.

"A group of girls read the same book and discuss it over dinner. It's fun. I'd invite you to join, but it's ladies only."

Bahar's description of a book club makes me realize that's what Baba and Maman have, the two of them reading the same books and discussing what they've read over dinner.

"Maybe Luis can answer some of your questions," she continues. "At the very least, he can show you that gay people can be happy. Maybe then . . . I don't know, maybe it won't be so scary to imagine what I think you're imagining."

I don't want to meet this Luis guy. I certainly don't want to know what life is like for men like him. But then again, I don't want to go back home either. To my lonely bed. To the realization that Shirin is now my past. To my hopelessness.

"Each one of us has a choice in this life," she says. "Between fear and curiosity. Which do you choose?"

I look into her eyes. "I'll choose curiosity tonight. But I can't make any promises about the future."

"Well, what's the future anyway?" she asks. "Just a concept that doesn't exist."

"The light shines only now," I whisper, realizing that what Baba often told me to remember came from the very poem he had me give Margaret. *The light of the beloved shines only now.*

"Rumi?" she asks.

"Yes," I say wistfully. "It's one of my father's favorite poems. He would often recite it to me."

"He sounds like a good father."

"I thought he was." I avoid her gaze. "Now . . . I don't know anymore."

Bahar opens the door to a piano bar called the Other Side. "After you," she says.

"I was raised better than that. Ladies first." I hold the door open and insist she go inside first.

She smiles demurely. "Thank you, sir." As I follow her inside, she adds, "But you do realize the whole concept of chivalry is sexist."

"Is it?" I ask, as I take in the space. "Is it impossible for a man to respect a woman and open doors for her?" She laughs at that as she searches the bar for her friend. The room is bathed in dim red light and filled with live music from a small stage. It has the same feel as the cabaret Baba and Maman took me to once. But instead of Googoosh's angelic voice, there's an effeminate man singing something provocative as a Santa Claus doppelgänger plays piano. Bahar is one of the only women in the room, though there is femininity everywhere. Men crowd the tables together. They hold hands. They giggle like schoolgirls. Some embrace their lack of masculinity, wearing hints of makeup, shirts that glitter, pants that shimmer. Others overdo their masculinity, wearing leather, sitting with their legs open wide, like an invitation. It all feels obscene.

"There he is!" she squeals happily. I look up and see a handsome man waving excitedly at her. His brown hair is messy and long, and his shirt is unbuttoned so low that his whole hairy chest is on display. Next to him is a tall, lanky guy with shorter dark hair and a shiny stud in his right ear. "Come on," Bahar says as she guides me to their table and gives Luis a big, warm hug. He swings her around in his arms before putting her down and introducing her to the other guy, Enrique. "And this is my amazing new friend Saeed," Bahar says proudly. Luis and Enrique both shake my hand firmly before we all sit.

Luis flags the waiter down and asks for "Four Cokes, please." I breathe a sigh of relief. At least I won't be expected to drink alcohol.

"Coming right up, sweetness," the waiter says with a wink to Luis. "I'll be sure to leave room in the cups."

He quickly returns with four half-empty glasses of Coke. Luis pulls a small bottle of rum from his pocket and tops his drink off with alcohol. Then he fills Enrique's cup up. "I know Bahar doesn't drink. You . . . Sorry, I forgot your name."

"Saeed," I say. "No rum for me either."

"More for us." He puts the bottle away. "And now for the first toast of the night." He holds his cup up. Enrique and Bahar follow his lead, and I reluctantly do too. "I'd like to make a toast to my friend Bahar, who has taught me so much about kindness."

"Stop it." Bahar blushes.

"It's true," he continues. "Most of my sister's school friends are so judgmental. They're so obviously uncomfortable with me being gay. They stare at me like I'm some zoo animal. But you've always been different. A good heart and *those* eyelashes—you're the full package, bitch."

I flinch at his casual use of such an offensive word, but Bahar doesn't look the least bit offended. He's right about her eyelashes. I didn't notice them before. They're thick and long. They curl up like a wave at high tide. In this mood lighting, I can finally see how attractive she is. And it's not just the lashes. It's her smile, her aura, her whole beautiful being.

We're about to drink when Luis says, "Wait. I'm not done. I'd also like to drink to Bahar's friend Saeed, who will hopefully be my new friend too, because if Bahar is any indication, Iranians are the coolest people around."

Everyone drinks and puts their cups down.

"Do you guys prefer to be called Persian or Iranian?" Enrique asks.

Bahar shrugs. "I think people can call themselves whatever they want to. Persian. Iranian. We should all define ourselves however we want to. There are more serious things to argue about than words."

"See," Luis says. "Brains and beauty on this one. I like

to call myself queer and Enrique here thinks it's—"

"It's an awful word," Enrique says. "It's the word I heard every time I was bullied. I use the word 'gay.' It feels, well, happier."

"But listen to Bahar," Luis suggests. "There are more serious things to argue about than words. You're gonna rule the world someday, Bahar."

"Thankfully, I have no interest in ruling the world," Bahar says. "Only deeply unhappy people want that much power."

I look at her and smile. I'm starting to discover how uniquely intelligent she is.

"So we're here for a specific reason, right? To help Saeed come to terms with being gay." Luis looks at me.

"Oh, no, I'm not . . . you know." My whole body tightens. "That's not at all why—"

He puts a hand on my shoulder. I instinctively push it away. "I know this is all new to you," he says with unsettling kindness. "And it's a lot at first. Trust me, it wasn't easy for me to come out. But you're not alone. There are a lot of us out there. That's why I brought Enrique. He's a new gay. He's only been out for three months."

Enrique rolls his eyes. "Which is exactly how long I've been with Luis. Coincidence?"

"Okay, fine, I *encouraged* you to come out!" Luis exclaims.

"You told me you wouldn't go on a second date with someone who's in the closet," Enrique declares with both gratitude and annoyance.

"And aren't you better off for it?" Luis asks.

Enrique nods. "I am, actually. But still, I think we have to be careful with how much pressure we put on people to come out. Like you, Saeed. I mean, if you don't feel safe coming out to your parents, then you shouldn't. Your safety comes first."

Luis takes Enrique's hand in his and kisses it. I feel my stomach turn. "You teach me so much, baby."

"I think there's, um, a misunderstanding," I stammer nervously. "I'm not . . . I'm not, you know, homosexual, or gay. Is that what you told him, Bahar?"

Bahar looks over at me, apparently unbothered by their assumptions. "No, of course not. I just said you wanted to ask some questions about gay life."

Luis takes a big sip of his drink. "I'm sorry to be nosy, but why? I've never met a straight guy who's interested in us unless he wants to beat us up or craves a midnight blow job."

"A midnight what?" I ask.

"Don't worry about that." Bahar narrows her gaze at her friend. "Come on, Luis, be nice. Saeed has a . . . a friend he just found out is gay."

"Ah," Luis says. "Okay. Well, please don't stop being his friend."

"Yeah," Enrique adds. "We need all the support we can get from our friends and families."

"So what do you want to ask?" Luis says.

I don't know where to start. I guess I want to know why. Why is my father like this? Why is anyone like this,

189

when you could be with a beautiful woman? I'm briefly distracted by a man in a leather vest and tight jeans who whispers something to the piano player, then starts belting out a song in a surprisingly moving voice. "*'Kiss today goodbye,'*" he sings. "*'The sweetness and the sorrow.'*"

"So, what brought you to America?" Luis asks.

"What brought *you* here?" I ask. "You don't look American."

"What exactly does an American look like?" he asks with a raised eyebrow.

"Mean and dumb," I say, and everyone laughs.

When Luis stops laughing, he says, "I was born here. But my parents were born in Mexico. Complicated story, but they should've been born here. Their parents were expelled from America in the 1930s, despite being citizens, because that's what America does when it doesn't like the color of your skin."

"Why do you stay?" I ask.

"Because it's my country, for better or worse. And maybe I can make it better."

I swallow down hard, because he sounds just like me. Just like Shirin. Just like all the dreamers in Iran.

"Now why are *you* here?" he asks.

Onstage, the man in leather and denim raises his arms up in the air as he hits a high note. "*'Won't forget, can't regret, what I did for love.'*" He could be singing about me. What I did for Shirin's love. And now, what I'm doing out of love for my lying parents. But I don't want to get into all that with two strangers, so I say nothing. The singer gets a standing ovation, and I join in because he really is great, and because I want to avoid answering the question.

"Okay, he's a musical theater fan," Luis says with a smile.

"My father is a music teacher," I explain. "I appreciate all music." Then I suddenly ask, "Were you always like this?"

"You mean, gay?" Luis shrugs. "As long as I can remember."

"So you can't change?" I ask.

"Like, make myself straight?"

"Well, yes. Could you love a woman?"

"Of course." He leans in. "I love my mother more than anyone who walks this earth. I love my sisters. All my best friends are women." He looks at Bahar with a smile. "Women are the superior sex, there's no doubt in my mind about that. If I could love a woman the way I love Enrique . . ."

Enrique swats him. "I'm right here."

"I was going to say I wouldn't want to change because I'm so happy with you." Enrique accepts the answer by giving Luis a kiss.

I look away from them. It's too much for me. Bahar squeezes my knee under the table and eyes me sternly.

"But what about, you know . . ." I don't know how to put my thoughts into words.

"Sexually?" he asks.

"Yes," I say, thinking of my parents. I hate thinking

of them having sex, but they must have done it if they created me. For some reason, I need to know that this was an act of love.

"No, I'm pretty much all gay," he says. "Just men on the menu for me." He laughs and repeats the word, "*Men*-u," with a sly smile.

"Men?" I ask. "Or one man?"

"Uh-oh," Luis says. "I'm sensing some judgment."

Bahar eyes me carefully. "No judgment, just curiosity. Right, Saeed?"

I nod, though of course I judge him. I've heard this about men like him. They sleep with any man they can find. How could they know true romantic love when it only exists between a man and a woman? "Just curiosity," I say, trying to sound convincing.

"The truth is . . ." Luis is about to answer the question when the waiter arrives with a fruit bowl. "Fruits for the fruits, on the house."

"That's nice of you, thanks," Bahar says.

"Don't thank me," the waiter says. "All the fruit's about to go bad, so the manager said we may as well give it away."

Bahar picks a stem of grapes from the bowl and pops one into her mouth. Ever the Iranian, she serves the rest of the table. She hands a grape stem to me. Then hands one to Luis.

"I still can't eat a grape," he says. "I know the boycott is over, but somehow I still feel like a traitor to my people if I so much as look at a grape. It's weird, I know."

"I'm sorry," Bahar says gently. "I don't know about the boycott, but if you'd rather I didn't eat a grape, I won't."

Luis laughs. "Oh, please enjoy the rotting grapes. The boycott's over. It was a way to fight for the rights of Filipino and Mexican farmers, who wanted things like, you know, basic medical care and retirement funds. But back to the reason we're here. I want to help you be a good buddy to your friend who came out, Saeed. How else can we help? We'd be happy to meet him if he wants that."

I want to scream out that it's not my friend who's gay, it's my father. And my mother. The people who raised me and who I know nothing about. The lying parents who admonished me for breaking one promise when they lied to me for my whole life.

"Where were we?" Luis asks. "I think you wanted to know something about sex."

"No," I say. "I really don't want to know anything about that."

Luis laughs. "Okay, then," he says. "We won't say a word about what goes on in bedrooms or in the baths."

I avoid Bahar's gaze. This is too much for me. The sexual frankness. The intimacy. And in front of an Iranian girl, no less.

"What are the baths?" Bahar asks. Her curiosity is innocent, but I can't help but cringe. I don't want to know more.

"Bathhouses," Luis explains. "You know, a spa. With steam rooms and saunas."

"Like a hammam?" she asks.

I think of the Turkish hammam that Baba took me to for my seventeenth birthday. He told me that his father took him to the very same place when he was seventeen.

"Yeah, I guess," Luis says. "Except this one's for, you know, for gay men to, you know . . . well, Saeed said he doesn't want to hear about sex, and I'm not in the business of shock and offense."

Bahar laughs. "Luis, I think this is the first time you've ever held back from explicitly speaking your mind. You've already had an impact on him, Saeed."

"You know . . ." Luis leans in. "Everyone thinks gay sex is about physical pleasure, while straight sex is about love and intimacy. But really, it's all the same. I don't care if you're a man and a woman in a bed, or two men meeting for a night in a bathhouse. They're both intimate. They're both love."

"Okay, I don't know about that," Enrique says. "You can't love someone you meet for one night in some sad bathhouse."

"Baby, don't be one of those self-loathing queens," Luis says. "The baths are sad if you use them to escape loneliness. And they're wonderful if you use them to celebrate yourself."

"Okay, fine, but my point is that you can't love someone you meet for one night *anywhere*," Enrique clarifies.

"Well, I loved you the moment we met," Luis says to Enrique.

Enrique smiles. "And I loved you . . . a month later."

"And I'm good with that," Luis says. "Just keep loving me."

I cringe at their constant use of the word *love*. I don't know that they'll ever convince me what they feel is love, no matter how many times they throw the word around.

"What do you think, Bahar?" Luis asks. "Do you believe in love at first sight?"

"I think love is time and trust," Bahar utters quietly. "If it's given too quickly, it can be taken away just as quickly."

"The superior sex has spoken!" Enrique exclaims triumphantly.

"And now it's time for the superior sex to sing," Luis says with a smile. He takes the last sip of his drink. "My sister might have told me that one of her book club friends is a great singer, and maybe that's why I suggested the Other Side."

"The piano player and I won't know any of the same songs," Bahar protests. "I prefer to sing in Persian, and I'm guessing he won't know how to play 'Aalam e Yekrangee' or 'Bekhoon Bekhoon' or 'Soltane Ghalbha.'"

"I have no idea what you just said, but if you don't get up and sing one of those songs a cappella, I'll never forgive you."

"I'm not singing a Persian song a cappella in a gay bar in Los Angeles." Bahar motions for the check.

"I bet Saeed can play," Enrique says. "Didn't you say your dad was a music teacher? What music teacher doesn't teach his kid to play piano?"

Luis squeezes Enrique's cheeks and kisses one of them. "Ugh, I love what a good listener you are. I swear, sometimes I think all I do is talk and all he does is listen."

"That's why we work so well together," Enrique says.

"Baba mostly teaches the tar," I say.

"So you don't play piano?" Luis asks. "Because I don't think the Other Side has a tar handy."

I look to Bahar. I'm not sure what she wants. But what I want is to hear her sing a song that reminds me of home. So I tell the truth. "I do play piano, and I know all those songs and more."

Bahar smiles shyly at me. "Okay." Then, whispering to me in Persian, she asks, "Which one should we sing?"

"I'm playing, you're singing," I say.

"Fine, fine," she says. "But which song?"

"I'll surprise you."

As we walk toward the piano, I hear Luis tell Enrique how beautiful he thinks Persian is. Bahar approaches the piano player and asks if I can take his place for one song, and the piano player agrees.

I sit at the piano and take off my jacket, throwing it on a nearby ottoman. Then I close my eyes. I play a single key. It brings me right back home. But it's not my home anymore. Not my country. Not my parents.

"Saeed," Bahar whispers. "Everyone's waiting."

I take a breath and start to play "Do Panjereh." I know she'll know it. Every Iranian knows the Googoosh classic. It's a song that seems to sum up being an Iranian these days. A song about being stuck, at an impasse. It's about love, but it could be about a parent and a child, or about a country and one of its many dreamers.

Bahar starts to sing, and her voice makes me forget everything. What she possesses is rare—the ability to make you feel. I open my eyes. My fingers play on their own. Muscle memory, Baba would call it. And my eyes, they're glued to her. No one speaks. She's put the crowd into a trance, even though they don't understand a word she's saying.

I wish they could understand the words, though. Maybe hearing these words would help them understand us as people. Two windows, she sings. Two windows are trapped in a stone wall. She's one of those windows. Her lover is another. She dreams of a world where the stone wall can be smashed, so she can die with her lover and go to another world. A world without hate. A world without walls.

A tear falls down my cheek when I play the final note. I cry for Shirin, my other window, who will be kept away from me by a stone wall for the rest of my life. I cry for my parents, who lived a lie and broke my heart. And I cry because Bahar just reminded me that there is beauty even in sadness. I was broken when I met her, and she's made me feel that there is hope again.

The audience gives us a standing ovation. Luis and Enrique hoot and holler for us.

"Come here and take a bow with me," Bahar says.

I join her in front of the piano. We hold hands and

bow as the crowd showers us with applause. I start to laugh at the absurdity of it all. Two Iranians singing in a gay piano bar. It's ridiculous, and also, it's the most fun I've had since arriving in Los Angeles.

"Why did you pick that song?" she asks me as the cheers keep going.

I answer honestly. "It reminds me of home."

"The end of the song is so tragic," she says. "I don't know why the two windows have to die to be together."

I think of Maman and her blueprints. "The stone wall keeps them separated, but they're a part of the stone wall. So if you break the wall, you smash the windows and they die."

She looks at me meaningfully. "Then I guess we need a world of windows. Where everything is visible. No walls, secrets, or division."

I nod. I know what she's saying. That I can't divide myself from my own parents, or from the men in this piano bar, or from any human being. And maybe, with her by my side, I can be that openhearted.

When we get back to the table, the check is already there. I see Bahar pull her wallet out and try to stop her. "Don't even think about it."

"I initiated this meeting. I'll pay." Bahar pulls some cash from her wallet.

"Absolutely not," I insist. "We're only here because of me."

Bahar looks at Luis and Enrique. "What you're observing is the Persian ritual of *tarof*," she explains. "We will fight over the check until one of us somehow wins."

"Usually in some covert way," I add.

"That's ridiculous," Luis says. "You're in our hood. We'll be paying."

"You're no match for us when it comes to *tarof,*" I say. "Watch and learn." In a flash, I snatch the check from Bahar and rush toward the waiter. I hand him ten dollars and tell him to keep the change. Bahar and Luis try to stop me, but I've paid for our Cokes, and that simple dance of fighting over a bill, along with a song I never expected to hear in a gay American piano bar, made me feel like I was right back home.

Bahar plays a Googoosh cassette as she drives me back home. She tells me she got the tape from a man who sells Iranian music out of the trunk of his car in Westwood.

"I'm impressed with you," she says when we reach Margaret's house.

"Because of my piano playing?"

She shakes her head. "That was a nice surprise, but no. When you came over and told me about your parents, I thought you'd be a typical Iranian man. You know, patriarchal. Closed off. Fearful of people who are different from you." I'm all those things, but I don't dare contradict her. She ejects the Googoosh cassette and replaces it with Pink Floyd. The music is trancelike when it begins. I look at her, surprised. "What? You think I only listen to sad Persian music? No, I also listen to sad British music."

I laugh as we pull up to Margaret's house. I feel that I'm supposed to lean in now. Kiss her in the car like they do in American movies. But kissing Bahar now . . . it would feel like cheating on Shirin. "Thank you," I say. "For everything. I'm not sure how to repay you for your kindness." Being with Shirin felt larger than life, like floating. Being with Bahar feels steady, grounded.

"There's only one way to repay kindness. And that's with more kindness."

I nod. I don't even give her a kiss on each cheek, as is customary in Tehran. I'm just not ready for that. Her skin against mine. Her breath in my ear. It's all too much.

Margaret is polishing a ceramic rabbit as she watches an old Marlene Dietrich movie when I arrive. "It's late," she says without looking up at me.

"I was out," I say.

"Yes, obviously." Is she angry? Curious? Her eyes offer no clues.

"I was with a friend," I say.

"A girl?" she asks.

"Yes."

She nods. "Well, thank God for that." Onscreen, Marlene Dietrich dances in a gorilla costume. "They don't make 'em like they used to. Movies now are all blood and tits." She puts the rabbit down and begins polishing another one.

"You love those rabbits," I say.

She looks up at me, with more warmth than she's offered me yet. "Funny, isn't it? For decades, I avoided rabbits. But when I divorced Willie, I couldn't stop. They were the only thing that made me happy."

I channel Bahar and continue asking questions. "Why is that?"

"Your grandfather, he used to call me Bunny because he said I reminded him of a rabbit. Smart and affectionate when I wanted to be." Clearly that's not something she wants to be anymore. "And willful and spoiled when I wanted to be." That sounds about right. "He bought me a rabbit as a present. A real one. It was silly, but it meant something. When we would spend time together, I would always bring the bunny, and we would pretend we were raising it together. Like the child we would raise together someday." She puts the ceramic animal down. "Obviously, that never happened. The rest is history."

"What was he like?" I ask. "My grandfather. He died when I was six. I really have no memories of him."

"I know when he died. You think I didn't keep track of him? We don't let go of the people we love. Even if we never see them again." The flicker of love in her eyes stuns me. She still hasn't let go of my grandfather, not completely. Just like I'll probably never let go of Shirin, not completely. "That's enough for now," she says. "And you've already learned far more than your father wanted me to tell you."

"I'm sorry," I say.

"Oh, stop apologizing," she snaps. "I hate people who apologize when they did nothing wrong. Your father is the one who should apologize. He's the one who deserted me. Left for Iran for what was supposed to be a visit and never came back. Barely ever spoke to me again. Didn't invite me to his own wedding, perhaps because I could've told people it was all a farce."

I nod, stunned, thinking I would also like an apology from my father, for lying to me all these years.

She claps her hands together. "What's done is done. I can't stand people who dwell on the past like it can change anything."

She hates so many things. And yet she embodies so much of what she rails against. What is polishing ceramic rabbits if not dwelling on the past? Her whole home feels like it's stuck in another time.

"Good night, then," I say. She doesn't respond. I want to hug her, but something tells me I shouldn't, so I head to my room and throw myself on the bed. I don't have the energy to brush my teeth, or change my clothes. I kick my shoes off and close my eyes. All the events of the day swirl around me. It's too much to make sense of. I open my eyes and turn to my bedside table. There's my stack of poetry books. Baba always said that when the world didn't make sense, the answers could be found in poetry, in the words of our ancestors. I pick up a Saadi book. I flip the pages. I've read every poem, know a handful by heart. I love these verses. They contain wisdom, and memories, and they connect me to my father.

But maybe I don't want to be connected to him right now. Maybe all his artistic tendencies are what made him the way he is. I push all the poetry books from the bedside table onto the floor. For the first time in my life, I fall asleep without reading a poem. It feels like the end of something. I'm not my father's son anymore.

The next morning, Baba and Maman call the house. Margaret answers, and after an obligatory "hello" and "how are you," she calls out to me. "It's your parents for you."

I grab a slice of bread for breakfast. I want to hear their voices. I want things to be like they were. But they never will be again. "Tell them I'm late for class," I say icily.

"Tell them yourself," she says, holding out the receiver for me.

I stare at the phone, imagining my parents holding their own telephone, wondering why I won't even say a quick hello to them. "I'm sorry, I . . . I'm really late."

"Well, take your jacket," she yells as I slam the door behind me. My jacket. I suddenly realize I took it off at the piano bar and never put it back on. I'll have to go retrieve it.

I look for Bahar at school, hoping she'll return to the bar with me. But I don't know her class schedule, and we don't run into each other all day. Finally, after a long day of classes, I take the bus back to the Other Side. The bar feels different without Bahar in it. There isn't a single woman inside, which changes the energy. Everything feels more charged. In a corner, two men kiss each other with sloppy passion. Santa Claus is still at the piano, as a bodybuilder type sings "I Cain't Say No."

I approach the bartender. "Excuse me, I was here last night—"

The bartender smiles. "I remember you. Solid piano playing. What'll you have?"

"Oh, I don't need a drink. I need my jacket. I left it near the piano. It's gray with big buttons."

He nods. "I'll go check the lost and found for you." Then he pours me a whiskey neat. "On the house, for entertaining us last night."

I take a sip of the drink, letting it burn its way down my body. It feels good, so I take another. The body-builder sings in an exaggerated accent about how he can't say no when a fella gets flirty, and the crowd eats it up. The alcohol warms me up and relaxes me. I need a bathroom, so I cross the room and enter the men's restroom. From the one stall come a man's muffled cries, almost like he's gagged. I don't want to see the source of these frightening noises, but I have to pee. My only option is a long steel trough, where a tall man stands, his pants unzipped. I hesitate before going to the opposite end of the trough before I unzip. The tall man's eyes are on me, and he touches himself. I close my eyes. The faster I pee, the faster I can get out of here. But nothing comes out. I'm too nervous.

"Hey," the man whispers.

I say nothing. I can't go to the bathroom. Not here. I zip myself back up and turn around to leave. But just as I'm about to head out, the stall door is kicked open, revealing the source of the muffled yelps. His shorts and underwear are around his ankles. He's found a way to sit on the toilet with his legs on a man's shoulders. The man thrusts into him. I'm frozen in place. I can't look away. Because this is who my father is. He's a man on his back, being invaded by other men. It's disgusting. If Bahar could see this, if she understood the way of men, she would know why I can never accept this.

"Oh shit, you kicked the door open," the thrusting man says. He moves aside, revealing the other guy's face, and . . . it's Luis. I run out of the bathroom.

"Saeed!" he calls out.

I rush back into the piano bar and hear the bartender call out to me. "Hey, your jacket."

I grab my jacket and bolt out into the fresh air. Luis follows behind me, flustered and breathless. "Hey, I'm sorry about that. I thought the door was locked."

"I— I have to go." I hear the disgust in my voice.

"Look, Saeed, I know why you came back to the bar. There's only one reason." He smiles. "Anytime someone tells you they need advice for a friend, the friend is them. It's obvious you're gay, and—"

"No," I blurt out aggressively.

"Come on," he says. "You're safe here." I've never felt so unsafe. "I won't judge you."

"I'm here because I forgot my jacket," I seethe. "That's it."

He obviously doesn't believe me, because he keeps going. "If you're scared your family won't accept you, I really get that. My family had a hard time with me

205

being gay, sure. But they never stopped treating me like their son. And from what I've learned from Bahar, your people are the same. We value family. You have no idea how many American kids are kicked out of their homes for being queer."

I look him directly in the eye and speak with icy precision. "Please listen to me. I. Am. Not. Gay."

"I know labels are hard. Don't label yourself if it doesn't feel right yet."

"I am not gay," I repeat, exasperated. "And I'm definitely not like you. Cheating on someone he supposedly loves."

"I wasn't cheating," he says, annoyed by the accusation. "We're in an open relationship."

"A what?"

"We love each other, but we're allowed to sleep with other people. I'm not a liar or a cheater. I'm all about honesty."

I swallow down hard. This is probably what my parents have. An open relationship. The thought sends shivers down my spine, and I wonder who they did these things with. For some reason, it's easier for me to shake off the thought of Maman with other women. But Baba, the thought of him with men, doing what Luis was just doing . . . it feels repulsive.

"Anyway, I can give you a ride home if you need one."

"I like the bus," I say curtly.

I walk away from him without saying goodbye. The bus takes me back to Westwood, where I walk again, toward Margaret's house. She's watching some old musical when I walk in. Onscreen, Rita Hayworth tap-dances with Fred Astaire. "Where were you?" she asks.

"Studying," I say. I lie so easily to her. Maybe Luis is all about honesty, but I'm not. I come from liars. Deception is in my blood.

The morning after that, my parents call again. Margaret answers. I tell her I have an assignment due and don't have time to talk. The morning after that, another call. Margaret answers. I just shake my head, and she lies to them. "He's not here." When she hangs up, she pours me a cup of coffee. "They're not calling for me, you know. Your father's avoided me for the last forty years. You're going to have to talk to them eventually."

"I never want to speak to them again," I say defiantly.

She nods. Sadly, she says, "I see you've inherited your father's ability to cut a parent out of his life."

"I suppose I have." I hide any trace of emotion from my voice.

They keep calling. I keep ignoring their calls. And then, one morning, they don't call, and I panic. The next morning, no call. And again, and again.

"They haven't called in a week," I tell Bahar as we sit on the UCLA lawn. College students are all around us, some racing to class, some lounging with a book, others throwing Frisbees or practicing dance routines or walking into dormitories in their pajamas. It's nothing at all like Aryamehr University. We don't have dorms in

Iranian universities. We live with our parents until we're married. I don't know that I'll ever adjust to student life here. I may have learned the language from a young age, but the way of life remains foreign to me.

"What do you expect?" Bahar asks. "You ignored them for, how long?"

"I just didn't know what to say to them. How do I tell them on the telephone that I know they're both—you know what they are." I haven't mentioned to Bahar what I saw Luis doing, and I assume he hasn't either, because she definitely would've asked me about it.

"They're gay," she says matter-of-factly.

"Exactly. That's not something you just blurt out from twelve thousand kilometers away. Why do they deserve my honesty, when they weren't honest with me?"

"I'm not telling you what to say to them, but they're your parents." She leans in closer to me. "You need to talk to them. Look what happened between your dad and his mother. This is how it begins. You don't speak for a week. Maybe two. And then pretty soon, a lifetime has passed and you find you have no relationship with your own family. That's not right."

"But if I do talk to them, it won't be a relationship. Not a real one. It will just be me pretending I don't know what I know. It'll be a lie. Maybe that's why Baba stopped speaking to his own mother. Because their whole relationship was a lie, and what's the point in that?"

"So in summary, you won't tell them what you know over the telephone. But you won't talk to them until you can tell the truth. But if you go back to Iran, they'll throw you in jail. So you're giving up."

"That's not how I would characterize it," I say, defensive.

"And why is that?" she asks. "Because a macho Iranian man doesn't like being called a quitter?"

"I'm not a quitter," I say. "I'm just . . . taking time to figure out my next move."

"Oh, your next move." She's playfully teasing me. "Is this a chess match? What kind of move are we talking about here? Let me know the rules."

"There are no rules, that's the whole problem. My family destroyed the playbook."

She puts a hand on mine. Her soft skin feels so good. "Then write a new playbook. Don't give up." She smiles before adding, "Quitter."

I laugh. "Stop."

"Quitter," she says, poking me with her finger.

"Pest," I say, poking her right back.

We keep repeating the words, like a tennis rally, until her poking turns into tickling and then tackling, and we fall onto the grass together. Her brown hair cascades onto the green grass. Her hands lie at her sides, so close to my face. She looks at me like she wants me to kiss her.

We stare at each other, our breath heavy from the laughter and the tickling. I should kiss her now. All around us, American students are making out, groping each other. They have no problem putting their affection on display. And yet, I do. But I also have affection for

Bahar. That much becomes clearer every time I see her. If anyone can inspire me to get past my fears, it's her. I want to tell her everything that haunts me. Perhaps, with her help, I can stop seeing Bijan's face in my nightmares. But first, I need to kiss her. I move closer. I close my eyes.

"Bahar, we're late," a voice yells. One of her girl-friends hovers over us. Bahar leaps up. I've missed my chance. "I'll see you soon," she says.

"Of course," I say, disappointed. "I'm not going any-where."

I can't stop thinking of our almost-kiss for the rest of the day. On the bus ride home, I close my eyes and imagine what the moment could've felt like if only we hadn't been interrupted. I'm still thinking of it when I unlock the door to Margaret's. I notice a suitcase by the door. It's black with a red tag around its handle. My heart feels like it drops into my stomach.

This is Baba's suitcase. He's here.

BOBBY

1939

Los Angeles

Mother has been on edge all week. Her mood swings have been even more pronounced than usual. On Monday, she burned toast and said it was a curse. On Tuesday, she spent six hours cleaning. On Wednesday, she went to church for the first time in, well . . . at least five years. On Thursday, she took me to a street fortune-teller. "Look at his palm," Mother told her. "Is that the palm of a star?" The fortune-teller traced the lines in my palm and agreed. "You know what I think?" Mother said. "I think MGM is playing hard to get. Is that what you see?" The fortune-teller nodded.

It's Friday now, and Mother is frantic backstage. She's got me and Willie standing in front of a mirror. She brushes his thick blond hair back. Spits in her hand to paste it down. Then does the same to me. I dream of a day when my mother's spit won't be in my hair.

"You look perfect," Mother says to Willie, squeezing

his football player's body from behind. "The new suit looks very handsome, and what do you boys think of my new dress?" She twirls, shimmering in silver brocade.

Willie grabs Mother and pulls her close. "You look gorgeous, Mags," he whispers in her ear. Willie is always giving Mother these kind of compliments.

Onstage, a comedian is audible. He's new, I think. I've never heard his very particular laugh before. He finishes laughing at one of his own corny jokes and then announces, "Up next at Slapsy Maxie's, we've got that family band you all love, the Reeves Trio."

I find my spot onstage at the piano. Willie sits on a stool with his new Gibson guitar, which Mother bought for him with the money we all earned. And Mother takes the microphone. I start to play "Embraceable You." It's our first time playing the song for an audience. I close my eyes and think of Vicente. I wish I could tell the whole world that I chose this song for him.

When I open my eyes, he's in the audience. Vicente. He never comes to my shows. His dad doesn't like him out late. Why is he here?

"'*Embrace me, my sweet embraceable you. Embrace me, my irreplaceable you.*'"

We end the song with my improvised piano solo. I deconstruct the melody, letting it turn into something mysterious and surprising. When the song ends, no one claps louder than Vicente. I wonder if he knows I'm playing these notes for him. I close my eyes and imagine we're the only two people in the room.

When our show ends, I rush backstage and throw my coat on. "What's the rush?" Mother asks. "We're having a late dinner. I asked Vinnie to join."

"His name is Vicente."

"Oh, please." She rolls her eyes. "Vinnie is easier."

"Why did you ask him to come?" I ask, genuinely shocked. Mother thinks "Vinnie" is a boring jock.

"He's your friend," she says. "And I wanted tonight to be special for you. I'm not a monster, you know. I want you to be happy."

We stay at Slapsy Maxie's for dinner, which wouldn't exactly be my first choice for food, but at least Vicente is here with me. I feel the heat of his legs next to mine under the table. I wish more than anything that we were alone.

"So," Mother says. "Shall we share the news with our Bobby boy?"

The whole table smiles. "What is it?" I ask.

Mother takes some papers out of her purse and puts them on my plate just as the waiter arrives with the food.

Seeing the papers on my plate, the waiter pauses. "I apologize, should I . . ."

Mother laughs. "Should you put a steak on top of my son's MGM contract?" she asks lightheartedly. "No, you should not."

The whole table looks at me now, waiting for my reaction.

"MGM contract," I whisper.

"Aren't you excited?" Willie asks. "This is what you've

always wanted. We're all proud of you, son." Willie's sincerity feels heartbreaking to me. He really is proud, even though I've always kept him at arm's length.

I look at Vicente, wishing he could answer the question I'm asking myself. Is this what I've always wanted? Or is it what Mother always wanted?

I feel sick to my stomach, but I force a smile. Because if I don't, I'll make everyone uncomfortable. And why would I do that when this is awkward enough?

"All our dreams are coming true," Mother says.

"You can put the food down," I tell the waiter, as I lift the contract up and start leafing through it.

"Oh, you don't need to read it," Mother says. "I can do that for you."

But I can't stop myself. My heart beats when I see how much they'll be paying me. Well, paying *her*, since I'm a minor. "A hundred dollars a week?" I practically yell.

"Not bad, huh?" Mother asks, proud of herself. "I told them not to offer a penny less. I know what you're worth."

I gulp down hard. It's a lot of money. At the same time, shouldn't a mother think her son is priceless? I keep reading. "It says here that I'm tied to the studio for seven years, but they have the option of dropping me every six months."

"That's standard," Mother says. "All the stars have that in their contracts. But don't worry. They won't drop you. Not with your God-given talent."

"It's not them dropping me I'm worried about," I

whisper. "It's just . . . seven years is a long time."

"Oh, I'm sorry." Mother cuts her rare hamburger in half, blood oozing from the meat onto her plate. "I didn't realize you had better plans than being an MGM star."

I flip through the final pages of the contract. My face must go white when I see the last page, because Vicente says, "You should eat, Bobby. You look tired." He knows me so well. He can read me in a way my own mother can't.

I cut some steak and stuff it into my mouth. I read in silence. The very last clause is a morals clause. It says the contract player will conduct himself with "due regard to public convention and morals." It says I won't ever act in any fashion that might "degrade me in society or cause me and the studio public humiliation or offend the community."

I look at Vicente as I read these words. I would burn this contract if it would mean I could kiss him. I don't want convention and morals. I want him.

"Well," Mother says, digging into her purse again and pulling out a pen. "Sign it."

I stare at the morals clause and then at Vicente's eyes. It all feels like a sick choice between being successful and being myself. But as Mother shoves the pen into my fingers, I feel like I have no choice at all. I sign the contract.

It's my last day at our school, and Vincente and I are on the tennis court. "*Love*-forty." I put even more emphasis on the love than usual, because I might not have a chance to be on a tennis court with Vicente again. I start my life as an MGM contract player on Monday and I'll be attending school on the lot.

I flub both my serves, one in the net, the other way out of the court.

"Game. Set. Match," Coach Lane bellows.

We all head to the net to shake each other's hands. Under his breath, my doubles partner says, "At least it's your last match, Bobby. Because honestly, tennis isn't your thing."

"Shut up and be a gentleman," Vicente says.

He and I linger behind like we always do, walking slowly. Our last walk from the courts back to school. Our last time avoiding showering with our teammates. More distressingly, our last time showering side by side. If I ever get to see him naked again, it won't be because of a school-sanctioned extracurricular activity.

"How do you feel?" he asks, as the cold, hard water hits our backs.

"I don't know," I say. It's the truth. I feel scared, like I'll be exposed as a fraud once I make it to MGM. I feel sad that I won't be starting and ending every school day with Vicente. And I feel excited, because there's new possibility in my life. All I can hope for is that stardom will give me the power to be with him the way I want to be.

"You know I'll still be your best friend, right?" he asks softly.

"Yeah, I know." I can't hide the sadness in my voice.

"But things will change." I stare at his body. I feel so cold, and so hot. I feel myself get hard, and I turn to hide the evidence of my lust from him, or worse, from the next person who might walk in at any moment.

"You okay?" he asks.

"Yes," I say too fast. Then just as quickly, "Not really."

"Bobby, look at me."

I cock my head back, but I don't turn my body. I can't have him see how hard I am. What if it disgusts him? I can handle so much, but not that.

"Turn around and look at me, Bobby."

I cup my hands over my erection and turn. I hold his gaze. And then I look down. And that's when I realize he's hard too. We both smile nervously. I don't know what I'm supposed to do or say next.

"I know why you wanted to be alone with me the other day," he whispers. "I've always known."

"You have?" I ask, my heart starting to pound. "Why didn't you say something?"

"Same reason you didn't." He sighs. "I'm scared."

I nod. "Me too."

"Maybe we can give each other courage." He takes my hand again and guides it to his crotch. I rub him. He gets even harder in my hands. I can feel the pulse inside him, his beautiful beating heart.

"We have to be fast," I say. "Someone could come—"

"I think I just did," he says after he climaxes into my hand.

I smell my fingers. I hesitate, and then I boldly lick

them clean. "It's so sweet," I say with a shy smile.

He looks over his shoulder. No one there. He reaches over and grabs me in his hand. "Your turn."

"I don't know, maybe we should stop now."

The hungry smile on his face makes it impossible for me to say no.

For some reason, I felt less nervous when it was me touching him. But now, all I can think of is Coach walking in and seeing us. Or one of those pasty boys. Or, God forbid, one of our parents.

"Vicente, we got lucky. Let's stop before someone comes in."

"What're they going to do? Expel you on your last day of school?"

"They could expel *you*," I say.

"Let them try. Goodbye, tennis championship." He speeds up his strokes. "Come on," he says. "Let go of them. It's just us right now. It's only—"

I can't hold it in anymore. I explode into his hand. My body erupts, shivers, like I'm levitating off the ground. It's blissful, but when the moment passes, I feel awkward and exposed. I don't know what to do, so I laugh nervously. He laughs too.

"Why are we laughing?" he asks as the jets wash all evidence of our passion away.

"I don't know," I say with a smile. "What just happened was kind of funny, and incredible."

"I'm going to miss you." His voice cracks.

"Me too," I say. Without his heat next to mine, the

cold water feels horrible. "What if I mess everything up at MGM? What if I don't find another friend there?"

He turns to me. "If you do find a friend, they better not replace me. No matter what happens, no matter what girls we marry, we'll always be best friends, okay?"

I want to tell him that I want more than that. I don't want to marry a woman I don't love, bring children into the world with her, pretend Vicente is my friend when he's so much more. But I don't say any of that. Because I know it's silly. It's a fantasy even too absurd for the movies, where a man can fly or cast spells, but can't love another man.

"Yeah, we'll always be friends," I say sadly, as I pull him close to me again. And there, under the shower-heads, in the same building as all our classmates and our teachers, we hold each other.

Willie drops Mother and me off at the gates of MGM. We stand outside until we're greeted by a woman who is even tighter and more rigid than Mother. Her red hair is yanked back into a small bun, stretching the skin of her forehead in a way that looks painful. Her pencil skirt and blouse are both fitted to her bony body. Even her shoes look a size too small. She holds a clipboard, which she nervously taps with her unmanicured fingernails. "My name is Mildred Butler, but you may call me Mildred. Bobby, I will be your personal publicist. Do you know what that means?"

I open my mouth to speak and realize how awfully

nervous I am. My mouth feels chalky and dry. "I don't."

"It means she will be in charge of your publicity," Mother says, as if it's such an obvious answer.

"Not exactly," Mildred says.

Mother's nostrils flare.

"At Metro, everyone is assigned their own personal publicist," Mildred explains. "Think of me as your shadow. I'll be guiding your every move."

I keep my eyes fixed on the ground under my feet. My shadow is caught between Mildred's and Mother's shadows, like I'm trapped between two dueling forces.

"I report directly to Howard Strickling," Mildred says. "Do you know who that is?"

Mother speaks up proudly. "He's the head of publicity at MGM."

"Someone has done their homework." Mildred sounds dismissive, and Mother flinches. "If I do my job right, then you will never meet Howard, do you understand?"

"Yes," I say.

"And for me to do my job right, then you need to behave, do you understand?"

I think of that contract again. Morals. Decency. Public humiliation. I feel invisible and ashamed, like Mildred can see right through me.

Mildred doesn't wait for me to answer. Instead, she grabs my face hard, her hand digging into my cheeks. "Now I'll give you the welcome tour. Follow me." She leads us to a soundstage where hair and makeup men and women work furiously on dozens of actors sitting in front of mirrors. They put dark makeup on the actors' skin, contouring their eyes to make them all look threatening. "We're shooting an adventure picture right now. These extras will be playing the Arabs who try to take our hero hostage."

Mother blinks rapidly when Mildred says this, with a nervous vulnerability I've never seen on her face.

One of the men playing a villainous Arab approaches us. He seems to be one of the only ones who doesn't need his skin darkened for the part. He stands behind me, staring uncomfortably at the two of us in one of the mirrors.

"Yes, Frank?" Mildred asks.

"Who's this?" Frank asks.

"Bobby, this is Frank Lackteen." I notice that Mildred doesn't even bother to introduce Mother, almost like Mother doesn't exist.

"You look just like my nephew," Frank says.

At this, Mother snaps, "I'm certain that's quite impossible."

I say nothing. I just look at myself next to Frank in the mirror, and think that Mother is wrong. It's very possible.

Mildred walks so fast that we can barely keep up. She talks even faster. "Here we have Lot One, the epicenter of Metro. This is where a lot of the magic happens. Lot One has soundstages and dressing rooms and rehearsal halls, where you'll hopefully be spending a lot of your time if you're cast in anything."

"He'll be cast," Mother says haughtily.

Mildred leads us around Lot 1. She points at all the important offices. She says there are labs and film vaults here, and warehouses where all the different departments who help make movie magic set up shop. It's awe-inspiring.

Then she leads us past Lot 1, into the surrounding stages.

"Keep up. Do you want to see the zoo or not?"

"The zoo?" I ask in shock.

"Where do you think we get the animals from?" Mildred asks. "MGM has its own police force. Its own firemen. Its own transportation system and hospital. Think of this as its own country. You're no longer just an American. You belong to the nation of Metro now."

"How exciting." I can tell Mother is trying to ingratiate herself to Mildred, but it's not working.

"Next to the zoo are the stables. Do you like horses?"

"I've never actually met a horse."

"Well, you'll need to take riding lessons, then. Imagine if they cast you in a Western, and you can't ride a horse. That would be a disaster." Mildred leads us to the outdoor sets. "Keep up. We don't have all day." One moment, we're in Renaissance Italy. The next we're in New York. Then we're in France, outside the Eiffel Tower. Then in Egypt. Then in a desert, where all those Arab extras are now congregating.

Finally, Mildred stops in front of a quaint white building with a red tile roof. Outside the building is a playground with children playing on slides and jungle gyms and a sandpit.

"And here we are at last," Mildred says. "This is where your mother and I will say goodbye for now."

"Goodbye?" Mother asks.

"Well, yes. You didn't think you'd stay here all day, did you?" Mildred asks.

Mother doesn't answer. Clearly, she thought she *would* be here all day.

"What is this place?" I ask.

"Why, this is your school," Mildred says. "MGM's Little Red Schoolhouse. You'll need a minimum of three hours a day of schooling. Proper schooling, that is. The rest of the time, I'll be setting you up with lessons. Voice and diction and riding and roller skating and ice skating and piano—"

Mother interrupts. "My Bobby boy could *teach* the piano lessons."

Mildred rolls her eyes. "Every mother thinks her child is the best. The truth is only one mother was ever right about that."

Mother tries to play along. "And who would that be? Garbo's mother?"

Mildred looks at her in absolute shock. "The Blessed Mother, of course," she says dryly.

"Oh, of course, of course," Mother stammers, as if she cares one bit about church.

"Now go inside. Your teacher, Miss Mary, is expecting

you," Mildred says. Before I can turn away, she adds, "But remember, Bobby, I'm your shadow. If you misbehave in school, at home, or anywhere else, I'll hear about it. So don't misbehave."

"I won't," I whisper, but all I want is to feel Vicente's heat next to mine again.

She pulls a card out of her pocket and hands it to me. "That's my work number, and my private number below it. You can call me anytime. It's part of the job. Do you understand?"

"I do."

"Good boy. I'll pick you up in three hours for your first riding lesson."

I wave awkwardly as Mildred yanks Mother away from me. I don't know what I expected from my first day at the studio, but seeing my mother put in her place by a woman named Mildred wasn't one of them.

The routine of my life changes fast. I still sleep at home, but there's no time for Reeves Trio rehearsals on weekdays anymore. The studio keeps me busy all week with a constant schedule of classes. They don't cast me in anything, not yet. For now, I'm just being paid a weekly salary to learn. A month into my contract, Mildred enters the classroom and says she needs me. I follow her to an outdoor bench, where we sit next to each other. Not a cloud in the sky as she says, "It's been exactly one month. How have you been doing?"

"Oh, good," I say.

It's not really true, though. I miss Vicente. Seeing him only on the weekends hurts. And even my weekends are busy, because it's the only time I can rehearse and perform with Mother and Willie. When I do see Vicente, it feels different. We're growing apart. And we haven't even discussed what happened in the shower. Sometimes I think I imagined it. With each day that passes, it feels hazier and hazier, more like a distant fantasy.

"Well, I have exciting news," Mildred says. "Billy Haines is having a party. Do you know who he is?"

"No," I say. "I'm sorry."

"He's an interior decorator. But that's not important. What's important is his best friend is Joan Crawford." My heart stops at the mention of her name. "And where Joan goes, *everyone* goes. Casting directors. Producers. Directors."

"Oh," I say. "Am I invited to the party?"

"Of course not. They need a piano player, and you're it, kid. It's a theme party. The New Testament."

"Sorry, that's the—the theme?" I ask. It seems like such a strange theme for a party. Religion and parties don't exactly seem to go together.

Mildred shakes her head in disgust. "It's tasteless, if you ask me. But Billy has requested entertainment at the event. He wants *Salome*'s 'Dance of the Seven Veils,' accompanied by a pianist. He's a big fan of Oscar Wilde, if you know what I mean."

225

I don't know what she means.

"And he asked us for our best young piano player to accompany his Salome."

"And that's me?" I ask.

"Of course it's you," she says. "Play. Smile. Charm the right person, and perhaps you'll be cast in something. Oh, and be sure to see the studio doctor the morning of the party. You have an appointment with him at ten."

"Am I sick?" I ask, realizing what a strange question it is.

"Not at all." She slaps my knee. "The doctor will make sure nerves don't get the best of you, that's all. Now go back to class. What are you still doing here?"

The Friday morning of the party, I go see the studio doctor, who barely asks me anything before handing me a bottle of Benzedrine and telling me to take a pill just before I leave for the party.

"What is it?" I ask.

"Oh, it's nothing," the doctor says. "Just a little decongestant."

"But I'm not congested," I say. "I can breathe fine. See?" I take a deep breath to show him.

"It will give you energy," he explains.

"Is this because I've been tired? It's just more work than I'm used to, but I'm not sick. I can handle the work, I promise." I hear the concern in my voice. Being sent to a doctor feels like punishment, like I'm being warned to step it up or lose my contract.

With a reassuring smile, the doctor says. "You've done nothing wrong. We offer this medicine to many contract players. It does wonders before performing, and you're about to perform."

"But I'm used to performing," I plead. "My mother and my stepfather and I, we've been performing for years."

The doctor gives me a stern look. "You're not performing for a bunch of drunks at a greasy spoon tonight. You're performing for the people who could make you a star. I'm your doctor now. You need to trust me and take the pep pill."

That night, I do as I'm told and sneak a pill into my mouth. I swallow it down with some water. Frisco paws at me the way he does anytime I put something in my mouth. "It's not food, boy," I say with a laugh. I hear Mother and Willie arguing in the living room.

"First you won't let me come to the studio," Willie says. "Now you won't let me come to the party. Don't you think I'd like to meet Joan Crawford too?"

"I *bet* you want to meet her," Mother snaps.

"You know it's not like that," Willie declares breathlessly. "I only have eyes for you. But sometimes it feels like you only want me to be his father when it's convenient for you."

"I'm not having this conversation right now," Mother shouts. "Tonight is not about you. It's about *my* son, so stay out of it."

Mother's voice sounds frightening. I lift Frisco into

my arms and hold him tight.

"I may not have adopted him yet. I may not look like him. But I think of him as a son." Willie sighs deeply. "And you told me I'd be his dad, remember?"

I look at myself in the mirror. The truth is, I don't really look like either of them. I certainly have something of Mother in my bone structure. But that's it. My skin is darker than theirs, and my eyes are a mystery even to me, because I have no idea who I got them from. I pull my journal out. Vicente gave it to me for my last birthday, but its pages are still blank. I guess I'm too scared to put any of my true feelings on paper.

"Bobby, are you ready?" Mother sings out cheerfully, as if I didn't just hear her and Willie fighting.

Ten minutes later, the medicine kicks in. And I feel like I'm flying.

It's hard to describe how I feel when I enter the party, like some mythical version of me. I glide into the room on a cloud. All my fear and insecurity is gone, replaced by a newfound confidence. I belong in this room of stars.

Mildred greets us in the foyer of the home. She looks disappointed to see Mother there. "Hello, Bobby." After a pause, Mildred says, "And Margaret. You're here too."

"Of course I am," Mother says. "You think I'm going to let him attend a party without a chaperone? He's a child. What kind of a mother do you think I am?"

From the dismissive way Mildred looks at her, I can tell she knows exactly what kind of mother Mother is.

My eyes dart around the room. The guests are unbearably glamorous. Not everyone has embraced the theme, though some have. I guess it's not hard to wear biblical clothes when you have a studio costume shop at your disposal. There are men and women dressed like they're in a Cecil B. DeMille picture. And then there are people dressed like they're at a movie premiere, fitted tuxedos and body-hugging gowns. Platinum-blond hair everywhere.

"Mother!" I interrupt her and Mildred. "Mother, look."

Standing by the grand piano, next to two dashing men, is Joan Crawford. She doesn't look like she did on the bicycle, all freckles and windblown hair. Her skin is translucent now. Her hair is slicked back in a dramatic style that only serves to accentuate that face. Those eyes, huge and searching and steely and determined. Those lips, powerful and dramatic. She's tiny, and yet also a giant. She laughs at something one of the men said.

"I prefer Garbo myself," Mildred says. "But Garbo doesn't go to parties."

"She looks just like she does in the pictures," Mother whispers to me.

I smile, so happy to feel bonded to Mother in this moment. I turn to Mildred. "We've seen every Crawford picture. Every single one."

I feel a surge of gratitude for my complicated mother, who pushed me to these heights, who spent all our cookie-jar money on movie tickets, who would clutch me tightly during the close-ups.

"Do you want to meet her?" Mildred asks.

"Yes!" I squeal. I thought maybe Mother was pushing me into something I don't want, but in this house, with that face in front of me, and this decongestant coursing through my veins, I've never wanted anything more than my own close-up.

Mildred puts an arm around my shoulder and leads me to Joan. Mother follows behind us.

"Miss Crawford, I'm so sorry to interrupt."

The two men step aside so Joan can take center stage. "Mildred, right?" Joan asks. "How is your father? He was ill?"

Mildred blushes. "Yes, but he's much better now. I can't believe you remembered, Miss Crawford."

Joan smiles, and then looks at the two men she's with. Throwing her head back playfully, she cracks, "At least she has a father."

I freeze for a moment. Perhaps this is another reason I see myself in Joan Crawford. Neither of us has a father.

My thoughts are interrupted when Mildred says, "This is Bobby Reeves, just signed with MGM a month ago. And he's a big fan."

Joan looks over at me with a magnetic smile. "Here I am. And these are my friends and your hosts for the evening, Billy Haines and Jimmie Shields. Isn't their home lovely?"

The men shake my hand, then shake Mother's after I introduce her, but Crawford doesn't move. She just stands there, as if she knows she's on display. We thank Billy and Jimmie profusely for having us. And then I turn to Joan and gush, "Miss Crawford, I don't want to bother you, but, well, I think you're the greatest star of all time. I just want to say that I've seen every film you ever made."

"Not *every* film," Billy says with a laugh, and Joan kicks his shin with her heel.

"Bless you, child," Joan says. And then she adds wryly, "When Mr. Mayer pulls you in for a meeting, make sure to tell him everything you just told me. Maybe then he'll give me better pictures."

"Oh, your pictures couldn't possibly be any better," I say.

Joan shrugs, like she doesn't agree, and mumbles something about Norma Shearer I can't quite hear.

Then the two men give Joan a pep talk about her career, and I don't hear every word because they talk fast and low, and also because I'm just looking at her. Like the whole world has disappeared and I'm staring at her close-up.

I realize something. The feeling I have at the pictures, it's the very same feeling I have when I'm with Vicente. Like the world around us disappears.

Joan says something to Billy. "You don't know what Mayer will do with me. Look what he did to you."

"He didn't do a thing to me," Billy says. "I made my own choices, and I have no regrets. I'm happy, really I am."

To my surprise, Billy squeezes the other man Jimmie's

back when he says this. My eyes can't look away from this gesture. A man's hand tenderly resting on another man's back, in public, at a party, in *their* home. It almost feels like a hallucination.

Then Billy, who seems ready to end this part of the conversation, announces the evening's first performance. My heart starts to beat. My fingers twitch a little. My mouth suddenly feels dry in anticipation of hearing my name.

But it's not me. The first performance is Cole Porter at the piano, accompanied by a young starlet dressed as Mary Magdalene. Porter plays magnificently. And the starlet is riveting, singing those suggestive words. *"Love for sale. Appetizing young love for sale."*

The crowd goes absolutely wild for them. I'm clapping so delightedly that I don't even hear Billy announce Salome's dance as the next performance. I feel like my brain shuts down when I sit at the same piano Cole Porter just played. The doctor was right. If I didn't have the added boost of the pep pill, I might have crumbled under the pressure of this moment. Who am I to follow Cole Porter, to play for Joan Crawford? And yet, all my doubt is vanquished by the surging confidence I suddenly feel. My fingers travel across the keys with more passion than they ever have before. I add flourishes that I hadn't planned, improvising on the spot. The dancer playing Salome keeps up with my every move, and I wonder if she's taken a pep pill too. At one point, I take my right hand off the keys and use it to bang on the side of the piano like a drum. Salome hops atop the piano as I turn the piano into a percussion instrument. The crowd goes wild. When it's over, the applause is like a waterfall, and I realize I was good. No, I was great. I am a star.

I catch my breath after taking a bow with Salome, and instinctively make my way outside. Mother and Mildred follow me, each one trying to outdo the other in their gushing praise for me, like it's a competition. They argue over who to introduce me to first. A few feet away from them, I see a bar and quietly head toward it. Mother and Mildred don't even notice me disappear.

"A Shirley Temple, please," I say to the bartender, a movie star of a man who happily obliges in mixing me a kid's drink.

"Amazing, isn't it?" a voice asks.

I turn and see someone standing next to me. A man, but he wears makeup and a fur stole over his tuxedo, which both scares me and piques my curiosity.

"What is?" I ask, staring at the man in disbelief. Is he allowed to dress like this?

"Shirley Temple," he says. "She became a star not so long ago, and already she has a drink named after her. It's my favorite drink, too." To the bartender, he says, "One more Shirley for me!"

The bartender laughs, like making a kid's drink for a grown-up is hilarious. But he makes one quickly and hands it to the man.

"You were wonderful," the man says to me. "Cole Porter better watch his back."

"Oh, thank you," I say, sipping on my Shirley. I hadn't realized how parched I was. I must still be staring at the man, because he says, "What's the matter? You never seen a pansy before?"

"No." *Unless I look in the mirror, of course.*

He laughs good-naturedly. His laugh is big and warm. "That's because the cops throw us all in jail these days. The only thing that's left for us to do is perform. We're criminals on the streets, but they *adore* us onstage."

"You perform too?" I ask.

He nods. "I'll be performing at the party. But you'll probably be in bed by the time I go on, kid."

"I'm not a kid," I say defensively.

The man named Jimmie who was standing with Joan approaches him and they have a quick conversation, asking after each other. Then Jimmie notices me. "Oh, it's you again. The kid at the piano."

"Oh, don't call him a kid," the man in makeup says. "He doesn't like that. But he was good, wasn't he? I told him Cole Porter better watch his back."

"Instead of watching other people's, um, backsides," Jimmie says, and they cackle with glee.

"My name is Bobby," I announce, observing the strange confidence in my voice. I realize I haven't gotten the man's name. "And you are?" I ask.

"By night, I'm Zip Lamb," he says, offering me a limp gloved wrist. I shake his hand firmly, overplaying my masculinity. "And by day, I'm . . ." He pauses for comic effect and says, "Oh, who am I kidding? I sleep all day.

I'm nocturnal, like a honey badger."

Jimmie laughs. "You were truly wonderful," he tells me. "Even Joan was impressed, and Joan is rarely impressed."

I beam at the praise. "Thank you," I say softly.

"I should get back to Billy," Jimmie says. "I'll see you at the Hollywood Rendezvous later?" he asks Zip.

Zip raises his arms up in the air and freezes in a pose. "You'll see a lot more of me at the Rendezvous than you will here. I go on at midnight, and you've never seen *anything* like what I have planned."

Jimmie leaves, and I turn to Zip, wanting to ask him a million questions. First of all, are Jimmie and Billy . . . a couple? Because it sure seems that way.

And if they are a couple . . . Well, it means the world isn't what I thought it was. I never believed that men could be together openly like this. But if they can, then who's to say me and Vicente won't be the same someday? Maybe we can share a home, a life. My mind spins. No, the whole beautiful world spins.

I turn to Zip. "Hey, what's the Hollywood Rendezvous, and what happens at midnight there?"

I don't get the answer because Mother and Mildred find me. They don't even acknowledge Zip. They pull me away, and Mildred says they've agreed on a list of who I should meet before I go home. They push me around the room, introducing me to casting directors and conductors and publicists and directors and even writers.

"Don't bother impressing the writers," Mildred says.

"They're the least powerful people in Hollywood."

"And they're all Communists," Mother adds.

When ten o'clock rolls around, Mildred says it's time to go. "The party's over now."

"But it's not," I say. "Zip Lamb hasn't even performed yet."

"Who?" Mother asks.

"The man I was talking to at the bar. The one in the . . ." I don't want to point out that he was wearing makeup and fur, so I say nothing.

"The *pansy*?" Mildred asks dismissively. "Oh, sweetie, he's not performing for you or me. It'll be a fruits-only performance."

I look around and see that it's not just us leaving. A whole group of people are clearing out. A smaller group—mostly men, but some women, Joan included—linger behind.

"You will stay away from people like him in the future," Mother says. "He's disgusting. Men like him prey on boys like you."

"On that, we can agree," Mildred says.

As they lead me out, I realize this might be the first thing that has brought Mother and Mildred together: their hatred and disdain for the very thing I know I am inside.

I can't sleep that night. Thoughts are buzzing inside me, like they have a heartbeat of their own. I played piano in front of movie stars. I met Joan Crawford. But that's not the part of the night that keeps me from sleeping. It's those men I met. Billy and Jimmie. The way they touched each other. The way Jimmie said, "I should get back to Billy." It makes me realize something. That I should get back to Vicente. That I should tell him I love him.

Now, while this energy is coursing through my veins. Now, while I have the courage to imagine a better life for us. A braver life.

It's almost midnight. I throw a coat on over my pajamas. I need shoes. I curse Mother for her no-shoe policy.

I tiptoe past Mother and Willie's room. The door is cracked open. Willie snores lightly, his muscular arm draped over Mother's chest. I guess they've made up since their fight before the party. Willie always forgives her.

When I'm confident Mother and Willie are soundly asleep, I sneak my way to the front door. The hardwood floors creak in certain spots, and I do my best to avoid them. Finally, I get to the front door. I grab the shoes and sneak out. When I'm outside, I take a huge breath of freedom, put the shoes on, and run as fast as I can. I have so much to tell Vicente, things I have to get out before this feeling goes away. This rush of confidence and possibility.

Luckily, he lives on the first floor of an apartment building, so I don't have to do any *Romeo and Juliet* screaming or climbing or stone throwing. All I need to do is walk for twenty minutes, knock on his window, and wait.

I knock.

I wait.

I knock again.

Finally, the curtains part, and there he is. In a white T-shirt and white Jockey briefs that hug his athletic body. His fists rub his eyes. He pushes the window up, so we're facing each other.

"Bobby?"

"Hi." I smile.

"Bobby, what's wrong?"

"Nothing," I say. "Nothing at all. Everything is fantastic. I played at a party at Billy Haines's house. Do you know who he is?"

"Shh." He looks over his shoulder. "Keep your voice down. My dad's asleep."

"He's Joan Crawford's very best friend, as it turns out. But that's not the interesting part."

"Are you sure you're okay?" he asks. "You seem different."

"I am different. The whole world is different. We just didn't know. There's so much we didn't know. Can I come in?"

"Sure, just . . ." He looks over his shoulder again. "I'm going to make sure my dad's door is closed so he doesn't wake up. Be quiet, okay?"

I enter as he exits. I throw my body down on his bed. My head hits his pillow and the smell of him envelops me. This is happiness.

When he comes back, there's a look of dread on his face. I sit up. "I'm sorry," I say. "Did your dad hear me?"

"No." He sits next to me. "He's not home. I figured he worked overtime and snuck in after I went to bed. But he's not home. And it's midnight."

"Maybe he's still working," I say.

"No, it's too late." He swallows hard. "I'm worried, Bobby."

"Maybe he's still headed home. Long Beach is an hour away."

"Even with overtime, he's never worked past ten. That's when the plant closes."

"Maybe he's getting a drink with his friends."

"He's never done that. He doesn't leave me alone at night."

"Maybe he has a new . . ." I stop myself from saying what I'm thinking.

"I know what you're thinking," he says, taking my hand. "And I hope you're right. Because if he's not with a woman, then he's . . ." He doesn't finish the sentence. He's too worried to put it into words.

"I can stay here until he comes home," I offer. "I'll sneak out the minute we hear him."

He almost smiles. Maybe he's thinking what I am, that this could be a stolen moment for us to continue exploring each other's bodies.

"Do your mom and Willie know you're here?" he asks.

I ignore the question. I don't want to bring Mother or Willie into this.

"Bobby, you can't stay here," he insists.

"I'm not leaving you alone and scared," I say. "I'm your . . ." What exactly am I to him? Screw words and definitions. We're alone. In bed. I grab him and kiss his lips. He kisses me back. Our tongues explore each other. We let our hunger guide the way. Hands on thighs. Tongues on necks. Breathless grunts of passion. But when I reach under his briefs, he stops me.

"Bobby, I'm sorry, I—"

"I love you," I blurt out.

"Don't say that." He turns away from me.

"But it's true." I try to pull him closer to me, but he resists. "I love you, and I want to say it. I want you to hear it."

"I can't hear it. It's not right. Especially not right now, when my dad is . . . I don't know where."

I want to say that his dad is probably in some woman's apartment, doing exactly what he's stopping us from doing.

"I want to tell the world I love you." I can't believe what I'm saying, how sure of myself I sound.

"Bobby, come on, you know we can't think like that." He sounds defeated.

"Like what?" I ask defiantly. "Like we actually deserve love?"

"If we start to believe we can be together, it will make the inevitable harder."

"No, it won't." I hold his hands. "Because there is no inevitable anymore. Listen to me. The world is changing. Billy Haines, he's a successful designer. And he lives with a man. They're a *couple*. There are men living together in this very city, and they're happy. They're not sad. Or miserable. Or friendless. We can be like them."

"I can't be a professional tennis player and be with you. You know that. Athletes have to be, I don't know . . ."

"Exactly. You don't know. Neither do I. So let's invent our future together."

He pushes himself back to the head of his bed. He sits cross-legged, his legs bending around each other. "It would break my dad's heart to know . . ."

"That you love me?"

He doesn't look at me. He knows I love him now. I want to know if he loves me too.

"And it would break your mom's heart too," he adds.

"The difference is I don't care about her heart," I whisper.

"Yes, you do." He sounds annoyed. "She's your mother, and even though she drives you crazy, it's so obvious you want her love and approval." I bite my lips, realizing he's right. "And I'm all my dad has," he says, bringing the ghost of his mother into the bedroom.

"You're all I have," I counter sadly.

I see a loose thread in his blanket and pull at it nervously. My mouth feels dry. I'm afraid the effects of the medicine will wear off before I can convince him to love me back.

"Your hands are shaking," he says. "Your eyes, they look different. More intense. Did you drink alcohol or something?"

Or something, I think to myself. But I don't tell him about the pep pill. He treats his body like a temple. The last thing I want now is his judgment. Maybe the pill, thankfully still coursing through my blood, only served to free the real me from captivity. It melted away the fear that was holding me back. I wonder when it'll wear off. I curse myself for not bringing another one with me in case it does. I can't lose this feeling. Not now. Not ever.

I take his hand. "You know I'll never give up," I say.

He blinks a few times. He looks down at my hand gripping his. "I don't want you to. You know I don't. You know I . . . I . . . ."

"Say it," I whisper. "Please say it."

"I can't . . . ." He shakes his head.

"I need to hear you say it. Even if we can't live it, just say it. Please." I can hear the desperation in my voice as my hand squeezes his.

He closes his eyes when he finally whispers, "I love you too, okay?"

"You do?" My stomach flutters. I feel myself melt into this beautiful moment.

"I do, and I want to scream it too."

I kiss his lips, his cheek, his neck. He doesn't stop me. "I love you so much, and I want the world to know that."

"But it can't be this world," he says. "Another world, maybe. A better one than this."

He's in close-up now. We're floating in timelessness, in happiness, in beauty. I feel our faces getting all gauzy as my lips part and move closer to his.

"Vicente," I say. "All these years . . . we've been inseparable, haven't we? I don't want that to change. I want to
be like Billy and Jimmie. I want to be yours. I want you
to be mine."

"I want that too," he says. "But we have to be careful.
The world might not be as kind to us as it has been to
Billy and Jimmie."

"Shh, enough of that." I pull his hand close to my
body, until it's touching my nervous belly. I guide his
hand lower, until he's touching my hardness. Then I take
my coat off. And my pajamas. Until I'm naked in his bed.
"Let's do all the things we've never done." I pant through
my words.

He smiles. He pulls his briefs down. We just stare at
each other for a few breaths.

Our haze is broken by the ring of the telephone.

"I should get that," he says.

"Please, no," I beg. "Not now."

"It has to be my dad," he says, standing up and pulling his underwear back up. He disappears into the living
room. I can hear him pick up the phone, out of breath.
"Hello?" A few seconds later, "Okay, I'll wait for you
here."

He rushes back into the bedroom, his face frantic.

"What happened?" I ask, standing up.

"That was my aunt. My dad had an accident at work,"
he says. "He's fine, but she's bringing him home from the
hospital now. You have to go."

I don't move. I can't leave him. Not yet.

"Bobby, you can't be here when they get home. You do understand that, right?"

The sharpness in his tone shocks me. "Of course I understand. I'll go." I look at my pajamas strewn on his bed and feel like an idiot. This whole night, it's been a silly fantasy. And the harsh return of real life feels like a slap.

We look at each other in silence for a moment.

"I'm sorry I came here." I throw my pajamas back on. "I didn't mean to upset you, or push you, or—"

He moves his head closer to mine. His lips part. He kisses me one last time. A new kind of kiss. Bittersweet and full of hurt.

When I start to walk home, the feeling of invincibility I had evaporates. The energy coursing through my veins is disappearing, and in its place is a hollowness.

My feet are tired. But my heart, my heart tells me I have to fill this void somehow. And so, I don't head home. Instead, I walk to Cahuenga Boulevard, wiping my tears away as I keep moving. I ask where the Hollywood Rendezvous is until someone finally tells me.

Outside the Hollywood Rendezvous stands a man in a tuxedo.

"Hello," I say.

He just cocks his head.

"I'd like to go inside, please."

"How old are you?" he asks.

I don't even know how old you need to be to enter a nightclub. "Twenty-five," I say, erring on the old side.

The man laughs. "Sure," he says. "And Jean Harlow is alive and living in Catalina."

"I'm a guest of Zip Lamb," I say haughtily.

"Well now," he says. "You don't look like Zip's type. He usually enjoys a mature gentleman."

"Just tell him that . . ." I'm about to say my name, but I realize Zip may not remember my name, so I say, "Tell him that Salome's pianist is here to see him." The man opens the ropes for a handsome pair of men wearing green carnations on their lapels. He says hello to them. When he's done, I stare at him. "Well?"

"Well what?" he asks.

"Aren't you gonna tell Zip that Salome's pianist is here?" I plead.

"Oh, you were serious?"

I nod. "Extremely serious."

"Well, all right then, don't get your panties in a bunch," he says. Then he disappears inside. I could just jump over the ropes right now. But then they would ask me to leave. And I want to know what happens behind these doors too much to risk that. I want Zip to tell me that yes, there is hope for me and Vicente, and for all the boys who love each other, and the girls too.

I wait patiently, staring at the full moon above my head. Mother once said that the full moon makes her emotions go wild. Well, I'm ready to go wild. I long for it.

"Salome's pianist?" the man says. "Right this way."

The man opens a side door for me. It doesn't lead me

into the club itself. Instead, it takes me backstage, where Zip Lamb awaits me. I almost don't recognize him. At the party, he wore some makeup. But now he's dressed head to toe as a woman. A big blond wig. Rouged cheeks and ruby lips. A stuffed dress that gives him curves like the windiest stretches of Laurel Canyon.

"This is quite the surprise," he says.

Suddenly, I feel so childish. What in the world am I doing here? I spoke to this man for a few minutes at some party. And now I'm just showing up at his place of work like I'm his friend. Or worse, his responsibility. Because I'm a mess right now, a lost little kid, and he notices that right away.

"You've been crying," he says.

"Is it that obvious?" I ask.

"I hope it wasn't something that happened at the party," he says.

"Oh, no," I say. "The party was wonderful."

"Is it your mother?" he asks. "She seemed like . . . a lot of mother."

I laugh. "She is. But no, it's not her. It's just that I thought . . ." I stop myself. Why am I telling a stranger all my secrets? And then I think, Well, who else am I going to tell? "It's just, meeting you, and seeing Billy and Jimmie at the house, the way they lived together, as a couple . . ."

He nods, sensing I'm hesitant to say more. "Go on. It's okay."

"Well, I thought, maybe I could have the same thing.

You see, I have this friend. This best friend."

"Does he share your feelings?" he asks with compassion.

I nod.

"So what's the problem?" he asks.

I look at him with pleading eyes. "It's just . . . I don't want to hide anymore. And he doesn't think . . . He doesn't believe we can ever be together."

He nods. "Look, I have to go on in ten minutes, and what I'd like to tell you will take a lot more than ten minutes."

"You can start?" I suggest.

"To begin with, you're not alone. And neither is your friend. There are so many men just like you. Men who love men. Women who love women. They're your community, your family. Come with me." He leads me to the back edge of the stage. He pulls the curtain open, just enough so I can see the patrons seated at tables, laughing and dancing. They're mostly men, many of them wearing green carnations. Billy and Jimmie are among them. But there are women, too. Women sitting together. Women in suits. Women . . . holding hands. "You see what I mean?"

"I see," I say, my eyes open wide.

Onstage, an emcee announces the performance. Zip points to a table at the back. He tells me there's an empty seat there that I can take, and that I can put another Shirley Temple on his tab.

I make my way to the table and order my Shirley

Temple. The crowd goes absolutely wild when Zip takes the stage with a woman named Kitty Doner. Zip is in his dress and Kitty is in a suit. I clap as loud as I can, the energy coming back to me. If I wanted hope, then I'm getting a huge dose of it just seeing them onstage. They start to sing a song in perfect harmony, and the lyrics say it all.

"'Masculine women, feminine men. Which is the rooster, which is the hen? It's hard to tell 'em apart today.'"

They dance as they sing. Kitty leads, of course. They part briefly, dancing side by side. And then, the real showstopping part of the number begins. Slowly, they each begin to disrobe. And then, when they've stripped down to their undergarments, they begin to put on the other's clothes. Zip puts on the suit Kitty was wearing, and Kitty squeezes herself into the gown and wig Zip had on. It's utterly captivating, like nothing I've ever seen before.

When they're done, they link hands and hold their united fists into the air. They bask in the applause. And I bask in the feeling of being among people like me. I stay for the next number, and the next, and the next. I can't leave until I've soaked up all the magic I can.

On Monday morning, I'm summoned to Mildred's office. As I walk there, I realize I now know my way around the studio. I know exactly which soundstage to make a left at, and what Parisian replica to walk straight through. When I see Myrna Loy being escorted to a photo shoot,

I barely blink. Not even the four giraffes being walked to Lot 1 shock me. I've gotten used to this place.

Mildred's secretary opens the door to Mildred's empty office for me. "Where is she?" I ask.

But the secretary isn't there anymore. She's left me alone in the office. I sit and wait. I cross my legs. I uncross my legs. I stand up and practice the latest tap dance I'm learning in dance class. I conjugate some French verbs Miss Mary taught us. I stand up and look out the window. In the distance, I see a giant musical number being shot outside a fountain. And then I glance at Mildred's desk. It's littered with files. Each one has a contract player's name on it. And at the very top is mine.

I tiptoe toward the file, as if anyone can hear me. I lift the cover, revealing the papers inside. There's my contract. And a memo detailing my skills—piano, voice, face, body. And a memo putting me in the "juvenile" category of actors, with a caveat that I could soon grow into a *leading man, unless he loses his looks as so many juveniles do.*

And then, just under these papers are a stack of papers, each marked with a date. The first date is my first day at the studio. It details, well . . . everything. What I wore. Who I spent time with. My entrance exam scores. Even everything I ate.

Lunch at the commissary. One hamburger with two slices of cheese. Potato chips. A slice of cheesecake with whipped cream. Two sodas. Note: Bobby has a sweet tooth. Extra exercise recommended.

I keep flipping the pages. My every move docu-
mented, sometimes with snide or complimentary little
asides.

*Acting class. Bobby was asked to cry. He could not. When
asked how he managed to cry for his screen test, he replied, "I
don't know." Concern is that he cannot act.*

They're not wrong.

And finally, I get to this past weekend. There's a
whole page about my playing at Billy Haines and Jimmie
Shields's home. It's one long compliment, adjectives liberally thrown in.

And then, on the final page in my file is something
that shocks me. A whole report detailing my every move
the night I went to Vicente's . . . and then to the Hollywood Rendezvous.

*On Friday night, Bobby snuck out of his home and went to
his best friend's house. Friend is Mexican. Then Bobby went to
a pansy club. We must ensure this does not happen again. We
know all too well how difficult it is to cover up the tracks of the
lavender set. Inform Eddie Mannix immediately.*

I close the cover of the file again and notice my whole
arm is shaking, with fear, but mostly with rage. I've been
angry before, but never like this. Not even Mother with
her harshness and her manipulations has ever stooped this
low.

I'm being watched. Spied on. It feels like the deepest
violation.

And yet . . . what did I expect? What is stardom if not
a violation of one's privacy? Or the giving up of one's

privacy in exchange for something else . . . adulation, glory, immortality?

I sit back down discreetly, praying Mildred won't know I snooped. But once I sit down, I see the huge windows in her office, and I let out a shocked laugh. They were watching me this whole time. They know my every move, so of course they know I read my files.

This is quickly followed by another revelation. This was all a setup. I was called into the office when it was empty, with my file visible for me to see, because they *wanted* me to read it. They need me to know that I'm being watched. It's the best way to get me in line.

"Ah, Bobby. Sorry I'm late," Mildred says.

I turn around. Mildred has a big, tight smile on her face. A smile that would be perfect for the Wicked Witch in *The Wonderful Wizard of Oz*. They should've just cast her.

"Hello," I say.

"Apologies for keeping you waiting." She squints at me, her eyes like blades. "I see you've kept yourself busy in my absence."

"I just do what's expected of me," I say. "Anyway, it's no use pretending I didn't read those files because you, or someone working with you, was watching me the whole time."

She smiles. This is a woman who obviously loves a chess match. "If you did what's expected of you," she says, "then you wouldn't be in my office right now. But here you are."

"I know," I say.

"Let me be clear." She walks toward me. Just her stance alone is a threat, but then come the words. "I am on your side."

"It doesn't feel that way," I say softly. I wish I had taken a pep pill this morning. It would give me the defiance I need to stand up to her.

"Case in point," she says. "I haven't said a word to your dear, sweet mother about what I know. I'm sure she would be horrified by your . . . tendencies."

I sink down into my seat, deflated. I want to take Mildred on, to stand up for myself. But just the mere mention of Mother reminds me of what I am: a scared seventeen-year-old boy. Scared of what my mother might do to me if she finds out what I am. If anyone knows how to hurt me, it's her.

"And why don't you tell her?" I ask quietly.

"Because I have no interest in your mother," she says. "And do you know why?"

I shake my head.

"Because women like her are a dime a dozen, dear." Mildred attempts a warm smile. "All the stage mothers are the same. I'm not interested in the ordinary. That's why I'm in show business. But you . . . You are extraordinary."

"I am?" I hate how flattered I sound by her praise.

She crouches down so she's on my level now. It's not a chess match anymore. It's something else. Something much more uncomfortable and strange. "I'm not interested in getting you into trouble with your mother or your stepfather. Do you know what I'm interested in?" She loves to do this. Ask questions that I couldn't possibly answer. "I'm interested in you fulfilling your potential. You're a star, Bobby. You have that undefinable quality that makes people *notice* you. You don't want to waste that, do you?"

I shake my head.

"How much do you know about Billy Haines and Jimmie Shields?" she asks.

"I—I know they have an incredible house and that they're best friends with Joan Crawford and—"

"And you obviously understood that they're pansies."

I flinch. That word can sound irreverent when someone like Zip says it, but coming out of her mouth, it sounds like an attack.

"I'm not judging." She throws her hands into the air in surrender. "What people do in the privacy of their own homes isn't my business. But being a star isn't a private endeavor. And there's only so much we can cover up for you. Or that we're *willing* to cover up for you."

"I understand," I say, but I'm not sure I do. It's all so much, and my head feels dizzy with all the information. My life is changing so quickly that my brain can't keep up.

"Billy Haines was a star," she explains. "You may not remember because you're too young for the silent pictures. But he had *it*. Charm and humor and looks. He transitioned seamlessly into talkies too. Unlike so many of the silent stars, his voice worked. All he had to do was keep his private life . . . private. He didn't even have to stop seeing Jimmie, mind you, all he had to do was hide it."

I feel my whole body tighten. I think of what a lifetime of hiding your love would feel like. How it would eat away at you until there was no you anymore.

"Mr. Mayer offered him the world. All Billy had to do was get married. And do you know what he said?"

I want to scream that no, of course I don't know what he said. Can't she just stop asking me questions she's just going to answer anyway?

"He said, 'But Mr. Mayer, how can I get married when I already am married?'"

Mildred laughs at this. Like it's the most absurd thing in the world to her. I think back to the way Billy and Jimmie touched each other so lovingly. I imagine myself back in the home they created. Of course they're married, just like me and Vicente could be someday, and what's so funny about that?

"And that was that," she says. "Billy Haines's career as a star was over. If Joan hadn't hired him to decorate her house, he might never have had the career he has now. But Miss Crawford's loyalty is not my business. *You're* my business." She takes my shaky hands in hers. "So, what do you say?"

"I— Uh, what do I say about what?"

"You're done with your *amigo* and those awful clubs, aren't you?" she asks.

Finally, a question I should be able to answer. "I won't go back to the clubs," I say. I'm not sure if I mean it, but what else am I supposed to say? "But Vicente . . . He's my best friend. He's been my best friend since we were kids. How am I supposed to stop seeing him?"

"You want my advice?" she asks. "See him in public. With other people there. Tell him to find a girl, and keep telling yourself the same. You can have a friend as long as the studio doesn't suspect anything untoward is happening. Now go on back to class." As I walk out the door, she says one last thing: "And don't forget I've got my eye on you."

That's something I'll never forget.

On Saturday morning, there's a knock on the door. I'm still asleep, recovering from a long week of studio life, which isn't so different from my old life. It's just one lesson after another, with Mildred having replaced Mother as the woman watching my every move.

But it's Vicente's voice I hear when the front door opens. "Hi, Mrs. Reeves," he says.

"Isn't it a little early for a pop-in, Vinnie?" Mother asks, annoyed.

"I know. I'm sorry." I hear a sadness in his voice that's usually not there, and it gets me out of bed. I've called his home to check in on his dad twice over the week. His dad's fine, and Vicente's been friendly on our calls. Something else has happened.

"Well, come in," Mother says. "Bobby's still sleeping.

Can I get you something to eat or drink?"

"No thanks," he says. "I'll just wait for Bobby here."

I throw on the last pair of pants I wore, lying on the floor by my bed.

"Well, take your shoes off," Mother orders.

"Oh," he says. "Sorry. I figured if I stood here by the door—"

"It's a no-shoes home," she says curtly.

I hear Willie greet Vicente as I pick the last shirt I wore up off the floor and throw it on. "Vinnie, to what do we owe the pleasure?" Willie asks brightly.

Willie is aggressively shaking Vicente's hand when I make my way to the door. "Hey," I say.

"Hey," Vicente says. "Sorry it's so early. I didn't want to bother you this week, 'cause I know the days are long at MGM, and honestly, the days are long for me between school and tennis and . . ."

"And what?" Mother asks, leaning in curiously.

"You know, can we go talk somewhere else?" he asks me. "I know it's early, but would that be okay with you, Mr. and Mrs. Reeves?"

Willie pulls Mother in close and kisses her on the cheek. "Fine by me."

Mother pushes him away, but she obviously loves the attention. I resent them for displaying so publicly what me and Vicente have to work so hard to hide.

"Go have fun," Mother says, turning to me. "You deserve a break after your hard work this week." Forcing a smile, she adds, "I'm proud of you, Bobby boy."

She turns her attention back to Willie, who massages her shoulders.

I plaster a smile on my face and say a thank-you before putting on my shoes. Vicente does the same. His dad's car is parked outside.

"Oh, you drove," I say.

"Yeah," he says. "My dad doesn't need the car today, and I figured . . . I don't know . . . that we could go somewhere where we won't be interrupted or . . ."

"Vicente, is everything okay?"

He looks at me, his eyes welling up. "Come on."

Neither of us says a word as he drives toward Topanga, his favorite part of the city. I know exactly where he wants to take me. His favorite spot. He's told me about it, of course, but he's never taken me there. Because it's the place he goes when he needs to be alone with his own thoughts, and I want him to have that.

We climb a rugged hill until we get to its peak. We're surrounded by trees and a magnificent view. He loves the topography of Los Angeles. I've never been an admirer of nature myself. Mother certainly never exposed me to the natural world growing up. This hidden spot is perhaps the wildest and most rugged place I have ever been. "I love it," I say.

"Come sit," he says, patting the ground next to him. "Look at this. Untouched by man."

"It's really beautiful." I sit next to him, then turn my focus from the view to his face. "Just like you."

He smiles, but his face is full of pain. "It looked this

way before men decided Los Angeles was a habitable place, and it'll look this way forever."

"Vicente, what's going on?" I ask nervously.

"Then again," he says with a shrug, "it will surely all burn down someday. The honeysuckle and oaks, the sagebrush and walnut, all gone. I guess everything beautiful must be destroyed someday. That's the way of the world, isn't it?"

"Vicente, you're scaring me. Is it your dad? I thought he was okay. . . ."

"He is," he says. "The accident was minor. He has to wear a wrist splint for a few weeks, but . . ."

"But?"

We sit there for a few long breaths, everything eerily quiet but for a hot wind that blows past the canyon, barely rustling leaves and branches.

"I don't even know how to explain this. It sounds so unbelievable to me. But they used the accident as an excuse to fire him. He's being forced to go back to Mexico."

"What do you mean back to Mexico? He came here when he was a toddler. You can't force an American citizen to leave America." I feel my voice speed up, fear and anger overtaking me.

"You don't need to argue with me about it. I already know all this." He looks out at the trees. I wish he'd look at me. "But apparently, this has been happening for almost a decade. All the jobs went away during the Depression, and they needed someone to blame. And who better than the evil Mexicans, stealing the *real* Americans' work? So they've been quietly finding ways of getting us to go back."

"But how? You can't deport a citizen."

He's still looking out at the view. I can sense that the minute he looks into my eyes, he'll break. He's trying to stay strong. "They don't call it deportation. Like true Americans, they've found a way to repackage it. They're calling it repatriation."

"Repatriation?" I repeat, incredulous.

"They're trying to make it sound like some voluntary thing. Like Mexicans want to go home and be a part of their true country. But how voluntary is it when you're being forced out?"

"But he doesn't have to go, right?" I plead. "He has a passport."

"He already met with two lawyers. There's nothing he can do. He's lost his job. He's been told he won't be hired anywhere else. No government help whatsoever. And you want to hear the kicker?"

"Not really," I say.

"They gave him a train ticket. One week from today. Along with a settlement check if he stays in Mexico for three months. He said it didn't sound like a suggestion. If he doesn't leave . . . they'll make sure he never has a good life here again."

I tug at his arm. I'm desperate to look into his eyes and show him my love and support. "I'm so sorry," I say, painfully aware that my words aren't enough.

"So this is it," he says. "We always knew we couldn't be together. Not in this life. Not in this horrible place. We just never knew this would be the reason. Or that it would end this soon."

"You can't give up," I say. "He can't give up. The federal government has laws. People have rights."

He laughs bitterly. "The lawyer explained this all to us. The federal government has been looking the other way for the whole decade, encouraging states and counties and even companies to do the dirty work of getting us out of the country. The lawyer said we should consider ourselves lucky. We're not like the other Mexicans who were rounded up in downtown raids and sent packing. We're being treated 'respectfully' in their eyes. Train tickets. A settlement check."

"Respectfully? You're citizens. You can't leave. You have tennis. You have me. Your dad can come back in three months. You can live with your aunt."

"She's leaving too," he says. "She doesn't work. Without her relief checks and my dad's job, she can't pay her rent."

"They cut her relief checks too?"

He gives me a hard look, like I'm not understanding what he's saying. "They want us gone, Bobby."

"What if you lived with us?" I feel dizzy. Desperate for a solution. I push my hands into the dirt underneath me to ground myself.

He shakes his head. "I can't leave my family." Then he

asks, "You know how many American citizens of Mexican descent have been repatriated? At least half a million. *At least.* The lawyer said it could be a million. Nobody knows, because it's all hidden."

"I'm so sorry," I say again. "I don't know what else to say. I'm just . . . so sorry."

He finally looks at me. And the tears start to fall. "Don't be sorry. You're the best thing about this awful place."

I put a hand on his cheek. I let his tears flow into my fingers. Then I kiss his wet cheeks, his eyelids, his forehead, his neck.

"Bobby," he whispers apprehensively.

"We're in the middle of nowhere," I say.

"We're in Topanga," he counters.

"No one's here." I let my hands explore his body.

He takes his shirt off. Then pulls mine off. Our sadness turns into hunger. For fifteen minutes, we're connected, whole, happy. Until we explode and fall atop each other on the crackling leaves, pants around our ankles, our bellies sticky. That's when the sadness comes back. The longing.

"Vicente," I whisper.

"Shh, let's not talk," he says. "There's nothing to say."

But there is, and I'm going to say it. "Promise me you'll consider staying here," I beg. "I'll convince Mother and Willie to let you live with us. You'll be in college soon. It's not for very long."

"Bobby." It's all he says.

"Promise me," I say. "Just that you'll consider all options."

He holds me close. He guides my head to his chest, my ear on his beating heart. "Okay, I promise."

I close my eyes. I let myself feel hope again.

The man at the door recognizes me as soon as I approach. "Salome's pianist," he says. I know it's risky for me to be here, but I just have to see Zip. "Mr. Lamb isn't here tonight," he says. "This isn't his home, you know."

"Oh, well, where is his home?" I ask.

"You want me to divulge his home address to you?" he asks.

"Well, no, but can you—can you tell me where he is tonight?"

"I'm pretty sure he's at Club Bali on Saturday nights," he says. "It's just down the strip."

I walk down Sunset Boulevard, the headlights of passing cars like spotlights on me. The Club Bali doorman lets me in right away when I say I'm a friend of Zip Lamb's. I enter into a tiki lounge. Red couches and straw umbrellas everywhere. The waiters wear sarongs as they serve tropical drinks to the patrons. Each drink has a tiny little umbrella in it.

Zip is onstage, wearing a sarong and a long red wig, alongside a man in a doctor's uniform holding a notepad. As Zip feigns different pains around his body, he sings . . .

"Rich and poor, black and white, ring his bell all day and

262

night. My doctor!"

Zip falls into the doctor's arms. The crowd eats it up, showering the two of them with applause. At the end of the performance, the man playing the doctor takes his white coat off, revealing a perfectly fitted tuxedo. He makes the rounds on the floor, greeting the crowd like he owns the place, which I'm pretty sure is true. Eventually, he's joined by another man, who stands by his side as they make the rounds, holding hands.

I follow some of the sarong-wearing waiters past the stage and into the kitchen, where I find a thirsty Zip drinking out of a pineapple.

"Hello," I say.

He looks up at me. "Well, if it isn't my lovesick piano player. How are things with your friend?"

"That's why I'm here," I say sadly.

"That doesn't sound good." He puts the pineapple down and hands it to a waiter. "Can I have another? Just juice, please. I'm parched. Whoever thought living in a desert was a good idea wasn't a singer."

The waiter grabs his pineapple and starts pouring juice into it, then grabs a bottle of liquor. "Hey!" Zip screams. A flash of anger. "I said *just* juice." Zip stands up and marches toward the waiter. He swipes the pineapple away from him and approaches me again. "So, you're really touring all the pansy spots, aren't you?"

I think about how cruel that word sounded when Mildred said it. But coming out of Zip's mouth, it sounds celebratory. Proud, even.

"Mr. Lamb, I don't know what to do, and I didn't know who else to talk to."

"You can ask me anything as long as you don't call me Mr. Lamb. Zip is fine."

"Is that your real name? Zip?"

The man who was performing with him approaches him from the back. With his arms around Zip, he says, "It most certainly is not. Zip named himself after his favorite invention, the zipper."

"Hush now," Zip says. "He's a child."

"And you, my dear friend, are not a teacher anymore. So there's no need to pretend you're an upstanding member of the moral brigade."

Zip sighs.

"I'll go change, and then we can talk," Zip says to me. And then, in a world-weary tone and with a glance to his friend, he adds, "Can't let the LAPD catch me masquerading again, can I?"

Zip and I walk down the Strip together in silence. Somehow, it's harder to speak to him out in the fresh air than it is in the covert spaces we've been together in so far. I'm not ready to ask him what I should do about Vicente. Instead, I turn to him and ask, "So were you really a teacher?"

"Does it surprise you?" he asks.

"Well, it's just—I suppose—" I search for the right words. "I guess I've never had any teacher as interesting as you."

He smiles. "I wasn't this interesting when I was a teacher. I tucked everything that made me the fascinating creature I am now away to please principals and superintendents and parents. They wouldn't even let me teach what I wanted to teach. Oh no, one must stick to a *curriculum*. Students must learn exactly what their parents learned. God forbid they question the world they live in. Which, if you ask me, is the purpose of education. To learn to ask the right questions." He laughs. "I'm sorry," he says lightly. "I can get a little passionate about the things I care about."

"Your students were lucky," I say.

He stops walking for a moment. He looks at me curiously. "I couldn't even say goodbye to them." He's somewhere else now. Swimming in some sad memory. "They made me pack up my desk on a Tuesday night. They told my students I was leaving Los Angeles to get married . . . to a woman."

I don't know what to say. His sadness is filling me now, like it's my sadness too. The tragedy of people like us.

"What choice did I have? I left." He takes a deep breath. "All I want is to teach again, but I have a police record now. That part of my life is over."

"Mr. Lamb, what happened?" I ask. "Why did they do this to you?"

"Municipal Code 52.51," he says sadly. "You know what that is?"

I shake my head.

"It states that masquerading in the streets is illegal."

"What is masquerading?" I ask.

With a smile, he says, "It's when a person dresses as a member of the opposite sex."

"Oh," I say. Then, confused, I add, "But you perform in the nightclubs. And Marlene Dietrich, she wears tuxedos in movies and—"

"They like us when we're their evening 'entertainment,'" he says. "But when we do it in the streets, well . . . that's a step too far for them."

"Oh."

"And don't think the vice squad doesn't raid our nightclubs and restaurants. They make a meal of it when they want to. Their specialty is luring men like us into public restrooms and then arresting us if we so much as peek at them. They're evil. Pure evil."

"I'm so sorry that happened to you," I say.

"What's done is done." He starts walking again, and I follow closely behind. "Once they knew that I dressed in women's clothes at night, they couldn't possibly have me teaching their precious children. What if I exposed their children to frightful ideas? What if I told their children the true history of this city of angels? Imagine if everyone knew that before we displaced the native people of this land, men loving men and women loving women wasn't just a fact of life, it was celebrated. And then the Spanish arrived . . ."

"And then what?"

"And then they introduced shame to this place," he says. "Shame is humanity's enemy. It's the root of hatred and division. You know, before they came, we could marry each other."

"Marriage? Really?"

"Yes, really," he says. "Even tribal chiefs could marry men."

"Wow," I say.

"Yeah, wow." He talks faster now. "This is what I *wanted* to teach my students. That the missionaries didn't bring progress with them. That's a myth. We've convinced ourselves that the world just gets better and better and better. That time can't help but bring progress. But that's all wrong. Do you know what those missionaries did? They taught people how to be *ashamed* and how to hide. And we're still hiding. Sure, we perform in clubs. And sure, we can be together in the privacy of our homes. But in the streets, in the schools, on the screens . . ."

"We're invisible," I say.

He looks at me sadly. "Yes," he says. "But we'll rise up. This whole state is named after a lesbian novel, and someday it will belong to us again."

"What state?" I ask.

"California," he says. "You see, no one knows these things. Imagine if we were taught about our real history in schools, or by our parents." He sighs. "But they don't let us become teachers or parents, so that'll never happen."

"I'm sorry." Why am I always apologizing for things I'm not guilty of?

"So why'd you come see me anyway? What's going on?"

I take a breath and launch into Vicente's situation. I tell him everything, but mostly what I try to convey is how much I love him and how scared I am of him leaving. "So I guess what I'm asking is . . . How do I make him stay?"

"Oh, you sweet boy," he says. "The first rule of love and life is that you can't make anyone do anything." He thinks for a moment. "Poor choice of words. Of course you can. Too many people make others do things. The rule is that you *shouldn't* make anyone do anything."

"But he has to stay. You don't understand." I feel breathless. Desperate.

"Of course I understand. You think I haven't loved and lost?"

"You have?" I ask.

"Most of us have. If there's one thing that connects us all, it's heartbreak."

"So I do nothing?" I ask, disappointed.

"You can remind him that you love him," he says gently. "You can ask your mother if she'd be willing to take him in. Or perhaps another family, or his tennis coach."

"That'll never happen," I say.

"You can give him options, is what I mean. But it needs to be his choice. If you force his hand, he'll resent you. And nothing destroys love like resentment. Trust me."

I think of all the stories about Zip I don't know. Who has he loved? Who has he lost? And is it appropriate to ask him?

"It's getting late," he says. "And this is my next stop."

We're standing outside a two-story Spanish bungalow. "What's here?" I ask.

He sighs. "A man I'm seeing."

I smile. "That's wonderful. So you're in love too."

An even deeper sigh. "I wouldn't use that word in this case. He's married."

"Oh."

"His wife travels for work. She's a dancer. They hate each other. And truth be told, I hate myself for doing this, but . . . I don't know, I suppose I need to feel wanted once in a while."

I nod. I'm not sure what to say.

"I'm so sorry," he says, shaking off his self-loathing. "I forget you're a kid sometimes. I don't want to bring you down or anything."

"I was already down," I say. "You helped. You always do. Just knowing you're out there, that you exist . . . it helps me."

He smiles. Then he pulls out a piece of paper and a pen from his leather satchel and writes his phone number and address down for me. "I'm always a phone call away. You need me, you call."

"Okay," I say. "I will."

"And get yourself home safe tonight. You need me to call you a taxi?"

"No, I'll walk right home. It's past my bedtime and I'm exhausted."

He nods. "Last time, you closed the club down."

"Last time, I was on a pep pill that the studio doctor

gave me."

His nostrils flare when I say this. I'm shocked by the sudden change in him. "Those pills are the devil."

"I—I'm just doing what I'm told. The studio doctor gave it to me."

"And that's a reason for you to do it?" he asks angrily.

"I guess not. But it was just that once."

"You're not yet eighteen," he says. "And you don't know a thing about pep pills and liquor, so stay away from that crap till you're old enough to be smart about it."

I feel chastised, but also grateful. I think back to Zip in the kitchen of the Bali. How upset he became when the waiter almost poured booze in his pineapple juice. I don't ask, but I start to think that despite making his living in nightclubs, Zip doesn't touch liquor. "I'm sorry, Mr. Lamb. I really am."

He shrugs off his dark mood. "You didn't do anything wrong," he says. "But you can't trust the studio to have your best interests at heart. You're a product to them, not a person. Do you understand me?"

What strikes me when he says this is that I *do* trust him. Despite having just met him. In fact, he may be the first grown-up I trust who isn't related to Vicente. That's something pretty extraordinary, and it makes me say something very odd. "Mr. Lamb," I say, "I've spent all my life wondering who my father is."

He looks at me curiously.

"And I guess—I guess you're exactly what I hoped

he'd be."

After a melancholy moment, he says, "And I've spent all my life wishing I could have a kid someday." He lets out a yearning exhale. "But that'll never happen."

"I wish it could, Mr. Lamb," I say.

"Bobby, you gotta stop with this Mr. Lamb nonsense. Call me Zip. Lamb isn't my real name anyway."

"It isn't?"

"I changed it when I was fired. I didn't want anyone to find me. Especially since I was supposed to be leaving town to marry my sweet lass." He laughs at this.

"Why Lamb?" I ask. "You're like—well, like the opposite of a lamb."

"I didn't take the name because of the animal. I took it because of a man named John Lamb. He was a banker. He was also one of over thirty men arrested in Long Beach for . . ." He pauses. "Well, I think you can figure out what they were arrested for."

"Oh," I say.

"The *Los Angeles Times* published his name in connection with the arrests. You know what he did?"

I shake my head.

"He swallowed cyanide." Zip closes his eyes, fighting back emotion. "He wasn't the only one. So many men wanted to end their lives because of the incident that Long Beach had to temporarily ban the sale of cyanide. Can you imagine?"

"I—I don't want to imagine," I say.

"Well, I couldn't let their memory die, so I took his

name. Zip Lamb. It has a nice ring to it, doesn't it?"

"It does," I say, but now I want to know the name he was born with. And where he's from. And how he got to become who he is now.

But the most important question on my mind is . . . How can I convince Vicente to stay in the country? I won't make him stay, but I will convince him.

He must sense Vicente's on my mind because he says, "Good luck with your friend. Remember not to force his hand. Just speak from the heart. Present him with options. And support him no matter what he decides."

"I will," I promise.

"I'll see you soon, I hope." He waves goodbye and knocks on the door of the bungalow. I stand and watch, too curious not to see the handsome married man open the door and welcome Zip inside. I pray that someday we'll live in a world where men like them can just be together instead of pretending. I close my eyes and pray that world arrives before it's too late for me and Vicente. When I open my eyes, I look around, wondering if someone from the studio is watching me, waiting for Mildred to reveal herself hiding behind a jacaranda tree. But no one's there. Maybe they took their eyes off me. Or maybe they were too busy chasing Garbo and her girls tonight to bother with me.

On Wednesday morning, I make myself a peanut butter and jelly sandwich as Frisco bounces excitedly near my feet, desperate for a crumb. Mother enters the kitchen in her nightgown, loosely tied. Her hair is messy, her makeup not yet caked on. The charms on her necklace jingle-jangle near her heart. "Good morning, darling." There's a lilt in her voice.

"Good morning, Mother," I say as I smear some jelly on top of the peanut butter. I've been waiting since Saturday for the right morning to ask Mother about Vicente living with us, but she's been in a nasty mood all week. This morning is it. "Mother . . . there's something I've been meaning to ask you."

"Is it about the studio?" she asks. "Mildred says it's going well. She suspects they'll be casting you in something very soon. Don't lose faith."

"No, it's not that." I press the two sides of my breakfast together. "It's about . . . well . . . Vicente's dad has to move back to Mexico—"

"Good for him," she says. "He'll probably be happier there. He's such a sad-looking man."

I flinch, and immediately pop to Mr. Madera's defense. "I think that's because his wife died, not because he doesn't belong here."

She shrugs. "We've all loved and lost. We don't all mope about it."

I take a deep breath to stay calm. "The thing is, there's only a little bit of senior year left. And it doesn't make sense for Vicente to leave the country so close to graduation. So I was wondering . . . Well, I was thinking maybe he could live here. With us. Very temporarily."

"Where would he sleep?" she asks. "We hardly have

room for another body."

"He could sleep on the couch," I suggest.

"And who would pay to feed him? And the extra water costs? People are expensive, you know."

I gulp down hard. I didn't even think about money. But then I remember I'm earning my own money now. Weekly paychecks from the studio, even though I've yet to be cast in a movie. "I'll pay," I declare proudly.

"You're a juvenile. You can't spend that money without our approval."

"Then give me your approval," I beg. Next to me, my sandwich sits uneaten. I'm not hungry anymore.

"Look, I know he was your best friend—"

"*Is* my best friend."

"But you're becoming a star now. Maybe this is a sign that it's time for a new friend who you have more in common with."

"I'll never meet anyone I have more in common with than him."

"Like what exactly? He's an athlete and you're an artist. You're American and he's—"

"American," I spit out before she can finish.

"You know what I'm saying," she says softly. "I know how it feels to say goodbye to someone you're close to. I really do. But it's an inevitable part of life."

"So that's it?" I ask.

Suddenly, I hear Willie's footsteps. He enters the kitchen still in his briefs, a loose shirt swimming over them, almost covering his thighs. He was obviously listening, because he asks, "You didn't think I should be a part of the conversation about your friend moving into our home?"

I realize in that moment that I think of this as Mother's home. She lived here before she met him. She makes the rules. But maybe Willie can change her mind. "I'm sorry," I say. "I just figured I'd ask Mother first. Of course I was planning on asking you too."

"Well, I think—"

Mother cuts him off. "Willie, darling, it doesn't matter what you think. It's settled, and I need to go get my face on. I'll drop you off at the studio, Bobby boy." She puts a hand on my cheek. "I'm sorry, sweetie. I know you're sad, but it'll pass."

When Mother leaves, Willie points at my sandwich. "You going to eat that?" When I shake my head, he grabs it and takes a bite.

Vicente's train to Mexico leaves on Saturday afternoon. We've planned one more morning together before he's gone. I knock on their apartment door, and I'm surprised to hear Coach Lane's voice when Vicente's aunt Rosa opens the door.

"It would be a real loss for the sport if Vicente were to quit," Coach Lane says.

I approach the living room apprehensively. Rosa sits next to Mr. Madera on the couch. The splint on Mr.

275

Madera's wrist reminds me of the injury that started this horrible chain of events. Vicente and Coach Lane sit across from each other on wood chairs. Coach Lane is way too big for his chair, and it creaks under him, looking like it might snap at any moment.

"Hi," I say. "I can wait outside if—"

Vicente stands up. "No, come in, Bobby. We're done here."

"I just arrived," Coach Lane says.

"And now you're leaving," Vicente says calmly. The room is tense, but Vicente just smiles. He's been wanting to tell Coach Lane to screw off for years, and this is his chance.

Coach Lane stands up and faces Vicente. "You're making the wrong decision. Your dad has to leave, but you don't. We can figure out a place for you to stay."

"Where?" he asks.

"I don't know," Coach Lane says. "It appears you and Bobby are still friends. Perhaps—"

"My mom said no," I whisper. "I tried." I can't believe Coach Lane and I are allies in this situation, both of us desperate to keep Vicente in the country. Coach Lane selfishly wants him to stay so he can train a tennis star and reap all the rewards of his success. And I selfishly want him to stay so I can love him.

"Where there's a will, there's a way," Coach Lane says. "Isn't that what I always tell you kids?"

"That's what you tell the other kids," Vicente says. "You usually just scream at me. Bait me into getting angry just so you can give me a penalty. Or two penalties. Or—"

The tables are turning. Vicente is in charge now.

"If I'm harder on you," Coach Lane says, "it's because you're the only one with any talent on the team."

"Or is it because I'm the only Mexican kid on the team?" Vicente asks coldly.

Instinctively, Mr. Madera and his sister stand up. They go to either side of Vicente. They each put a protective arm around him.

"No," Coach Lane says unconvincingly. "I promise that's not why."

"Then why haven't you invited me to stay with you?" Vicente asks. A challenge.

Coach Lane shakes his head. "Think what you want of me, but you're making a mistake if you leave now. There's no tennis establishment in Mexico, not like there is here."

"Daniel Hernández," Vicente says.

"That's one player," Coach Lane says.

"One *Mexican* player. Playing for Mexico. And I'll join him. If this country doesn't want my dad, then it doesn't deserve me." Vicente's tone is defiant. Proud.

Coach Lane refuses to admit defeat, which doesn't surprise me. "I'm talking about the support system you'll need. Coaches and courts and amateur tournaments. Southern California is the epicenter of tennis right now. Perry Jones. The Southern California Tennis Association. The Los Angeles Tennis Club. They've created the stars of the game. A tennis player moving from California to Mexico is like . . . it's like Bobby saying he wants to be a musician or a movie star and moving to . . . I don't know, Timbuktu!"

"Bobby, you're not moving to Timbuktu, are you?" Vicente asks, laughing.

"I guess I would if the government makes me," I say slyly.

Mr. Madera laughs at this. So does Rosa. The laughter is a relief, because it puts an end to Coach Lane's plea. "I can show you out," Mr. Madera says. He puts a hand on Coach Lane's shoulder, and Coach flinches. The small gesture is one of power. As Mr. Madera leads Coach Lane out, he says sternly, "If you're lucky enough to have another Mexican kid on your team, I hope you show him more kindness than you showed my son."

I stand awkwardly in the living room when Mr. Madera comes back in. "Now that he's gone," Mr. Madera says, "let's discuss the plan. Rosa and I will finish packing up and get the suitcases in the car. And Vicente, you'll meet us here in an hour and a half."

"Correct," Vicente says.

Mr. Madera looks over at me, real empathy in his eyes. "I'm sorry to say goodbye to you, Bobby."

Rosa smiles as she extends her hands to me. She clasps my hands in hers. "Take good care of yourself, okay?"

I feel a tear form in my eye. I hug her tight. I've been thinking so much of Vicente that I haven't even processed that I'll also miss his dad and his aunt. They've meant so much to me. They've shown me that grown-ups can be caring and supportive. If I ever have kids, I'll be like them.

Mr. Madera pulls me into a hug next. "We'll let you know our number and address when we get settled in, okay? There are no goodbyes in this world. Just see you soons."

"Come on, Juan," Rosa says. "Let's go pack and let the boys have their time."

Mr. Madera releases me. I notice his eyes are welling up like mine are. Rosa leads the way to the master bedroom, and Mr. Madera follows. Finally, Vicente and I are alone.

"So," I say.

"So," he says.

"What should we do?" I ask.

"I don't know," Vicente says.

"We could go burn down our old high school," I joke.

"It is Saturday," he says with a sly smile. "No one'll be there."

I laugh sadly. I guess sometimes the only way to deal with a situation that's too painful to handle is by cracking jokes. Then I ask, "Should we go to Topanga?"

"I don't think we have time."

"Walk around the neighborhood?" I ask.

He nods. "Yeah, that sounds good. This place just makes me sad now. Like I'm standing in the past."

I lead the way out. We walk side by side, past kids playing in front yards, past jacaranda trees, past memories we've shared together on these streets. The block we're on is where we learned to ride bikes together.

"Do you think your dad was right?" I ask.

"About what?"

"That this isn't goodbye." I gulp down hard. Why would I ask a question I don't want the answer to?

"I guess that's up to us." He doesn't look at me. His tone is flat.

"I don't want it to be goodbye. Do you?"

"You know I don't," he says. "But I'll be there. You'll be here. And even if we were together, it would still be impossible. We know that."

I want to remind him about Billy Haines and Jimmie Shields. But I know what he'll say. That's them, not us. And he would never do that to his dad. We don't talk much after that. We circle the neighborhood in silence. But there are three words I need to say to him when we reach his home again and it's time to say goodbye. "I love you."

"Bobby, please." He moves away from me. Just a few inches, but it feels like I've already lost him. "Don't make this harder than it already is."

"But we can find a way to—"

"No, we can't. I don't want to live with you like those men you met. I don't want to explain to my devastated father that his son is . . . is . . ."

I look down. "It's okay. You don't have to say it."

"You see, I can't even *say* it, and yet you think I can *live* it."

We stare at each other. "I'm kissing you goodbye right now," I whisper.

"Me too," he whispers back softly. I keep my eyes glued to him as he walks away. That's when the tears come. A few tears at first. And then, what feels like a river.

I'm alone, all alone. And the only thing I want is a way to make this gnawing pain inside me disappear. I wish I was the one leaving. It's easier than being left. Maybe the only way to get over this heartbreak is to make a new beginning, somewhere far, far away, where I can be a new person.

MOUD

2019

Tehran

Watching Peyman and his family feels like being in some kind of fun-house mirror of my dad's life, had he never left Iran. This is the beautiful, living wife he could've had. These are the perfect heterosexual teenagers he might've had. This is the extroverted, boisterous man he could've been. I sit on a corner of the couch, a spectator to this happy reunion of former best friends.

"Remember Behzad?" Peyman asks, and my dad nods. "He turned into a conservative asshole. Totally in bed with the regime."

"What happened to Morteza? The one who was always top of the class?" my dad asks.

"He married the daughter of a Russian oligarch and lives in Moscow."

They continue like this until Peyman has filled my dad in on where each of their classmates ended up. A guy named Manuchehr died in the war with Iraq, may he rest in peace. And a guy named Omid turned into one of the ayatollah's henchmen. "May he fuck right off," Peyman says defiantly. That's how Peyman speaks, with Persian swear words liberally thrown in, much to the delight of his wife and kids, who find him hilarious. The son is a freshman in college. The daughter is headed to college next year. Their ease with their dad makes me realize this is also a fun-house mirror version of me. This is the laughter and warmth *you* could offer your father, Moud.

When we've finished the homemade *kashkeh badem-joon* and used the lavash bread to scoop up every bite, I stand up and collect people's plates, stacking them atop one another. My father gives me a nod to acknowledge my good manners.

"Mahmoud *jan*, you're the guest here," Peyman says. "Put those dishes down."

"I'm happy to do it," I say. "There's no need for *tarof* between us." It must be the first time I've said anything other than hello, because they all erupt in laughter at my American accent, and I wish I could be invisible again.

"We're not mocking you," Peyman says. "It's adorable."

"I sent him to Persian school on Sundays for years," my dad says. "But it's hard when you don't hear a language all day. . . ."

"You didn't speak to him in Persian at home?" Peyman's wife asks.

"I did," my dad says. What he means is that he barely spoke to me at home at all. The few words exchanged

283

between us could never have been enough for me to master a native accent.

"Say something else," Peyman begs. "It's so rare to hear an authentic American Persian accent."

I smile, trying to play along. "These dishes won't clean themselves," I say in Persian. They all laugh.

Peyman leaps up. He throws his arm around me warmly. "Come on, I'll lead you to the kitchen."

As we walk to the kitchen, I hear the son ask my dad questions about America. The questions make it clear he dreams of transferring to a college in the United States.

"Sink is there," Peyman says, pointing to a big sink facing two windows inches from each other. "Just put the dishes inside and I'll clean everything later."

I place the dishes in the sink, briefly entranced by the pomegranate trees outside. Each window offers a view of a pomegranate tree, like two perfectly framed paintings. "We have pomegranate trees in Los Angeles too," I say. "Maybe that's why so many Iranians moved there."

"No," Peyman says. "It's because Iranians are obsessed with status and celebrity. There's a word I love for it in English. What is it? When you just want to sleep with celebrities?"

"Starfuckers," I say quietly, afraid of my dad hearing me.

Peyman claps his hands together. "Yes. You see, people say the Persian language is so poetic because we have words no other language does. And it's partially true, of course. What other language has two words for fart? Only Iranians would make sure nobody ever mixes up a loud, dry fart with a silent, wet one."

I laugh. "Actually, we've got two words in English too. A *gooz* is a fart. And a *chos* is a shart." This is the relationship you could've had with your father had you both loosened up.

"Stop right now and teach me this new word. Shart, you say?" He laughs.

"Yeah, you know, like . . . shit and fart together. Shart."

He slaps my shoulder like we're old friends. "Never let anyone say the English language doesn't have its own poetry." This is the relationship you could've had with your father if you both weren't grieving for so long. "If Iranians and Americans could stop talking about nuclear enrichment and sanctions long enough to realize they both have two words for farts, maybe there could finally be peace. That's a special thing. Tell me, Mahmoud, do the French have two words for the gas that passes through us? The Russians? The Chinese?"

"I . . . I don't know, maybe . . ." I run the water and pick up a sponge. Put a little detergent on it.

He's still laughing as he reminds me that I'm not doing the dishes.

"I like cleaning, really," I say. I cleaned a lot in our house, because my mom was gone. I don't say that, but I sense that he knows it.

"Fine, then I'll dry." He grabs a dish towel, and I hand him the first plate.

"Teamwork makes the dream work," I say in English.

"You see, one more thing America and Iran have in

common. You have a cliché for every occasion. We have a poem for every occasion."

"Please tell me you don't know five poems by heart," I say, thinking of Siamak's rules for being a good Iranian.

"Five?" he asks. "What kind of person can recite only five poems?"

I laugh as I hand him another dish. He dries as he recites, "'*Be grateful for whoever comes, because each has been sent as a guide from beyond.*'" He eyes me with a nod, then adds, "In case you missed it, that's me using Rumi to let you know I'm happy you and your father are here."

"Me too." I'm surprised by the emotion in my voice.

"I realize you're here for sad reasons. Your baba . . ."

"Yes." I keep my eyes glued to the dishes.

"And I was sorry to hear about your mother. I never met her, but—"

"Thank you." I hand him another dish. "I didn't meet her either. I mean, I did. But . . . I was four. I have no memory of her."

"Of course you do," he says. "You just don't know it. Not every memory is accessible to the conscious."

I hand him the last dish. I say nothing. Maybe he's right. Maybe she exists in my subconscious somehow. Maybe she shaped me more than I know.

"I spoke to her on the telephone a few times." Peyman dries the last dish. "After she died . . . That's when your father stopped calling me as often. Grief made him pull away. And then time sped up. And here we are."

He puts the last dish on the rack. We stand side by side

with no purpose anymore. No dishes to clean. And yet, I'm not ready to go back into the living room, because I need to ask this man one question. "Do you know who my father is looking for?" He doesn't answer. I look at him, my gaze sharp and perhaps a little desperate. "Please tell me. I know he couldn't find her, but he won't tell me who she is."

He pauses briefly, then gives in. "I tried to help him locate her, but I failed. I don't believe she lives in Iran. Probably somewhere in Europe. Maybe she lives in Los Angeles. Wouldn't that be something, Shirin and your father living in the same city all these years?" He's lost in some distant memory. He and my dad are kids again.

"So her name is Shirin?" I ask.

He nods. "Shirin Mahmoudieh."

My heart skips a beat. Her last name. Mahmoudieh. My first name. Mahmoud. Was I named for a woman I've never heard of? "He loved her?" I ask.

"What has your father told you?"

I look away from him. "Nothing," I whisper.

"Why don't you ask him?" Peyman suggests. "If he hasn't told you anything, it's probably because he wants to honor your mother."

As Peyman puts an arm around me and leads me back to the living room, my mind reels. Peyman may not have told me much about who Shirin was and is, but he confirmed something. If telling me about her risks dishonoring my mom, then it means my dad did love her. In the living room, my dad answers politely as Peyman's kids shoot questions about America at him. Staring at my stoic father, I realize I've never seen him in love.

"Mahmoud *jan*, my children have a proposition for you," Peyman's wife says.

The college kid launches into an idea. "When you and your dad go back to Hollywood, we want you to create a television show."

"Okay," I say as I sit. "You do realize my dad's an aerospace engineer and I'm in high school."

"It's Hollywood. Anything can happen."

The daughter takes over pitching duties. "So it's a reality show called *Tehrangeles Swap*. At the beginning of the season, a group of people in Tehran swap places with a group of people in Los Angeles. And throughout the season, you track them to see what they learn, what silly trouble they get into."

"You need a prize," Peyman suggests. "Americans love a prize."

"Maybe at the end, if a pair of people agree to stay swapped, they each get a million dollars to start their new life."

I laugh. "I mean, I can totally see it."

My dad shakes his head. "Except for the fact that a television network in the United States isn't allowed to send a cent to Iran, let alone a million."

Peyman slaps my dad's shoulder hard. "Stop killing my children's dreams, Saeed." Peyman laughs. Everyone laughs except my dad. What's he thinking? What's going on in his mysterious head?

* * *

On the car ride back home, my dad anxiously turns the radio dial from one station to another. Every time he does land on a station, it's a news reporter reading out propaganda. Crackle, propaganda, crackle, propaganda. Finally, he lands on music. A baritone voice singing a song I think I recognize. I think about how women aren't allowed to sing publicly here. How can a country that raises women as fierce as Ava not allow them to use their voices freely?

My dad sings along to the song, using the music to avoid talking to me. But I have to talk to him. "Dad," I say.

He just gives me a "hmm," then goes back to singing.

"I liked meeting your friend," I say. "He's really cool."

"He always made me laugh when we were young." There's a genuine smile on his face.

I take this an opening to say more. "You know that if you ever loved someone other than Mom, it wouldn't . . ." I hear my voice shake. "What I mean is that it wouldn't hurt me, or make me think less of you, or . . ." We reach Baba's neighborhood. Out on the streets, a group of young men flex their muscles and smile for a selfie. "I mean, what I'm saying is that I want you to have love in your life, just like I want you to want me to . . ." Stop, Moud. This isn't about you. "What I mean is that I know about Shirin, and—"

"Mahmoud, the reason I didn't tell you about Shirin is not because I'm ashamed of having loved someone before your mother. Your mother knew all about Shirin. There were no secrets between us. And I need you to under-stand that what I felt for Shirin was youthful infatuation. That's a kind of love, of course. But the love I shared with your mother, it was different. Deeper. Grounded in respect." He pauses, but I don't say a word. I want him to keep talking, to tell me everything. "Your mother was so wise. Much smarter than me. When we first met, she told me that love too easily given can just as easily be taken away." He sighs. "The love your mother and I shared wasn't easily given. It was earned over many years, and it only grew stronger over time."

"I'm sorry," I say.

"You have nothing to be sorry for." He places a hand on my knee and squeezes it quickly before placing it back on the steering wheel.

"No, it's just . . . I mean, I lost my mom, but I never knew her. You lost the person you shared your life with. And I'm sorry."

"Me too," he says sadly. "But I didn't share my life just with her. I also shared it with you."

I can't help but smile at the bittersweet truth in his words. "Was I named after Shirin?" I ask. "Her last name is Mahmoudieh."

My dad smiles. "You were named after your mother's grandfather. But your mother knew Shirin's last name, and she appreciated that your name honored my own past as well as hers."

I nod. "Is that why you won't call me Moud? Because it would wipe her away?"

He thinks for a moment before saying, "I don't know. Maybe." With a sly smile, he adds, "Or maybe it's simply because Moud is a ridiculous name."

I laugh. "So why didn't you ever tell me about her if Mom knew?"

"The reason I haven't told you about Shirin is that . . ." He turns onto Baba's street. "To tell you about her would be complicated. Explaining why I stopped pursuing Shirin . . ." He trails off as he pulls into Baba's driveway.

"Dad, tell me, please. I know you don't have the strongest emotional immune system, but—"

"The strongest what?" he asks, laughing as he puts the car in park and turns the engine off.

"It's just a term Shane taught me."

"Well, it's absurd," my dad says. "We don't have an emotional immune system."

"I know, it's just that I want to know everything about you."

We sit in silence for a few breaths. No radio to distract us from the discomfort of the moment. "There is something your grandfather has been wanting to talk to you about for a long time. And when he does tell you, he will probably tell you that I was the one who discouraged him. Which is true."

"Discouraged him from telling me what?" I ask.

"It just didn't make sense. At first, you were too young to understand. And then when you told me that you were, you know . . ." He strains to say it, but finally says, "Gay."

"Uh-huh." I'm so confused by where this is going. I was trying *not* to make this about me, but it's somehow become about me.

"I suppose when you told me you were gay, I didn't want him encouraging you or confusing you. Certainly not over the telephone. It felt like something you should talk about in person, and it will happen on this trip because your baba, well . . . I think he blames me for not talking to you before Maman died."

"Talking to me about what?" I ask.

My dad opens the car door. "Your baba blames me for a lot." He looks away from me. "I think you do too."

"No," I say, but we both know that's a lie. Of course I blame him. He's my only parent. Who else am I supposed to blame?

"Just know that I blame myself too. For so many things." He still won't look at me. "Maybe if your mother had lived . . . She brought out the best in me. But when she left me all alone with you . . . I wasn't equipped to be a single father. I didn't know what to do. I was so angry. At myself for all my mistakes. And at my parents. Had it not been for them, I would've had a different life."

I get out of the car and stand next to him. I don't know what he's saying, but there are things I do know. That we both blame our parents for the hurt we've felt in our life, because who else is there to blame but the people who chose to bring you into the world, and failed to change the world into the perfect place we all wish it could be?

"I always thought the best thing I could do for you as

a father was protect you from pain," he says.

I nod, because he did do that.

"Maybe I was wrong." He finally looks at me. "Your mother would have been so different. She was so open. Curiosity was her constant state."

"Yeah?" I want to know more, but I'm afraid of ruining this fragile moment.

"It will probably hurt you to learn all the things you didn't know. And I know it will hurt you deeply to lose your baba. But if I've learned anything in this life, it's that I always had an inner strength inside me. The first time I felt pain, true pain, was leaving Iran. Losing my country, my parents, and yes, Shirin. But the pain was nothing compared to what happened next."

"What happened next?" I ask.

"I met your mother. I discovered a deeper love than I had ever known. And I realized I had it in me to be one of the survivors rather than one of the ones who is knocked down. Your baba is the same. He's survived almost a hundred years in a world that was often cruel to him. I think you're a survivor too."

When we head inside, my dad leads me to Baba's study. We don't interrupt Baba as he plays his tar. But when he finishes, he looks up at us.

"Baba, it's time to talk to Moud," Dad says. With a heavy nod, he adds, "About . . . everything."

Baba takes a moment before he wheels himself closer and smiles. "I've been waiting a long time to hear you say that."

Baba has Hassan Agha lay out some tea and sweets in the kitchen for us, and then gives him the rest of the day off to go be with his son. Now we're all alone in the house. Three generations of Jafarzadeh men.

Baba takes his first sip of tea. "Before I die . . . ," he says.

"Baba, please don't talk like that," I beg.

"I'm not scared of death," he says. "Perhaps that's because I've lived. Really lived. And I want you to know about my life. My whole story. Ever since you told me you were gay too—"

"I'm sorry, what?" I blurt out.

Baba laughs. "That was an awkward way to tell you I'm gay, wasn't it? But I had to do it somehow."

I don't say a word. How can I when my jaw is still open from the shock?

"I'm sorry," Baba says. "Let me start at the beginning, if it won't bore your father."

My dad shakes his head. "You're many things, Baba. But boring isn't one of them."

So Baba tells me the whole story about how he once lived in Los Angeles, where he loved a tennis player and almost became a movie star thanks to his stage mother, Margaret, who my dad went to live with during his college years but who died before I was born.

"What was she like?" I ask. "My great-grandmother?"

"Intense," Baba says.

My dad laughs. "Very intense."

With a smile, Baba says, "But she was my mother, and we made peace by the end of her life. I was happy about that." Baba seems to anticipate all my questions. When he tells me that Maman was also gay, he quickly adds, "But I did love her. I shared my life with my best friend. We were a team."

But when Baba reaches the part about my dad giving Shirin up to protect him and Maman, I have to stop him. I turn to my father. "Dad, I don't understand. You never looked for Shirin because . . ."

My dad finishes the sentence. "Because Shirin's father found out about Baba and Maman and threatened to expose them if I ever spoke to his daughter again."

My jaw drops again. My dad gave up a woman he loved to protect his parents.

"That's also how I found out about Baba and Maman," my dad says.

"So if it weren't for that," I whisper, "you might have married a different woman, had a different kid. . . ."

"You can't think like that," Baba says. "History is a quilt. You pull one thread and everything changes. I'm here. Your father is here. You're here. We can't change that. But we can be honest with each other."

It's all so unbelievable, but at the same time it answers so many questions I've always had. It's like my life has always been an untouched coloring book, and finally, someone is coloring it all in for me.

When the facts are out, I realize how late it is. We've talked for hours. "Do you have any more questions?" my dad asks.

I think about it. "I guess, just . . . why didn't you tell

me sooner? Like, when I came out? Or, I don't know . . .
just sooner."

"I wanted to," Baba says. "But your father didn't want
me to, and you're his son. I had to honor his wishes."

I turn to my dad, my eyes pleading to know why he
waited so long to tell me the truth about my history.

"I don't know," my dad says regretfully. "I suppose I
felt . . . I felt that the moment you and your grandfather
spoke, there would be no chance that you might change."

"Change? Like, become straight?" I ask.

"I don't know." My dad sounds embarrassed. "It's not
rational. I know this isn't a phase. I understand. But I didn't
want you to have a hard life. I wanted you to be happy."

"But Dad, what I need to be happy, truly happy, is
your love." I feel my voice crack.

My phone rings. It's Shane. I silence it quickly. I don't
want to talk to him. I can only imagine his response if I
told him all this. He would think it's the ultimate tragedy,
a man and a woman pretending to be straight in a bigoted
country. And yet, there's so much more to the story.

"Baba, is Dad right? Were you unhappy?" I ask, thinking of Shane. "I mean, do you wish you could've been
with a man instead of with Maman?"

My dad shifts uncomfortably in his chair. He hates
this. All this truth. And all this gayness. I understand
something in this moment. My dad wasn't just struggling
to accept me coming out to him. He was struggling to
accept his parents being gay. And he blamed their sexuality for costing him his first love. Maybe all this time, it

wasn't about me. Or yeah, it was about me, but in ways I didn't fully understand.

Baba looks at me earnestly as he thinks of how to answer the question. "When I was your age, I dreamed of a world where I could live with a man. Not just any man. Vicente. We were boys then, and I wanted to grow into men together. But it couldn't happen. For so many reasons. The life he wanted, the career he wanted . . . it was impossible for him, for us, back then. But regret is no feeling for a happy man. And I am a happy man. I'm proud of the life I lived. If I regret not being able to make a life with him . . . If I ask to go back in time and change the world . . . then you wouldn't be here, Moud. And you wouldn't be here, Saeed."

My dad looks down. He looks like a little kid. Small and unsure of himself.

"When I think about what I've done here, what your maman and I did . . . I know that in the eyes of the West, I lived a hidden life. But that's not what it felt like. We have a real community here, and I've been able to help so many young people in meaningful ways."

"Does Ava know?" I ask.

Baba nods. "She does, and I'm quite impressed that she didn't tell you. She seems like a gossip, but deep down, she's a good girl. And many of her friends . . . well, many of them have been my students, and have sought guidance on how to accept themselves." I remember Siamak and Ava sharing a glance when Baba's name came up, and now I understand why. Baba probably helped Siamak.

"Her parents?" I ask.

Baba laughs. "Those idiots, absolutely not. They don't deserve to know a thing about my private life. I've had to learn who to trust here, and who not to trust. Ava's parents might speak out against the regime, but deep down, they're bitter and mean. They would bring me down just to take this land from me."

"I'm sorry," I say. "I mean, I know you're happy and I think I understand why—"

"Because I lived a life of purpose."

"But to live your whole life thinking your own family could destroy you—"

"And you think that doesn't happen in the West, where parents kick their children out of the home for being like us?"

"Yeah, I know." I glance at my dad, who may not have joined PFLAG, but who always sat across from me at the dinner table. "I'm lucky I didn't have that kind of dad."

"You deserved a better dad than you got, though." I've never heard my dad sound so emotional. "If your mother had lived, maybe I could have been a better man." A tear falls from his eye. "But she didn't. And when you told me you were gay, it wasn't her compassion I felt. It was the fear and the shame. The best of me died with your mother."

I wait for Baba to console my dad, to tell him he is a good man. But he lets my dad travel through his own remembrance of my mother.

"There's still plenty of time for you both," Baba finally says with a nod. "And I'm starving, so one of you is going to have to be my sous-chef, since I gave Hassan Agha the day off." Baba turns his wheelchair and heads to the fridge. He surveys what's in there. "There's no time to make a *khoresht*, but maybe we can do something different tonight. Have you ever had spaghetti *tahdig*, Moud?"

"No," I say.

"It was the only dish your maman would cook. She left the cooking to me, but when I was too busy, she would make spaghetti *tahdig*." He pulls some tomatoes from the fridge. "Come on, Saeed. Chop these up and throw them in a pot."

My dad dutifully takes the tomatoes. He washes them in cold water, then places them on a cutting board.

Baba points to a high cupboard. "Moud, there's spaghetti up there. Get it out, and don't overcook it. Very al dente. We soften it just a bit before we burn it."

Baba leads us through the steps of making the spaghetti, and we laugh about how Iranians say *eh-spaghetti* instead of spaghetti, and *eh-ski* instead of ski, and I'm suddenly reminded of my upcoming trip to Shemshak. Of kissing Siamak. And of how my grandfather and father have now been more honest with me than I'm being with Shane.

Shane calls again as I'm going to bed. I silence it again. He texts me. *You there?* I stare at the text. If I start to respond, he'll see those little three dots and know I'm here. And I want him to think I'm asleep. I don't want to talk to him. If I do, I'll have to tell him all this. And I don't want to hear his take on it. I don't want to hear any takes. I'm so sick of people who feel they have to have a take on other people's lives.

My phone in my hand, I go to Siamak's contact. I debate calling him instead, but that feels strange since we've never called each other. A text seems less invasive, but what do I say? I type out a text: *Excited for our eh-ski trip.* It feels dry, so I add one exclamation point. Then another. I remove the second exclamation point. Then I delete the whole text. Why am I texting him anyway? This guy I shouldn't have kissed.

I attach my phone to the charger and put it on airplane mode. Unreachable. I close my eyes. I try to imagine Baba at my age, showing up to work at MGM every day, in love with another boy. I feel so sad for him. I try to imagine my father mourning one lost love as he fell for my mom. Then I picture my mother, telling my dad that love easily given can be easily taken away. I can feel her presence. I may not have a memory of her, but she's with me. And I cry. I'm weeping because she left me too soon. She would have loved me. Accepted me. Fought for me. She would have taught my dad how to be a different person. Baba said a happy man can't have regrets. Well, maybe I'm not happy, because I'm full of them right now.

The next morning, I wake up to the magical sound of Baba playing the tar downstairs. The sound travels up to my room, filling me up with its beauty. I turn my phone on. There are more texts from Shane. *Babe, will you just let me know you're okay?* And, *Okay I'm officially worried.*

And, *I'm heading into class, but my phone's on vibrate.* And, *Please call me, things are really shitty here and I need to talk to my boyfriend.*

I have to call him. I have to tell him everything. About Baba, sure. But also about kissing Siamak. I can't ask for honesty from my family and not give the same to Shane.

"Thank God," he says when he picks up the phone. He's in his bedroom.

"I'm so sorry," I say. "I'm here. I'm fine."

"I was worried." He sighs. "But maybe I deserved the silent treatment for how stupid and offensive I was on the phone the other day. I've learned a lot in the last twenty-four hours."

I'm curious about what he's learned, but I need to confess first. "Shane, there's a lot I have to tell you about what's been going on here."

"Same." He sighs. "I really fucked up, Moud."

I stare at him on the screen. He looks defeated. Guilty. Holy shit, did he kiss someone else too? Or more?

"Did you listen to yesterday's live podcast?" he asks.

I flinch in surprise. I thought he was going to confess to cheating. "I can't listen here," I say.

"Oh, right. Well, probably for the best. It was a disaster. We were talking about Caitlyn Jenner and whether we should be down with her, you know."

"Okay . . ." I have no idea where this is going.

"And I was saying that while we should obviously support her transition, we don't have to support her politics. I mean, she voted for Mango Mussolini. She said he'd be good for women. Good for women? A man who grabs them by the—"

"I know what the fucking president said." I sit up. "Shane, what's this about?"

"So I was just saying that part of what's so important about being queer is finding your tribe and holding on to them tight. Because so many of us have straight families—"

I don't, as it turns out. But I don't interrupt him.

"Straight communities. Straight teachers and classmates. Blah, blah, blah. And I just kept saying that we have to have high standards for who's in our tribe."

"Uh-huh," I say.

"I'm well aware I'm not supposed to use the word 'tribe' anymore, but in the heat of the moment, I just kept saying it."

"Okay," I say. I still don't understand why any of this matters. My grandfather just came out to me. I kissed another guy. Why are we talking about his use of a word?

"And also, I guess I've used the word a lot in the past, always in the context of finding your queer tribe, but like, it's not our word. Obviously. I mean, if you're queer and Native, that's different. And if we're going deep into the root of the word, it comes from the Latin word *tribus*, which was used by ancient Romans and—"

"Shane, just apologize," I suggest. "You're an expert at communicating. You'll find the right way to say you're sorry."

"Well, I mean, yeah, I'll obviously apologize, but . . .

Well, so this guy, a queer Native guy with a very large TikTok following . . . I guess he listens to the podcast, very closely, as it turns out. And he made this TikTok where he spliced together bits of me using the word. And he lip syncs to it."

"Oh," I say, starting to understand that Shane's beloved internet has turned against him.

"And also, he included that time I said Gaga in the 'Paparazzi' video is my spirit animal, and that time I said I'd give anything to powwow with the Spears family and convince them to Hashtag Free Britney. . . ." I'm cringing now, realizing how badly he messed up. "And he hashtagged his TikTok compilation of me Peak White Gay, and well . . . it's viral."

"How viral?" I ask.

"Very, very viral."

I'm quiet for a moment. There's so much I could say. Shane has turned into the exact people he hates so much. But I don't want to knock him when he's already down.

"I think I'm going to stop doing the podcast," he finally says.

I say nothing.

"Do you think I should?" he asks.

"Shane, I don't know. I think you should do what feels right to you. I mean, Sonia's your podcast partner. What does she think?"

"She thinks we should take a break and think on it." The humility in his voice is so shocking. All that arrogance is gone. "But like, if we were a real podcast with a real company or advertisers or whatever, we'd definitely be toast. So maybe we should be toast."

"Maybe it's okay not to have an answer right now," I suggest to the guy who always has answers. I want to say that maybe this is an opportunity for him. Maybe if he stops spending his time talking so much, he can start listening more, start asking new questions.

"Anyway, I'm working on an apology, 'cause it makes me feel sick to think I offended a whole group of people, especially the people who my fucking ancestors displaced and stole from. And I have no place telling others what they should and shouldn't do, 'cause I'm no authority and I'm one of the people who . . . Well, you know what we did. I mean, we as in Americans, not we as in me and you. Because I understand the ways in which you are an American and the ways in which you're not now. And I guess, well . . . I want to apologize to you."

"Okay," I say, surprised that he's making this connection.

"I guess it took being publicly mocked to realize I can be a bit of a know-it-all, or a major know-it-all. And that last argument we had, it was, for lack of more poetic words, Peak White Gay."

I laugh. "I guess it was."

"So yeah, I'm sorry, and I want to learn, and I was thinking . . . what if I came to Iran before you come home?"

I'm so shocked I don't say anything.

"I know it's crazy, but I want to understand your culture and meet your grandfather and—"

"You need a visa," I say. I realize I don't want him here, not right now at least. Not when I've yet to tell him all my own secrets.

"I know. I looked it up. It usually takes ten days. If I apply now, I could get there before Christmas."

"You also need an invitation letter," I say. "It's complicated."

"I know that," he says. "Maybe it's a dumb idea. Maybe I won't get the visa in time. But I'll try, if you want me to." He takes a breath. "Do you want me to?"

I feel overwhelmed. I called to tell him about Baba, about Siamak, not to ponder whether he should come visit me here. Which would make this trip all about him, the American in Iran.

"It's just . . . I thought you didn't believe in visiting countries where gay rights were—"

"I know what I thought, and what I said, and how it came off. And what I'm saying is I was wrong."

This is so big for him. The guy who is always on the right side of things, accepting that he's been wrong. Perhaps coming closer to accepting, through his own mistakes, that no one out there can always be right.

"You can think about it," he says. "I mean, obviously I'd start the visa application and all that. But you can think about it, and if you don't want me there—"

"It's not that I don't want you here," I say. "It's just . . . complicated."

"I know. But listen, can I have your blessing to at least try to get the visa? If I fail, I won't come. If you tell me it's too much, I won't come. But can I try?"

I know him too well. He needs to escape his guilt, and the only way he knows how is to take action. I can't take that away from him right now. "Sure," I say.

He smiles. "Okay, enough about your asshole of a boyfriend. How are you?"

I freeze. I had every intention of telling him everything. But now, it just feels wrong. I can hear my dad heading down for breakfast. If I tell Shane I kissed another guy now, it'll be like kicking him when he's just been knocked down. It would be cruel. Maybe it can wait. If Baba and my dad waited seventeen years to tell me the truth about their history, then I can wait a day or two to tell Shane about my momentary mistake and about Baba.

"I'm good," I say, forcing a smile. "But it's time for breakfast here, so I have to go."

"Hey, thanks for putting up with me. And thanks for not breaking up with me 'cause of what I said."

I'm not sure which part of what he said he's referring to. The things he said to me, or the words he used without thinking. It doesn't matter, really. He's finally realized he's not always right, and that's enough for today. I still feel disconnected from him, though. I still need to tell him the truth about kissing Siamak, about Baba. But that's for another day.

* * *

The next few days in Tehran feel magical. I've never felt so close to my family. It's like we opened some kind of Pandora's box of memories, and now they come flooding out. Baba tells stories about Maman, and about Margaret. My dad tells stories about my mom, about how she would constantly tease him for being so quiet, so unable to access his emotions, how naive he was to believe that Khomeini would be good for women. I think about Shane when my dad tells this story, what he said about Caitlyn Jenner saying Trump would be good for women. Once again, the lines between Iran and America blur, just like the lines between then and now. Borders feel more fluid than ever.

My dad and Ava take me shopping for ski clothes, and Ava says she's going to drag me onto the slopes even if she has to carry me there herself. My dad buys me an old-school one-piece ski suit from Ava's friend who designs stuff from vintage clothes. It's actually three old ski suits patched together. The arms are white, the body of the suit is red, and the legs are green. The colors of the Iranian flag. I love it, not because I want to tumble down a ski slope representing Iran, but because the way these three suits have come together to create one piece feels like the perfect way to acknowledge what's been happening to my family. My grandfather, my dad, and I are slowly, finally, becoming one.

The day before our ski trip, I'm packing in my room when I hear the front door slam. "Baba!" Ava yells. "Moud! Baba!" Her voice is hoarse and desperate.

I rush out of my room and run into my dad in the

hallway. "What's happened?" I ask.

"I don't know," my dad says.

We descend the staircase together as Baba wheels himself to the front door.

"Ava *joon*, what happened?" Baba asked. "Is it your parents?"

"It's Siamak. They arrested him. He's in jail. And not just him, three other art students who model for him. One of the students' dads is in the Sepah, and he found some photos Siamak took of the boys to make his pieces."

"What kind of photos?" my dad asks.

"Siamak makes paintings inspired by old Persian miniatures," I say. "But he makes them . . . very gay."

My dad squints, probably wondering how I know this. But it's not the time to ask about that.

"A father had his own son and his son's friends arrested," Ava says with disdain. "Can you imagine?"

"Unfortunately, I can." Baba shakes his head. "This is going to be very difficult if the father is in the military. They'll show no mercy, but we'll find a way."

Ava's lips tremble as she speaks. "I don't know what to do. I'm freaking out."

The room spins around me. It's not just that I care about Siamak. And about the whole community I met at that party. It's that this could be me. It could be my grandfather.

"Maman had so many lawyer friends who could possibly help us," Baba says. "I can make some calls. We need to stay calm."

"How can I stay calm?" Ava says anxiously.

Baba wheels himself to Ava's side. He holds her hand. "Breathe, Ava *joon*. You know the authorities here usually just want money."

"How much money?" she asks.

"I don't know yet," Baba says. "Give me time. I'll contact some lawyers. See who's willing to help us."

"They usually leave us alone. Why now?" Ava's desperation fills the room.

"They do this when they're on the defensive," Baba explains. "Fuel prices are surging. People are angry. There's talk of more protests. What better way to distract people than with a little moral outrage?" He could literally be talking about America again.

Ava is taking deep breaths now. Her voice is calmer when she says, "Would you talk to his parents and his brother with me? They didn't even know he was gay, and I don't know how to tell them alone."

Baba nods. "Of course."

"Thank you, Baba," Ava says. "I don't know how I would cope without you. How any of us would."

Baba shrugs. "I'm no hero. The people who take to the streets to protest this disgusting regime, they're the heroes. They're the ones risking their lives. I just sit in my study and play the tar."

"You do so much more than that, and you know it," Ava says.

"The people protesting in the streets," my dad says. "I was one of them a long time ago. Protesting a different regime. And I regret it so much. Look at what the revolution did. We wanted more freedom, and we got this bullshit." My dad rarely swears, and hearing how angry he is about this injustice against queer people makes me feel like he has my back.

Baba nods solemnly. "Power corrupts. The Shah had people killed. Khomeini had people killed. The Russians killed my poor father in the 1940s. I had so little time with him, and they took him from me. The Americans kill people all over the world to maintain their hold on power. The only thing I understand is *people*. Individuals, not groups. That's how I've lived my life. Just being good to as many individual people as I can."

"Remember the protest in Jaleh Square?" my dad asks Baba.

"It was just before you left Iran," Baba says.

"I never told you this. . . ." My dad takes a breath. It appears we haven't run out of memories to share with each other. He tells us all about a boy named Bijan Golbahar who was shot in front of him. Dad tried to find him, but never could. And he still wonders if Bijan survived. He turns to me and says, "It was your mother who helped me work through my feelings about that day. I would see his face in my nightmares until Bahar helped me accept what happened."

Baba moves from Ava to his son. "Maybe we can find him now," he says.

"Now?" my dad asks. "It was over forty years ago."

"Forty years is nothing in Iran."

We stand by the front door, the four of us together. A family marked by tragedy and connected by love. We say nothing to each other until my phone rings. It's Shane. I silence it. I have to tell him he can't come to Iran. The truth is I don't want him here. It's too complicated. This trip is about my family, and he's not that.

"You can talk to your boyfriend," my dad says. "It's okay."

I flinch at my dad's use of the word *boyfriend*. It's the first time he's ever used that word to describe Shane. If only he knew that he was finally accepting my relationship just when it's at its rockiest precipice. I'm so filled with doubt about who I am that I'm not sure I can even be in a relationship anymore. I think I might need time to figure out who I want to be. But how do I tell Shane from thousands of miles away that I want to end things?

"Thanks, Dad," I say. "But I can call him back. I just want to be with you guys right now."

"I'm going to start making calls." Baba wheels toward his study.

"I'm coming with you," Ava says.

Baba and Ava disappear, and I face my dad. "I guess I'll go unpack," I say. "I'm obviously not going skiing."

"You want to play backgammon?" he asks.

"Now?"

He shrugs. "What else are we supposed to do?" He leads me to the living room and finds Baba's backgammon board. It's made of wood and leather. My dad sets up the pieces.

"I barely remember how to play. We haven't played since I was a kid."

"You'll see how quickly it'll come back to you." He hands me a set of dice, and a dice cup. "This is the set I learned on. Roll just one dice to see who goes first."

"Die," I correct him.

"Oh, I see." He smiles. "I'll teach you backgammon and you'll teach me how to speak English."

I laugh. *Die* is a word I'd rather not think of right now, because I've never felt closer to death. My grandfather's imminent death. Siamak in prison, probably fearing for his own life. And my mom, whose voice I don't remember, whose smile I have no memory of, but who is with us right now.

"Dad?" I roll the dice and move my pieces. "I think I might want to end things with Shane, but I'm not sure."

"Do you . . . love him?" my dad asks, taking a long pause before using the word *love*.

"I do," I say. "But I also think I need time to just . . . I don't know, be alone."

My dad picks up the dice for his turn. "I think the reason I didn't know the word is because dice come in pairs," he says, looking at me. "They're never alone."

SAEED

1978

Los Angeles

Baba's suitcase feels like a threat. I've been ignoring his calls since finding out who he really is, since giving up the love of my life for him and Maman. And now he's here to force me into a confrontation. I tiptoe past the living room, where Baba sits on the chair and Margaret sits on the couch. They're both silent, until Baba says, "We hear you, Saeed. We know you're home."

I enter the living room. I'm so nervous that I'm sweating through my shirt. My mind is flooded with the awful things I saw Luis doing in that bar bathroom, the same thing my father has probably done. "Baba?"

Baba stands up. "You think you can just ignore your parents," he says sternly. "Your poor mother has been devastated that you won't speak to her."

"I'm sorry," I whisper.

"She would be here too, but she's afraid of planes. I've brought along a letter from her." He fishes an envelope out of his inside jacket pocket and hands it to me. "It explains her side of a story that I assume you know. I can't think of another reason why you would avoid us."

"I don't want to talk about it," I plead.

"I'd like to explain my side in person," he says. "Perhaps tonight. Perhaps tomorrow. I can stay as long as it takes for you to understand."

"I'll never understand," I manage to say.

"Time has a way of helping us adjust to new ideas. You look a little tired. Let's all go to sleep, and talk when we're well rested."

Margaret stands up. "Great idea. It's all been too much for me. Seeing my son for the first time in forty years. Hardly recognizing him when I opened the door."

"Stop being dramatic, Mother," he says, and I flinch at him calling her Mother. "You recognized me."

"Hardly," she says.

Baba shakes his head. Seeing them together is like my first glimpse of what he must've been like as a teenager. "Don't make this about you, Mother," he snaps.

"Why would I do that?" she asks. "It's not like I'm the one who was deserted by her own son. Not like I'm the one who took in the grandson she never knew—and saved his life."

"We thanked you profusely," Baba says. "You repaid us by telling Saeed what we asked you not to."

"There you go again, always assuming the worst about me," Margaret says. "I didn't tell Saeed a thing. Your secret has always been safe with me."

"You were always good with secrets," Baba says softly, obviously referring to something else.

"I didn't tell you who your father was to protect you," she whispers. "All my life, I tried to protect you. I could've told the whole world you were gay. Could've ruined your precious life at any point. Could've ruined your little boyfriend's tennis career. But I never did. Because I've always been more of a mother than you've ever given me credit for. I even loved the dog you deserted until he took his last breath."

"That's not fair," Baba argues. "I wanted to take Frisco, but I couldn't."

"You were more distraught over leaving that dog than leaving your own mother."

"We're not talking about the past," Baba says firmly. "That's over. What you did. What I did. It's almost forty years ago."

"It still feels like right now to me," Margaret says.

I feel invisible, a spectator to a scene that was first performed long before I was born.

"If Margaret didn't tell you about me and your mother, then who did?" he asks me in Persian. "How did you find out?"

I hate this. I don't want to say Shirin's name out loud again. It just reminds me of what I've lost. But how else can I explain? "Remember Shirin, the girl I wanted to propose to?"

"Of course," Baba says. "I did everything I could to

get in touch with her, but her father—"

"Her father," I say with venom. "Exactly."

"He wouldn't let me talk to her, but he did take your phone number," Baba says. "But what does she have to do with—"

"Her father called me here. He told me about you. And Maman. He said if I ever contact his daughter again, he'll tell the authorities about you."

Baba is silent for a few breaths. "Did you . . ."

"What?" I ask.

"Try to find a way to talk to her?"

"No," I say quietly. "I'll never contact her again."

Baba nods. "Thank you, son."

He reaches his arms out to hug me, but I pull away. "I'm going to sleep now," I say.

"I can come read you a poem before bed like we—"

"I've stopped with that crap," I say in English. "I'm not the same person I used to be."

I hear Margaret as I head to my room. "You see?" she spits out. "Didn't I tell you that living a life of secrets would catch up with you someday? You chose this. For once, you can't blame me."

"I don't blame you, Mother," Baba says, dejected. "Just myself."

I stop outside my bedroom. Lean my head against the hallway wall. I want to shut them out, and I also want to hear everything they say to each other.

"You know, Mother," Baba says. "I don't need you anymore. I have enough love in my life now. And yet, being here again, it makes me realize that . . . Well, I still want your love."

There's a moment of silence. And then the television is turned on. "Sit down," she says as she turns the volume up. Classical music streams out. I recognize the piece. Baba loves it. Tchaikovsky's Violin Concerto in D Major. I let the strings sweep over me.

"Joan Crawford," Baba murmurs.

"*Humoresque*," Margaret says. "She made this years after you left. You quit, but she kept going."

"I never quit," he says. "I still play every day."

"You wasted your gift," she says. "Teaching isn't for people with your talent. You should've been one of the greats."

"Teaching is the greatest gift," Baba says calmly. "It's how we pass down what we've learned to future generations."

"You could've been immortal," she says. "Like her."

"She was unhappy and beat her child," Baba says.

"You're unhappy and lied to your child," Margaret replies.

"Then I take after you, I guess."

At that, Margaret cackles. "Touché," she says with a laugh.

They sit in silence. The concerto ends and Joan's voice travels through the house. I tiptoe back to the living room and there they are. A mother and a son, scooting just a little bit closer to each other on the couch, enraptured by the same images, the same sounds, the same fantasy.

* * *

I don't remember falling asleep. The last thing I remember is the sound of more classical music and Joan Crawford's deep, melodramatic voice lulling me to sleep as I stared at the ceiling.

"Good morning." Baba holds a cup of hot tea. "Just like I make it at home."

I sit up and take the teacup. He does make the best tea. And the best food. I wish I could tell him how much I miss his cooking. I haven't tasted anything that good since I arrived in America.

"I thought I could take you on a tour today," he says gently.

"I'm not a tourist," I say. "I live here."

He nods. "A tour of my past." He releases a deep sigh. "Parvaneh and I discussed telling you the truth many times, you know. When you were young, it just seemed too soon. Too much for you to comprehend. And children can't keep secrets, certainly not you. You would tell the other kids at school when you wet the bed."

"I never wet my bed," I say.

"Of course you did." Baba puts a hand on my arm and squeezes it. "You know there are things about you that only your maman and I know. What you were like as a baby. How we taught you to be an adventurous eater by blending different *khoreshts* into baby food. You know what your first word was?"

I shake my head.

"Baba," he says, smiling sadly.

318

The tea is starting to wake me up. It's just sweet enough, just strong enough, just hot enough, and yet it's still not enough to melt away my resentment.

"When I went to Iran, it was to meet my father for the first time. Your grandfather. I didn't think I would stay forever. But what I found when I arrived was, well . . . a revelation. A country full of people who looked like me." A country I wish I could return to. "But it wasn't just the country I fell in love with, and I did, as you know. The poetry. The music. The community. I love it all. But above all, it was my father. He let me in. In a few weeks, I felt closer to him than I ever felt to my mother." He shakes his head. "It's a horrible thing to say, but it's true. I've learned that there are people who let you in and people who shut you out. My mother was someone who shut me out. Maybe she and I will get a second chance now. But my father . . . he let me in immediately. He told me how he felt. He showed me who he was. And that helped me figure out who I could be. Who I wanted to be."

"A liar?" I ask, my words like a blade.

Baba doesn't flinch. He accepts my anger calmly. "I want to let you in now. I've tried to be a good father to you. To love you and support you. But you're right to be angry. I wasn't honest with you. It's time now."

"What if I don't want that?" I ask sadly.

He sighs. "Are you angry because I lied to you, or because you think I'm disgusting?"

I look at him with confusion. "I don't know, Baba. Both, I think."

He accepts my answer with a nod. "Take a shower and change your clothes," he suggests. "I've rented a car."

I don't say yes. I don't say no. But I take a shower and get dressed. Because there's no turning back now.

Baba takes me to the house he grew up in. It's in Hollywood. It's still there, small and unkept. We knock on the door, but no one answers. He tells me about his schedule, the constant training Margaret put him through. He tells me about his stepfather, Willie. How they would all perform together in nightclubs when he was a teenager. We wait a half hour for someone to come home and let us into his old house, but no one does, so we keep moving. He drives me to where he took piano lessons (still there), where he took voice lessons (a restaurant now), and where he took violin lessons (a parking lot now). He takes me to what used to be Louis B. Mayer's kingdom, where dreams were made, where stars roamed the backlots.

"History is a strange thing," Baba says as we drive away from the once imposing lot. "We think certain monuments are indestructible. I thought MGM was like the White House. That it would reign forever. But look at it. Fires destroyed some of the sets. Others were demolished. The grandeur is gone. Nothing physical is indestructible. The only thing you can't destroy is love."

"It turns out you *can* destroy it," I say, thinking of Shirin.

Baba looks at me. "I know how hard heartbreak is.

I've been through it. There was a boy. His name was—"

"Please," I beg. "I don't want to hear about you and your boys."

"Not boys," he says. "One boy."

"What about in Iran? What about all the boys you teach?" I immediately want to take it back. I know it's a horrible and untrue accusation as soon as I fling it at him.

"*Aziz joon*," he says quietly. "I would never touch one of my students."

"I'm sorry, Baba. I know that. It was an unfair accusation."

"No, it's all right. If you don't speak your fears out loud to me for fear of offending me, then I won't be able to tell you they're false. My students . . . Some of them are homosexual."

I tap my leg nervously.

"We're a small but tight-knit community in Tehran. Many of us know each other. And when a young person feels lost, we help them. Some of my students came to me less for musical instruction than for, well, support and acceptance. I had someone like that. Here in Los Angeles. His name was Zip Lamb."

I look at him like that's the most absurd name I've ever heard.

"It wasn't his real name," he says, reading my thoughts. "He changed his name when he became an entertainer. Also because he was arrested. Like I was."

"You were arrested?" I blurt out in shock.

"So many of us were then. So many of us still are now.

Maybe that's something you can empathize with, since you had to escape a country you're not safe in. Being targeted by the police . . . it's something we have in common."

"But . . ."

"But what?" he asks. "You think I deserved to be arrested, don't you?" I hate how he always knows what I'm thinking. I can't hide anything from him.

I don't answer his question.

"His name was Vicente," he says.

"Who?" I ask.

"The boy I loved," Baba says, and I cringe at his use of the word. "I won't tell you his last name because he has a successful career, a wife, children."

"So he lies to them just like you did," I say.

"We don't know that," Baba says. "Perhaps he's bisexual. Perhaps his family knows everything, even if the world doesn't."

"Does he live here?" I ask.

"No," Baba says, "but we're about to pull up to his old home, which hopefully hasn't been torn down." Baba turns a corner and slows the car down. He doesn't say anything for a long time. He gets out of the car and knocks on the door of a small home. A woman opens the door. Baba exchanges a few words with her, and then waves for me to join him. He locks the car and we enter the house. The woman tells us she's lived in it for ten years now. Baba marvels at how little it's changed. The light fixtures. The floors. All the same. When he reaches an office, a small sob escapes his lips, almost by mistake. "This was his bedroom back then," Baba says, his eyes wet. He crouches down and runs his fingers along the decorative floorboard. I have to squint to see what he's touching. Initials carved in the floorboard. *VM* and *BR*.

"This meant a lot to me," Baba says to the woman with startling sincerity.

"My pleasure," she says. "I've always wondered about the history of this place."

And then we thank the woman and leave.

"So his last name begins with an *M*," I say when he starts to drive. I'm remembering finding out that Shirin's last name starts with an *M*. Trying to playfully guess her name so I could find her again. I wish I could go back to that moment. All mystery. All possibility.

"Yes," he says. "It does. But please don't go asking questions about him. He deserves his privacy. We all do."

"I already know more than I want to," I say.

He ignores my snideness. "There's one last place I'd like to take you to." He stops at a flower shop and runs inside while I wait in the car. He comes back with a dozen green carnations in his hand.

"A peace offering for Margaret?" I ask, shocked.

"No," he says. "Although come to think of it, that's not a bad idea. We'll get her some flowers on the way back from the cemetery."

"The cemetery?" I repeat quietly.

He drives us to the Hollywood Forever Cemetery, and I'm shocked to find it's full of tourists taking photos of themselves in front of graves. Rudolph Valentino. Jayne Mansfield. Tyrone Power. It feels so wrong, people swarming a place of grief like this. Smiling as they point at someone's grave.

"Here he is," Baba says when we reach a small tombstone. He places the green carnations next to the name: *Patrick Berry, 1901–1955.* "That was his real name. Zip Lamb."

"He died so young," I say quietly.

"We wrote each other letters for many years." Baba looks at the grave, then up to the sky, like he can't decide if Zip is down in the dirt or up in some afterlife. "He was fascinated with my stories about Iran. He always said he'd come visit, but he never did. And I thought someday I would come back here, but I never did."

"You're here now."

He looks at me tenderly. Places a hand on my cheek. "Yes, you're right. Too late for him, but not too late for you."

"How did he die?"

"He was arrested again," he says. "I think he was too ashamed to write to me about it. But he left me a letter, and one of his friends sent it to me."

"A letter?" I ask.

"A goodbye letter," he says sadly. "He took his own life. Swallowed pills. Which is especially heartbreaking, because he wouldn't touch liquor or pills of any kind."

"I'm sorry," I say, and I feel a sudden chill, thinking it could be my baba in that grave. "I may not agree with what you are, what he was, but . . . I don't want you to die."

He nods. "What a tragedy. Can you imagine the loneliness?"

I shake my head. I can't. I think of Shirin's mother, who also took her own life. I feel so grateful I've never known that much despair.

"I wish for a world where everyone can love who they want to love openly," Baba says. "But that's not the world we live in, is it? My mother and my father were torn apart by her parents. I couldn't love Vicente. And now you and Shirin."

I want to tell Baba that it's not the same. Shirin and I are a man and a woman. It's different. But I don't dare say it.

"I'm so grateful I found your mother," Baba says. "We love each other. Maybe not the way you thought we did." I think of their separate bedrooms. "But we're partners. We support each other. We brought you into the world, and you're an incredible young man. We're proud of you." I avoid his gaze. I don't want to feel his pride right now. Not when I'm still not sure if I'm proud of him. "All things considered, I've had a pretty good life."

"Stop talking like it's over," I say. "You're not even old yet."

"Let's go," he says. "We'll pick up flowers for your grandmother. She deserves our gratitude for taking you in."

We walk across the cemetery grounds, past more smiling tourists and a few genuine mourners crying at their

325

loved ones' graves. The contrast is startling and seems to sum up the contradictions of being human. We have the capacity for joy and grief, often in the same moment.

I hand Margaret her bouquet when we get home, but I tell her they were Baba's idea.

"They're lovely," she says as she puts them in water.

When Baba comes to wish me a good night, he tells me he'll be heading back to Tehran in two days. "I think, or at least I hope, that this visit means you'll be answering our calls again."

I nod. He's my father. She's my mother. I can't change that, and I don't want to make them suffer. But also, I don't want to hear more. I don't want to know about their open relationship, or his gay students, or the boy he loved when he was my age.

"Baba," I whisper. "I'll always be your son. I'll answer your calls. But I don't want to know more than I already do. I just . . . don't need to know every detail of your private lives."

He pauses, and I can hear the disappointment in his voice. "I understand." He gives me a kiss on the forehead. "You haven't been brushing your teeth enough," he says. "I can see them getting yellow. Teeth are so important. If you don't care for them, they rot like fruit."

"Okay, Baba," I say. "I promise I'll brush regularly."

I take a deep breath as he leaves the room. This is what we'll be from now on. A father and son who talk about teeth and weather. I'll tell him how my classes are going. He'll ask if I need money. We'll wish each other a happy birthday. And hopefully, that'll be enough, because it's all I can give.

The next day at school, I find Bahar on our lawn and tell her everything. I can't tell what she thinks of it all. She barely speaks, but when she does, it's to ask a short, probing question. Every time I try to tell her what happened, she asks how it made me feel. How it felt to find out my teenage father once loved a boy who is now a married man. How it felt to stand at the grave of a man who helped my father accept himself. And how it will feel to say goodbye to him.

"I don't know," I say. "I suppose in a way, it'll be a relief."

"But won't you miss him?" she asks.

I nod. "Of course I will. I just wish we could go back to what we used to be like. He would cook for us. We would play backgammon for hours. We would laugh."

"Maybe you'll get back there someday."

I look at her, unsure.

"Everything good takes time." She surprises me by taking my hand in hers. Her fingernails are bitten off, a small detail about her I've never noticed before. Wavy eyelashes. Chewed-up fingernails. And the softest skin.

"Like love," I whisper.

Her eyes glimmer. "Love?"

"Isn't that what you said? When we were at the piano bar . . ."

She laughs. "I'm sorry, sometimes I say things in the

moment and then I forget them. It's terrible."

"No, it's not," I say. "It just means you're living in the moment. Not holding on to the past. Not consumed by the future."

"I'm not so sure about that," she says.

"What you said is that love is time and trust," I say, reminding her.

"Oh, right, of course." She squeezes my hand. "I do believe that."

"And you said that love too easily given can be easily taken away."

"I believe that too." The smile she flashes me reminds me of Baba's advice about teeth. Hers gleam. "Tell me something, do you remember every piece of spontaneous wisdom I throw out there?"

I blush. "Have you ever been, you know, in love?"

She shakes her head. "My parents already think I'm an old maid. They have very old-fashioned values for two academics. They're already trying to set me up with Agha Faripour's son the medical student and Agha Asghari's son the personal trainer."

"The what?" I ask.

"He holds the weights as people exercise. He has very big muscles. You should see him. He could probably bench-press you."

"I'd rather not see him," I say, laughing. "And honestly, I'd rather you not see him either."

Now she blushes. "Not to worry, he's not my type. The only muscle I'm interested in is the brain."

"Bahar *joon*," I say seriously. "The brain isn't technically a muscle, it's an organ."

She laughs. "Thank you for proving you have a brain. Although I would guess Agha Faripour's son the medical student also knows that."

"How would your parents feel about an engineering student?" I ask, moving a little closer to her.

"What my parents think is beside the point." She raises her head up proudly. "I'll choose my partner in life when the time is right. But you should know I'm not interested in rushing into marriage and motherhood. I have my own ambitions, and my own plans for my life."

"I like that about you," I say. "You have a strong sense of self."

She laughs. "Most guys your age like big breasts and long legs. But you like a strong sense of self. You're a very serious person, you know that?"

"I do know that. And what I'm seriously saying . . . trying to say . . . is that . . . Well, if love takes time and trust, then I'd like to see if we can build up to that kind of love."

She squeezes my hand. "Does this mean you're not thinking about her anymore?"

I don't know how to answer that. The truth is that I'll always think of Shirin, as a happy memory, and also as a sad memory. But that's what she is, a memory. And I'm not going to let that stop me from living. "The truth is . . ." I stop. I want to say the right thing. "The love I had for her is exactly what you described. It came easily.

It was taken away easily. I want a different kind of love now."

She seems to accept that answer.

"I'd like to give you something." I pull the turquoise ring out of my pocket and present it to her.

"Saeed *jan*, please tell me you're not proposing when I just told you I'm not ready to be a wife."

"It was my mother's ring. And then I was going to use it to propose to her."

"You can say her name."

"Shirin."

We sit in silence for a moment, and I suddenly realize we're not alone. There are other students all around us. Other lives. But I feel so alive, so in this moment, that I hadn't even noticed them.

"So let me get this straight," she says, smiling. "You are *not* proposing to me with a ring you were going to use to *actually* propose to another woman."

"I . . . It sounds awful that way."

"I'm teasing you." She takes the ring from me. "Turquoise wards off evil."

"So I'm told."

"If I accept this ring, what does it mean?"

I take the ring back and place it tenderly on her index finger. "It means that you will carry a piece of me, and of my family, with you at all times. That would make me happy. Maybe it means that, at some future date when we've had enough time and trust, and when you're ready, I will propose for real. And hopefully, you will accept."

"I'll accept this ring on one condition. I'd like to meet your father before he leaves. I don't suspect I'll ever return to Iran, and I'd like to meet the man who might be my future father-in-law at some future date when we've built enough time and trust."

I nod. "Then you're coming over for dinner tomorrow night. I'll have him cook for you. He makes the best Persian food you've ever had in your life."

"My mother might disagree, but I'll be the judge of that."

I smile. "Bahar . . ." I feel a heaviness inside me. "Why do you say you won't return to Iran?"

"Why? You want to return? You just arrived."

"I came here to escape, but if the revolution succeeds . . . if there's a new regime . . . then it will be safe for me again. And maybe . . ."

"The things I want for my life, my ambitions, I just don't know if I'll be able to achieve them there."

"But if the revolution succeeds—"

"Then what? Khomeini *is* the revolution now. You think he's going to be a champion of women's rights?"

"I do," I say. "I really do. He'll listen to the people who put him in power. Women. Students."

"We'll agree to disagree on that." She shrugs. "Anyway, we can't predict the future. But what I know is that my future is here. I love being Iranian, but I want to be an Iranian here in America."

I feel a sense of amazement at how well she knows herself. She knows what love is without ever having been in love. She has the strength of will to dodge her parents trying to rush her into marriage. She knows who she is, who she wants to be, and where she belongs. I want that feeling. I want to learn from her, to experience life with someone as grounded as her by my side. Maybe going back to Iran is just a silly fantasy. Even if there is a new regime, and even if I wouldn't be arrested, my parents will always be there. And I'm not ready to live in their home again. I want to make my own life, build my own history.

"Do you have any favorite dishes?" I ask. "I want Baba to cook you the meal of your dreams."

She laughs. "The meal of my dreams, huh?" She stands up. "Come on, we'll both be late for class if we don't start walking." As she leads the way to what all the students call the awkward steps, she lists her favorite dishes. "*Tahchin* is number one," she says. "*Fesenjoon. Kookoo sabzi.* Do you know where the best Persian supermarket is?"

"No, but I'm sure you'll tell me."

She does tell me. She will be my guide to the best Persian supermarket, to making my way in this new country I don't belong in, and to being a better person. Maybe if she's by my side, I can change from a person who shuts people out to a person who lets people in.

BOBBY TO BABAK

1939

Los Angeles to Tehran

"Well, that took forever," Mother says when I get home from saying goodbye to Vicente. "Are they gone?"

I look up and find her stretching in the living room, Frisco licking her bare feet. "They're gone," I say. My voice sounds distant. Numb.

"Willie's picking up Chinese food from Golden Pagoda on his way home," she says. "I told him to make sure to get mushroom egg foo yong for you."

"Thanks." I give her as much of a smile as I can muster. Maybe she's not the parent I wish I had, but at least she remembers my favorite dish from Golden Pagoda. I take a breath. With Vicente and his family gone, I'm determined to find things to love about my own family. What other choice do I have?

"Pull my arms, will you?" she asks. "I can never get a deep stretch without you."

I dutifully take hold of her forearms and gently pull

her forward until she gives me a nice long *aah* and taps me to let me know it's enough. "I'll be in my room for a bit," I say. "Can I take Frisco with me?"

"Be my guest," she says. Then she rubs Frisco's head and adds, "Thanks for the pedicure, you little nut."

I hold Frisco as I enter my bedroom. I grab the journal Vicente gave me. I place Frisco on my lap and I stare at the blank pages. I want to write about how empty I feel with Vicente gone, but I have no energy, no motivation. I feel lifeless, and all I want is to feel alive again. And that's when I remember. There are still pep pills in my bathroom cabinet.

I leap off the bed and head toward the bathroom. I find the bottle in the cabinet. I put one in my mouth, then run the sink water. I lower my head into the sink, letting the cold water hit my tongue. I swallow sideways, the pill finding its way into my body. It works almost immediately. I feel a rush of energy. I suddenly have the confidence to put my feelings down on paper. I grab a pen and start to fill those blank pages. I put all my energy into writing about Vicente in my journal. I write about our love, and about my heartbreak.

By the time Willie gets home, I've filled almost the whole journal. I go to the kitchen, where Mother and Willie have laid all our favorite dishes on the table. Chicken Picon for her. Pineapple fried shrimp for him. Frisco sits at our feet, hoping one of us drops some food for him. I push the food around my plate. I put a bite into my mouth. It's the same meal I always love, but I have no appetite. I want to walk. To talk about Vicente. I need to find Zip. "I'm not hungry," I say. "I'm sorry."

Willie looks sad. "I went all the way downtown to pick up food from your favorite restaurant because your mom said today would be a hard day for you, and you don't even want it?"

"No, I do. And I really appreciate it. Can I have it tomorrow?" I'm stuck on the fact that Mother had him pick this up because she knew I'd be going through a hard time after saying goodbye to Vicente. Maybe she does know me, or care about me, even if she has no idea how to show it. Or maybe this is her way of showing it.

"I'll put it in the fridge for you," Willie says.

"Thanks. I'm going for a walk, if that's okay." When Mother gives me a nod, I go to the door and put my shoes on, and then I walk toward the Strip, toward Zip.

The Hollywood Rendezvous doorman knows me now. "Salome's pianist," he says with a smile.

"Hi, I'm here to see—"

"Zip, who isn't here."

"Oh right," I say. "He's at Bali on Saturday nights."

"Not this Saturday night," the doorman says. "Bali was shut down by our friends in the police department last night. On the downside, they're investigating Bali for allegations of homosexual conduct—"

"That's horrible," I say.

The doorman watches as a group of handsome young men, green carnations on their lapels, approach the door. He lets them in, no questions asked, probably because of how good they look. "On the bright side, Bali's closure—temporary, we hope—has led to an increase in customers for us. You can join them if you like. Now that you're an old friend."

I want to go find Zip. To tell him everything about Vicente's departure. But then the doorman opens the door for a young guy who looks a bit like Vicente. Dark hair, slicked back like Tyrone Power. Pants that hug his athletic legs. Long, elegant fingers. Tyrone looks back at me as he enters. His eyes sparkle. He looks close to my age. I'm entranced by how much he reminds me of Vicente. Maybe this is a sign. Maybe I'm meant to go inside. I hear the music that flows from within the doors. It beckons me in. "Well, sure, I'll go in for a bit, thank you."

I follow Tyrone inside and take it all in. There's a band playing the fastest version of "Dardanella" I ever heard. The speed of the song matches the speed of my heartbeat, racing with energy because of the pep pill. A dance floor is packed with joyful people, shaking their hips and laughing as they attempt to keep up with the beat. I want to join the festivities, to dance away this energy, but I need a bathroom first. I push my way through some boisterous tables of patrons toward the bathroom.

I'm about to lock the door when Tyrone pushes his way in behind me. "Oh, sorry," he says. "I didn't realize someone was in here."

"It's okay." I smile. He really does remind me of Vicente, and I want my love and my best friend back so badly. Where is he right now? Did he make his connection to Mexico City? Is he safe? Does he miss me?

"It's just that I really need to, you know, piss, but I can wait my turn."

"You can go first," I say. "I'll wait—"

Before I can say I'll wait outside and exit, he unzips his pants and starts to piss in the toilet. He watches me as he does, a smile on his face. I'm frozen and confused. Part of me wants to give him his privacy, but if I open the door now, I'll risk exposing him to the patrons standing outside. So I stand there like a fool, trying and failing to stare at anything but him.

"Your turn," he says when he's done. But he doesn't zip himself back up.

"I don't usually, well, you know . . ."

"We're both men. What's the big deal?"

I look into his gleaming eyes. I do need to go to the bathroom. And I do like his attention. I unzip in front of the toilet. I'm about to urinate when he smiles at me. I smile back. Then, suddenly, his face turns cold.

He pulls a badge out of his front pocket. "You're under arrest for lewd conduct."

"But I . . . I didn't . . . I didn't do anything . . . You're the one who . . ."

"Put your cock back in your pants and—"

"But I really do have to, you know, go to the bathroom. That's why I—" He stares at me so hard that I do what he says. I zip my pants back up. I feel fear. Shame. I thank God that Vicente and his family are gone, because now I can make sure he never finds out about this.

"Sure you did. We both know why you lured me in here."

"I didn't— You're the one who—"

Everything goes black when he cuffs my hands behind my back and I piss myself, my pants getting wet.

"Oh, come on, that's disgusting," I hear him scream, but I don't see anything. The world has gone dark. Hazy. The music never stops as I'm led out. No one even seems to notice that a guy who looks like Tyrone Power stands behind a kid who's covered in his own urine. He stands so close to me that they probably don't notice the handcuffs. Maybe they think he's taking me home for an illicit tryst. Maybe they think this is what new love looks like. I wish I was in my body so I could scream for help. But no one who feels the shame I do could ask for help. Because shame makes you want to disappear. That's all I want right now—to disappear into the darkness.

At the police station, I'm checked in by a group of officers who gleefully call me names. "Don't worry, swishie," one of them says. "Plenty more guys like you in jail."

Another officer makes a limp wrist as he lisps, "Maybe not as pretty as this little buttercup, though."

Only one officer treats me like a human. He pulls me aside and quietly says, "You should get a lenient sentence because you're a minor."

"Thanks," I manage to say.

"You know," he says as he fills out some paperwork,

"my church has incredible success ridding homosexuals of their impulses."

I say nothing. He's only being friendly because he wants to change me.

"You get one phone call," he says. "Are your mom and dad home?"

I want to laugh at the assumption that I have a mom and a dad. When the truth is that I have a Mother and a Willie. "My dad should be home," I say. "I'll call him."

He hands me the telephone and I'm grateful for my memory again. I remember Zip's number. *Please be home,* I pray silently. *Please be home, please, please, please—*

"Hello?" he says.

"Mr. Lamb," I whisper. "It's um, Bobby. Reeves. It's Bobby Reeves, you know, the—"

Zip laughs. "Bobby, I know who you are. Is everything okay?"

The cop looks at me, confused. "Your own dad doesn't know your name?" he asks.

I ignore the cop. "I'm, um . . ." I take a breath. I hate saying it, but I have no choice. "I'm at the Hollywood police station. I've been arrested for lewd conduct, but I swear I did nothing wrong and—"

Zip's voice takes on a sudden urgency. "Listen to me, kid. Even if you did something wrong, you did nothing wrong. Do you understand me?"

"I think so."

"I'll be right there."

He arrives in record time. They let him bail me out. I

hate that I've ruined his night. Cost him money. Probably reminded him of his own arrest, of the injustice that destroyed his teaching career.

As he leads me out into the street, a group of officers laugh at us. Tyrone is one of them.

"You should be ashamed of yourselves," Zip says.

Tyrone cackles. "*We* should be ashamed? We're not the fruits, sunflower."

"You love to call us fruits and flowers, don't you?" Zip smiles defiantly.

"Mr. Lamb, don't . . . They could . . ."

But Zip knows exactly what they could do. And he doesn't care anymore. "You know what fruits and flowers have in common? Their lives are short. They wilt. They rot. But when they're alive, there's nothing sweeter or more beautiful. That's a sweetness and a beauty none of you will ever know. Because your hearts are bitter and ugly."

Before Tyrone or his cronies can say another word, Zip leads me away. I can feel the adrenaline in his footsteps. In how fast he moves me far away from them. He needed to say that. He needed to fight back in some small way, even if he'll never win the battle or the war.

When we're far enough from the police station to relax, he stops walking and catches his breath. And I catch mine. "You okay?" he asks.

"No." What else is there to say?

"Kid, you smell terrible. What'd they do to you?"

I feel tears coming. "I pissed myself," I say. "I was in the bathroom with him."

"Him?"

"The police officer. The one who looks like Tyrone Power and also like Vicente, who's gone. He's gone. He's in Mexico by now. A whole border away from me, and I'm alone and I have a police record and I pissed all over myself."

"Oh, Bobby. I'm sorry." He hugs me for what feels like a second, or maybe an eternity. I don't know. But I'm so thankful for this kind man, who cares so much about me he'll hold me, even when I reek of my own urine.

When he lets go of me, I wipe the tears away. "Aren't you going to be angry with me?"

"Of course not," he says. "Don't think that I could ever—"

"But you warned me and I didn't listen. I'm an idiot. You warned me. You said the vice squad's specialty is luring men like us into restrooms and then arresting us if we so much as peek at them. You said they were pure evil."

"And they are," he says firmly. "They're the evil ones. Not you. I'm not angry at you. I don't blame you. Do you hear me?"

I say nothing. Because I'm angry at myself. I took the pill. He warned me to stay away. And the effects of that pill led me right into a trap.

"Do you hear me?" he asks again.

I ignore the question. "What do I do now?" I ask. "I have a police record. If this ever happens to me again, they won't be lenient. Isn't that what you said?"

He nods. "It can't happen again, unless . . ."

"Unless what?" I ask, anxious for a solution, for some way to turn back time and wipe this whole day away.

"I have friends in the movie industry," he says. "The studios, they have fixers. Very powerful men who can get police records expunged. They do it for all their stars."

"But I'm not a star," I say.

"If they think you'll be one someday . . ."

"If I tell them, they'll tell Mother, and if Mother finds out . . ." I swallow hard. I don't even know what would happen if Mother found out. Would she just ignore it? Would she try to change it? Would she kick me out of her house?

"Listen, it's your choice, but if you want it off your record, that's the only way."

"Would you have done it? If you were under a studio contract, would you have asked them to help you when you were arrested?"

He looks up to the sky. I can tell he hates thinking of his own arrest, and I wish I could take the question back. But that's not how words work. Not how actions work either. There are no second or third takes in life. Just one take. But what we do have is the chance to grow, to learn, and to forgive. "Yes," he says eventually. "I would do anything to have a clean record. I could teach again. I could do what I'm meant to do. I would do anything for that."

"Okay," I say. "But can we call them from your place? If anyone else sees me tonight, I want to be wearing clean pants."

He manages a laugh. I do too. We walk to his place in silence. I'm enthralled when he opens the door to reveal his home. It might be a tiny little studio apartment, but it's so full of life. He has a Victrola player with stacks of records next to it. There are photos of mysterious men and women haphazardly taped to the wall. Men in makeup. Women in suits. A few people I recognize. Oscar Wilde. Joan Crawford. Walt Whitman. His bed is really just a mattress, and it's covered in clothes. A mess of fabric and feathers, ruffles and lace.

He leads me to the bathroom and lays out some clothes for me. "These should fit," he says.

He closes the door behind him, and I strip the clothes off me. My pants are crusty and vile. I turn the shower on. The jet feels so good on me. The hot water cleans me. Revives me. It washes away my tears, helps me release this day, this long, horrible, evil day. I hear him put on a record. I don't recognize the song, but it's full of fire and life. I close my eyes. I pray that wherever Vicente is, he's happier than I am right now. Part of me hopes he never finds out what just happened to me. Another part of me wants him to know how lost I am without him.

I dry myself and throw Zip's clothes on. The pants swim on me, but he gave me a belt, so I tighten it around my waist to hold the pants up. The shirt he gave me swims on me too, but I don't care. I like wearing his clothes. It feels like a new skin.

I find him sitting next to his Victrola. I sit next to him. "Who's this singing?" I ask.

"Ma Rainey," he says. "One of the great artists of our time."

The lyrics of the song stun me. *"Went out last night with a crowd of my friends. Must've been women, 'cause I don't like no men."*

"Wow," I say. "They let her sing about how she likes women."

He laughs. "Well, they let her get away with it eleven years ago. Back when you were . . ."

"Six years old," I say with a smile.

"You see," he says, "people like to think society only moves forward, only gets better. And sometimes it does. But the truth is sometimes things get worse. And things can get a lot worse for those of us who don't hold the power, do you understand?"

"I do, Mr. Lamb." I'm thinking of Vicente and his family. Of how one second they're citizens of America and the next they're being forced out, along with hundreds of thousands of their brothers and sisters, mothers and fathers, aunts and uncles.

"You're wearing my clothes and sitting on my floor. I think you can call me Zip now."

"Okay. Zip." I take a breath. The record ends, and I'm left with my thoughts. And all I can think is that as much as I hate to, I have to call Mildred. She has to make this go away. "I think I'll make that call now, Zip."

He leans over and grabs the telephone. He yanks it toward me. "You remember the address here?" he asks.

I nod. "I'm a pianist. I've been trained to have a good memory." I dial the private number Mildred gave me for emergencies.

"This is Mildred Butler speaking."

"It's Bobby Reeves," I say, hating the meekness of my tone. I'm afraid of her judgment.

"You're in trouble," she says. Not a question. Why else would I be calling?

"I'm so sorry," I say. "I didn't mean for any of this to happen, and I swear I'm innocent—"

"Of what?"

"Sorry?"

"Innocent of what?"

"Of . . . well . . . I was arrested for . . . well, lewd conduct . . . But the officer followed me into the bathroom at the Rendezvous."

"You went back to a pansy club?" she asks curtly.

"Yes," I croak out.

"Then let's stop with the proclamations of innocence, shall we?" There's a long pause. I'm afraid she'll give up on me. Tell me the studio will terminate my contract now. "Hollywood police station?" she asks.

"Yes," I say.

"We have good relationships there." She's terse. All business. She has no interest in talking to me. Just in doing her job. "You do understand that your mother will have to know about this."

"But—"

"I'm sorry, but once the police are involved, parents must be notified."

"Okay," I say.

"If it happens again, you won't be this lucky. This is your last chance, kid. You haven't even been cast in a movie yet, and you're already a pain in the neck."

She hangs up on me, and I clutch the phone tight, like she might come back at any second to keep shaming and berating me. Zip takes the phone from me and places it back on the receiver. "How're you doing?" he asks.

"Not great," I say. "I messed up so badly. I did everything you told me not to. Took a pep pill. Let myself be lured into a bathroom with—"

"Stop," he orders. "I won't hear any more self-flagellation from you. When all this passes, we can have some more words about those pills. But right now, you need to understand that you were trapped. What happened to you is happening to men and women like us all over the country." The anger in his voice takes a physical shape, like it's a weapon. "You know what they did when Prohibition ended in New York?"

I shake my head.

"They passed a law barring establishments from serving homosexuals. From even letting us gather publicly. God forbid we have spaces that belong to us."

"God does forbid it, doesn't he?" I ask. "That's what Mother and Mildred would say."

"With all due respect, screw Mother and Mildred.

God loves us as we are. I know that. And the sooner you know that, the sooner you'll stop blaming yourself." I look up and notice a small cross above his mattress. "It's not your fault. It's not our fault. They won't allow us to congregate. Won't allow us in their precious military. Won't allow us to teach. Won't allow books or movies to talk about us. Don't you see what they're doing?"

"They're trying to make us invisible," I say.

He takes my hands in his. "But we're not. We exist. We always did. We always will. And wait until they all die and get to heaven and realize God was on our side the whole time."

"Maybe they won't go to heaven," I say. "Maybe they'll go to hell."

"I don't believe in hell," he says. "Here on this messed-up planet, there's good and evil, justice and injustice. But that's our doing. We raise kids to be hateful. We teach it to them. Up there, in heaven, in God's eyes, we're all good. We're all forgiven."

I nod. I want to be able to hold those two thoughts in me like he does. That someone can be evil in this life, and yet worthy of forgiveness in the afterlife. I don't know if I'm there yet.

"We should get you home," Zip says.

"Oh, you don't . . . What I mean is, my mother and Willie, well, Mildred is going to tell them what happened and they'll be very upset—"

"Which is exactly why I'm offering to be with you. If you need my support."

I think about it for a moment. Would I rather face Mother and Willie alone? Or would I rather have Zip by my side? The answer is obvious. "Sure," I say. "Thanks. For, you know, for everything."

"If you want to thank me, take care of the next generation when you're my age," he says.

"I don't understand."

"I had teachers. Guides. People who helped me find my way in a world that tried to make me invisible, as you so eloquently said yourself. If you want to thank me, then you need to do the same. When you become a man, be a teacher, a guide. Help young people who are made to feel invisible feel the opposite. Make them feel seen. Without guides and mentors, our community would be lost."

"I will," I say. "I promise."

He stands up. Offers me a hand to help me up. He looks at me before we head out. "Chin up. Never forget that no one can take your pride away from you."

Mother and Willie are waiting for us in the living room when we get home, just like I feared. The first thing I notice is how scared Frisco looks. He's in the corner of the living room, curled up around himself like he gets when Mother and Willie fight. They must have been screaming. The second thing I notice is my journal, filled with page after page about my love for Vicente. It's in Mother's grip. I knew I should've left those pages blank.

"Hi," I say quietly when we enter.

"Who are you?" Willie asks Zip.

"My name is—"

Mother cuts him off. "We met at the Billy Haines party." She shoots a piercing gaze at Zip. "Is this all your doing? Corrupting our youth is your specialty, isn't it?"

"He didn't do anything," I say. "He wasn't even there when it happened. He helped me."

"Helped you do what exactly?" Willie asks, approaching Zip. Willie towers over Zip. He leans toward Zip threateningly. "If you laid a hand on my boy—"

"Willie, stop!" I plead. "He didn't touch me." Frisco leaps up and rushes toward me protectively. He yaps at my feet.

"I would never hurt a child," Zip says. "All I want is what's best for Bobby."

"What's best for Bobby is not to have his mind filled with crazy ideas." Mother holds up my journal. "I read this after getting a call from Mildred. You're mentioned a few times in here, Mr. Lamb. Seems like you encouraged him to become a homosexual."

"Not to become a homosexual," Zip says calmly. "You see, he already is one. I'm encouraging him, and both of you, to accept it."

"Accept it?" Mother asks. "I've devoted my whole life to giving my son the life he deserves. And now you want me to let him throw that all away so he can perform in fur stoles like you."

Zip looks at me with sorrow in his eyes. "What I wish is that Bobby didn't have to choose between the career he deserves and the love he deserves."

"Well, he does," Mother says curtly. "That's the way the world works. Now I'd like you to leave, preferably far away, like Vicente. Thank God he's in Mexico."

"Take that back," I say. "Take it back! What happened to the Maderas, it's not fair. It's un-American."

Mother just laughs. "If you think that, then you don't understand America."

"This is your son," Zip says. "He's been through a lot today. Perhaps instead of judging him, you could support him."

Mother's gaze is fixed on me as she says, "If I don't judge him, if I don't punish him, then how will he ever learn never to do this again? You might enjoy playing the fairy godfather, but I'm his mother."

Zip won't back down. "You can't change a person. Has life not taught you that lesson yet?"

Willie, who has been silent too long, finally snaps at Zip. "Enough, please. You need to leave. This is something for our family to discuss."

"But you're not my family, Willie!" I yell, holding Frisco tight to my chest so I don't scare him with my anger. "You met Mother three years ago. You married her two years ago."

Willie looks hurt, like I just struck him. "We all share a last name," he utters. "I have every intention of adopting you when your mother says it's okay."

I know Willie wants to be my dad, and I know he doesn't deserve my spite. But I can't help but be honest in this moment. "What about asking *me* if it's okay? I have a dad out there, somewhere. I know I do, and I want to know who he is."

"You love some imaginary father more than you love me?" Willie asks.

"He's not imaginary." I bite my lip too hard. "He's my *real* father."

Willie flinches. "Your *real* father?" he echoes nastily. "Wow." He turns to Mother. "Give me that key on your necklace, Mags."

"Willie, stop!" Mother demands.

"Give it to me." Willie moves toward her. "I've done everything you asked of me. But he'll never see me as his father, because you don't treat me like a father. You treat me like an employee. Now give me the necklace."

My heart flutters. I always knew there was a secret behind Mother's necklace.

"I'll never forgive you, Willie," Mother says, with a tremble that makes me see she's really scared.

"Give it to me, or I'll just tell him."

"Tell me what?" I ask. "Mother, what's he talking about?"

"Willie, please don't," Mother implores. "We agreed when you proposed. You promised. . . ."

"No, what we promised each other was that we would be a family. That I would have a son. A real son." Willie turns to me. The despair on his face is heartbreaking. "I really thought I could be the father you needed. I did. I swear. But I can't. You deserve to know who your real dad is."

"Mother?" I utter. "Willie knows who my dad is?"

Mother nods. Then she pulls out the necklace she never removes. Clutches the tiny gold key dangling on the chain. She heads to the tall armoire next to the fireplace, climbs atop a chair, and pulls a hidden box from above the armoire. She places the box down on the coffee table. There's a look of dread on her face as she puts the key in the lock and opens it.

"Why?" Mother cries. "Why are you making me do this, Willie?" I've never seen her so defeated and vulnerable. She looks at me and asks, "Are you sure you want to know?"

I nod. "I have to know, Mother."

She opens the box. I pull away from Zip and look inside. There's a photo of Mother and a dark-skinned man. She's so young in the photo. Happy. Innocent. She's lovingly holding a white bunny rabbit in her hand. And the man in the photo . . . His arm is around her tenderly. But that's not what makes my heart skip a beat. What stuns me is that the man looks almost exactly like I do right now. He must be around my age in the photo.

"My God," Zip whispers. "It's you."

It really could be me in the photo standing next to my young, beautiful mom. I put the photo down and pull a piece of paper from the box. I recognize Mother's handwriting on the paper. She's written a name at the top, and under it a series of addresses and phone numbers. She's crossed out most of the addresses and numbers, except for the ones at the bottom. I stare at the paper, then at Willie, then at Mother, then at Zip. I speak the name out loud. I can barely pronounce it. "Hah-seen Je-fahr-ze-day."

"It's pronounced Hossein Jafarzadeh," Mother says sadly.

"Lalehzar. Tehran. Iran." I speak the words quietly, almost to myself.

"I've always kept track of him," she says. "Just in case . . ."

"Just in case . . . ," I repeat. I pick up the photo of them again. I look at her misty-eyed as I say, "You loved him."

Mother closes her eyes. Maybe she can't look at me right now. Or maybe she's traveling back to when she was that young girl. "Yes. I loved him so much." She opens her eyes and looks at a defeated Willie. "I'm sorry. I think my heart closed up when I had to leave him."

Willie just shakes his head sadly.

"Why did you keep him a secret from me all these years?" I ask.

"I can't . . . It's too long of a story for today. I'll tell you. I promise. But please, not tonight. Not after what we've been through."

"Just tell me . . . Does he know I exist?"

She nods. "He asked me to name you Babak before I left Iran. Before you were born. I never told my parents. They wouldn't have let me name you Bobby if they knew it was my small way of keeping him with us."

"Babak," I whisper. "That's who I could've been. Babak Jafarzadeh."

"I had no choice," she says. "Staying with him would've meant losing my parents. And I couldn't do that. They were my family. I needed them to help raise you. I needed their support."

"Their money?" I ask. Mother never told me much about my grandparents, who both died when I was a toddler. But two things were always obvious to me. She resented them. And we lived off the money she inherited from them until it ran out.

"Yes, their money," she says. "But also their emotional support. I was just a girl. I couldn't stay in a foreign country all alone, raising a child without them. They were furious with me, but much more furious with him. They forbade me from ever speaking to him again. I didn't know what else to do."

"That's his phone number, isn't it?" I ask, running my finger along the number at the bottom of the paper. "I want to call him."

"You can't," Mother says. "We don't have a long-distance telephone plan."

"I do," Zip says. We all look at Zip, surprised. "I have a group of friends who moved to Berlin years ago. It was safer for them there."

"I'm going to call him," I tell Mother.

"Please, Bobby." Mother sounds depleted. "I know I've been hard on you. And I know I didn't tell you who your father was. But what was I supposed to do? If I was hard on you, it's because I saw potential in you. I didn't tell you about your father to protect you. What good would it do for people to think you're a foreigner? Look what happened to Vicente and his family. That could happen to you too. They could expel you at any moment if they don't like who you are in this country. I understand the way the world really is."

I face Mother. I want to hate her. But I don't. I pity her. Because she didn't have the strength to live the life she truly wanted.

"If this country doesn't want me, and it doesn't, then I don't want it either," I say.

"You don't know what you're saying."

"Yes, I do." I push my shoulders back. "And you of all people should understand. We're the same, aren't we? You weren't allowed to love my father. And I wasn't allowed to love Vicente."

"It's different," she says. "Hossein and I, we didn't sin. We created you—"

"I'm not a sinner, Mother," I say calmly. "God loves me." I look at Zip, who gives me a supportive nod. Then I turn back to Mother. "All I want is to live my own life. Make my own choices. And I'm choosing to go call my father."

"Then what? Think ahead. It will only hurt Hossein to hear from you. You're just an idea to him. Something distant and invisible. When he hears your voice, it will break his heart."

"I've learned something today," I say. "A broken heart is better than a heart of stone." I give Frisco a kiss on the head. "At least a broken heart can heal."

I head out, still holding Frisco. Zip exits by my side. "Come on, you can make that phone call from my place." Giving Frisco a pat, he adds, "You're welcome too."

From an open window, we can hear Mother scream at Willie. It's all his fault, she yells. She wants him out of her house.

It's clear their marriage is over.

And my life is just beginning.

MOUD

2019

Tehran

I'm on my phone doing research when Shane calls. It's morning in Iran, night in Los Angeles. I silence the call. It's the fourth time he's called me without getting a response. I just don't know how to tell him everything that's happened, everything that's on my mind. I go back to my search, scouring the world for Shirin Mahmoudieh. I know her name, and that she studied biology and wanted to be a medical researcher, and that she had a brother who lived in England. But the only two Shirin Mahmoudiehs I find are the wrong age. One too old, living in Rasht. The other too young, living in Munich. I can't find another Shirin Mahmoudieh anywhere, which means she either has no digital footprint, or she's married and changed her name. I want so badly to find her single, still pining for my dad. I have a fantasy of giving my dad a second chance at life, at love. Maybe he can be happy again. And if he's loved, maybe he can love me in a new way, a deeper way. I sigh. Maybe this whole mission is selfish, just a way for me to transform my father into the dad I always wanted. Shane calls again. I can't keep ignoring him, so I click accept on the video call. "Hey," I say.

"Hey." He looks different. He's buzzed his hair off. It looks strange on him, like he's somehow punishing himself.

"I'm sorry I haven't called you back—"

"Or texted. Or emailed. Or used any of the ample means of communication at our disposal to say, 'Hey, Shane, I know you've been having a hard time. How are you coping?'" He scratches his head.

"Coping?" I parrot quietly. I don't want to judge him. I know problems are all relative. I know that being called out is a nightmare for him, but it's so hard for me to listen to his dramatic language when I'm thinking about Siamak in jail, about the love my father gave up, the life my grandparents could never have. Then again, how can I expect him to empathize with the things I'm going through when I haven't told him any of it?

"I shaved my head," he says.

"I can see that. It looks . . ."

"What? Say it."

"I mean, it looks good," I say. "It's just not you."

He nods. He shifts in his bed. "I guess . . . Well, I've been doing a lot of thinking about myself. Which obviously means I'm been thinking about us, because who am I without you?"

I feel a lump in my throat. The fact that he thinks

of me as a part of him makes me remember everything we've been through together, all the memories and confidence he's given me. Who would I be without him? Probably still closeted. Probably someone who would never have built up an emotional immune system, as he would say. My dad modeled how to escape emotions for me. Shane taught me how to face them.

"And I guess . . ." He pauses. Chooses his words deliberately. "I guess I think we should take a break."

"A break?" Why is he breaking up with *me* when I was ready to break up with *him* days ago?

"I'm sorry," he says. "I didn't want to have this conversation over the phone. Obviously."

"Obviously," I say.

"But I also felt like putting it off would be disrespectful to you. I have to tell you what's on my mind, you know. Because if we stop being boyfriends, we'll still be best friends. I hope. And it's not about you. It's me, it's all me and my stupid shit. I need to take a step back and figure out who I am without a podcast, without all my loud-ass opinions."

I sit in shock for a few breaths, and then I laugh. I can't help it.

"Okay, this isn't the response I was expecting, but I guess it's better than tears."

I put a hand over my mouth, my warm palm stifling the laughter. When I've found my equilibrium again, I finally speak words that belong to me and not to him. "I'm laughing because . . . Well, not because this is funny, but because I was thinking the same thing."

"You wanted to break up with me?" he asks, an ache in his voice.

"I guess I also need time to figure out who I am. This whole trip, it's been . . ." It's been a lot. But what do I tell him about first? How do I even begin?

"It's been . . . what?" he asks.

"There's just a lot I didn't know about my family, and I guess it's made me realize there's a lot I didn't know about myself. And how can I be with you when I don't know who I am yet?"

"That's exactly how I feel." He takes a breath. "It's weird, right? We're miles apart, but in a way we've been having the same experience."

I shake my head. "We really haven't, Shane."

"The same *emotional* experience."

I stand up. I let out a deep sigh. I pace the room as I talk, my thoughts flowing now. "No," I say. "We haven't been having the same emotional experience. I love you for wanting to feel connected to my experience, for wanting to connect with *the whole world*, but you don't know what it feels like to find out your grandparents were gay and couldn't be themselves—"

"Wait, what?"

"And that your father gave up his first love to save his parents' lives—"

"Slow down, Moud," he begs. "I don't understand."

"And I kissed someone," I blurt out.

"Wait, you cheated on me?" he asks, not making

any effort to hide the hurt.

"I stopped it as soon as it happened," I explain. "And it's not like I can even see him again, because he's in jail now."

"In jail?" he echoes in shock. "Why?"

"Because he makes gay art, and you can't make gay art here." I'm stunned by his speechlessness, so I keep going. "And I didn't tell you because I hate that I kissed someone else, or let him kiss me, or whatever, because there's really no difference." I take a small breath. Wait for him to say something, but he's still at a loss for words. "And I didn't tell you because . . . Because if I told you he was in jail, that three of his friends who modeled for him are in jail too, it would just give you all the ammunition you need to say I told you so."

"No," he whispers quietly. "Don't think of me that way."

"What way?" I spit out, shocked by my venom. "Aren't you the one who didn't want me to step foot in a backward country that kills gay people? Well, here I am. You were right, okay? You've always wanted to be right—"

"That was the old me. That's not—"

"It doesn't matter," I say. "It doesn't matter anymore. Siamak is in jail. My grandfather's about to die. I just . . . I just . . ." I just break down. The rage turns to sadness.

"Moud, let it out," he says.

"I'm sorry," I blubber. "I'm so sorry I kissed someone else."

"Oh, babe, stop. You *kissed* someone. It doesn't make you a bad person. Is your friend gonna be okay?"

I sit back down on the bed. "I don't know. My grand-father is calling lawyers to see what we can do."

"So there's hope," he says.

"There's always hope." I manage a smile. "Shane?"

"What?"

"Are we officially broken up?" I ask.

"I guess so." He smiles sadly. "But can I be here for you as a friend?"

I nod. "Yeah, I'd like that. And I can be here for you too. If you're ever having a hard time."

"You'll answer my calls now that you're not hiding anything from me?" he asks.

"Yeah," I say.

There's a knock on my door. "Moud," my dad says loudly from behind the door.

"Um, did your dad just call you Moud?" Shane asks.

"I guess he did," I say. "My dad's said a lot of surpris-ing things on this trip." This could be my I-told-you-so moment, but I don't want to be spiteful, so I just say, "Come in, Dad."

My dad enters. He's dressed for the day. "Your grand-father wants us downstairs. He has news."

"About Siamak?" I ask.

"I don't know." He hovers awkwardly by the door, then asks, "Is that Shane on the phone?"

I nod. "You want to say hi?"

My dad shrugs, and I turn the phone so they can see each other.

"Hey, Mr. Jafarzadeh," Shane says. He picks up his

ukulele and nervously strums it. Being around my dad has never been easy for him.

"Hello, Shane. How are you?" my dad asks.

"I'm okay, all things considered," Shane says.

"We decided to split up," I tell my dad.

My dad isn't sure how to respond to this. The old him would have just nodded and ignored it, like nothing was ever said. How could a relationship end when he didn't even acknowledge it to begin with?

"It's okay," Shane says. "It's best for us both."

"Perhaps," my dad says. Then, in his driest tone, he adds, "But your emotional immune system must be feeling very compromised right now, Shane."

I burst out laughing. "Shane, that's my dad mocking you, which is a very Persian way of showing affection." That gets a sly smile from my dad.

"I'll see you downstairs," my dad says before he leaves. "Goodbye, Shane."

I can hear my dad's heavy footsteps as I tell Shane I should go.

"If we don't talk until you get home, I just want to say that was a profoundly weird moment with your father, and also . . . good luck with everything. I'll be thinking about your friend. If there's anything I can do . . ."

"Shane, there's nothing you can do."

"That's not true. I could start a GoFundMe, or contact nonprofits. I mean, there has to be a way to help."

"You know, when Americans want to help people in the Middle East, it usually goes very wrong," I say.

"Yeah." I can tell how much he hates his powerlessness. "Well, I'll see you in 2020, I guess."

"See you in the Roaring Twenties." I wave goodbye to him.

I feel a strange emptiness when I hang up. Empty because we're no longer Shane and Moud, we're now our own separate beings. Strange because the emptiness feels full of possibility. It feels right.

I get dressed and go downstairs. Baba and my dad wait for me by the front door. Baba hands me some toasted *barbari* bread. "Here, breakfast," he says. "Eat it on the way."

"Where are we going? Did you find a lawyer for Siamak and his friends?" I ask.

"Not yet," Baba says. "But I have a call with one early tomorrow morning. Today, we're going to pay an old friend a visit in Karaj."

"We're all going?" I ask.

"Of course," Baba says. "I need your dad to drive."

My dad smiles. "I have no idea where we're going, but I do know you shouldn't be alone after your . . . breakup."

I smile. "Yeah, thanks, Dad."

There's a sense of peace on Baba's face as he watches me and my dad connect. Then he says, "Go to the bathroom now, because we'll be in the car for an hour or two."

I think of Shane on the drive from Tehran to Karaj. My dad drives and Baba sits in the front, his wheelchair in the trunk. I'm alone in the back seat. No one speaks, maybe because there's both too much and nothing to say. But the wheels moving, the topography changing, the trees and the highways and the skyscrapers passing by us, the small protest over gas prices we drive past, they all help me process being without Shane. *Process.* An American word my dad would probably mock. But I like the word. It acknowledges that everything we go through has no beginning or end. Not really. Shane and I might not be a couple anymore, but we're not done. My mom isn't gone; she's here in me, in my dad. If being in Iran has taught me anything, it's that we carry history inside us.

We park outside a modern four-story apartment building in Karaj. The street is a mix of urban and residential, with honking cars and crowds of people filling the tree-lined street. The smell of exhaust overwhelms me as Baba wheels himself up the wheelchair ramp and presses a buzzer.

"Yes?" a woman's voice answers.

"It's us," Baba says. "The Jafarzadehs."

We're buzzed in. My dad holds the door open for us both. "Thank God these modern buildings are wheelchair accessible," Baba says as he wheels himself in and presses the elevator button. We ride the elevator up to the third floor and ring the bell.

To my surprise, a young boy answers the door. "Welcome," he says in a singsong voice. "I'm Bijan."

I turn to my father. There's a tear forming in his eye as he looks into the little boy's eyes and realizes who we're here to see.

"Hello," Baba says. "I'm Babak Jafarzadeh. This is my son, Saeed. And my grandson, Mahmoud, but he prefers to be called Moud. We're here to see—"

"My baba, I know. He told me."

My dad's voice is quiet as he asks, "Were you named after your father?"

"I was," the kid says. "But I'm the superior Bijan Golbahar, and my dad knows it."

I look at my dad as he realizes that the boy he helped at the protest all those years ago is alive, and has a very precocious son. My dad looks to Baba with gratitude in his eyes. "How did you find them?"

"I know people," Baba says. Then, turning his attention to the boy, he adds, "And you know something, Bijan? Children should always be superior to their parents. I know my child is."

A woman rushes to the door, holding a kitchen rag. She wears a simple chador over her hair, puts an arm around the boy, and smiles at us. "Please come in. I'm Behi. I'm behind schedule because Bijan is late coming home from work."

As we enter the living room, my dad looks around and says, "This is a lovely home." My dad's right. All the little details that indicate a life well-lived. The colorful old carpets. The child's drawings taped to the walls. And of course, the framed photos of that same family through the years.

"Sit," the woman says. "Bijan, be a good boy and come help me set the coffee table."

Behi leads her son into the kitchen. My dad and I sit next to each other on the couch. Its old cushions make us sink surprisingly low. Baba parks his wheelchair next to my dad. Behi and Bijan rejoin us quickly. Bijan sets down a tray of sweets. *Zoolbia-bamieh* and *gaz* and *halva*. Behi sets down a tray with a pot of tea next to five glass teacups and sugar cubes. "Everything is homemade," she says as she pours the tea.

We sit in silence for a moment, just the sound of slurping tea. Finally, my father speaks. "I've wanted to find Bijan for so many years." His voice cracks.

"We know," Behi says. "Because he was also desperate to find you. But he couldn't remember your name. Just your face. And by the time we learned your name, it felt too late, too invasive to—" The front door creaks. "There he is," Behi says, relieved.

The sound of footsteps gets closer as the elder Bijan's booming voice fills the room. "I'm sorry I'm late. There was a protest blocking the streets. I think this fuel crisis might really be the thing to finally topple the—" When Bijan enters the room, he immediately freezes in front of my dad. "It's you." His eyes open wide with the shock of recognition. "It is you. I would recognize you anywhere."

My dad stands up. He doesn't say a word. He just moves close to Bijan and hugs him tight. My dad's not a hugger, but right now, I can tell he doesn't want to let go.

When they finally let go of each other, Behi makes official introductions and then everyone sits down again. Bijan sits on a chair, his son jumping on his lap. Bijan looks deep into his son's eyes as he says, "This is the man who saved my life. He could have escaped. But instead he took the time to remove his belt—"

The younger Bijan finishes the story. "And he turned it into a tourniquet."

"That's right," the elder Bijan says. Shifting his gaze to me, he asks, "Did you know that your dad saved my life?"

It doesn't feel right to say that I didn't know until very recently. So all I say is, "I do know that."

"Saeed *jan*," Behi says, refilling his teacup. "Bijan has always wondered what became of you."

"Just like I always wondered about you, Bijan *jan*," my dad says. "I prayed you were alive."

Bijan nods in understanding. "And I prayed that you lived a good life. I prayed that God gave you many blessings for the gift you gave me."

My dad nods too. "I have tried to live a good life. To be a good man. But I'm afraid I haven't always . . ."

"He's been a good dad," I say with a certainty I couldn't have imagined before we came here.

My dad looks at me, his eyes misty. "Have I?"

"And a good son," Baba adds.

My dad shakes his head. "I don't know. I blame myself for so much. When I think of us in those streets, Bijan. Everything we believed in. And look at this country now. Sometimes I feel like I failed my family and my country."

"You obviously didn't fail your family," Bijan says softly. "I can see that clearly." He looks at his own family now. "As for our country . . . I've apologized to my wife and to my son many times for being a part of that stupid revolution."

"Don't speak like that," Baba says. "What you did wasn't stupid."

"It was," my dad says. "And you of all people know it, because you warned me not to go into those streets."

"And everything a father says is correct?" Baba asks. "Tell me, Moud, has your father always been right?"

"Definitely not," I say with a smile.

"There you go," Baba says. "You had a strong will, Saeed. You evidently did too, Bijan. You weren't stupid. Just young. And hopeful."

"Look what our hope turned into," Bijan says. "We wanted freedom, and we got worse corruption, more death, more war, worse injustice. . . ."

"You can't blame yourself for what Khomeini did to this country," Behi says. "He politicized a spiritual doctrine. He made disobeying him a sin. That's *his* doing, not yours."

The young Bijan, who has been following the conversation with great interest, leans in as he speaks. "But aren't people marching again? Maybe things will change this time."

The elder Bijan shakes his head. "Like they changed during the Green Wave ten years ago? I let myself feel hope then, and once again nothing changed."

"But someday things will change," the boy says passionately. "They have to."

Baba smiles. "Listen to the young. He's right. Change

is the only constant in this life. Our history is long, and none of our energy is wasted."

"You really believe that?" my dad asks.

"I have to," Baba says. "Maybe this won't make sense to you until you're as old as I am, but you can't leave this earth without hope. I have to believe there's a better world coming for my son, and my grandson, and all the future relatives I'll never know."

I feel a sudden chill. Baba talking about his death scares me. So does the implication that I might have children someday. What kind of father will I be? I know one thing. If I do have kids, I'll make sure they know everything about Baba. And about Dad.

My dad takes a sip of tea before asking his next question. "Behi *joon*, you mentioned earlier that by the time you found out my name, it felt too late to contact me. How did you find my name?"

Behi nods. "She found us about ten years ago."

"Less than that," Bijan says. "Bijan was already born, remember?"

Baba and I both look at my dad, as all three of us realize they can only be talking about Shirin. "Was she . . . Is she . . . happy?" my dad asks.

"It was one phone call," Behi says. "She did want to tell you. To contact you. But she also didn't want to insert herself back into your life. So she told us your name in case we ever wanted to find you."

My dad's voice is soft as he asks, "Do you know how I can contact her?"

Behi stands up and digs an old address book out of a drawer. She flips its pages until she finds what she's looking for. She tears the page out and hands it to my dad. "Here you go."

My dad lets go of our hands and stands to take the paper. "Shirin Carmichael," he says almost to himself.

So she did get married. And she changed her name.

"She lives in London," Behi says. "That I remember."

"Thank you," my dad says. "You have no idea what today has meant to me."

The elder Bijan stands up and shakes my dad's hand. "I have every idea what today means to you."

Behi insists we take half the sweets with us before we leave. As we head out, I can hear little Bijan asking his mom why she gave us all the delicious sweets. Behi laughs. "Bijan *joon*," she says. "There's plenty left for you. There's enough sweetness in the world for everyone."

We drive past a protest on our way home. Outside, people chant, "Death to the dictator." Others chant, "We have no money. We have no fuel." Others chant, "This is your last month, Khameini, it's time to go." Others chant, "Death to the Islamic Republic." I roll the back window down and take in all their faces. Most of them are young. Young men just like my dad once was, marching these same streets, fighting a different enemy but the same fight.

"Do you think these protests will change anything?" I ask.

"I hope so," Baba says. "The government will do what

it always does. It will kill people. Jail people. But people are angry this time. People can't afford fuel. Many can't afford to live. Inflation has made people's savings worthless. Poverty is everywhere again. And those connected to the ayatollah don't pay taxes on their millions and billions."

My dad sighs. "It all sounds so familiar."

"Power corrupts," Baba says firmly. "But someday, the people of this beautiful country will get the government they deserve. It won't be in my lifetime. That much I know. I hope it's in yours, Saeed *jan*. It's what you've always wanted. A truly free and abundant Iran."

"Yes." My dad nods. "But Baba, my lifetime is your lifetime. As long as I'm here, as long as Moud is here, you'll be here too."

"'*When I am dead, open my grave and see . . . ,*'" Baba says.

"'*The cloud of smoke that rises round your feet,*'" my dad continues. It takes me a moment to realize they're reciting a poem.

They finish the poem together. "'*In my dead heart the fire still burns for thee.*'"

"Who wrote that?" I ask.

"Hafez," Baba says. "My father and I would read poetry together every night. He loved our poetry."

"What was he like?" I ask, imagining my great-grandfather sitting next to us. Wishing there were four generations of Jafarzadeh men in this car.

Baba smiles. "He was warm. Charismatic. You know,

when I flew to Tehran to see him when I was seventeen, the visit was meant to last a week, not a lifetime. I didn't expect him to help me get out of my MGM contract. I never thought I'd end up finishing high school in Iran."

I ask, "What was it like? Coming to Tehran for the first time? Meeting your dad?"

"The first place he took me was to a hammam," Baba reminisces. "He asked me so many questions as we sat on those hot rocks. And he answered so many of my questions. When the man came to exfoliate me, I was shocked by how much dead skin was coming off me. I think I knew in that moment I would never leave. Because it felt good to be this new person, in a new skin." Baba's voice cracks when he says, "It felt good to be his son."

My dad nods. "I'm sorry I broke our tradition of reading poetry together, but if it's not too late, we can begin again tonight."

"I'd love that, Dad." I give him a nod, then turn my attention back to the changing landscapes outside my window.

"Of course, to truly appreciate our poetry, you'll need to learn to read Persian," Baba says. "The English translations are often terrible, especially the Rumi translations."

"I'll do my best," I say, excited for the challenge.

"You're young," Baba says. "I had never even heard the Persian language until I was your age, and look at me now. The young can learn anything."

"Teach me a poem now," I say. "Teach me one of your favorites."

"You're his father," Baba says to my dad. "You teach him one of your favorites."

"'*How can I know anything about the past or the future*,'" my dad recites from memory.

"Ah, Rumi," Baba says. "You know that poem was my father's favorite too. It was the first poem he shared with me, my very first night in Iran. '*How can I know anything about the past or the future—*'"

Suddenly, a guy on a motorcycle cuts my dad off as we turn onto Lalehzar Street. My dad almost runs him over. He honks angrily. Raising his voice, my dad says, "Idiot. One thing I don't miss about this place is the crazy drivers."

Baba laughs as my dad parks outside the house. We help Baba into his wheelchair and enter the house. Hassan Agha greets us and asks Baba if he needs anything.

"I'm okay," Baba says. "I think I'll go play some music."

As Baba wheels himself toward his study, my dad calls out to him. "Baba, I wanted to say . . ."

Baba turns his wheelchair around.

"Just . . . thank you," my dad says. "For finding Bijan, and for . . . for forgiving me for being ungrateful for so many years. I am grateful for you."

"Thank you, my son," Baba says with a wistful smile. "But what I want is for you to forgive yourself."

My dad and I are heading up the stairs when the sound of Baba's tar fills the house. "It's so beautiful," I say.

"You should learn from him while you're here," my dad suggests.

"Can you play?" I ask.

"A little," he says. "I was always better at piano."

"You play the piano?" I wonder if my dad and I will ever run out of things to learn about each other. I hope not.

"I used to." He puts an arm around me. "And your mother was a fantastic singer. One of our first nights out together was at a piano bar." He pauses when we reach the top of the staircase. "A gay piano bar."

"That sounds like quite a date for a heterosexual Iranian couple in the 1970s," I say, laughing.

"It wasn't a date, not really. But your mother did sing 'Do Panjereh' with me at the piano, and the crowd gave us a standing ovation." My dad shakes his head happily at the memory. "All right, it's been a long day. Let's get some rest."

I watch as he heads to his room and closes the door. There's so much more I want to say to him, ask him. But when I walk toward his room, I hear his voice. He's calling Shirin. It sounds like he's leaving her a message.

I don't disturb him. But he does come to see me before bed. He reads me a Khayyam poem, in Persian and then in English. We recite it together until I know it by heart.

I'm woken up by Ava's voice the next morning. Not just her voice. Her parents too. Everyone is assembled in the living room, their voices loud. I look at my clock. I slept in, exhausted by the emotional events of the previous day. When I get to the living room, I find my dad and

Baba sitting on one side. Ava sits between her parents on the other side.

"Baba, are you sure about this?" Ava asks.

"Ava *joon*," her dad, Farhad, says. "Baba said he wants to sell the land—"

"I know," Ava says. "And obviously I want him to as well."

I sit next to my dad, confused. Ava was always opposed to Baba selling the land and letting Farhad build a high-rise.

"Then let him," Farhad says. "The sooner we move, the sooner he'll have the money in hand."

"I want it before January," Baba says.

"I'm sure that can be arranged," Farhad assures him.

Ava's mom, Shamsi, leans forward. "Baba *jan*, I know this isn't what you wanted, but I hope you'll be happy. And even after you pay the lawyer and the judge, you'll have more than enough money to buy a great apartment. Something wheelchair accessible and easy."

I catch Ava's glance, and she waves to me. "What's going on?" I ask quietly.

Ava lets out a heavy sigh. "Baba found a lawyer who will help Siamak and his friends."

"Wait, that's great news," I say. "So there's hope?"

"In Iran, money can buy anything, even hope," Baba explains.

I'm starting to understand what's happened. "Oh, so you're . . . you're selling the house and the land so you can free them?"

Ava explains, "That's how it works here. Judges can be bought if the right lawyer knows how to navigate the system." For all the love she has for Tehran, Ava sounds repulsed by her country right now.

I take this all in. The corruption of it all. I guess sometimes that's the price of freedom. Still, I can't help but ask, "What would've happened to them if Baba wasn't sitting on land that was worth this much?"

"Don't ask questions you don't want answers to," Baba says. "People who can't bribe their way out of trouble here shouldn't be here. They should be seeking asylum elsewhere."

I swallow hard. Our evil president has waged war on asylum seekers and immigrants, leaving people like Siamak to fend for themselves in this stew of corruption. For every Siamak who finds a way out of jail, there will be others who don't. I close my eyes, the weight of it pressing down on me. The leaders of both countries I belong to don't care at all about people, just about power.

"Baba *jan*," Farhad says. "If you come to my office, we can get all the paperwork sorted out quickly. We want to file today to get things going."

Baba nods. "Let's go then. I'm ready."

As Baba wheels himself forward, I see the determination on his face. I feel so proud to be his grandson. My grandfather is a man who is willing to tear down his own home to save four boys. I turn to Ava. "How're you doing?" I ask.

"I don't know." She gets up so she can sit closer to me.

"I guess I'm happy that my friends will be okay. And sad that this house, with all its memories, will be gone."

"I'm sorry." I wish I could find better words.

She suddenly stands up. "Let's take pictures of it. Every room. Every corner. Every closet. That way, if we ever forget what a part of it looked like, we'll be able to look at the photo." She takes her phone out and starts snapping photos from every angle. Eventually, she points the camera at me. "Come on, *baba*, give me a good pose." I pout my lips. Anything to make her smile again. "Much better."

We photograph the downstairs first. Then we move upstairs. By the time we get to the bedrooms, we're giddy. Ava tells me her favorite story from each room. That bathroom is where Maman used to color her hair. That window is the one Ava broke with a tennis ball when she was ten years old. Ava sets her camera to timer mode, and she makes me pose with her in each room, directing us to make a happy face, a sexy face, a shocked face.

We go back downstairs to photograph Baba's study last. His instruments are there. His tar. The grand piano. A tombak and a daf and a guitar.

"Siamak took lessons from him," Ava says.

"I figured."

"Anytime I met someone struggling with their sexuality, I sent them to Baba for music lessons. But it wasn't just music they learned." She snaps a photo of the room as she talks, then another. She doesn't ask me to pose. The mood has changed from giddy to reverent. "They came to him to learn about their history. To learn that they're not alone. That they were always a part of our country, and always will be. That's what Baba and Maman did for people."

I nod. I run my hands along the smooth neck of Baba's tar, this instrument that I hope to play someday.

"Pretty cool to be a part of this family, isn't it?" Ava asks. "Not everyone is as lucky as we are."

I just look at her and smile. This trip has brought up so many conflicting emotions for me: heartbreak, sadness, regret. And also, love, connection, purpose. Ava's right. I am lucky.

Siamak and his friends are released on the last day of the Western calendar. There are still months before the Persian new year, months for them to recover from the brutality they experienced before welcoming the rebirth our new year symbolizes. Ava brings them all by Baba's house that morning so they can thank him in person. The boy whose father started this whole horrible chain of events has tears in his eyes when he says, "Mr. Jafarzadeh, were it not for my father, none of this would have happened. I've told everyone how sorry I am, but I need to tell you—"

"Stop," Baba says gently. "I'm the one who is sorry that you don't have a father who loves and accepts you. I hope that someday he does. But if it's not safe for you to go home, you're welcome here. And I have many friends who could take you in as well. Our community has always needed mentors to guide and protect us. I'm nothing special."

"But your house . . . You gave up your home," the boy says with aching sadness.

"It won't be demolished until next week." Baba looks around the place. "I still have plenty of time to enjoy it. And I did pretty well for myself from the sale. You have nothing to feel guilty for."

When enough gratitude has been expressed, the boys all leave except for Siamak, who lingers behind. He and Ava invite me to an *abgooshty* with them for lunch.

"Go ahead," Baba says. "But be careful in the streets. The protests are getting worse."

"Don't worry," Siamak says. "I'm not risking prison again."

My dad takes a deep breath. "*You* shouldn't risk it," he says. "But I will. I helped bring this disgusting regime into power. It's time I stood up against them."

"Saeed *jan*," Baba whispers. "Please. Not this again."

"I thought you were proud of my bravery," my dad says.

"I am. I was. But . . ." Baba trails off.

"Why don't Siamak and I go to lunch and let you guys discuss this in private?" Ava suggests. "Moud, are you joining us?"

I shake my head. "I think I'll stay here, but I'll walk you out."

Ava and Siamak give Baba and my dad a kiss on each cheek before we leave together. As Ava unlocks her car, I can't help but think back to the night she picked me up for the party where I met Siamak. Dalida was blaring from her speakers as she drove me to a new reality. I feel like a different person now.

"You sure you don't want some *abgoosht?*" Ava asks me. I shake my head. "I mean, I love *abgoosht.* But if my dad's going to the protest, I want to go with him."

"Moud, be careful." Siamak speaks urgently. "You know what the government here can do now."

"But he's my dad." The emotion in my voice surprises me. "I can't let him go alone. And I can't expect him to stand by my side if I don't stand by his."

Ava impulsively grabs ahold of me and pulls me into a hug. "*Vay.*" She squeezes my cheeks hard. "*Vay.*" She moves my face toward Siamak. "What am I going to do when my cousin leaves, Siamak? Look at this sweet face. What will I do?"

"You'll do some tequila shots and dance away your sadness," Siamak says, smiling.

Ava slaps his shoulder playfully. "You asshole, that's exactly what I'll do. You know me too well."

"It's not goodbye yet," I say. "We still have a few more days."

"And don't think I'm not coming to Hollywood to visit you when you do leave," Ava says. "I expect you to take me to Tehrangeles, and to that place where Marilyn Monroe put her footprints, and I'd love it if you could introduce me to my future husband, Sam Asghari."

Siamak laughs. "Only you would try to steal a man from Britney Spears."

Ava points a finger at Siamak. "She's Britney *joon* now.

And we can share him. I'm all for polyamory."

I can't stop smiling as I watch the two of them banter. But when the banter ends and it's time to let them go, I realize that while I will see Ava again, this might be the last time I see Siamak. "Ava, would it be okay if I said goodbye to Siamak? I may not see him before we go home."

"Go ahead," she says, but she doesn't move.

Siamak and I both laugh. Then he says, "Ava, I think he was asking for a private moment."

Ava shakes her head. "You have to spell things out for me sometimes." She gets into the car and turns some Britney on, which makes us both smile.

Siamak and I face each other. "Are you okay?" I ask.

He nods. "I think so. I don't know, honestly. It'll take me some time to process what happened."

I want to reach out and hold him, but I don't. "Sometimes I can't believe we're the same age. The things you have to think about . . . they're so different from the things I have to think about."

"Everything is relative." He glances at Ava before asking, "Does she know? About our moment?"

I shake my head. "I didn't tell her. Not that I want to keep secrets from her. You can tell her if you want."

"Not everything that's unspoken is a secret," he says. "Some things just belong to those who experienced it."

I think about that. I'm not sure how to tell the difference between withholding a secret and honoring a private moment. Maybe I'll figure out where that line is someday. "I did tell my boyfriend." I quickly correct myself. "Ex-boyfriend."

His face suddenly looks ashen. "Oh no, I'm sorry. I hope I didn't—"

I quickly assuage his guilt. "We didn't break up because of our kiss, don't worry. It was just time for us to go our separate ways. But also, what I wanted to tell you is . . ."

He leans in, waiting.

"Well, thank you." I look into his soulful eyes. "I know that party, that kiss, it might have been just another night to you."

"It wasn't," he says sincerely.

"Good." I smile. "Because it meant so much to me. Knowing you, seeing your art, hearing about your life." I pause before saying, "And kissing you too."

"It wasn't a bad kiss," he says with a sly smile.

"Not bad at all. And even if we never kiss again, I just want you to know that you opened my eyes to how much more there is out there. I'm really grateful for that, and really happy you're free."

"Good, because I want you to introduce me to my future husband, Sam Asghari, too." Just as I'm about to laugh, he leans in and gives me a quick peck on the lips. "Goodbye for now, Moud joon. We'll always have Tehran."

The music might have stopped Ava from hearing us, but she saw the peck. She rolls her window down and screams, "What in the world is going on?"

"Nothing for you to worry about," Siamak says as he

gets into the passenger side.

"I always worry about the people I love," Ava says. "I was born that way."

Siamak laughs. "You're the best, Ava."

"Yes, she is," I say loudly as I wave to her.

"Yes, I am," she screams as she hits the gas and takes off.

When I go back inside, Baba and Dad are still arguing about the protest. Baba pleads with my dad. "Saeed *jan*, if you're going out there, be careful. Stay on the sidelines. Let your voice be heard, but don't take unnecessary risks."

"I'll make sure he doesn't," I say. "Because I'll be with him."

"Absolutely not," my dad says. "It's not safe for you."

I move toward my dad. Until I'm uncomfortably close to him. "Dad, you want to go. It's important to you."

"Nothing is more important to me than your safety."

I love him for saying this, but I say, "You've kept me safe all my life. Sometimes that's meant hiding yourself from me. I don't want that anymore."

"You don't understand what might happen."

"Maybe you're right. But I understand what will happen if we don't go. You'll regret not being a part of it."

We're at a standoff. Quietly, almost to himself, Baba says, "The things you regret are the things you don't do, not the things you do."

My dad turns to his father curiously. "What's that, Baba?"

"It's what Zip told me when I wasn't sure about coming to Tehran to meet my dad." Baba looks at us with a sense of purpose. "Go. Go for me. Go for all those who came before you, and especially for those who will come after you. Go, but stay safe. I beg you to please stay safe."

My father and I head out into the streets. We walk toward the sound of protests. I can barely hear the ring of my dad's phone over the chanting ahead of us. "Death to Khameini. Death to the Islamic Republic. The Supreme Leader lives like a God, we live like beggars." My dad answers his phone. "Hello?" He stops walking. Frozen in place. "Shirin?" he says. "My God. Shirin. It's you." I watch my dad as he listens to her on the other end of the line. "I'm with my incredible son right now. And you?" He nods and smiles. "Shirin *joon*, can I call you when I have more time? There's so much to say." He nods some more before saying, "Goodbye for now, then." He hangs up the phone, but he holds it up for a moment, like he can't believe that she was ever on the other end of it.

"Dad?"

He's entranced.

"Dad, are you okay? Is she okay?"

He snaps back to attention. Puts his phone in his pocket. "She seems fine. She lives in London. Maybe we'll visit her one day."

"I'd love that," I say.

He starts to walk toward the chanting again. I follow, walking by his side.

When we reach the protest, the crowds scream that the

internet has just been shut off because the government is scared of the truth getting out. I'm about to step closer to the protest when my dad puts a protective arm in front of me. "I can't," he says. "I know how this ends—with young lives being taken too soon. I won't risk that life being yours."

I look into his eyes as he pulls me back, farther away from the crowd. Police suddenly swarm. They pin people down, shoot guns into the air as warnings. My dad puts a protective arm around me. "Did they really turn the internet off?" I ask.

"I'm sure they did." He looks back at the protest before continuing to guide me away from it. "In my day, it was easier to control what the public heard. Now, with the internet . . . they have to work harder to shut down communication."

I take my phone out and try to load a website, any website. Nothing. I open the camera on my phone and videotape the protest. I zoom in on police officers firing guns, pinning innocent people down.

"Moud, what are you doing? Let's go." My dad pulls me away.

"Hold on," I beg. "Just another minute." I keep filming, trying to catch as many details as I can.

"Moud, enough," my dad orders.

My dad and I rush back to the safety of a house that will be razed in a week's time, soon to be replaced by a high-rise. Change is the only constant in this life.

As the chanting and the guns and the voices screaming for a better world get farther and farther away, my
dad whispers, "*How can I know anything about the past or
the future when the light of the beloved shines only now.*"

I look into his eyes. "That's beautiful."

"Never forget it." He puts an arm around me and leads
me back into the house.

I rush to the landline to call Shane. I get his voice
mail. It's the middle of the night there. "Shane, it's me,"
I say. "Listen, I'm going to send you a video as soon as I
can. Post it. Share it. They've shut down the internet in
the whole country here. We need you to get the word
out. Use your voice. It's what you do best."

When I hang up, the sound of Baba's tar floats toward
us, replacing the violent sounds we just left behind with
timeless beauty.

"Let's go tell your grandfather we're safe," my dad
says.

My dad's arm is around me as we walk into Baba's
study. I close my eyes. With each step, we get closer to the
music. The melody feels like sunlight peeking through
the fog I've spent so much of my life in. It warms me
and illuminates the darkness. It reminds me that the light
shines only now. I will never forget that again.

AUTHOR'S NOTE

My kids once asked me, "What's your favorite day ever?"
Perhaps they were expecting me to say it was the day
they were born. Or the day I was married. But after giving it some thought, I told them my favorite day was
today, because it holds every preceding day within it.
This book, in some ways, was born from that conversation, from wanting to understand the way my present,
and our collective present, holds the past within it.

I've always been obsessed with the past, nostalgic for a
time I never lived through. I think that's because, when I
was young, so much of my history was hidden from me.
My parents, and many of their generation, didn't speak
about Iran, perhaps to shield the next generation from the
pain of their memories. Similarly, when I started to realize
I was gay, I knew nothing of queer history. It certainly
wasn't taught in schools when I was young. As a kid, I was
too scared to dig into my Iranian and my queer history.
And so, my obsession with the past took other forms. I was
consumed by Old Hollywood. I lost myself in the fantasy
world of Joan Crawford, Marlene Dietrich, Jean Harlow,
Rita Hayworth, Marilyn Monroe, Judy Garland, and so
many others. The first version of this novel wasn't about
Moud, Saeed, and Bobby. It was about a young girl making her way in Old Hollywood. That story guided me to

a different story, to a much more personal tale. In some ways, the process of writing this book mirrors the process of my life. What began as an escape through fantasy ended with me having to face the reality of my history and identity. Creating art has been one of the true gifts of my life. It's given me a tool to piece together the histories that were hidden from me, and in doing so, to become more whole.

This book is, among other things, about the resilience of the human spirit. In particular, the spirit of Iranian people and queer Iranians. Iran's former president, during a visit to the United States, famously said, "In Iran we don't have homosexuals like in your country. In Iran we don't have this phenomenon." Those comments still enrage me. Through family and friends who live in Iran, I know of many queer Iranians living in Iran, though they must hide their queerness from the government. Perhaps that's what makes me the saddest about those comments. They remind me of how often I felt invisible in my home and my community growing up. And they remind me of how many people, especially queer people with intersectional identities, feel *too* visible in some spaces, and invisible in others. And yet, somehow, community still forms.

This book is also an ode to the bonds of family, and to the power of forgiving those we love, and forgiving ourselves. If there's one thing I love about Persian culture, it's the way it values family. When I struggled with my family's and my culture's difficulties in accepting my sexuality, many Americans I knew turned my family and the Iranian community into the bad guys. They spoke the language of American self-empowerment, which tells us that if someone doesn't accept us as we are, we should shut them out completely. I spoke the language of immigrant families, which taught me that family loyalty comes before everything else. My family and my culture may have struggled with me, and I may have struggled with them, but we never turned our backs on each other. And I'm so grateful for that, because now I have a family who accepts me, and a vibrant, ever-changing community that welcomes my voice. We've never been perfect, but we've always been there for each other, and we've always forgiven each other.

This isn't meant to imply that we should keep our families close if they threaten our safety. Nor is it meant to imply that we all have the option of healing the wounds of our families. Many family bonds are broken by emotional and physical abuse. Many members of our queer community can't come out for fear of their own safety. No one should come out if they don't feel safe.

I hope that those who are moved by this book are inspired to dig into their own past, and their own invisible histories. Perhaps, by shining a light on all the histories that were once invisible, we can honor those who paved our path for us by making the world a place of greater empathy, forgiveness, and understanding, a place where every today holds the spirit of every yesterday within it. Because all we will ever have is this moment, and we owe it to those who fought for us to make it as beautiful as possible.

ACKNOWLEDGMENTS

I'm deeply grateful to the Iranian people currently fighting for a free Iran. As I write this, Iranians are over one hundred days into protesting the brutal regime they suffer under. The spark of these protests was Jina Mahsa Amini, but the inclusive women-led movement has also shined a light on Iran's ethnic and religious diversity. Every Iranian holds their own unique history within them. As those of us in the diaspora have struggled with how to honor the bravery of our fellow Iranians, we've heard a common refrain: Be our voice. I hope this novel does that, but it is one story. This book isn't meant to represent all Iranians, and I hope that if it moves you, you'll dig into more Iranian art from diverse voices, and into the history of Western intervention in Iran and throughout the region. Acknowledgments are not only about gratitude. Acknowledging something is to recognize its existence, and if we want a better future, we must acknowledge the wrongs of the past. To every queer Iranian and to all queer people who grow up in cultures that aren't ready to see or celebrate you yet, you're not alone. Ours is a global community.

Alessandra Balzer has helped me be my own voice. Over the course of four books, she has guided me deeper into my own heart. I'm grateful to have a literary healer as an editor. Big thanks to Team Balzer + Bray/HarperCollins: Caitlin Johnson, Michael D'Angelo, John Sellers, Erin DeSalvatore, Mark Rifkin, Andrea Pappenheimer, Kathy Faber, Kerry Moynagh, Patty Rosati, Mimi Rankin, and Almeda Beynon. The book jacket is art directed by Alison Donalty and designed by Julia Feingold. The art is by Safiya Zerrougui. I'm truly obsessed with what they created.

John Cusick at Folio Jr. has the honesty, generosity, and tenacity that makes for a truly great agent. Thank you, John, and the entire Folio team, especially Madeline Shellhouse for working to get this book published around the world. As a polyglot who has lived in many countries, I want my books to travel and feel borderless.

This book is an ode to family, and creating it was a family affair. My cousin Lila and my aunt Azar generously guided my research. I wouldn't have been able to achieve authenticity without them. My mom's cousin Mandy Vahabzadeh took my author photo. Mandy showed me at a young age that being an Iranian artist was possible. I'm forever grateful for that. I love everyone else in my vibrant, garlic-hating, life-loving family. Al, Maryam, Luis, Dara, Ninzzz, Mehrdad, Vida, John, Moh, Brooke, Youssef, Shahla, Hushang, Azar, Djahanshah, Parinaz, Parker, Delilah, Rafa, Santi, Tomio, Kaveh, Jude, Susan, Kathy, Zu, Paul, Jamie, and all Aubrys and Kamals. To my parents, Lili and Jahangir, and to every immigrant who left their country and worked to create a new life for their family, I'm in awe of the resilient beauty of your hearts.

Mitchell Waters, Brant Rose, Toochis Rose, you've been crucial to my journey as a writer. Major thanks to the four superstar authors who took the time to read this book and give it their seal of approval: Arvin Ahmadi, Firoozeh Dumas, Jason June, Julie Murphy. Feeling community in the solitary job of writing a book means so much. To all the readers who have supported me, I see and appreciate you. Brasileiros, você me fez sentir visto como um contador de histórias de uma forma que eu nunca poderia ter sonhado. Obrigado fofos.

I have so many friends who keep me going. Thanking them all would make these the longest acknowledgments ever. From Choate to Columbia to writers' rooms and sets, if we shared laughs, tears, creative partnership or a dance floor, I appreciate you. For keeping me going in the strange years this book was written in, I'd like to thank Lauren Ambrose, Mojean Aria, Tom Collins, Jazz Elia, Jennifer Elia, Susanna Fogel, Lauren Frances, Ted Huffman, Mandy Kaplan, Ronit Kirchman, Erica Kraus, Erin Lanahan, Joel Michaely, Busy Philipps, Melanie Samarasinghe, Sarah Shetter, Jeremy Tamanini, James Teel, Serena Torrey, Lauren Wimmer, Nora Zehetner.

Jonathon Aubry, I'm so lucky to be your husband. I never imagined a life as abundant and beautiful as the one we have. You keep me grounded and you let me fly, a magical combination. I love you more with each passing day. Toujours L'amour, my true blue Pal.

Evie and Rumi, it's you, it's you, it's all for you, everything I do. You're my heart, my life, my pride, my joy, the answer to every question I've ever had. Watching you both grow into your beautiful, unique selves is the greatest gift I've ever been given. I could write a hundred books and dedicate them all to you two and it still wouldn't cover all the ways you inspire me and everything I want to tell you. The most beautiful moments are the ones I share with each of you.

I hope and pray that by the time this book reaches you, the Iranian people will have the freedom and human rights they—and all people—deserve. Zan Zendegi Azadi.

—Abdi Nazemian, January 1, 2023. Los Angeles, CA